MARS NATION 1

Hard Science Fiction

BRANDON Q. MORRIS

BRANDON Q. MORRIS
HARD SCIENCE FICTION

Contents

Mars Nation 1

Sol 3, NASA base

THE SUN FLOATED RIGHT ABOVE THE HORIZON IN A ROSY SKY. Lance squinted at it. It looked much smaller from here than it did from Earth, but its light could still blind him if he gazed right into it. After a few more arc minutes around the sun, the sky shifted to blue. Sharon, the pilot whose studies had also included meteorology, had told him about this, but he hadn't believed her. He needed to apologize to her, even though the others knew by now that he was one of those who had to see such things with his own eyes.

"Everything alright?" he heard Mike's voice say over his helmet radio.

"Yes, Commander. It's very romantic."

"You have things to do."

Thanks, Mike, he thought. *Like I didn't know that already.* Lance took his time anyway. It was to be his first step onto the new planet that would be his home for the next six months. Until now, all he had done was travel across the Mars surface from the landing site of the *Endeavour* to their quarters inside the Rover's pressurized cabin, which he reached via a pressurized tube.

He squinted again at the distant sun. It looked white from here, not yellow like from Earth, which might explain why it felt less warm. Of course, that wasn't the fault of the color, but rather the distance. "We need to optimize the disembarking process," he said. "If it takes us six hours every time, we'll never get any work done."

"Don't worry," Mike replied. "Even after the sun sets, it will stay light for a while. The dust in the atmosphere will keep reflecting the sunlight even after the sun has dropped below the horizon."

"No shit," slipped out before Lance could catch it.

The commander's know-it-all commentaries always rubbed Lance the wrong way. They had received more than enough information about what a day was like on Mars during their intensive training. However, it never paid to let himself get annoyed. He was lucky Mike was always insensitive to stuff like this. And, there were the times when no one except Mike had a handy answer for something. It wasn't a surprise to find out that the man had finished his college physics degree by the age of nineteen.

Lance braced his hands against the roof to their quarters and pushed downward. Ninety percent of the base was buried under the Martian surface to protect its residents from radiation. The roof was composed of the now unneeded heat shields that had once belonged to the explorer robots that had built the base prior to the humans' arrival. A thick layer of Martian dirt was spread across the metal. Lance finished pushing his torso up through the hatch. He pulled his legs out, knelt on the roof, and finally stood up. His breathing was heavy. After so many months of weightlessness, every activity seemed astonishingly difficult. What had been the point of pedaling like crazy on that exercise bike all the time?

"Okay, I'm out," Lance said.

"Looking good," Mike answered. "At least from what I can see on the screen. But your heart rate! You're really out of shape, aren't you?"

"Watch it, boy, or I'll show you what shape I'm in at arm wrestling later on."

Diplomatically speaking, Mike was notably underwhelming in terms of physique. It was nothing short of a miracle that he had made it through the training process. His intellect probably compensated for everything else, but he didn't stand a chance beating Lance at arm wrestling. Lance took a cautious step away from the hatch toward the sunset. He expected to hear a hollow tone as he moved forward, but the air was probably too thin and the sensitivity of the external microphone too low for that.

"You know you're supposed to wait, right?" Mike asked.

Of course, he knew that. The airlock was so narrow that only one person in a spacesuit could fit through at a time. Once outside, they were always supposed to move around in pairs, which was why Sarah, his buddy for this walk, would emerge through the hatch in a minute or two. But it wouldn't hurt if he looked around a little, would it?

He walked over to the edge of the roof. From here, it was only about twenty centimeters down to the Mars surface. Should he? He had yet to feel like he was actually standing on the planet. What would happen? The ground looked dry and stable. The area right around the base had been reinforced during the construction process. Lance glanced back toward the airlock, but Sarah was still nowhere in sight. He slowly extended his right leg, scooted it forward, and lowered it—and himself—toward the ground. He gingerly placed his foot down, beginning with his heel, and had to burst out laughing. The situation was hardly humorous, so the outburst had to be a subliminal overreaction. He was the first person to ever set foot on Mars! Although he didn't feel up to celebrating, he couldn't stop the laugh. Lance shifted his weight onto his right leg before bringing the left one down to the ground. He stood there then, and laughed again.

"Are you feeling okay?" Mike asked. "I assume that, despite our agreement, you didn't wait for Sarah. We're lucky we're the only ones here. How would it look to the bigwigs if they knew you disregarded my direct orders about the exiting process?"

"But I didn't, Mike, promise," he replied.

"Earth is asking how everything's going with the suit," Mike said.

By this point the first images had been transmitted home. That meant twenty minutes had gone by, assuming that Earth had responded immediately. Lance gazed at the glowing numerals on his wrist. Exactly. However, that also meant that one-twelfth of their maximum shift of four hours was already gone. Sarah should be here any minute. The mission's doctor was supposed to help him clear the dust from the top of the base so that everything would look in tip-top shape for the TV transmission. Mission Control never left anything to chance. The international mission had cost too much to open it up to criticism.

Lance looked down. The suit was very form-fitting, and it looked quite good on him if he did say so himself. But that was definitely not what Mission Control wanted to hear. Although... maybe. Compared to the older models, which had ballooned around the astronauts' bodies, the new suits were significantly more photogenic. The only part still pressurized was the inside of the helmet, while the suit's elastic material was wrapped tightly around his body. He had noticed how agile he felt when he climbed out of the hatch. During the training on Earth, he had gotten to know—and to hate—the old, stiff spacesuits.

"I really like it. Kudos to the developers!" he said.

He then tapped the glowing numerals on his arm, thus activating the projection screen inside his helmet. Earth would soon be bombarded with data, the extent of which blew his mind. Locational and directional specs, temperature, pressure, wind direction, the composition of the stone on which he was standing. It was too much, within the confines of a space helmet. He tapped his arm again, and the digits and arrows gradually vanished. He really didn't need to know anything else besides the cardinal direction in which he was looking at the moment.

"The data stream on my screen is a little much," he said.

"Oh, the suit is tracking your position. Don't worry," Mike replied.

"Lance?"

He turned around at the sound of Sarah's voice. Her head was just emerging from the round hole in the roof. He couldn't make out her face due to the reflection of the setting sun in her visor.

"Need some help?" he asked.

"I've got it, thanks," she assured him.

Her English was spoken with a faint accent. Sarah hailed from Switzerland. Nobody on board had yet managed to pronounce her last name correctly. Jaeggli sounded a little like Jacqueline, but in Sarah's mouth, it was something completely different. Lance enjoyed teasing her that she didn't look anything like the stereotypes about her country. After all, people always imagined Swedes as tall and blonde, but she was short and dark-haired. She calmly kept reminding him that she came from Switzerland, not Sweden, which she knew were hard for an American to keep straight.

As a precaution, he climbed back onto the roof. They didn't know yet how well Sarah would adjust to the unfamiliar gravitational pull.

"Are you both ready?" Mike asked from inside.

"Looks like it," Lance said.

"Alright, then. You know where the tools are."

They had already been through this. There was a crate of sorts on the northern edge of the building. Lance let Sarah lead the way. Her muscles strained slightly against the suit's elastic material. *Yes, they are definitely suitable for TV.* He gave himself a mental shake. Lance had vowed to not get involved with his female colleagues. His girlfriend was waiting for him at home, after all. If he made it back in the next twelve months, they wanted to start trying to have children. Before departing for Mars, he had arranged for extra sperm to be frozen because of the potential radiation damage.

"Opening the crate," Sarah said.

The Swiss woman leaned down, while Lance watched

from a safe distance of about three meters. She undid first the left latch and then the right, before reaching for the center of the lid and lifting it.

"Oh!" she cried, springing backward.

"What is it?" Mike shouted nervously.

Lance covered the distance to Sarah in long strides, but there was nothing to see.

"Gotcha!" she crowed with a laugh. "What were you two thinking? That there was a spider in the box?"

Sarah had a good sense of humor, he had to give her credit for that. He looked around inside the box. It was stuffed full of objects whose purposes weren't immediately evident.

"Thanks, Sarah. I almost had to change my pants," Mike said over the radio.

The doctor chuckled as she leaned back into the crate. It looked like she knew precisely what she was doing, although it was more likely that she was just following the instructions on her helmet screen. Sarah pulled out a tube about one meter in length.

"Here. Hold this," she said, pushing it into Lance's hand. She then looked back inside, reaching down along the right edge of the crate. She tugged out a round tank.

"There it is," she declared. "Okay, give me that back." Lance returned the tube to her, and Sarah stuck it into one end of the tank and handed the assembly to him. "Turn around," she instructed, making a little circling motion with one hand. He obeyed, and she rummaged around in his backpack. He could guess what she was doing as she pressed a cable into his hand. "The outlet is on the side of the tank."

After locating the small slot, he connected the cable. The old-fashioned vacuum cleaner in his hands was being powered by the life support backpack strapped across his shoulders.

"Get going," Sarah said. "I'll take care of the measurements."

"Sure," he said as he started to suction the dust off the base's roof.

"How about a little light?" Lance asked over his radio.

The light was fading faster than they had expected. This was probably due to the high density of dust in the atmosphere. Thanks to the low gravity and the lack of rain, the dust remained in the air for quite some time after a windstorm.

In lieu of an answer, several strips of lights flashed on along the roofline. The result looked spooky. A paler corridor now glowed around the base. In the sunlight, the dust hadn't been nearly as visible as now. In fact, it had taken on a resemblance to fog.

"Will you be done out there soon?" Mike asked.

"We're almost finished with the spring cleaning," Lance replied.

A pail full of water sat beside him. He had just finished washing the portholes, and he only had one more thing to take care of. He opened the lid on the pail, and steam swirled around him. In the thin air, only one-thousandth as dense as that on Earth, the heated water inside the pail evaporated very quickly. Hence, the lid. He submerged his sponge and had to hurry or risk losing the moisture. The dampness vanished as quickly as alcohol on Earth. At least he didn't need to dry the glass.

Where was Sarah?

"Sarah?" he called.

The doctor didn't respond.

"Can you see Sarah on your screen?"

"Yes, Lance. She is about two hundred meters south of your position.

He turned around and gazed into the specified direction,

but he couldn't see anyone. The light, however, only reached about fifty meters by this point.

"Sarah?"

Nothing. Should he be concerned?

"Can you see her readings?"

"Yes, but based on privacy laws, I can't—"

"Mike, don't be stupid," Lance said impatiently.

"Okay. She's doing just fine. Her heart rate is a little elevated, but other than that, everything's good."

"You're not worried about anything?"

"We'd see if something happened."

"Hmm," Lance said. "I'm going to check it out, anyway."

After depositing the sponge on the pail lid, he stood up. He then called up Sarah's position on his helmet screen. After walking twenty meters it was so dark that he could only see the vague outlines of his feet.

He tried contacting her again. "Sarah? Are you there?"

What a dumb question. The instruments were clear in their readings. Lance felt himself growing increasingly concerned. How could his colleague have gotten lost out here? Even if a dust storm had hit them, they never would have been in real danger, thanks to the thin atmosphere.

Was he scared of little green Martians? Lance's screen told him that he should have just reached Sarah. A bulky black shadow materialized right in front of him. He was startled, but it only took a moment for him to realize that it was just a boulder. He really was seeing ghosts. He strode around the rock and almost stumbled over something soft. It was Sarah's leg. She pulled it back and jumped to her feet, though she still didn't say anything. However, she looked almost as surprised as he did.

"I turned off my radio," she said breathlessly. "What's wrong? Why are you here?"

"To find you."

"What for? The base has my vitals. Or did I suffer a heart attack without noticing it?"

"No, I just thought... ah, forget it."

"You were worried about me. How sweet," the doctor said. "I simply wanted to be alone for a minute. We've just spent seven months sharing the same forty cubic meters and were together for a long time during our training. I really needed this."

"Got it. I didn't mean to disturb you."

"Next time I'll let you know."

"Greetings, turtle doves," Mike interrupted from the base.

Haha! 'Turtle doves,' my ass, Lance thought. Sarah was thirteen years older than himself. There was no way she'd be interested in a kid like him.

"What is it?" she asked Mike.

"You should head back to the base."

"Why? Don't we still have about an hour? It feels marvelous out here."

She's laying it on a bit thick, Lance thought. At that moment, his suit heater cut on. The surface temperature had dropped to minus 30.

"It looks like I need you back here."

"Has the TV ceremony been postponed?" Lance asked. One of the presidents of the mission's sponsor nations had probably just called in at the last minute with a special wish or something.

"No, there's a problem. A distress signal has come in," Mike replied.

"What does that have to do with us?"

"A whole lot, Lance. It's coming from close by."

"The crazies."

"You guessed it."

May 23, 2042, MfE ship Santa Maria

"Get it started!"

Henrik shouted so loudly that Ewa covered her ears as he slammed his fists onto the silvery console in front of him. This was now the second time that the pilot had lost his temper. Ewa shook her head disapprovingly, but she didn't say anything. Something like this didn't typically happen. However, there was nothing typical about this flight, which had seemed to be ill-fated from the start. It was understandable that patience was in short supply among some of them, especially considering they only had three or four days to get the engine repaired. If they failed to do so, they wouldn't reach their orbit around Mars, and they would have to make another full loop around the sun.

"Just calm down," Chuck said. The Brit, a former bomber pilot, was their commander.

He stopped beside Henrik and rested an arm across his shoulders. Ewa found this an odd picture, knowing the two of them as she did from the selection procedure in which they had competed against hundreds of other applicants from around the world. Henrik, the slim, intellectual Dutchman, had maneuvered their group through many trials with his calm, thoughtful demeanor. On the other hand, Chuck had always shot ahead, trying to solve problems in a hands-on manner and failing along the way. But now he was the one holding the crew together. It was amazing how wrong you could be about people! If it had been up to their group, Chuck wouldn't have been named commander. However, a volunteer team of psychologists had made the decision. This was in keeping with the other aspects of the trip, which were also being handled by volunteers.

And that was increasingly proving to be a problem.

"This fucking engine! Who conned us into buying it?" Henrik demanded as he spun his seat around to face Chuck.

Out of the corner of her eye, Ewa noticed that Piotr had stood up. He was the third crew member assigned to this shift in the command module. Piotr came from an influential Russian family, and he had acquired the engine for the Mars for Everyone project through his connections. This engine was supposed to bring them into Mars orbit and eventually down to the surface.

"We'll figure it out," Chuck said.

Ewa noticed that he shot Piotr a hard look. *Just let it go*, his eyes said, but the Russian was not a man who could leave well enough alone if he felt he was being mistreated.

Piotr drew closer. "The engine is rock-solid," he said quietly. "The model was tested over many years, and we got it for pocket change. We couldn't come close to affording any of the engines the private manufacturers offered us. You wouldn't even be sitting here if my uncle hadn't known someone who—"

"Maybe it would be better if I weren't sitting here," Henrik shot back angrily.

"Do you want to go back to your Mama?" Piotr asked. "Wee Henrik would like to be fished out of the ball pit? As soon as a few problems pop up, you Westerners start whining. I'm right, don't you agree, Ewa?"

Ewa said nothing, but she retreated a few steps, sensing they were on the verge of a real fight. If anyone had told her before today that Henrik would raise his hand against any of their fellow travelers, she would have simply laughed, but now Henrik seemed angry enough to hit someone.

She had to agree with Piotr in part. It felt like a clear boundary line ran down the crew, and it seemed to have something to do with the former Iron Curtain, despite the fact it had been gone for over fifty years already. The enthusiasm for the Mars colonization project, which was funded through donations, had whitewash covered this boundary, but the thin paint was now flaking away and the line had reappeared.

"I—" Henrik said, balling his fists.

"You? You can't take any more?" Piotr just had to keep picking at him.

"That's enough!" Chuck cut in as if he was dealing with two yapping dogs. All that was missing was him grabbing them by the scruffs of their necks. The glares continued.

"Enough," he repeated.

To Ewa's surprise, the warning worked.

"Idiot!" Henrik muttered, sitting back down.

He leaned over the control panel as if he needed to check something. Piotr hadn't seen that coming. He opened his mouth several times, but couldn't seem to come up with anything to say. Then he spun around. As the floater—who would cover either the pilot or the commander in their absence—his place was in the corner of the command module.

"Just stay calm," Chuck said. "The technicians have sworn up and down that they'll have the engine back up and running soon."

Whatever... Previous experience had proven that these promises were relatively hollow. The engine had obviously sat around a little too long in the old spaceship dockyard where Piotr's uncle had found it.

"Besides, I contacted the *Endeavour* expedition on Mars yesterday. They are considering if and how they might be able to assist us," Chuck continued. Piotr and Henrik whipped around to face him as if the commander had detonated a bomb on the bridge.

"You did what?" Henrik asked.

"You heard me. I'm Commander of this ship, and it's my responsibility."

"You should've asked us," Piotr said, now back up on his feet. "According to the foundation's statutes, we're supposed to collectively make any decisions that impact our day-to-day operations."

"We aren't on Earth anymore. You might have forbidden me to establish contact."

Ewa attempted to visualize a team discussion. Chuck was probably right. Among the twenty people on board, there were several who placed a high value on the independence of the MfE project. That wasn't all that surprising. After all, everyone here was crazy enough to have left the security of their home planet without the prospect of a return ticket. Some of the crew hadn't only broken off their own personal contacts, they were fed up with the old human race in general, which was represented in the international *Endeavour* Mars expedition. Adding to that was the mentality of 'us up here, them down there.' MfE—Mars for Everyone—had been painstakingly financed through donations, while the four astronauts, who had taken the first step on Mars before them, were being paid through tax funds.

"You shouldn't have done that," Piotr said.

"But it's done now," Ewa said. "And so what, really? It's just one option. We don't have to accept their help. We can keep circling the sun and try again in a year to enter Mars's orbit."

Chuck shot her a grateful look. Continuing in orbit around the sun really wasn't an option. They didn't have enough supplies to last out another year.

"And what did the folks down there say?" Henrik asked.

"They have to figure out what their options are. And there's still a chance the technicians will fix the engine."

Ewa had heard enough. Besides, her watch had just

vibrated. It was time to feed the animals. She was actually a chemist, but on this project, everyone wore several hats. At least she had always been interested in agriculture.

"See you later, boys," she said in farewell before floating over to the hatch that connected the command module with the rest of the ship.

The MfE initiative hadn't been able to afford a large ship like NASA's, or even the SpaceX colony ship that was following them. Instead, they had purchased two recycled Dragon modules and arranged for them to be shot into space as secondary cargo. As a practical measure, the construction crew for the final design had traveled on the ship with them. Back then—must have been almost three years ago—Ewa had followed the TV coverage of all the developments. The media had dubbed them 'the crazies' because they wanted to undertake, on a minimal budget, a voyage without a planned return. And yet hadn't the settlers who had moved lock, stock, and barrel to the Wild West been just as crazy? Most of Ewa's fellow travelers would have seen that journey as a form of insanity, and many of them still thought like that. In any case, their ship had almost reached Mars!

Something told her that she had seen and heard enough. It was time for her to leave. Ewa opened the hatch to the interior space. The stench washed over her like a wave, making her feel slightly nauseous. Of course, there was a reason for everything. It didn't stink because the crew refused to bathe, but rather from the ever-present dampness. They had been living for over five months in a balloon-like structure, which was filled with damp air and cooled from the outside by the chill of space.

Between the two cone-shaped Dragon modules, they had constructed a framework out of a titanium alloy, the most expensive they could afford. And then they had fastened fabric panels to the framework, similar to the way that tarps can be attached to an internal structure. When that was done, they pumped the entire thing full of breathable air. The *Santa Maria* was a gigantic balloon, but in this instance, the whole structure wouldn't pop if the surface developed a hole in it. This was because, like an anorak, the flexible walls were divided into various chambers that were filled with water. The water provided excellent protection against the interplanetary radiation, and it offered stability in the frigid temperatures that existed in space.

The boldly-adventurous construction had been another reason that most people on Earth predicted that the project would fail. However, the reality was different—they had made it. Ewa floated through the hatch and closed it behind her. Warm, jungle-like humid air enveloped her. As little of the humidity as possible was allowed to enter the command module, where it could damage the electrical systems.

During their long journey, several problems had developed that made it clear that the spaceship builders had been somewhat lacking in terms of their building technology knowledge. The life support system was large enough to transform the exhaled carbon dioxide into oxygen and to purify the wastewater. However, nobody had thought about the large amount of perspiration that would be produced. It clung to the walls as droplets, but because of the state of weightlessness, the moisture didn't separate from the surfaces. Since it didn't roll down and gather into puddles, it was impossible to wipe away.

Over time, the drops coalesced into a film that spread everywhere and grew thicker. The only way to cope with this dampness was to continually dry the walls, but this was like tilting at windmills. The free shift that each of the twenty crew members had, once their primary duties were finished, was filled with working out and cleaning. In other words, their days were divided as follows: twelve hours of work, four hours of athletics, and eight hours of sleep.

Ewa had observed her fellow travelers. The psychologists had obviously done an excellent job evaluating them, considering they hadn't devolved into murder and manslaughter despite the absence of any private space. Of course, there were regular conflicts. Shortly after their departure, three couples had quickly formed. This was part of the plan reflected in the selection of ten women and ten men. Mars for Everyone had been imagined as a colony that would grow naturally on the Red Planet. However, the relationships hadn't even lasted a month. The *Santa Maria* wasn't exactly optimal for couples. Would this change in the hard reality of Mars?

She floated past her colleagues, en route to the lower area, greeting a few of them. The one crew shift was hanging on the lateral walls in their sleeping bags, looking for all the world like plump bats. The others were either working out or cleaning up the condensed moisture. They chatted quietly to avoid disturbing the sleepers. Everyone agreed that the best invention ever was the super-lightweight, sound-absorbing headphones that an electronics manufacturer had sponsored. One advantage of being weightless was that the headphones hardly rubbed at all, regardless of your sleeping position. They functioned amazingly well.

The animals were kept in the lowest level of the second space module, the terminus of their balloon as it were, a drainage plug of sorts. At least this meant that the animals weren't contributing to the stench in their space-traveling tent. Ewa truly enjoyed her time in this area. This wasn't really due to the animals, which she viewed more as her responsibility than as her darlings. However, the climate control in this module operated at just the right capacity. Thus, the air down here was as fresh as in the command module, and yet she had something here that was a rare commodity on the ship—peace and quiet.

Ewa slipped through the hatch and into the 'zoo module,' as it was jokingly called. They had been given animals that reproduced easily and could provide valuable nutrition. This menagerie included a guinea pig family, several rabbits, and bantam chickens that laid remarkably large eggs.

Nonetheless, they were placing their highest hopes in the insects that were living in their own boxes. Ewa had never been scared of bugs, which was why she didn't mind taking care of the locusts and other insects. Ewa opened the first box. Her eyes were met with a great scrambling. Golden mealworms, which were a precious source of protein, twisted and turned in mounds of wheat bran. She had to search for the pupas and transfer them to a different box, since these would soon turn into mealworm beetles that would eventually lay more eggs for new worms.

Not long after their departure, complaints had arisen that her zoo occupied the entire module. However, when she warned her fellow crew members that a few bugs might occasionally escape from their boxes, the protests had fallen silent. Since that time, she hadn't been disturbed even once while at work.

Ewa had been surprised by how little the weightlessness had affected the insects. They had already reproduced enough to supply one or two meals for the crew, but no one had ever asked for them. The chickens were grateful for the fresh food, though. She shut the box and turned to the buffalo worms, the larval form of the lesser mealworm beetle. Lastly, she checked on the locusts, the so-called 'desert shrimp.' *Honestly,* she thought, *they taste more like chicken.*

The chickens always seemed to do well. There was an almost endless supply of worms for them, and in return, they laid a steady stream of eggs. Back on Earth, these birds were ground dwellers, but up here they flapped around happily. The ability to navigate space seemed to be deeply rooted inside them.

She always saved cuddling the guinea pigs and rabbits for last. They hadn't adjusted to weightlessness as well as the birds, and they sometimes somersaulted like helpless fuzz balls inside their cages. This was why Ewa had installed several low ceilings in their terraria so that they now had use of a cave-like space. Since then, the animals' appetites had increased substantially. She gingerly lifted one of the rabbits into her arms. He snuffled her sweetly, and she scratched his fur.

"So, how are you doing today?"

His fur was smooth and shiny, and his breathing even.

This was the first rabbit to be born on board. Ewa was interested in seeing how it would deal with gravity once they landed.

A deep rumble suddenly resonated throughout the ship. The sound came from overhead, but she could feel it even in the module's intermediate floor. It sounded as if someone had pounded several times in quick succession on the lid of a giant barrel.

Sol 4, NASA base

THE GROUND WAS VIBRATING.

Lance could feel the unbelievable power of the robotic drill. The tiniest of tremors planted themselves in his spinal cord and then climbed to the top. He recalled how his father had once let him hold a hammer drill. The tool, which seemed to have been almost as large as he was at the time, had felt like a strong, angry animal—perhaps a bear—but it had responded to even his littlest movement. He had been in control of powers that far exceeded his own. That had been the moment he decided to become an engineer.

He didn't have to push the drill into the ground with his own strength. The machine could do that itself, and the more progress it made, the more successful it was at doing this, since the weight of the stone that it was removing from the ground was making it heavier and, therefore, more powerful. He controlled the tool with the assistance of a small remote control. The sensors were linked to his helmet screen. Whenever he looked down he could see the green outline of the drill, as well as the type of stone it was presently removing.

It's actually too easy, he thought. *We're here on a strange planet that we've never even stepped foot on before now, and we already feel at home. Or no, it's more like we're on a trip to an exotic locale. Everything is packed. We've been vaccinated against the worst infections, and we are dutifully peeling our fruit before we eat it.* There didn't seem to be any real dangers—or was that just pure arrogance?

Lance walked to the other side of the machine. It was run by two chains and reached the height of his chest. Its task was to construct a ditch that ended precisely at the base. This was where the first extension would go. A laboratory. The stone that the robotic drill was gathering would be partially melted down and then poured to form the slabs that would become the walls of the lab. For a roof, they would set a large iron slab on top of the walls to increase the insulation against the intense radiation from outer space. Since Mars had no ozone layer, too much of this radiation reached the planet's surface.

Lance gazed around. Until recently, this area had still been quite virginal. But over the past two years the robots had been cruising around and preparing for the landing of their lords and masters, who had finally assumed their thrones. Humanity had conquered a second planet. It sounded strange, but the thought of it made him proud.

"Hey, you two," Mike hailed by radio.

"Yes?" Sarah responded.

Just this morning Mike and Sharon had complained that they still hadn't been allowed to leave the base. But Lance was in charge of its construction, and Sarah had insisted on accompanying him as the medical officer. She wanted to keep an eye on him for health reasons. There hadn't yet been a good reason for either Mike or Sharon to go out for a walk on the surface. Curiosity wasn't a deciding factor. The expedition was being too tightly run for that.

"Sorry, but you have to come back inside," Mike responded.

"What about my work?" Lance asked.

"The drill will get on just fine on its own."

"And if it comes across something that it can't assess?"

"Then it will wait for you. I need you in here more than it does. Your mind, primarily."

"What's wrong, Mike? The crazies?"

The Mars for Everyone project had been a pain in his ass

even back on Earth. How could anyone be so reckless? The fans had reminded him of adolescents. But if they'd gotten themselves into danger... well, they were adults, after all.

"You've nailed it. But it's much worse than you're thinking."

AS THE SLIDING DOOR SHUT BEHIND HIM, HE HEARD A woman's voice coming from the loudspeaker. Her voice had a faint Eastern European accent. Five minutes later, he and Sarah had peeled off their suits and joined the others in just their training suits.

"Ewa Kowalska from *Santa Maria,*" Mike said as an introduction. "And this is Sarah Jaeggli and Lance Leber. Lance is our engineer. If anyone can help you, he's the one."

"The *Santa Maria?*" Lance asked.

The young woman smiled. She had short blonde hair and blue eyes. Her nose looked like it had been broken in the past. "After Christopher Columbus's flagship."

"Ah, right. I hadn't made that connection."

The woman didn't really look all that crazy. She radiated something that he couldn't identify at a distance, but he could still sense it. "How can we help you?" he asked.

"I have already filled Mike in," she replied. "Shortened version: When we tried to reactivate the command module's engine, it tore free from its mount. This caused the pressure in the module to plummet."

"Oh. I assume there were casualties?" A shiver skittered down Lance's spine all the way to his tailbone.

"Yes. Five all told, including our commander, Chuck Manners."

"My deepest sympathies." Lance reached for the back of Mike's seat as his knees went weak. Five people had just died fairly close by. When you found yourself so far away from humanity, several million kilometers felt like a stone's throw away. "Have you figured out what happened?" he asked. In situations like this, he preferred to focus on the technical discussions.

"Since everyone who was there is dead, we don't know. Right before the depressurization, our sensors indicated a strong negative acceleration. However, the modules' systems are independent, which is why we don't have access to the engine data. We're planning an EVA for tomorrow."

"Are you sure you want to go out and see all that in person?"

"We have to. Like I already told Mike, the command module's engine was supposed to slow us down and bring us into orbit."

"But it's destroyed anyway, right?"

"There's a second module at the other end. We're now turning the ship with its vernier thruster. We need to know what happened so we don't make the same mistake again."

"And if it works, will everything be all right?"

"Not quite. The second module propelled our ship after launch out of Earth's orbit. It only has enough fuel to land on Mars."

"In other words, if you use it to decelerate, you will reach orbit but won't make it to the surface."

"Even if we could land, we'd be unable to."

"What do you mean?"

"There are still fifteen people and a few animals up here. We can't all fit in the one module. It had just barely worked with both modules, although it was a really tight fit."

"A Dragon module, right?" Lance asked.

"Yes, exactly," Ewa said.

In recent years, the price of those things had dropped drastically. Their manufacturers were producing them on assembly lines like Henry Ford manufactured his Model-T a century ago. Dependable and affordable enough that a privately funded organization could manage the cost. Well-used modules were practically given away. *If the new owners forgot to arrange for a thorough refurbishment, then what?* Lance thought.

Lance tried to imagine ten people stuffed into a landing module. He recalled seeing photos of five people jammed into an Indian motorcycle rickshaw. That's what it would be like. But with fifteen people? Impossible.

"Hmm," he said.

"Hmm?" Ewa echoed.

"I don't know if you've already discussed it with Mike, but there might be one other possibility."

He glanced at Mike, who was simply shaking his head. *What does that mean? Shouldn't we try to help these people?*

"We could pick you up," Lance said.

"You would do that?" The woman he had never met in person scooted very close to the camera, though she seemed strangely neutral. It seemed as if she had drawn a boundary between words and emotions. It had to be the shock.

"The *Endeavour* is tanked up in case of an emergency return to Earth. We could fly up to you, transfer enough fuel for the deceleration, and then bring part of your crew down to the surface."

"That would be cutting it damned close," Mike said. Lance suspected he didn't like the idea. At any rate, he didn't appear pleased with this solution.

"We cleaned it out yesterday," Lance added. "Even if we only take an additional five people on board, that will only be about one-third of its normal landing weight."

"We have to be sure about the calculations," Mike muttered through clenched teeth.

"Of course, we'll be careful," Lance said.

"The *Endeavour* won't be so easy to steer with them on board," Mike remarked.

"Sharon will take care of that, right?" Lance looked over at his Brazilian colleague.

"Absolutely," she said with a confident smile.

"You should keep the majority of the fuel, which you'll need for your own landing," Ewa cut in. "Even if we can't make it with the one module, we can save at least five of our people."

Lance nodded. They couldn't withhold this assistance. Doing so would have legal ramifications.

"Good. Check into what went wrong with the defective engine. The plan will only work if you can manage to slow down the second module. We will run our calculations in the meantime. Mike out."

Ewa's face vanished. The monitor once again displayed its standard background, a snow-covered mountain on Earth. Mike tapped it with his finger.

"If we run into any problems," he said, "you've just given away our ticket home. Are you clear on that, Lance? Those crazies might feel otherwise, but I want to get back to Earth. There's no way I want to waste the rest of my days on this godforsaken planet."

Lance had never seen Mike so upset or this determined.

"You won't have to," Lance replied. "It'll take another eight weeks for us to produce enough hydrogen and oxygen from our supplies for the return trip. We could fill the *Endeavour's* tanks three times over and still keep to schedule."

"Then all I can do is hope you're right, Lance."

May 24, 2042, Santa Maria

Ewa looked around panic-stricken. She had just woken up but had no idea who she was or where she was located. How had she ended up in this chaos? Her eyes fell on a yellow slip of paper that was taped to the wall on a level with her head.

'Wait 30 seconds' was written on it in her own handwriting. She took a deep breath and released it. Then everything fell back into place. She had experienced another of those strange fugue states. They never lasted longer than a minute. And they were terrifying because her mind felt completely blank during them. She had suffered from epileptic seizures since puberty. Her parents, both in the military, had arranged for her to have surgery in a military hospital when she was seventeen. They said it was a brand-new kind of therapy. Since then, she hadn't had a single seizure. However, the blackouts had started three years ago, and recently they had become more frequent. Did it have something to do with her epilepsy?

Ewa shook the thoughts away. She had things to do.

"Theo, I'd like you to come with me."

Ewa pointed at the dark-haired, shirtless man sitting across from her. She knew that Theo was German, but he had the same surname she did and came from Berlin. He was tattooed, wore earrings, and was sitting at the center of the thirteen remaining crew members. Ewa had no idea why it happened, but right after the catastrophe, suddenly everyone started doing what she suggested. It had been her idea to contact the NASA crew at the Mars base for help. But it had also been the logical next step considering that before his death, Chuck had told her about the request for assistance he had sent down there. She had decided not to tell the others about Chuck's unauthorized contact. It didn't matter anymore, as it were. The commander was dead, and they were out of options when it came to entering the orbit around Mars. Everyone had agreed that she should contact the base.

The result had been that the others were now sitting across from her as if she had some special status. It actually made her feel uncomfortable. She didn't want anyone to hang on her every word. Ellen and Nancy, the two youngest crew members, seemed to look up to her as a big sister. She scanned the faces one more time to evaluate her decision. Five men were floating there in various positions. Andy wasn't there because Gabriella, the doctor, had sent him to bed due to circulatory problems. In addition, there were eight women. What had been the ideal gender balance when they had launched was now obviously skewed. The women had the upper hand. Would this change the character of the journey? Ewa didn't know.

"When do we go over?" Theo asked.

Yes, he had been a good choice, even if it had been a fairly intuitive one. The German seemed quite resourceful. Before now she hadn't paid him much attention, even though he was hard to ignore in light of the numerous tattoos that he enjoyed displaying.

Did she really have to be the one to go out right now? Probably, as otherwise it wouldn't feel like the natural next step. Ewa remembered the moment she left the command module through the hatch. What was the last thing she had seen and heard? Chuck had been explaining something, and she had said something like, 'See you later.' She would honor this promise, even if it frightened her. She felt a lump rise in her throat as she thought about Chuck. She had never imagined him dying. And what was all this for anyway?

"I'm sorry, Gabriella, but we need Andy," Ewa said.

Andy—Andrej—was the best information engineer on the crew. If anyone would know how they could collect the data, he was the one.

"I'll get him," the Italian doctor replied, floating toward the wall. Her flowing hair fanned out behind her.

Ewa watched her. The doctor opened one of the sleeping bags. Ewa hadn't even suspected that someone was inside it, considering how flat it looked. Gabriella cautiously unwrapped the occupant, removed his earphones, and woke him.

"Don't be worried, Andy," she said as she gently patted his cheeks.

"What's going on?"

"We need you right now. I'm sorry. You can rest some more later."

"Uh, I'm feeling better already. What do you need?" he asked.

"Ewa will cxplain it to you."

The two of them rejoined the group.

"Here we go," Gabriella said.

"We need to get the data from the engine, Andy," Ewa said. "I hope we'll be able to find that in the damaged module."

"That would be the only place, if at all. The two modules are on autonomous systems—as is the belly of the ship," Andy replied. He looked exhausted and pale. This was the way Ewa imagined most hackers looked. His sharp nose cast a shadow across his face.

"If at all?"

"The computers might've been destroyed during the incident. I wouldn't be surprised if that was the case."

"And what does that mean for us?"

"You could try to start them up. If that doesn't work, you'll have to bring me the memory boards."

"Which ones?"

"All of them, ideally. It will be a while before we get any new supplies, so we can definitely use any functional replacement parts we can get."

"Good to know, thanks. We'll pack up everything we can get our hands on."

"Can I go lay back down now?"

"For an hour, until we're done with the pre-breathing process. Then you'll have to be ready to help us boot the computer. Maybe we'll get lucky and it'll start."

"Sure. See you later."

Andy turned around and headed back to his sleeping bag. How could anyone be so skinny? And yet, he had passed the athletic examinations with flying colors, better than the majority of the other ten thousand applicants. She shouldn't be fooled by his appearance.

EWA CLIMBED DOWN FROM THE BIKE, DRENCHED IN SWEAT. Ellen held out the lower section of the spacesuit so Ewa could climb inside it more easily.

"The two of you should actually rest a while," the doctor said.

"I know, but everything will just take longer then. We need to know now what caused the accident."

"That's why I'm allowing you to stop the pre-breathing process early."

As ship's doctor, the Italian was now the highest-ranking officer. That reminded Ewa that they still needed to resolve the commander problem, but not until she had paid her last respects to Chuck. She stretched out her arms as the Hard

Upper Torso, known as the HUT, was lowered on top of her. The other Mars expeditions were using more modern suits, but the MfE organization had been forced to take the more economical route.

The old Russian models had the advantage that they could be repaired with supplies they had on board. However, the suits were quite awkward to move around in. Ewa checked the instruments in her tech pack. Everything was running. She pulled on her helmet and began to breathe the air being supplied by the life support system.

It smelled surprisingly good inside. Since she was now enclosed in a suit that had been sweated up numerous times —and probably also been thrown up in at least two or three times—the air right outside the suit would have smelled abominable to a newcomer. However, they had been living like this for months. It was astonishing how quickly a person could get used to such things.

"Doing alright, Theo?" she asked over the radio.

The German turned around and smiled. He had obviously heard every word she said. Theo was about twenty centimeters taller than she was. He floated in front of her toward the airlock. Although he was quite slim, he now looked more like the Michelin Man balloon they recalled from old photos.

The airlock was located in the second Dragon module on the lower end of the ship. Actually, it would have been more convenient to exit right out of the ship's belly. However, it hadn't proven feasible to slice a pressure-tight airlock into it.

"It's just the two of us," Ewa said soothingly.

She didn't want to startle the animals, which was why she let Theo take the lead while she closed the hatch between the module and the ship. Theo was already unlatching the airlock.

"Want to go first, or should I?" he asked.

"We'll go at the same time. It'll be easier on the animals."

"Whatever you say."

Ewa blocked the airlock door so that none of the animals

could slip inside. Theo crawled ahead, and she crept after him, pulling the door shut behind her.

"All clear?" Theo asked.

She glanced around. There were no animal stowaways in the chamber, which was very tight. She could hardly move without brushing against Theo.

"Go ahead," she said.

The chamber was filled with a whooshing noise. As Theo released the air, Ewa checked the readings on her suit. Everything was in order.

"Ready," Theo said.

"Then let's go take a look."

At her prompt, he opened the outer door with the help of a crank handle. "It's a little stiff," he said. "I bet it's been a long time since someone used this back access."

The door swung open into the darkness beyond it. Ewa thought she could feel a slight draft, but that was impossible. Something inside her felt drawn to where the disaster had transpired. Shouldn't she be scared?

"I'll go first," Theo said.

"That was always a given," she assured him.

The German swung his legs outside and then hooked himself to the guideline that ran around the Dragon module. After that, he lowered the rest of his body out of the lock. Ewa followed him, hooking her safety line right away, too. She was about to push herself out of the airlock when Mars appeared in her line of vision. She didn't move as the image seared itself into her memory. She could still remember what Earth had looked like when they had left its orbit. Mars was completely different. It looked about as large as the moon in the night sky. Only one half of it was illuminated by the sun, and that half was covered in reddish-brown spots. The other side was dark, but not completely black. It was quite apparent that this was a sphere in front of her and not a disc. This wasn't a stage set, no, it was stark reality. They would soon reach a new planet.

"Do you see it?" she asked.

"Yes, amazing. We've almost made it."

Ewa glanced up, then down at her feet. She needed to generate an artificial horizon, a line against which she could orient herself. Otherwise she would lose her balance. Theo stood next to her, two steps away. It looked as if he was leaning to the side, about to tip over. This effect was the result of the module's round shape.

"We have to get over there," Ewa said as she pointed at the hill that rose before them. This was the *Santa Maria*'s balloon-shaped center connector. The bow was located on the other side of it, and this was where they would find the damaged module.

"The lead rope has to be around here somewhere," Theo said.

During the construction phase, the builders had suspected that someone would need to make their way along here eventually, so they had attached a rope between the bow and the stern along which the astronauts could pull themselves hand over hand.

"You go to the left, I'll go right," Ewa said.

They went their separate ways and searched for the rope with their helmet lamps.

"Found it," Theo called.

Ewa moved down the module to his position. The magnetic boots were really very practical. Walking down the module's metal surface almost felt like walking on Earth.

"I'm hooking on," he said.

He leaned down, released the carabiner of his safety line from the module's guideline, and connected it to the lead rope. He then pushed off and slowly floated up the incline. Ewa did the same thing. However, she didn't want to float to the top. She tried to walk along the balloon's hull, shortening the length of her safety line to stay close against the ship. Her feet brushed against material that looked like an anorak shell. But there was nothing soft about it. She should have expected that, but she was still a little disappointed because she had imagined this would feel something like wading through a ball pit. At least she was covering the distance quickly.

It only took her a minute to crest the hill. Ewa adjusted her lamp to shine on the damaged module situated beneath her. She could only make out a few vague shadows. Was that the silhouette of a person? She felt cold, but shook off the feeling. It couldn't be a person. The shadow was too large for that. They had to get closer. Ewa inched forward, holding her line in tension. At least she had something to hold onto.

She came to a stop two meters away from the module. Theo joined her. The porthole glittered in the beams of her lamp. It looked like a tear had welled up in it. Ewa was suddenly overcome by a wave of sorrow, as if there were an injured animal in front of her. That had to be the stress talking. She shook her head and took a step forward.

They couldn't see the true extent of the damage to the module until they were standing right in front of it. The module was shaped like a flattened can, and its base looked as if a giant had pushed its finger into it from the back. Ewa felt like it looked as if something had tried to rape the ship. Tears pooled in her eyes. *No.* She didn't have time for that now.

"The engine must have started up on its own," Theo declared, his voice sounding flat.

"Maybe," she said.

"I'll take a closer look at it," he replied.

A good idea. He knew engines better than she did. It then occurred to her that there was something she had been suppressing—to recover the data, they would have to go inside the module. She would have preferred to do the engine evaluation. The module's hull was ripped at the base, which was what had caused it to lose air. However, a person couldn't fit through the gash.

"I'll give the airlock a try," Ewa said.

"Alright. Just call if you need me," Theo replied.

I'd like you to take over this job, Ewa thought. Imagining something was one thing. Actually having to witness it in person might exceed her abilities. Still, she didn't say anything.

"Andy, are you there?" she asked into the radio.

"Yep, as fresh as a daisy."

It was good to hear his voice. He was so... alive.

"I'm going in now."

"Have..." Andy faltered. He had probably been about to say, 'Have fun,' but had caught himself. "Good luck!" he said instead.

Ewa was already turning the lock. The door moved toward her. There was still air in the lock! Anyone who could have made it in here would have probably survived. But it had been too late by that point. She left the hatch behind her open. The internal door unlatched easily. If there was still any air in the module she would receive a warning, and even if the module lacked power, the door would remain locked for safety reasons.

But that didn't happen. The universe was behind her and in front of her. She floated through the open hatch into the command module. There they were, all three of them. They were lying on the floor, which on her last visit had still been the ceiling. Chuck, Henrik, and Piotr, their bodies strangely twisted. Ewa had to avert her eyes while she choked down the bile in her throat.

"Can you see this?" she asked. It had just occurred to her that the others could watch what was going on around her via her helmet camera.

"Yes," Gabriella murmured.

"Do you need some kind of diagnosis from me, Gabriella? Official time of death or something like that?"

"No, Ewa, they suffocated. That's obvious."

Ewa looked back at the three bodies. She had imagined death in a vacuum as more gruesome. Burst eyeballs and stuff, but there wasn't anything like that here. Ewa wished she could say that they looked at peace, but that wasn't true. They didn't look peaceful, more like they had fought to the bitter end.

"Ewa? Shankar and Asha are still missing."

The two technicians. A couple. They had both come from the Indian subcontinent and met during the training. Since then they had been inseparable, wherever they were. At the time of the accident they had been trying to start the engine. Ewa studied the circular floor. She caught sight of the wide gash that the engine must have created, causing the module to rapidly lose all of its air.

The engine room was located below this floor. Shankar and Asha had probably died before the three men up here. She searched for the access hatch, which was partially covered by Chuck's body. She had to nudge him a little to the side, which took a considerable amount of effort on her part, but she had to do it. Ewa gave a start when his hand suddenly moved. That had to be caused by some kind of tension that was building up as rigor mortis set in.

She opened the hatch. The space beneath it was tiny. Could the two technicians have even fit down here? But then she saw them. They were wrapped in each other's arms. It would have been heartwarming if it hadn't been so unbelievably sad. She found herself imagining their conversation before they had climbed down here. 'You or me? I'll do it. No, let me. Alright, let's do it together. It's tight, but we'll manage.' Ewa switched off her microphone for a moment. Nobody needed to hear her sniffling or how deeply she was gulping air. When she got herself back under control, she reactivated the mic.

"They're dead, too. You can see that."

"Thank you, Ewa," Gabriella said. "That's enough for the report. We all saw it and are witnesses."

"We should pay them our last respects," Ewa said.

"We'll do that. Later. First we need the data," was Gabriella's reply.

"Alright," Ewa said. She slowly stood up again. After brushing imaginary dust from her knees, she shut the hatch.

The computer consoles were hanging from the ceiling. Ewa had to reorient herself. She shut her eyes and envisioned her last visit here. In her mind, the ceiling reverted to being the floor. She activated her angular thruster and slowly rotated 180 degrees. She opened her eyes again. The computer was now underneath her. *I can't look up*, she thought. *If I do that, the bodies will fall on me.* It was an insane situation, so crazy thoughts had to be expected. She propelled herself over to the computers with a few arm strokes.

"Andy, are you there? Can you see this?"

"Yeah, it looks like the power's out."

"But where is the light in the module coming from?"

"The lights along the walls have their own buffers."

"Understood," she said. "What should I do?"

"Do you see the green switch there in the front? Flip it forward then backward."

She followed his instructions, but nothing happened.

"Okay," Andy said. "The computer isn't responding. There isn't much more you can do. Or do you have an emergency generator with you?"

"I could try to divert the power from the backpack attached to my suit."

"That wouldn't last long. Just bring me the memory panels."

"If you can tell me—"

"You can access everything right beneath the console," Andy said, interrupting her. "There you'll see some thin tin sheets. You need to bend them forward and pull them out."

Ewa knelt down. The memory boards were protected by metal sheets that were suspended in grooves at the top and the bottom. She needed a tool. Ewa reached into her suit satchel. Her fingers brushed against a screwdriver. That should do the trick. She shoved the blade along the bottom edge between the groove and the metal and pushed down on the handle. Through this lever effect the thin tin first bulged, then popped off its track, enabling her to remove it.

"Well done," Andy said.

Ewa was startled by this, but then she recalled the helmet camera. "And now?"

"Do you see the boards? They're in three rows of twelve."

"Which ones do you need?"

"All of them, if possible. I don't know when I'll have access again to so many replacement parts at one time."

"Really? I'm supposed to leave our friends lying here while I grab spare parts for you?"

"I'm sorry. That's not how I meant it. The memory is on the three right-hand boards on the upper row."

She touched the first of these boards with her glove. "You mean these?"

"Yes, exactly."

Before leaving the zoo module, Ewa had attached a bag to her tool belt. She now took it off, carefully extracting the boards and placing them inside the bag. "I hope they survive the transport," she said.

"They're space-seasoned," Andy replied. "No worries."

Ewa ignored a temptation to hurl the bag with the memory boards against the wall. *What good would that do? It would just give Andy other dumb ideas.* "Theo, how's everything with you?" she asked.

"I'm done with the engine. I was about to ask if I should join you."

He was probably already outside the airlock, waiting. But she could understand his hesitation. She wished she could have spared herself the sight of all this. Ewa picked up the bag and floated toward the airlock.

Before she left there was one thing she still had to do. She looked up at the ceiling. It looked as if Chuck, Henrik, and Piotr were waving at her. She squeezed her eyes shut and left the damaged module.

"I'M FINISHED," ANDY CALLED. HE WAS WORKING HIS WAY OUT of his sleeping bag, where he had retreated to evaluate the data.

"That only took you two hours," Theo remarked.

They had gathered at the center of the module—Andy, Theo, Gabriella, and Ewa in the middle, and the others grouped around them.

"What have we got?" Ewa asked.

"The analysis of the engine didn't reveal much. It's clear that it surged sharply at some point. The breach in the hull was a fatigue fracture. The material had already been subjected to a large number of accelerated states. Too many."

"So, if the engine had performed as normal, nothing would've happened?"

"That seems to be the case," Theo said.

"Then this was caused by a combination of human failure and material deficiency related to our need to cut financial corners?"

"No, Ewa," Andy interrupted. "Not if by 'human failure' you mean Shankar and Asha."

"Yes, that was what I was thinking of."

"The technicians couldn't do anything about it. It was obviously a software error. The navigational software failed. Or to be more exact: it reacted too slowly."

"Can a program be too slow?" Gabriella asked.

"You know how when you take a shower, sometimes you turn the water temperature up higher but nothing seems to happen? And then suddenly you're being scalded?"

"Yes, that happens to me all the time," Gabriella admitted.

"That's what happened with the navigational software. I assume that the fuel consistency was slightly altered somehow. The flow rate was different. The program gave the engine more gas to try to equalize the levels. And then the engine scalded us," Andy explained.

"That sounds plausible," Ewa said. "I think we can work with that." She was glad that Andy had found the perfect analogy.

"I can alter the program in the other module," Andy added. "I'm sure you were about to suggest that."

"Thanks, Andy," Ewa replied. "Our next business is to

take care of our dead and to give them a proper send-off. And we have to talk with the folks down at the Mars base. Could you handle that, Theo?"

The German nodded.

Ketut spoke up. "I would like to take care of the ceremony for Shankar and Asha," he said. "They were Hindus, like me, so there are a few special things to tend to."

"That would be great, Ketut. Thank you very much. Take however many people along as you need."

It felt like a stone rolled away from Ewa's heart. She had been afraid she would have to see the bodies again in their helpless state. She then noticed that her bladder had been trying to get her attention for hours now. She simply hadn't had time to take a few moments in private.

"I'll be back in a few minutes," she said, dropping to the lower level of the module.

The toilets were located in the back corner of the module. She closed the curtain around her and strapped herself down. She then held the suction tube between her legs. She was just starting to feel relief when someone tapped her on the shoulder. Could there never be any privacy around here?

"Excuse me, Ewa, but it's important."

"What can be so important, Andy, that you have to bother me right now?"

"That software error," Andy said. "What I said wasn't quite true."

"You misunderstood something? That happens."

"No, I did that deliberately. In the other module, which is completely identical to the command one in terms of its technical systems, the software is functioning perfectly."

"But that's a good thing, right?"

"No. It was functioning perfectly before I examined it."

"What are you telling me?"

"That someone might have tampered with the software in the command module. It would be highly irregular for there to be two identical modules, and for only one of them to run into a program error and the other not."

"You're talking about sabotage?"

"Yes, that's what people call it. Someone didn't want us to reach Mars."

Ewa felt herself grow warm. If Andy was right, they probably had an enemy on board, a murderer. They had to keep this quiet. "But it still could've been an accident," she said wistfully.

"Yes, that's why I didn't say anything earlier. It would've caused too much turmoil."

"You're right, Andy. Everyone would suspect everyone else."

"Precisely. But I wanted you to know. You're the one who knows what's going on around here."

"Why me? It was just a coincidence that I went over there and got the memory boards. And don't forget, I left the module right before the accident, as if I knew what was going to happen."

"You're not that cold-hearted, Ewa."

No I'm not, unfortunately for me, Ewa thought. The sight of the bodies had upset her greatly. She shook her head. "You don't know me," she said.

"Well enough, I do. That's why I'm going to suggest that you be made the new commander tomorrow."

"Me? You're crazy." Andy's suggestion was flattering, despite all that had happened. And the position would open up possibilities that had previously remained closed to her.

"True—otherwise I wouldn't even be here. Of all us crazies, you're the most level-headed. That's why you'd make the perfect commander. No, the only *possible* one."

"I don't know what to think," she said.

Andy left, and Ewa shut her eyes and tried to relax enough to finish emptying her bladder. She had never wanted command status. She leaned back against the wall and cried as her urine began to flow.

Sol 5, NASA base

"My name is Theo Kowalski."

Lance was disappointed. He had expected to see the blonde again, but she wasn't on the screen. Instead, he was facing a dark-haired man with earrings and a hard accent.

"Lance Leber. I'm responsible for the details of this taxi ride, or whatever it is," he answered.

"We've determined the cause of the explosion."

At least the guy wasn't beating around the bush. His accent indicated that he was German, though his name sounded Eastern European.

"Well?"

"A software error led to a fatigue fracture. We've made the necessary corrections."

How typical. Only rarely did catastrophes these days arise from a single cause. The safety mechanisms saw to that. During their training, they had analyzed the most tragic accidents of the past—Chernobyl, the Challenger explosion, the collapse of the Eiffel Tower, the Lunar Lander disaster, and so on. These were always one-of-a-kind events because people had proven themselves to be surprisingly teachable. However, the universe's capricious ability to invent new catastrophes seemed limitless. You couldn't be an engineer without acknowledging that reality.

"That seems reasonable," Lance said. "The module wasn't sufficiently tested before launch." *I shouldn't have said that,* he thought. *It was too late for it to matter anymore.*

"The budget," Theo replied with an eye roll. "However, nothing would've happened if the software error hadn't occurred. This is why I assume we should be able to slow down enough to enter orbit if we receive the fuel."

"That should go as planned. Our ship is already being prepared for launch. I estimate that we'll be able to lift off in three hours. We just need your precise course coordinates so that we can calculate the most fuel-efficient interception route. If needed, we can postpone our launch."

"ARE YOU COMING?" ASKED SHARON.

Lance set his tablet down on his narrow bed. His girlfriend smiled up at him. He had just made her his background photo because he realized that he was slowly forgetting her. How was that possible? They sent each other video messages daily, providing accounts of their days' activities, but they seemed to be drifting further and further apart. And yet it wasn't the millions of kilometers that were creating the distance, it was the time they were spending with other people. Would he even recognize her by the time he returned? They had been so certain...

With a shoulder shrug he got up to follow the pilot. As he walked out, his gaze went back to the screen.

Sharon followed his eyes. "Your girlfriend?"

He nodded.

"She looks nice."

"She is."

"How long have you been together?"

Lance was about to say *two years* when he realized that this was a complicated question. Over the past six months, had they actually been 'together?' And before that, during the training, when he had been gone multiple times for as long as two weeks? "I'm not sure how to answer that," he said.

Sharon stopped walking and looked at him. "The Mars blues?"

"I guess so."

She rested her arm lightly across his shoulders. Sharon was two years his junior, but right now, she seemed downright motherly. "It is inevitable that you will grow apart. And once you get back, it won't be the same as it was before. You'll both have changed. However, it can be even better than it was," she said.

"How do you know that?"

Sharon laughed. "I spent six months as a meteorologist for a research station in Antarctica. I could talk on the phone with my husband occasionally, but that was it."

"And after you got back, you were happy again?"

"We decided to get a divorce. After six months in the cold, I realized that my colleague from the university, the one who was overseeing my work, understood me a lot better than my own husband."

"Ah, that wasn't exactly what I wanted to hear," Lance said.

Sharon punched him lightly in the arm. "That's not my fault, my good man. But the moral of the story is—after that, I was better off. I learned some things about myself and my needs."

"I can't process that right now. I just want what I imagine to be reality. Your colleague from the university—what happened with him?"

"Are you asking if we're together? No, he was married and wanted to stay that way. I had to accept that. That was the only reason I even applied for the Mars mission. And now I'm here. From a poor neighborhood under Sugarloaf Mountain, all the way to humanity's first Mars base. That's pretty amazing, isn't it?"

Lance had to agree. It was amazing. He looked back one last time at his tablet, but the screen had already gone black.

IT WAS ONLY A SHORT DRIVE TO THE *ENDEAVOUR*. SHARON drove the Rover herself instead of leaving the work to the autopilot. Lance watched her from the passenger seat. They were alone. Sarah had offered to take them to the ship, but neither he nor Sharon had wanted that. It would have just made their farewells more uncomfortable. This wasn't anything significant, really, purely routine. They would fly into orbit, transfer a little freight, and return to the surface.

The final step, their landing, would be the most treacherous one, but even this had been practiced a thousand times. It was in this area that NASA had really profited from the private companies, particularly SpaceX and Blue Origin. For cost reasons, they had perfected the thrust-vector landing procedure. The old practice of a module landing in the ocean wouldn't have worked on the dry Mars surface. Thanks to the planet's much lower gravitational pull, however, it was significantly easier than on Earth to gently land on the surface with the help of the engines' braking ability.

It was entertaining to watch Sharon drive the Rover. She sometimes stuck the tip of her tongue out of the corner of her mouth. She looked very focused and very calm, a completely different person behind the wheel, calm and prudent instead of spontaneous and emotional, as was her norm. In all honesty, pilots weren't needed anymore, but Lance found he felt safer with her than he did with the autopilot.

"Did you also drive a Rover at the North Pole?" he asked when the silence grew uncomfortable.

"In Antarctica. At the *South* Pole," she corrected him.

He bit his tongue to stifle a smartass remark.

"But, yes. It wasn't all that different. There's more than just ice down there. There are desert-like regions full of stones and debris, which are about as cold as it is here. The only difference is that you can breathe there, at least until you freeze."

"And in the permanent ice?"

"That's a different story altogether. I'm already looking forward to us researching the ice cap at Mars's North Pole."

"Why?"

"Here in the ever-present desert, the problems are presented by the things you can see. Take that boulder, for example. I can't tell how large it is, but the laser can tell me, and so I know how far I have to drive to get around it. In the ice, it's the obstacles you can't see that present the problem. Antarctica is one giant glacier. You can find ten-meter deep ice caves that are only covered by a thin layer of ice. Even if you can see it with the radar, you have no idea if the layer of ice will hold. You often have to take long detours just to be safe. And, sometimes the overlay might be too thick for the radar, but still fragile."

"Sounds exciting and dangerous," Lance said.

"Absolutely. But as you can see, I'm still here. Everything is possible."

"Will you take me along the next time you go to the South Pole? If you crash the Rover into an ice cave, I can repair the chain or transform it into a helicopter."

"It's a deal," Sharon said, laughing.

"There it is. Isn't it pretty?" Lance observed.

They had just caught sight of the *Endeavour* in the gloomy twilight of a noonday Mars. The ship was standing in a mostly flat area devoid of obstacles. This spot had been selected as an optimal landing site by robotic explorers, before their arrival. The *Endeavour*'s nose was pointing proudly at the sky. Its curved lines looked feminine, and the fins on its sides added a note of elegance.

The *Endeavour* was standing on three support legs. A tube wound its way from between its legs like an umbilical cord, leading to a fully-automated fueling station that supplied the ship with nutritional matter which had been cultivated on

Mars. This included fuel for the engine—comprised of oxygen and hydrogen—as well as oxygen and water for the life support system.

Sharon steered the Rover right next to the rocket. She had to park in a very specific spot. Acoustic signals indicated how far off she was from that mark. After three minutes of small adjustments, the beeping stopped.

"We're here," she said, although it wasn't yet time to get out.

Before Lance was able to see that they were rising, he could feel it—they were being lifted up. A retractable rod raised the pressurized cabin up to the level of the *Endeavour*'s entry hatch. It jiggled slightly, as if they were being carried upward by elevator. Lance tried to see the base from their position, but either there wasn't enough light, or it was too well-concealed due to their position halfway down the curving surface.

The pilot released her safety belt, which her seat protested with an irritating beep. Sharon ignored it and reached for her fat, leather travel bag.

Lance got up, too. All he had was one small plastic bag in which he had packed an extra pair of underwear, a toothbrush and toothpaste, and a comb. *What could Sharon possibly need for two days?* A squeaking sound came from the back part of the cabin. An oval-shaped tube was now extending from the Rover to the *Endeavour*'s airlock.

Sharon pointed in its direction and said, "It's about time."

At that moment, an intensely green light flashed on, practically blinding Lance. "They certainly wanted us to see it," he said.

"Nobody could ever overlook that," Sharon agreed. She turned the wheel on the hatch to the left. "Let's go!"

She dropped to her knees at the hatch and crawled off, sliding the bag ahead of her. The tunnel in front of them was so low that you couldn't walk through it even if you crouched down. *Crawling on your hands and knees for a little over two meters isn't the end of the world, though,* Lance thought. He moved into the tube, closed the hatch behind him, and followed the pilot.

Once he reached the *Endeavour*, he immediately recognized the familiar smell of the past six months. Either their recently inhabited Mars base was missing something significant, or they hadn't spent enough time over there yet. In any case, the smell here was completely different from that over there. *More engine oil here, fewer people,* determined the mechanic in him. There were no oil stains to be seen—or smelled—in their base. It might be because of the life support system. The model on the ship came from the space technology industry, while the version for the Mars base had been designed by a renowned climate control manufacturer.

Lance glanced around. They had moved off the ship only five days ago, but it felt to him like much longer ago than that. The ship looked as if it had been abandoned for weeks. Maybe that was due to the dust that had gathered on the horizontal surfaces. In weightless environments, dust collected much faster in static electricity zones—and not on tables and shelves. With his sleeve, he wiped off the table they'd always used.

"We can clean later," Sharon called from the upper level, where the bridge was located. She was already sitting in her pilot seat.

Lance climbed up the ladder. The overhead light was off, but the room was still bright because the many little lights on the console provided enough illumination. Lance felt like he was in a science-fiction film. All that was missing was Mike beaming a hologram of himself onto the bridge. Instead, he called the old-fashioned way, over one of the monitors.

Sharon brought up his image on the seat screen. "We're ready," she said. "I've gone through the launch checklists with the autopilot and am just waiting on Lance."

"Where is he?" Mike asked.

"He's been cleaning the kitchen, but I think I hear him coming."

"Haha," Lance said. "You might laugh, but it's really

dusty down there. It's enough to bring out your inner clean freak."

"Whatever," Sharon said. "I need you for the launch procedure."

"First you want me in the kitchen, but now you need me up here?"

"You're a real couple of sweetie pies. Can you just tell me when lift-off is?" Mike interjected.

"What did you say, Mike? 'Sweetie pies?'" Sharon asked.

"Yes, 'sweetie pies.' Anything else?"

"What is that supposed to mean?"

"I'll explain it to you when you get back."

"Okay, deal," Sharon agreed.

"T MINUS TEN MINUTES," A COMPUTER VOICE ANNOUNCED.

Lance looked quickly at the clock. It was just past one in the afternoon. His lap was covered by a thick pile of old-fashioned paper from which he was reading off one question after the other.

Sharon checked to make sure that the data fell within the acceptable parameters. From time to time reports came in from the subsystems about things like the pressure in the oxygen tank, the wind velocity, or the angle at which the *Endeavour* was standing on the surface. Mike had calculated the launch time such that they would reach the rendezvous point with the *Santa Maria* with the lowest possible fuel consumption. The MfE ship had been deflected by Mars's gravitational pull and was flying in orbit around the sun. They had to stay beside it long enough to pump over fuel and bring five crew members on board.

"Tell me. If we have enough room, why don't we just take all of them with us?" Lance asked.

"Because they've asked us to only take five of them. Are you still working on the list?"

"GN&C?"

Sharon studied two displays to her left. "Complete."

"But what if they die?"

"I don't think they want to forfeit what they brought with them. And that's okay. How would we take care of fifteen additional people?"

"We have enough emergency rations for three years. We'd manage."

"The MfE people cannot go back to Earth. They want to stay here permanently, don't forget that. And now, let's keep going."

"T minus five minutes," the computer announced.

Lance continued through his list until Mike interrupted. "Ready to launch?" he asked.

"Confirmed," Sharon answered.

"Correct," Lance said.

"T minus one minute." This time it was Mike who said it. "Begin countdown."

The computer started counting down instantly. They didn't have much more to do except keep their eyes out for any lights that unexpectedly started blinking red. The computer monitored these. Lance leaned back in his seat.

"To the stars," he suddenly blurted.

"You poet," Sharon replied.

"T minus ten," he heard.

"Nine."

"Eight."

He thought about his girlfriend. *What is her eye color, again?*

"Three."

"Two."

Blue. They're blue.

"One."

"Launch."

The entire ship vibrated. It was a mind-blowing moment. Like a tiger gathering its strength before leaping, the *Endeavour* started its engines. The combustion process combined oxygen and hydrogen to create water. The dry Mars surface was instantly drenched in steam.

The ship lifted off. First, centimeter by centimeter, then faster and faster. The inertia pressed Lance into his seat. He could see on his monitor that they had just broken the sound barrier. No sound was produced by this, only the deep rumbling in the belly of the ship and the increasingly-loud whistling of the layers of atmosphere as they passed through them. The whistling dropped as the atmosphere grew thinner. Instead of a muddy, pinkish brown, the porthole was now filled with the black of outer space.

'To the stars,' Lance thought. *And there they are.*

May 25, 2042, Santa Maria

Ewa never liked it when she could remember her dreams. This was why she preferred to take a pill every evening, which sent her into a deep, dreamless sleep. This had been less necessary in recent times, but this morning her dream had seemed astonishingly real as she woke up. It had been terrible. She didn't want to think about the details. Suppression was the only way to alleviate her emotional pain. Nothing at all had changed.

The excitement must have caused it. Andy planned to follow through on his threat to suggest her as the new commander today. She knew he'd do it. On the one hand, she *was* excited. It was an incredible honor. On the other hand, she was scared. She wasn't afraid of the duties or worried that she wasn't up to the responsibilities. She was concerned she would fulfill them all too well. She was once again moving down the path she had started forging so long ago without consciously being aware of it.

Ewa felt torn. If she didn't accept the position—assuming the job was even offered—who would be the next choice? Andy lacked support. Theo was nice and was willing to get his hands dirty, but he didn't show any initiative. Gabriella maybe, but she wasn't the best speaker, and she sometimes demanded too much from people; she really was the embodiment of the stereotypical temperamental Italian. Chuck had been the perfect commander.

Ewa's mind turned to what all they had to do today. They had to inter their five dead comrades in space, rendezvous with the NASA ship, refuel, and decelerate. Then they could land eventually. But first and foremost, they had to reach Mars orbit.

Ewa unzipped her sleeping bag and turned back the shell. She flinched. The others had gathered around her sleeping spot. Andy called out something, but she couldn't hear anything. She took off her headphones and heard the others clapping.

"What's going on? It's not my birthday, is it?" she asked.

It was common practice in her homeland to wake up the birthday child with a serenade.

"In a way, it is," Andy countered. "I made you a treat."

"Yes, you did," she said.

"I have spoken to each crew member individually, so there wouldn't be any group pressure. And each of them, every person here on board, has confirmed my personal opinion that you are the optimal successor to Chuck."

Ewa had to admit that Andy really seemed to like her. She had never spent all that much time with him. She had tended to keep herself apart from the others. The only exception to this had been Chuck. If she had wanted company, she had spent time with him. He'd had something about him that made you feel safe.

"That is very nice of you," she said. Where were the right words when she needed them?

"We hope that you will accept our election," Gabriella said.

"You've already voted?"

The doctor nodded. "Fourteen ayes, one abstention."

"Ah, so you counted my sleeping as an abstention."

"We thought that was fair."

"Alright then. It wouldn't make sense for us to spend lots of time debating this. Someone has to do it, and you have chosen me, so I can hardly protest. Thank you very much, all of you, for your trust."

Everyone clapped.

"But now we should get to work. How far is it to the fueling point?"

"The rendezvous with the *Endeavor* will take place in about three hours," Andy said.

"I'm sorry to cause any stress, but we need to take care of our dead before then. Ketut, you offered to take over those duties, right?"

"Yes, Ewa. We have already secured Chuck, Henrik, and Piotr. Now we are dealing with the other two. We just wanted to wait until your appointment as our leader was official."

"Thank you. This is great. Just let me know when Shankar and Asha are over here, too." She looked at the German, who looked exhausted. "Theo?"

"Yes?"

"When was the last time you slept?

"Uh..."

"Please be honest."

"About thirty-six hours ago."

"Go rest for two hours. I can't manage without you for longer than that, and I'm sure you'll want to be here for the memorial ceremony, but those two hours are necessary."

"I promised the NASA people that I would report in thirty minutes from now."

"I'll take care of it. Now go to bed."

Theo nodded and floated downward.

Ewa looked around. It felt good to give the orders. She had been afraid of that.

SHE RECALLED HAVING SEEN THE MAN WHOSE FACE WAS ON THE screen, but she couldn't remember his name. It had a nice ring to it, though, something alliterative.

"Hello, *Endeavour*, Ewa Kowalska from the *Santa Maria* here."

"Lance Leber," the man replied.

Ah yes, Lance Leber, she repeated to herself, *A melodic name.* "Pleased to see you again. I'm the new commander."

"Under other circumstances, I would offer you my congratulations, Ewa."

"Yes, I would prefer for Chuck to be speaking with you right now."

"I can understand that," said Lance, abruptly going straight to the point. "What is your status?"

His commander had introduced him as an engineer, Ewa recalled. That get-to-the-point behavior would fit. "We've already turned the ship, and your base transmitted the course data. We will reach the optimal position in ninety minutes."

"Have you ever done something like this before?"

"Both modules were fueled in Earth orbit, so we aren't completely clueless about how this works. At the same time, Chuck was in charge of that."

"And on top of that, we'll be on divergent orbits," Lance said. "We'll be riding on a giant carousel. You'll just happen to pass us in a wide curve, and from our carousel, we'll extend out to you the humongous teddy bear we've just won at the shooting gallery."

He'd actually made her chuckle. "Nice metaphor," she said. "And all this will take place at a speed of five kilometers per second, not per hour."

Lance frowned and sighed. "It sounds worse when you put it that way. The fuel line is fifty meters long. We'll get as close to you as possible, and then our ships can drift apart by a few meters. Mike, our math genius, claims that we only need to transfer the necessary amount of oxygen. You have enough hydrogen, I've heard. Then you can slow down to enter orbit, and we'll have all the time in the world to get your people on board."

"That sounds good," Ewa said. "Hopefully, there will be no surprises."

"We'll handle any problems that might arise. That's why I'm here," Lance said.

He obviously sought to calm her nerves. She felt half flattered, half underestimated. This happened more often than not with people who didn't know her yet.

"One more thing," Lance continued. "Are you sure you don't want us to take your entire crew? That would be the safest course of action."

"You think so? Yes, that sounds reasonable," Ewa said. But then something in her mind clicked and she knew she had just made a mistake. "And I thank you for the offer," she said, correcting the course of their conversation. "However, how could we build our colony without all our supplies? We'll need people up here to handle the planning of that."

"Makes sense. The captain always goes down with the ship."

"True, you could put it that way if you wanted. We'll talk again in about eighty minutes. We first must hold a memorial service for our deceased comrades."

"*Endeavour* out," Lance declared.

"We're ready," Ketut said.

She hardly recognized him—he had shaved his hair off completely.

The Balinese man noticed her look. "This is the way the sons of the deceased normally show their sorrow. Since Shankar and Asha didn't have any children, and we can't really perform many of the Hindu rites, I wanted to do this for them."

"What would still need to be done for their souls' benefit?"

"We washed and anointed them while sitting up, as prescribed. We actually should have burned their bodies to release their souls. We will have to trust the sun to do that once we have sent the bodies out through the airlock."

Ewa didn't tell him that the bodies wouldn't fall into the sun. They would be moving much too fast for that to happen. Ketut probably knew that anyway. But eventually the sun would expand into a red giant and consume everything out to Mars's orbit. The souls of the two Hindus would be free at this point, at the latest. Eternity is a long time. There was something to be said for having an immortal soul. Ewa herself didn't believe in it, even though she had been raised Catholic.

"Good, I'm coming," she announced.

Ewa released herself from her wall strap and floated down to the connector to the functional module. The others had already gathered there.

To Ewa the bodies looked striking, almost beautiful. All five of them were wrapped in white cloths, and their faces were visible. Chuck, Shankar, Asha, Piotr, and Henrik appeared peaceful, as if they had left this world without any grievance. That was good. It would make it easier to bid them farewell. How had Ketut and his assistants managed this? Ewa remembered what she had seen inside the damaged, airless module. Henrik and Piotr had looked desperate, Chuck furious. The two Indians appeared filled with mutual love. The desperation, fury, and suffering were gone. What remained was the love. At least that was what she saw. Or was she just imagining it?

Seeming to sense Ewa's approach, Nancy turned toward her. That was a signal to the others. Ewa felt self-conscious, and her cheeks flushed. She needed a few deputies, someone else to stand by her. Theo, Andy, and Gabriella came to mind. But that was a problem she could take care of once they had landed. They were expecting her to say something. Ewa bit her lip. She had prepared something the night before. Hopefully, she could conjure up the words.

"Dear Chuck, dear Shankar, dear Asha, dear Piotr, dear Henrik," she began, slowly moving past them. "Like everyone else here, I was able to share this exciting time with you. It was, without a doubt, the most important years of your lives and mine. We took this path together, one that only a very few were courageous enough to choose. Of course, I was afraid to undertake this journey that had no return, and I'm sure you felt the same. However, your courage was greater than your fear, and this was our greatest commonality."

She paused a few seconds, then went on in an even more pensive tone. "I wish I could have spent more time with you. I'm still angry about the accident that ended your lives, and I'm sad that I will never get to talk to you again. But I have a feeling the purpose of this trip has been fulfilled for you. In a few minutes you will become satellites of our sun. Once we have completed our mission and our colony on Mars flourishes—a dream shared by every one of us here—then we will be able to look up at you."

Ewa pretended to wipe a tear from her eye, because it seemed like what should be done at this point.

"This is all a nice vision," she continued, "but it isn't a consolation. It is impossible to find consolation right now. At least I can't. I'm upset that you're no longer here, and I will always miss you. We will feel your absence every single day. We will eventually get used to it, but despite that, there will still be a hole in our lives that fate has created."

Ewa fumbled in her pocket for a handkerchief, but she couldn't find one. Theo noticed and handed her a package of tissues. She wiped her nose.

"This might sound like a contradiction," she picked up again. "I'm inconsolable, but I still find comfort in the fact that you will always be here. This is one of the contradictions that make us sometimes love—and hate—life so much. Dear Chuck, dear Shankar, dear Asha, dear Piotr, dear Henrik," she said, "it is time for us to say goodbye and to wish you safe travels. I'm certain that we'll see each other again someday."

It was strange. Although she didn't believe in an afterlife, she had spoken this last sentence with deep conviction. Ewa turned around as the tears flooded her eyes. She was crying for herself, but nobody knew that.

It was silent in the belly of the *Santa Maria*. Even the life support system seemed to be running quieter today. The others said their farewells to the dead in silence. The only audible sounds were whispers, rustling, and occasional weeping. Some tears had already dried up. She watched Ketut give a signal. Theo helped him carry one body after the other through the hatch and into the module. Somebody in a spacesuit floated up from the side. Ewa was surprised to read Ellen's name on the badge. Of everyone, this young woman was going to be the one to commit the bodies to space from the airlock? But she had probably volunteered for this duty.

Ellen disappeared into the module. Ewa couldn't see what was going on, but she could guess. Ellen was taking one body after the other into the airlock and pushing them out the hatch. It was hard work. When they had constructed the airlock, no one had given any thought to having a robot on board to do something like this. She needed to reevaluate her image of Ellen.

The young woman reappeared twenty minutes later. Her face was red, and she was sweaty. The spot next to the module's hatch, where just a few minutes ago five bodies had been lying, was now empty.

"Attention, *Santa Maria*!" That was Lance's voice.

"We're ready," Theo answered. His voice sounded muffled since he was outside the ship's hull at the moment.

Ewa was gazing at a screen divided into two fields. On the left, she could track the flight paths of the *Santa Maria* and the *Endeavour*. The right field gave her the view through Theo's helmet camera. There wasn't anything to see right now. The camera's light wasn't powerful enough to pick up the tiny points of the stars. Without them, the sky was eerily black.

Everything on the left side seemed to be taking place in slow motion. One dot was moving along an acutely elliptical course around Mars. The orbit had this shape because each time the *Endeavour* got close to the planet, it accelerated sharply. This was the precondition for the two different ships to reach a similar speed. However, she could only see a tiny section of this course, which meant she couldn't tell that the route was curved.

The second dot was the *Santa Maria.* It was still traveling at a faster speed and was slowly catching up to the other dot. In the strongly zoomed-in view that showed the courses of the two dots, the lines seemed to be running almost parallel.

"Can you see us yet? We have you on our radar," Lance reported in on the other side. "We're extending the hose now."

As Lance had explained to her, the hose would hold stable in space. There was nothing that could either slow it down or deflect it.

"Still can't see anything," Theo replied.

"Just wait. I'll count down the meters," Lance declared.

"Ninety... eighty-five... eighty...,"

Lance waited a few seconds between each number. The camera still wasn't picking up anything. There it was! The spotlight had caught a shadow. That must be the *Endeavour.* What was Theo feeling out there?

"I see you," was all he said.

"The line is on its way."

This was the trickiest moment, except for all the delicate moments that were still to come. Theo had to catch the half-meter thick hose that was coming toward him from out of the darkness. However good the *Endeavour*'s aim was, it wouldn't be able to hit the fuel tank neck. Usually a robotic arm took over this work. But during the construction of the *Santa Maria,* no one had thought about that. And even if they had, they probably couldn't have afforded one.

"I'm in position," Theo announced.

"Seventy... sixty-five... sixty...," Lance said. "You should—"

"Ha, I see it! You're two meters too high. I'll have to jump."

"Then do it!" Ewa called.

Theo was right, he had to jump. Surely he was on a safety line. He couldn't have forgotten that. Ewa glanced over at the left side of the monitor. The *Endeavour* had done its job too well. It had gotten closer to the *Santa Maria* than expected, which was why the hose was now off target.

"Ooof," she heard Theo say. "I... I've got it. I'm pulling myself back down."

It was only two meters. That shouldn't—and couldn't—take long. The image from the helmet camera swung back and forth. Obviously, Theo was searching for something to grab onto. Ewa held her breath in suspense.

"Ah," Theo said. Wheezing followed, then a metallic sound. Was he screwing the hose on? The helmet camera only showed the module's outer hull. Theo had other tasks more important than to document his work, and he knew what he needed to do. Ewa held her finger over the button that she must push shortly.

"Start fueling," Theo finally shouted.

Ewa hesitated, but then pushed the button. They were still okay on time. Whoever it was—whether Lance or Sharon—up in the *Endeavour* had been waiting on this. Liquid oxygen immediately shot through the line under high pressure. This was the only way the hydrogen they already had on board could combust.

Ewa switched over to the fuel gauge. Guillermo, the Mexican engineer, had done the calculation for her, so she knew the amount they needed for a successful deceleration maneuver. That was the most important thing right now. Once they reached orbit, they could refuel for the subsequent landing procedure. At first, the gauge moved slowly. Guillermo had warned her that at the beginning some fuel would be lost. They had thirty seconds.

The *Santa Maria* was gradually, but steadily, passing the *Endeavour*. The hose could reach a distance of about ninety meters. Ewa drummed her fingers on her armrest. The seconds seemed to go on forever. It was like they were filling the tank of their heavy-duty truck, while slowly passing a fuel truck to the left. Luckily, here in space, there weren't any potholes. The only danger they faced was the possibility of the process taking too long.

They wouldn't get a second chance. After their convergence, Mars's gravitational pull wouldn't give the *Endeavour* any choice except to circumnavigate the planet, while they would have to continue on their orbit around the sun. But by the time the *Endeavour* had circled the planet, the *Santa Maria* would already be so far away from Mars that no one could help them.

Two bars. It was going faster now. Why hadn't someone programmed a more precise gauge? *Because fueling isn't usually a time-sensitive matter,* she reminded herself. Six bars—that was the target.

"Fifteen," Andy said from behind her.

That wasn't good. Half the time was up already, but they still weren't at three bars. Was there anything she could do? Now was the only chance! Her thoughts swirled, and everyone was watching. She had to do something! If only she hadn't...

"Ten," Andy said.

Ewa shivered as if she were floating in the liquid oxygen. She rubbed her wrists. "Theo, get ready to disconnect the hose," she said.

The hose was equipped with a quick-release system. These had been developed for use with robotic arms, which were never as flexible as a human hand. But now it was practical, since all Theo needed to do was push a lever and the hose would detach itself. If it didn't react fast enough, the hose would tear. In that case, they wouldn't be able to fuel the module for the landing, which would mean that they couldn't reach the surface.

Ewa watched the screen. Four and a half bars and almost out of time.

"How does it look?" Theo asked.

"Bad," she said.

If Theo knew how bad it really looked, he would try to

postpone the moment. That would be risky. He had to push the lever at the exact second they had calculated.

"Four three two one," Andy counted down loudly.

"Disconnecting the hose," Theo said calmly.

Ewa watched him via the video stream from his helmet camera. The hose fell away rapidly, a white liquid streaming out of its end, instantly evaporating. Theo then turned his back on the scene. His work outside was done.

"Come on in, Theo," Ewa said quietly.

"How is it in there?"

It was quiet inside the *Santa Maria*. By this point, they all knew what had happened.

"Unfortunately, we didn't reach the amount we needed," Ewa said.

"And you're just hanging around there?" Theo practically shouted into the microphone. "You have to find another solution, right away! Pull yourselves together, all of you! Damn it!"

Ewa unbuckled her harness. They didn't have enough fuel, that much was crystal clear. Then Ellen suddenly touched her leg. She was floating below Ewa. Ellen, the young chick who had volunteered for the duty of sending all five bodies into space. Ewa had underestimated her. She had forgotten that each person on board had gone through the selection process. Although Mars for Everyone had never collected enough funding, there had been plenty of support behind the project. No one who had made it onto the crew could be described as ordinary.

"Yes, Ellen?"

"The tank isn't as full as we'd like it to be," she said.

"That's the understatement of the day."

"But not wrong."

"No, you're correct," Ewa managed to say with a smile.

"If I paid enough attention in my physics classes—and in all modesty, I hold a Ph.D. in physics, as well as degrees in astronomy and chemistry—then that is relative."

"What do you mean?"

"We want to slow the ship down to a certain speed."

"Right."

"Purely physically speaking, we want to transition a certain mass *m* to a negative velocity. The larger *m* is, the harder it will be for us to do that, because of the inertia tied to that particular mass. On the other hand, the smaller *m* is, the easier it would be to slow down. All we have to do is reduce our mass. For example, the damaged module—"

"Oh! Of course. That's... so basic."

Ellen looked offended.

"No, I didn't mean to criticize you, not at all. But I should've thought of that myself! Have you done the calculations?

"Only roughly. The Dragon V4 weighs about 5.7 tons, right?"

"No clue," Ewa said. "I'm actually a farmer."

"And a chemist. I read up on you. We're colleagues. But the size is right. The second Dragon weighs just as much. Now, it's just a question of how heavy the inflated module in between is. Unfortunately, I don't know that. It doesn't weigh more than a balloon, does it?"

"I'm afraid it does, Ellen. First of all, the walls are filled with water. Second, the supplies and machines. Third, the people. I don't think we weigh much less than fifty tons. But we should discuss this with the others."

THEO WAS THE LAST ONE TO JOIN THEM. HE TOSSED HIS rubber shoes into the corner. They moved in a straight line to the wall. Ewa watched them bounce off it with a squeak and a little spray of water.

"So, what's going on?" Theo asked, his torso damp and sweaty. His tattoos glistened as if he had just oiled them.

"We need to reduce our weight. So much so that the fuel we have will be enough to slow us down. And we have to do this in the next two hours," Ewa said.

"Good. Loud and clear. We should ditch the broken module right now."

"Slow down," Ellen said. Theo glanced at her. Ewa noticed his eyes held astonishment. He didn't know her like this. "We might need it to store other things."

"Sorry. I was too hasty," Theo replied.

"We were just in the process of taking suggestions from every division about what we can get rid of. The list is long, but it's still not enough to ensure that we can safely make orbit. Our belly is simply too full."

"Could we give some things to the *Endeavour*?" Theo suggested.

"That won't work. We won't run into them again as long as we stay on this course," Ellen said. She had taken the lead on this discussion, and that was okay with Ewa.

"And if we let most of the water out of the sidewalls of the balloon? We don't need the radiation shield any longer."

"That's not enough either, Theo."

"Then there's only one solution," he said. Ewa suspected that the others wouldn't like where this was going.

"Yeah? Then spit it out," Andy said. He also seemed to have a suspicion about this.

"We all squeeze into the functioning module and jettison the rest of the ship."

"You're crazy," Andy said.

"There aren't any other alternatives," Theo countered. "Besides, this is a very reasonable option. You're crazy if you flat out reject this."

"Just a minute, boys," Ellen cut in. "Theo's basically right, isn't he? We'll definitely have enough fuel if we only have to slow down the one module. But will we all fit inside?"

"It wouldn't be comfortable. The Dragon is only approved for eight passengers. However, I think the volume would suffice. Once we're in orbit, half of us can transfer to the *Endeavour*. That way we won't have to share the landing loungers as couples."

"You're forgetting something critical," Andy said, his

voice sounding threatening. "The middle part of this space ship is our mission. That's where the machines and provisions are that we'll need for our settlement. We can kiss our mission goodbye if we lose all that. Why have we gone through all this hardship if we're going to do that? We wanted to build something better than what the other humans have achieved down there. We can't give up so easily on that."

Ewa had never liked what seemed to her to be the proselytizing branch of MfE. And that was putting it mildly. Was Andy really part of that ideology?

Theo was watching Andy with a furrowed brow. He seemed to be trying to come up with a suitable response. "If we can't reach orbit, our mission is dead either way," he said. "Is that really so hard to understand?"

"I understand quite clearly what you want, Theo," Andy declared. "You've never been committed to this goal. There's only one thing you care about, and that's yourself."

Ewa was amazed that the German could remain calm. Either Andy was right, but it didn't matter to Theo, or the accusations were baseless and, thus, bounced right off him. She didn't know which was the case.

Theo didn't respond right away. He scratched his forehead and folded his arms. To Ewa, this looked like theatrical performance meant to symbolize composure.

"True, I want to survive," Theo finally said. "I have no interest in floating through space for eternity like the five good people we sent off today. But at least their deaths weren't pointless. Their deaths were regrettable, but it was something that happened to them, something they couldn't change. If someone had given them the option to either postpone or avoid death, they would've taken it. But nobody came and warned them. However, we have a choice. We owe it to Chuck, Henrik, Piotr, Shankar, and Asha to use this opportunity."

One-zero, Theo. And just like that, he got the others behind him. Who else might belong to the ideological contingent? That would become clear, sooner or later. At this point,

Theo the pragmatist was in the lead. That was obvious from the others' faces.

"I suggest that we draft a list of all the things that we absolutely *must* bring into the module," Ewa said. "Ellen will collect your suggestions. You all have one hour to do this, and then we'll talk about it. Each of you must keep in mind that we will be leaving behind many valuable items."

"May I say one thing?" Ellen added. "The items won't be lost forever. In the belly of the *Santa Maria*, they will orbit the sun, and will occasionally come close to Mars. We can fetch them then, if we still need them."

"As long as we're still alive," Andy said darkly.

"THAT IS VERY REASONABLE," SAID THE MAN FROM THE *Endeavour*. Ewa had both him and his colleague on the screen. They looked relieved.

"Before our landing, we will need to transfer a few passengers over to you," Ewa said.

"No problem. We'll reach you in two hours."

The image vanished, but then reappeared. The *Endeavour* had already slipped behind the face of the planet, so another orbiter had to be transmitting the signal.

"Thank you so very much, both of you. We will try to consume as few of your resources as possible. MfE is still planning to establish an independent colony."

"We can talk about that later."

The man—wasn't his name Lance?—smiled rigidly. He was probably worried that the NASA base would have to provide for fifteen additional people indefinitely. Ewa wanted to do everything she could to keep this time as brief as possible. Despite their willingness to help, the NASA people made her uncomfortable.

Ellen handed her the list of the few items they could rescue. She seemed quite disheartened.

“Don’t worry,” Ewa said. “What the ship has loaded in its belly won’t be lost. We’ll just be delayed by a year or so.”

“That’s a long time,” Ellen replied. “We have to offer the crew an alternative.”

“And what would that be?”

“Maybe... the initiative could send the next load of supplies from Earth a little early,” Ellen suggested.

“That’s not realistic,” Ewa said. “They didn’t have enough money to rent an Earth-based station to stay in contact with us, or even to procure a slot in NASA’s Deep Space Network, at the very least. Or did you believe the official excuse they gave, that no one could respond in a timely fashion due to the transit time of the messages? That’s why we were forced to break off all contact with Earth.”

Ellen sighed. “Then I guess we’re ready,” she said. “Anything else?”

“Just a minute.” Ewa skimmed the list. Her animals were on it, as well as the seeds. Those were the main things. All of the machines would have to remain in orbit, as well as a large portion of the supplies. They would bring along enough to feed the fifteen of them for a maximum of five days. So that the spacesuits didn’t have to take up unnecessary space, each person would wear their own. The landing would be torturous, since the suits weren’t made for this kind of strain. Nonetheless, they would reach their goal.

“What about the computer replacement parts?” Ewa asked.

“Andy wrote up his own list for this. He said it would take him too much time to jot down every chip and module, so I assigned him a general spatial volume,” Ellen said.

Ewa didn’t respond. She would have to speak with Andy later, once they were down on the surface. These kinds of exceptions shouldn’t be allowed. However, if she protested now, Ellen would feel unjustly criticized.

“Thanks,” Ewa finally said. “If everyone is content, I can live with that.”

"*Everyone* content?" Ellen laughed cynically. "*Nobody* is content, and they all blame me personally."

"That's normal," Ewa said. "But you've simply done your job, and I'm grateful for that."

"If we wait any longer, we'll miss our window of opportunity to jump into orbit," Andy declared.

Ewa first had to search for him, because a large, free-floating crate blocked her line of vision. Ewa caught the shoulder of a spacesuit hurrying past her. The occupant turned around. All she could tell through the view hole was that it was a woman. Ewa read her name. It had to be the astronaut from the Philippines.

"Marilou, could you please take care of securing this box? On Mars, it will weigh at least a hundred kilograms, and it shouldn't fall on top of anyone's head or toe."

"Of course," Marilou answered.

"Andy, how much time do we have?" she asked.

"Fifteen minutes."

"Then we'll start the orbit countdown in ten. There's too much stuff flying around here, and we need to strap it down."

Most of the others had put on their helmets, so she switched over to the general channel.

"The deceleration procedure will start in ten minutes. Our highest priority is to secure every single free-floating object in the module. Then go ahead and strap yourselves down. There are enough harnesses."

This set the crew in motion. Besides herself, there were fourteen men and women in the module. The walls had almost completely vanished behind all the objects that had been fastened to them. Only the area around the airlock was still open because once they reached orbit, this was the access point for the eight astronauts who would be transferring over to the *Endeavour*.

"Andy, it's time to release the module from the ship."

"Yes, ma'am!"

Ewa thought she heard a metallic click, but that must have been her imagination. It was too noisy in the module for her to hear something like that.

"Shit," Andy said. "The adaptor is sticking."

"On my way," Theo shot back.

The German must have suspected something like this might happen because he already had a crowbar in his hand. It was a good thing the entrance to the airlock hadn't been blocked. Theo exited the module in record time. Ewa pulled up the live stream from his helmet onto her screen.

"Theo, even though we're out of time, please be very careful," she said over her private channel.

"I'll see what I can do for all of you as well as myself."

That wasn't exactly what she needed to hear right then. Ewa didn't want there to be any more victims. The image from the camera wobbled severely. Theo seemed to be striding quickly across the module's outer hull. It was only about three more meters to the coupling mechanism. The picture stopped moving. Ewa watched as Theo examined the mechanism with his flashlight. At first, the nature of the problem wasn't apparent. The metal glittered in the flashlight's beam as if it were brand new. Due to the lack of oxygen, nothing in space rusted.

The camera abruptly zoomed in on the mechanism. Theo must have brought the camera very close to the material. "Do you see anything?" he asked.

Ewa wasn't sure what she was supposed to be seeing. There was a nut in the center of the ship's coupling ring through which an arm-thick metal rod, which was attached to the module, was inserted. The image seemed strangely familiar to her...

"These are the security catches. There are three of them distributed around the coupling connector. They keep the module strongly attached to this location. A barbed hook is attached to the end of the bolt," Theo explained. "It functions like a lock. When Andy tried to uncouple us, he simply turned the hook on the end of the bolt ninety degrees. The rods should've been released from the connectors, but one of them is sticking. This one."

The camera zoomed in a little more. Now Ewa realized what Theo wanted to show them. The slit between the bolt and the connector was a little narrower on the one side than on the other.

"It's jamming," Ewa said. *Theo has found the problem! What was the likelihood of that problem occurring?* she wondered.

"Exactly. That must've happened in Earth orbit when they put the ship together. Somebody was sloppy."

Or, it was sabotage, Ewa thought. The word echoed through her head, *SA-BO-TAGE,* as if each syllable were striking loudly against a church bell. She didn't say anything.

"Can't you just saw off the coupling rod?" Andy asked.

"That would take too long. But why do you think I brought this thing along?" The crowbar was held into view. Then Theo pointed the camera right at the spot beside the security catch.

"I'll brace myself against the module and use the ship for counterweight. My hope is that the lever principle will help me push all of you a few micrometers to the side so you can free up the bolt, Andy."

Once again, ancient physics trumped modern technology. Ewa suspected that this would increasingly be the case in their future. No, it wasn't just a suspicion. She was positive, without knowing where that certainty was coming from.

"Okay," Andy replied. "Don't be startled when I have to fire the directional thrusters briefly. The module is going to separate a little from the rest of the ship."

"I hope you're hooked onto the safety line," Ewa said.

Theo didn't answer.

"On your signal, Theo," Andy said.

"Okay," Theo replied. "Three—two—one—push!"

Ewa glanced up. When Andy fired the directional thruster, anything that wasn't strapped down would shift a little. But nothing happened.

"It didn't work," Theo said.

"We'll try again," Ewa ordered.

"I'm ready," Andy said.

"Three—two—one—push!" The muffled sound of exertion could be heard over the earphones.

"Shit," Theo gasped. "I'm not strong enough."

"I have an idea," Ellen cut in. She must have been following their efforts. "We could use the ship's inertia to break off the module."

"You will have to be more specific."

"We have to decelerate in just a minute anyway. That means that the engine is going to slow down the module. The fat belly of the ship won't be affected by this and will press closer to us. The fastening bolts will be pushed deeper into the lock. If the crowbar is placed at the right point, the ship's inertia will disengage the hooked end of the latching mechanism. The ship will exert many tons of weight against the bar, more than Theo could ever apply to it."

"But if we decelerate while we're still attached to the ship, then the ship's inertia will just keep pushing us through space," Andy interjected. "We'll need much more fuel because we'll effectively have to slow the entire ship, not just the module. And we'll end up missing the orbit window."

"That will only be true until the ship has broken the coupling mechanism. After that, we can fire the module's and the ship's directional thrusters and veer away from each other. That way we'll only need to slow the module down."

"Whew, Ellen! That's a completely unpredictable maneuver," Andy said. "We can't know when we'll be free and clear of the ship. I hate things like this."

"It seems to be our only choice," Ewa said. "Or does someone have another idea?"

"There is one other problem," Theo said. "But don't worry about it. I know how to solve it."

"You should at least tell us what it is," Ewa said.

"Just let me take care of it," he said confidently.

"No way," Ewa said in the tone of a direct order.

Theo sighed. "Someone will have to hold the crowbar in place until everything's over. Otherwise, the slightest vibration could make it fly off, and we'd be back to square one. I'll take care of it."

"What exactly do you mean?" Ewa asked.

Theo didn't respond.

"He will stay out there until I hit the brakes," Andy stepped in. "It'll be like he's dangling his legs off the back of a moving car while a semi races toward him at extreme speed. If we don't get out of the truck's path fast enough, Theo will be crushed. And even if we do manage to make a sharp turn, he'll run the risk of being thrown off and landing in the street when we drop our speed."

"I wouldn't have put it quite that concretely," Theo said, "but that's it in a nutshell. I would prefer to join the rest of you inside, but Ellen's idea really is our last, best chance."

"Theo, wedge the crowbar in as best you can, and come right down to the airlock," Ewa said.

"I'm sorry, Ewa, but I can't do that. It would jeopardize our mission."

"The mission isn't more important than your life. Do you really intend to disobey my orders?"

"It is one life against fourteen. A pretty good deal. We won't get a better offer. I accept the consequences for my insubordination and expect to be punished as soon as I return to the module."

"Deal, Theo. I'll get my whip ready, and you'll pay for this," Ewa said.

She pretended to accept the situation with humor, but she really didn't feel up for snappy comebacks.

"T MINUS SIXTY."

Andy had taken over the navigation. He could calculate the adjustments faster than anyone else, if that proved necessary. The seconds were counting down digitally on Ewa's helmet screen. She wished she could scratch a spot that itched, but the spacesuit made that impossible. On other launches, a feeling of anxiety had spread from one person to the next. Ewa had literally felt how the trembling of the person next to her had leaped across the space to her. However, this time everyone was stuck inside their own cocoons. The fears that were clogging her throat were her own. She couldn't even imagine herself catching these from the other crew members. This was mortal fear. Nobody enjoyed the thought of dying, and neither did she.

"T minus thirty."

Half a minute to go. Ewa switched over to the signal from Theo's camera. The view was very calm. Theo must have leaned his head against something, or he was holding it with both hands. No, that wasn't the case. Otherwise he couldn't keep the crowbar in the correct position. How did he manage to stay so calm? How did he blow off steam? She wished she could hear him whistling or singing, but he remained quiet.

"Three two one ignition," Andy said.

With a jolt, Ewa's back was pressed against the hard floor. Two seconds and it was all over. At the same moment, Andy had also fired the lateral directional thrusters at the midsection of the ship. They didn't have much force, and inside the module they hardly felt anything from them. If the plan had worked, the ship was now pressing on the crowbar and leaning slightly to the side.

"Now," Andy said. That had to be the moment. Either they would be free any moment, or... Ewa refused to think those thoughts through to their end. What did the instruments say? Why wasn't Andy saying anything?

"It looks like we're... People, we're free!" he cried.

Ewa couldn't celebrate yet. What had happened to Theo? Had the massive ship flattened him against the hull of the module like a mosquito?

"Theo?" she asked. "Theo, please report in."

All she could hear over the earphones was heavy breathing. The picture from Theo's camera was utterly black. That had to be the blackness of space. If the camera had been destroyed, she would have received an error message.

"Attention! I'm taking us out of the path of the ship and beginning the deceleration process," Andy announced.

The directional thrusters on the module were now working. Ewa could feel their effect as a slight pressure toward the left. They were pulling to the left of the ship.

"Can you wait to slow us down to enter orbit until we've heard from Theo?" Ewa asked.

"Negative," Andy replied. "Every second is costing us more fuel."

The counterthrust started, and the engine built up so much force that Ewa was suddenly one and half times as massive as she was on Earth. Someone in the corner yelped. Somebody had probably gotten jammed up against a crate. Ewa watched the module slowly separate itself from the ship on her helmet screen. The *Santa Maria*'s giant belly was gradually catching up to them.

"Crap, the directional thrusters are too weak," Andy said. "Prepare for impact."

The module took a hard blow to the side. Ewa saw how the ship's fuselage collided with the hull of the module. If Theo had happened to be standing there, he would have been squashed. She then felt the module start to spin. The collision with the passing fuselage had set the module in rotation. They couldn't slow down like this! The engine's thrusters stopped working and would stay offline as long as the module spun.

"Andy, can you stabilize us?"

"Already trying."

Ewa could feel his efforts. The engine seemed to stutter, but that was Andy's doing. He had activated it as a means of counteracting the rotation. He was really good at this.

"Theo?"

She once again heard groaning and heavy breathing. But he was still outside!

"Can we do anything?" she asked.

"Ooof."

He was back!

"That was a... wild ride... not making... progress."

The module slowly stopped turning. They were now about the weight they were on Earth.

"I'm heading to the airlock," Theo said.

Ewa imagined him crawling along the surface of the module. He wasn't weightless anymore. Along with his suit and backpack, he had to now weigh 150 kilograms. Could his safety line handle that?

"One... more... meter...," he murmured. "Man, this is hard."

"Theo, we need you in here," Ewa replied.

"Yeah, I'm coming already...," The transmission broke off. *No signal* flashed up on Ewa's screen. Theo's camera went dead.

"Andy, can you see anything?"

"Shit, no. Nothing!"

Ewa held her hand up in front of her view hole. This couldn't be true! In the last second!

"You shouldn't curse so much." That was Theo's voice. It was coming from the internal microphone in the airlock.

"What did you... You scared the hell out of us!" Ewa shouted.

"Something scraped past my helmet and took out my camera and antenna," Theo responded.

"Come in here now. I'm waiting with the whip," Ewa said.

"I'd rather wait here in the airlock until we're in orbit. There's more room in here than where you are."

"You're just worried about what's coming, you old scaredy-cat."

Sol 6, Endeavour

"You're lucky not to be in the base right now," Mike said. He looked really miserable on the monitor.

"Earth?"

"Lance, it honestly feels like the entire planet wants to make accusations against us. At least everyone who can contact us. We overstepped our authority, jeopardized our mission. The only thing they haven't tried to saddle us with is the civil war in South Africa."

"So, we were supposed to let the people in the *Santa Maria* just die?"

"Of course, nobody puts it in so many words, but I have the feeling we were supposed to just let them spend another year orbiting the sun. They probably hoped that this little problem would take care of itself. The official statement is that we should have asked for authorization for every step we took, and the experts might have been able to come up with better solutions."

"Do they really not get it that everything had to happen fast?"

"They would've likely preferred for everything to go at a bureaucratic pace. Then nobody would've been at fault when the *Santa Maria* failed to decelerate enough to enter Mars orbit. Didn't the experts always say that an expedition like that was insane and didn't stand a chance? In a way, that makes sense. Otherwise, a volunteer organization is going to show the nations of the world that someone can actually make it to Mars on a tenth of our budget."

"Well, they can be happy then. It's now proven that only the more expensive kind of expedition works."

"They're afraid, Lance, that these amateurs are going to ruin the professional show. When you get back down here, the base is going to look like some refugee detention camp in Jordan. The surroundings look the part already. No one will want to see pictures like this on TV."

"Does this mean we won't have to do the TV shoot? That would be great news!"

"Not exactly. I've managed to sell them the new situation as a hero story. Professionally trained NASA astronauts rescue amateur team from Europe. The TV freaks will be all over this one."

"But the MfE folks are from all over the world, not just Europe."

"Doesn't matter. It was a Dutchman's idea, so that project is European in concept. Everyone will enjoy a little Europe bashing."

"So we need to be prepared for some reporter to show up at the airlock?"

"Haha, Lance, maybe in a hundred years. No, I'll keep the two of you out of it, I promise. But when you get back down here, I don't think you'll be able to avoid one or two interviews."

"Thanks. If I had to give interviews from up here, I'd lose my mind." Lance turned the camera so that Mike could get a better view of the command module. "Look."

"That's about how I imagined it," Mike said.

"We were lucky they didn't have spacesuits for their sheep and goats, or they would be floating around here, too."

"I would rather not think about how it must smell because of them."

"Good point. The first thing I did was send our passengers to the showers. Seriously though, they make a very reasonable impression."

"And their leader, Ewa?"

"I would have liked to meet her, but she stayed on board their Dragon module. I'd like to know how she managed everything, despite all their problems. That woman has her head screwed on right."

"Careful, Lance. You've got a girlfriend."

"Come on, that's not what I meant."

"Well, in that case, have a good time with our guests. I'll see you soon. Mars out."

His stomach growled. The sound reminded Lance that he had wanted to eat something before his chat with Mike. He stood up from his seat. Sharon seemed to be asleep. At least her eyes were closed, and her breathing was deep and slow. How could she do that in the middle of this chaos? As Lance turned around, he slammed his knee against the hard edge of a box. "Ouch!" slipped out. That hadn't been there before. They really had to secure everything that the newcomers had brought along before they landed.

Greeting the guests at the airlock after they had refueled the module had been fun. Lance didn't really see himself as a social creature. He had never volunteered with a charity, and he only made donations because it was important to his girlfriend. Maybe the pleasure had been based on the fact that for the past months he had only been around the same three faces. Shaking hands with eight newcomers all at once had reminded him that he was part of a larger entity after all. However, unlike him, these people intended to remain forever in this desert wasteland. He had to respect that. For the rest of their lives they wouldn't see any other faces—unless they decided to produce new additions themselves.

But the coming weeks would be stressful. Ewa, the commander, had insisted that they would move as quickly as possible to their own MfE bases, but how would that function? They would have to put up with each other for a while. Mission Control wouldn't be happy about this, as they wouldn't be able to work on expanding the base as planned. They would need to loan their machines to the settlers. This wasn't a problem for Lance, since the base offered enough room for four scientists. The NASA crew that would be replacing them in twelve months would have to hurry the expansion along.

Lance floated a level down to where their guests were staying. He greeted them briefly and moved purposefully toward the supplies closet. He already knew what he was hungry for. He pulled out the drawer, and his mouth turned downward. Someone had emptied the tube of nougat cream. Every last gram had been quite artistically squeezed out. Lance knew what an empty tube looked like. He didn't even need to check. And the culprit dared to leave the container in the drawer to rub his nose in it. *You got here too late, Lance.*

He turned around, trying everything he could to keep his composure. It was just a sugar-fat confection with chocolate flavoring! "May I have your attention, please?" He still couldn't keep his voice from trembling. He held the empty tube up high.

"Oh, I'm sorry about that, Lance."

A young woman in a bra and underwear floated toward him. Lance turned red. Nothing like this had ever happened to him! He cleared his throat.

"I should have disposed of the tube. So sorry," the woman said.

Marilou. Now he recalled her name. She was clearly of Asian descent. He could tell that from her face, which was his current focus. "Uh, yes, that's what I was going to ask." He tried to keep his eyes locked on hers, but he couldn't manage to.

He wanted to give himself a slap. How would he seem to all of them? A lecherous guy who stared at a woman without saying a word. He had to end this. "Yes," he said. "This goes for all of you. The recycling area is located in the lower drawer."

He pointed at the corner of the room. The main thing was that this wasn't in Marilou's direction. He needed to take something out of the drawer, but all he found there were various varieties of cough drops. Cough drops? Who had packed those? It had to be someone from the *Santa Maria*. The stockpile was impressive, but where would they catch a respiratory virus around here?

Lance cleared his throat again. His throat actually did feel a little scratchy. He pulled out a package of lozenges and floated back upstairs with as much dignity as possible. As he did that, he passed by a mirror that hadn't hung there before and was shocked. It was apparently impossible in a weightless environment to move with dignity. He looked like a gigantic, fat fish flailing around on dry land.

"GLAD YOU'RE BACK!" SHARON RESCUED HIM FROM HIS embarrassment.

"What's going on?" Lance asked.

"The *Santa Maria* module is about to start its descent to the surface."

"Good for us. We'll have a box seat view for at least thirty minutes."

"That was the idea."

"What is their rationale for doing it now?"

"I think they hope that we can help them if there's an emergency," Sharon said.

"How do they imagine that? We can't just fly back and forth across the area. Changing our orbit would cost us at least one Mars circuit."

"I believe they know that, Lance. It's more about feeling like they aren't alone if we're in a good spot to watch everything."

A feeling? Lance couldn't imagine that this would really do much to help the seven remaining MfE members in the module. But he didn't want to argue with Sharon.

"*Endeavour*, please respond."

Sharon answered the call. The face of the blonde appeared on the screen. She was wearing her spacesuit, but her helmet was off. Her face was very flushed.

"Sharon here. Do you have everything ready?"

"We just initiated the deceleration process."

Sharon started laughing because a goat suddenly popped its head into view.

"This is Petey," Ewa said, chuckling in response to Sharon's mirth.

"Pleased to meet you, Petey," Sharon joked.

"I would like to send you our telemetry data. You might be able to catch irregularities before we're in a position to. After six months of weightlessness, the g-forces won't be a walk in the park."

"Of course, that's a good idea. We'll watch out for you."

"I know you can't really help us if something goes wrong, but an early error report might save us."

So much for feelings, Lance thought. Ewa had a very realistic understanding of her options. He liked her already, although he had yet to meet her in person.

THE PICTURE ON HIS SCREEN FLICKERED. LANCE THUMPED IT A couple of times from the back. This had helped him in the past, and he wasn't disappointed today, either. He was watching the module's landing. He had strapped himself to his seat for this. Until just a moment ago, it had been noisy on the lower level where the MfE astronauts were staying, but now a ghostly silence reigned. The newcomers were also following their friends' maneuvers on a monitor.

The data looked great. The module was moving right along its intended course. If this continued, they would make a model landing. At the moment, their engine was busy reducing the speed of the module by combusting hydrogen with oxygen and creating steam. Lance checked the temperatures in the combustion chamber, which at 3,200 degrees Celsius was within the normal range.

Presently the module's engine shut down. Its tanks weren't completely empty, but it would need the remainder of the fuel for the final meters. The Mars atmosphere now took over the braking process. Despite being so thin, the module was moving so quickly that each molecule it encountered acted as a negative velocity influence on it.

Lance switched to the module's internal camera. The seven individuals were lying in a colorful scattering across the floor. They seemed to be quite calm, although they were now technically at the mercy of their recycled, bargain-basement module.

The lower side of the landing module was heating up. That wasn't a surprise. A heat shield provided protection against this, but it wouldn't last indefinitely. Besides that, the Mars atmosphere wasn't thick enough to bring the module to a complete stop. There was nothing he could do. Everything had been programmed beforehand, but something made him feel anxious. *Shouldn't the parachute be out by now?*

And, there it was! It initially unfurled as a ring that resembled an unused condom. Even at this stage, it was a very efficient braking mechanism. And then the automated system blew air into it, and the condom expanded into a giant parachute. Lance focused the radar on it. The chute was over thirty meters in diameter.

"Looking good," he said to Sharon.

"Yeah."

On Lance's screen, the elevation profile of the landing sequence had a fairly sharp kink in its line about thirty kilometers from the base. This was where the module would have to release its parachute, since it would impede the journey over the last meters and would prevent the module from hitting its target. The screen showed the module as a blinking dot that was moving along its plotted trajectory. The point had just reached the kink—and overshot it.

"Did you—" he started.

Sharon had already opened the radio channel. "Your parachute hasn't released," she said.

"Yes, the mechanism has jammed. Damn it," Ewa replied.

"If you can't make it work, you're going to fly way past the base."

"I know. We're on it. Just a sec."

A camera image appeared on the *Endeavour*'s screens. The only sound that was being picked up was a loud whooshing. Lance switched over to Ewa.

"What is that?"

"Theo. He's climbing out."

Lance pulled the camera image back up. She was right. He had seen this once in an old James Bond film, where the hero climbed across the surface of an airplane in mid-flight. It was quite clear. He recognized the Mars surface, as the wearer of the camera crawled across a landing module that was dangling at the end of a parachute 1,000 meters above the ground. Nobody would believe him when he told them about this. The whooshing sound was the wind.

"Fifty-kilometer deviation," Sharon said.

The camera briefly swung toward the underside of the parachute. It was astonishingly far away. Had he just heard wheezing? It was impossible to guess what the man was trying to do. "Does he have a knife?" Lance asked quietly.

"A wire cutter," Ewa answered. "That isn't a normal parachute rope."

"How did he know that?"

"No clue. He had insisted on spending the landing in the airlock."

"But the wire cutter?"

"He had hauled a toolbox into the airlock with him. Wanted to be prepared for anything."

"That's insane," Lance said.

He really hoped that Theo survived. It was evident that

the people from the *Santa Maria* were crazy, but there was a method to this guy's kind of lunacy. *Theo would be an asset to the NASA base. Ewa would be, too,* he thought.

The image suddenly tilted. Lance's hands tightened around his armrests. But he wasn't following an endless fall. Theo had probably just managed to clip the first cable, which had caused the module's altitude to abruptly change. The man must be securely attached to a safety line. Theo seemed to give ample consideration to his crazy missions.

Another wobbling. That was probably the next cable.

"How many cables are attached to your parachute?" Lance asked.

"I don't know," Ewa replied. "I wasn't trained as a commander, so I hardly know the ship."

The camera tilted forward, momentarily transmitting a view of the abyss. They only have five hundred meters to go, Lance guessed.

"One hundred-kilometer deviation," Sharon noted.

It hadn't taken long for the module to cover a significant distance. How would the seven astronauts return to the base? But one problem at a time.

The fourth shaking. Four cables. Lance hoped that was all of them, but the module was still attached to the parachute. Lance took a deep breath and felt himself start to sweat.

Cable number five tore free. Theo now needed to be extra careful. Once he cut the last cable, the module would enter free fall. Hopefully, he could find a safe spot to withstand the impact. He wouldn't have time to reach the airlock since it was located on the side of the module, and the airflow there would be terrible.

"One hundred fifty kilometers," Sharon remarked calmly. That didn't matter. The most important thing was simply for them to make a soft landing.

The camera image jolted. That, for sure, was the last cable. Lance watched the screen as the module immediately accelerated. The camera now showed only gray metal. Theo was probably situated on the top of the module and holding on as tightly as he could. He only had to make it through several seconds. Lance watched the elevation trajectory. The engines should fire again as soon as they reached one hundred fifty meters above the surface. And—*Yes!*—they did! Sharon applauded. The landing unit slowed down. The surface looked good, no large boulders in sight. Fifty meters, twenty, ten, finally the module was on the ground. Lance heard noisy jubilation and clapping from the lower deck.

Ewa called in. She looked pale. Her task wasn't over yet. Sharon and Lance congratulated her. "Thank you for tracking us. Unfortunately, we still need your assistance. On our own, we won't make it to the base."

"We were already thinking about that," Lance said, "but we'll manage it. You needed to speak with Mike and Sarah. We still need to land ourselves."

"Just a minute," Ewa said. "Our crew was wondering if you could be part of the solution. If the *Endeavour* could land at a distance we could cover by foot, we could hike over to you and then handle things from there."

This initially sounded doable, but then completely impossible, because this would make their next launch significantly more difficult. The machine's fuel production only took place at its intended landing site close to the base. How could they transport liquid oxygen and hydrogen across a hundred kilometers of the Mars surface?

"We'll need to discuss that," Lance said. "But the most important thing right now is that *you've* landed."

Sol 7, MfE landing module

Ewa could feel her aching muscles as soon as she awoke. Working out on an ergometer was completely different from having to deal with a planet's gravitational pull around the clock. It had only been ten hours since they had landed, although it already seemed like an eternity. Since the chain of dramatic incidents had ended, time had returned to its normal, non-turbo pace.

Once they landed, they had all been too exhausted to even set foot on the Mars surface. Theo had climbed through the airlock into the module and had been welcomed as a hero. But then they had all succumbed to sleep. That was alright, though. Ewa didn't view this as a loss of time, rather a necessity. As long as they didn't leave the landing module, they weren't under any time pressure, since the life support system was sufficiently large and stocked with an ample amount of oxygen.

They would have to cross 150 kilometers before reaching the NASA base. This problem wouldn't be easy to solve, but Ewa had decided to postpone it for the time being. Before they tackled this, they would have to do what a scientist would do—feel the new planet under their own feet. She was confident the others would agree with her.

"Well, how about going out for a little walk?" she asked the group.

The faces of her fellow travelers looked weary, but her suggestion was met with all-around agreement.

"Absolutely," Ellen exclaimed. "I wanted to go out yesterday, but you all looked so exhausted."

"You could've convinced me to go," Andy said.

"Who wants to go first?" Ewa asked.

"I think Theo should be the first one to set foot on Mars. We wouldn't even be here without him!"

"Theo?"

The German opened his eyes. "Forget it," he said. "I'm so sore that even my bones hurt. Feel free to set off on your own. I need a break."

"We'll draw lots," Ewa suggested.

Ellen nodded.

There were seven of them. Theo didn't want to go, and as commander, Ewa decided, she would go last. She needed five somethings, four of which would be blanks. She looked around the module. It would be impossible to find paper in all this chaos. Ewa reached into her pocket. The tissue would have to suffice. She ripped it into five pieces and marked one of them with a pencil she found in the toolbox, before balling them up.

Gabriella drew the piece with the x on it. She would be the first volunteer from the Mars for Everyone Initiative to step onto their new home planet. The doctor smiled.

"Congratulations!" Ewa said, adding to the others' enthusiastic comments as they pulled on their spacesuits. Only Theo remained quiet, sitting in a corner.

They helped each other get dressed. Ewa and Ellen lifted Gabriella's HUT into place. The upper part of the spacesuit was bulky and heavy, especially in Mars's gravity field. Ewa finally realized that with their landing, she had lost something that she could never regain. She would never again float over to Theo. Gravity would accompany her and her children's children for the rest of their lives. A year ago, this would have seemed completely normal, because she didn't know anything else. But over the past six months, she had gotten used to weightlessness.

Ewa turned around. The animals were locked in a corner in a wire cage. What did they think about their new surroundings? Had they inherited the instinct to cope with gravity, or would they have to learn what to do? The mammals might still carry inside them a memory of Earth, but the current generation of mealworm beetles had been born in space. She would need to watch them carefully to see how this influenced their reproduction rate. However, she was basically optimistic. The more adverse the circumstances, the faster Mother Nature tended to speed up the life cycle process.

Gabriella entered the airlock. They no longer needed to go through the pre-breathing procedure since the normal atmosphere in the module had been replaced with pure oxygen, which had meant they could lower the pressure inside. This significantly reduced the risk of getting the bends, which occurred due to the presence of nitrogen in the air being breathed.

"It feels great," she said from outside.

The crew applauded. Andy was the next in line, while Ewa brought up the end of the line.

Ten minutes later, Ewa was also standing on Mars. She scraped her foot across the ground, which was solid, covered with only a little dust. It looked like California's Death Valley. Ewa knelt down and cleared a patch of ground. The reddish dust stuck to her glove. The surface looked as if it hadn't rained in a long time. It was riddled with cracks and ruts. And yet, it didn't look arid. The dirt reminded her of the contents of her flower pots when she forgot to water them for two weeks. Ewa crumbled a little dirt from the edge of a rut. It was crumbly but not uniform. It contained various components. When they added moisture and some organic materials, bacteria and other small creatures were bound to thrive—and eventually generate the fertile soil needed to grow crops.

But that was still a long way off. They had the seeds on

board, of course, but they weren't yet in a position to cultivate the plants that would grow from them. But the mission was far from being jeopardized by this reality. Ewa would have to keep going and fulfill her responsibilities, regardless of how many victims fell along the way. Only the goal mattered. She extended her legs in front, lay back, and stretched out on the ground. Her eyes wandered up to the sky, which looked strangely unstructured. There were no clouds here like there were on Earth. Neither Mars's hard, waterless ground nor its thin air which lacked oxygen bothered her at the moment. All she wanted to see for the rest of her days was the hazy, blurry, brownish pink of the sky. It was an alien sky, and yet she would now live under it forever.

"IT WILL TAKE ABOUT TEN HOURS FOR OUR ROVER TO REACH you," Mike said.

"We'll make it that long," Ewa replied.

"There is one problem, though. The Rover is running a low-pressure system without an airlock. This means you have to wear your spacesuit to get on and off of it, and all the air in the cabin will be vented out."

"That does present a problem," Ewa said, scratching her head. "We have all sorts of animals with us, and they don't have any spacesuits."

"Besides that, the Rover has a retractable pressurized tube. We use that to move from the base or the ship to the cabin of the Rover without spacesuits."

"You are explaining this like it isn't an option for us."

"Right. You lack the corresponding piece. The tube has to be attached to the outer hatch of an airlock so that it can stay airtight. You would need a coupling mechanism like that."

"Could we recreate it somehow if you sent us the specs?"

"I think that would fall somewhere between complicated and impossible. Or do you have a lathe on board that could cut a perfectly-fitting, one-meter metal ring?"

Ellen tapped her on the shoulder. Ewa nodded.

"My father always said that you could make anything work with duct tape. We have plenty of that. Couldn't we just secure the tube with that?" Ellen asked into the microphone.

"We just sealed a small leak with some duct tape yesterday," Mike said. "It was Sarah's idea. But would it be enough for a tube? You can try to figure that out. The challenge will be the module's curved external wall. The end of the tube is flat. On the top and bottom, the duct tape would need to have a thickness of at least thirty centimeters. Would the material hold in these cold temperatures?"

"Ellen will test it out," Ewa said. "Any other ideas? How large is the inside of the Rover?"

"Quite a bit smaller than the module, but we could take you in two trips."

"Pack up, people! They're coming to get us!" Ewa said. She felt like a teacher preparing her students for a field trip.

Everyone dutifully packed up their things.

"We can't take everything with us the first time," Ewa explained. "We will wait to take the non-essential items with us on our second round. If what you're leaving here has special handling instructions, you will need to jot them down and tape them to the object."

"Where do we get the paper and tape?" Andy asked.

"Use whatever you can find. Or take the fragile things with you on the first trip."

"Who'll come back on the Rover's return trip?"

"We'll decide that later, Andy. But I need someone to volunteer to stay behind and watch the animals. They will be brought on the second trip."

"Do you already know how we're going to get them to the Rover without spacesuits?" Andy asked.

"We have ideas, but no solution yet. But I'm optimistic."

"I'll stay," Rebecca volunteered.

Again, Ewa was taken by surprise. The black South African woman hadn't attracted her attention in terms of personal initiative. However, the reality was that in a smaller group, individuals often found themselves more likely to be challenged and engaged.

"Bad news," Ellen exclaimed over the radio. "I've been playing out here a little with the duct tape, but it looks hopeless. It would be easier to nail pudding to the wall."

"Thanks for trying," Ewa replied.

"We can't leave the animals here!" Ellen declared.

"Nor will we."

"Good. Then I'll come back inside."

ANDY SHOOK HIS HEAD AND POINTED TO HER HELMET. WHY didn't he just tell her what was bothering him?

"Do I really need to?" she asked.

Andy nodded, pulling on his own helmet. She did the same. A beep signaled that Andy was trying to contact her via a private channel. She accepted the request.

A text appeared on her helmet screen: "Please turn toward the wall so nobody can read your lips, and speak quietly."

He was really overdoing this. Andy was acting like he was investigating a conspiracy. Had the events prior to their landing perhaps rattled him? Ewa turned around so he would leave her in peace after this. Andy could be stubborn when he wanted to make something happen.

"Thanks," she heard him say. "What I'm going to tell you has to remain between the two of us."

"I promise," she replied, though she couldn't keep an annoyed undertone out of her voice.

"I get it that this isn't something that interests you right now," Andy said. "We really have better things to do than chat on a private channel like two conspirators."

True, Andy, you're right, she thought. What had he discovered? It really would be better for Andy if he didn't always have to obsess about things and could simply just let things go.

"Do you remember the moment we wanted to uncouple the module?" he asked.

"Of course."

"It didn't function."

"Yeah, that was why there was all that drama afterward."

Now he was hand-feeding her facts that she knew anyway. She was about to end their conversation.

"What would you say if I told you that wasn't what happened?" he asked.

"You mean we just happened to all have a collective hallucination? If you're about to tell me that, as your commander, I'll have to send you to the doctor. I hope—"

"Unfortunately, that's what I have to tell you. The module should've been released without a hitch. It just thought it couldn't do it."

"Andy, I've had it up to here with all this. The module can't think for itself!"

"I didn't phrase that well. The software reported an error, even though there wasn't one."

"But... why would it do that?"

"I can't tell you that. I don't know the motive behind it. I can only assure you that the software was manipulated in such a way that it registered a non-existent error."

Ewa's heart rate quickened. "Andy, but remember what Theo told us," she said. "He saw the jammed bolt with his own eyes."

"I'm not sure what he actually saw. Maybe he lied to us?"

"Theo saved us. Why would he have lied to us about what was wrong?"

"I haven't figured out potential motives behind all this. Theo might've seen what he wanted to see. When you briefed him, you told him that a bolt had to be jammed. But it definitely wasn't. We would've been able to uncouple the latch just like normal if the software hadn't been manipulated.

"And why are you so sure about that?"

"You brought me the memory boards from the other module. I was able to carefully compare our software to those boards by searching for clues to whatever had been manipulated in terms of the engine control. Hackers occasionally leave behind almost imperceptible signatures because they are proud of their work. Ideally speaking, no one is ever meant to notice them."

"Did you find anything?"

"No, but that only means that it wasn't freelancers who did the work on the engine."

"But instead?"

"Full-time paid programmers who didn't care about what they were doing. Or professionals maybe, who didn't want to risk the chance of someone catching onto them."

"But how would these people have known that we would want to undock the module? Our plans didn't include that step."

"That's also been bothering me, too, Ewa. At first, I was thinking that someone must have kept them informed about what was happening, and they had made the necessary adjustments."

"But you don't think that anymore?"

"No, I don't... I think the hacker was on board."

"You mean, you're sure one of us did it?" Ewa was appalled by Andy's words. His accusations were outrageous. This had to be kept from the others, and especially from the NASA team. They would never allow such a security risk inside their base!

"Yeah, relatively sure," Andy replied. "Our opportunities to communicate with Earth are limited. For the critical time span, I couldn't find a single message in the ship's memory that had been sent from there. That means that someone on board has to be operating solo."

"Couldn't the hackers have simply erased their tracks?"

"We're talking about security-relevant systems here that can't just be deleted. Every transmission is recorded along with its timestamp and duration. Only the content is later deleted."

"And if the hackers also have access to the security system?"

"Then they would have reversed the manipulation before we landed, before someone could notice it. But that didn't happen. Thus they were successful at implanting their code, but they didn't manage to remove it afterward."

"Andy, these are far-reaching accusations."

"These are just the facts. To make accusations, I need the culprits."

"But consider what would happen if you blame Theo. Most of them consider him a hero. You would just sow distrust and conflict."

"That isn't my intention. I just wanted to lay the facts out for you. It's up to you to decide what to do with them."

Ewa felt relieved, but she kept this to herself. She only knew that she couldn't trust anyone. "Thanks, Andy. I know to highly value your insights and leads. Please document them well in case you—"

"—encounter an unexpected incident? You've been watching too many crime shows, Ewa. I'm good at what I do. As long I don't make any errors, the conspirator won't know what I'm up to."

I hope so, Ewa thought. "I won't fill the others in on what you've found out," she said. "This should make your work easier. But please keep me up-to-date."

"Sure, Ewa. I hope I've done the right thing by coming to you."

"You hope? You don't trust me?"

"Trust is a big word. On a scale of one to one hundred, my trust in you is around eighty-five."

"Is that high?"

"It's only been exceeded by one other person."

"By yourself?" Ewa laughed. Andy's self-esteem was anything but shaky.

"No, by my grandmother. She raised me on her own after my mother ran away to the city, away from my alcoholic father. She sits at one hundred."

"And yourself?"

"A solid fifty, I'd say."

Sol 7, NASA Rover

Someone had to drive the Rover, and Mike lost the draw. He had absolutely no desire to chug across the desolate Mars landscape for ten hours. Fifteen kilometers per hour—he would have been faster on his mountain bike. Pity he hadn't been able to bring his bike along. With such low gravity, a tour through the Mars desert would have been exciting. And the jumps he could have nailed under these conditions! At least he didn't have to steer the Rover himself, since the autopilot was maintaining the course. If he had let the *Endeavour* land earlier, a MfE person could have been the one sitting in here, bored to death.

The plain he was currently crossing was a classic example of a barren Martian landscape. If only he could examine a few glacial valleys or enjoy a view of the twenty-kilometer-high Mons Olympus! Instead, the boulders lying around him were exceptionally small representatives of their category. He sometimes came across patterns that looked like tracks left by monstrously-large vehicles. They had been created by the wind, which had been blowing here unhindered for millennia. Like a gigantic grater, the sand had scraped across the substrate, revealing the hidden structures once buried deep within the rock.

Mike watched his gauges. If he increased his speed to

twenty kilometers per hour, he could reduce the remaining drive time by two hours. That would also cut the Rover's range from five hundred to four hundred kilometers. That was significantly more than he was planning to cover today, but in a life-threatening environment like this, it never hurt to have a safety reserve.

The Rover was being powered by a methanol fuel cell which, in addition to the energy required to propel the vehicle, also produced water and carbon dioxide. The carbon dioxide was expelled through an exhaust pipe into the atmosphere, which was already composed of this gas. On the other hand, the water was captured, and with the help of the electricity generated by the solar cells on the vehicle's roof, part of it was split into hydrogen for the engine, and oxygen for breathing, as well as for the engine. This meant that Mike didn't need to worry about either his water or his breathable air reserves. Quite the opposite—the faster he drove, the larger these grew.

There was one limiting factor, though, and that was the size of the methanol tank. NASA had determined that a range of five hundred kilometers per full tank was sufficient, since the range of operations around the base was supposed to occur within a radius of 100 kilometers. Unlike hydrogen, methanol was safe and easy to handle, so when needed, a supplemental container could be packed, allowing the range to be doubled.

Mike sighed. He had loathed long drives as a child. His mother had always driven him from the East Coast to the West Coast to celebrate Thanksgiving with his grandparents, due to her fear of flying. In the Midwest, the midpoint of those trips, the landscape became almost as bleak as the one here. However, back then, they had pulled off at a gas station every two hours or so.

If Mike needed to go to the bathroom on this trip, all he had was the portable urine container. He had packed seven extras for his passengers. For other bodily needs, there was a chemical toilette on board, but it wasn't large enough to accommodate the needs of eight people on a longer trip. However, the intuitive shame of the passengers would prevent this from becoming a big deal. The cramped interior of the Rover, with its eight square meters of floor space, meant there was no such thing as private toilette usage. The return trip should be a blast. It would probably make him nostalgic for the peace and quiet of the outward run.

"ARE YOU MAKING GOOD TIME?"

Mike jolted awake. He must have dozed off for a moment. "Yes, Sarah," he replied without looking at the instruments. The autopilot would have awakened him if it had registered a problem.

"The *Endeavour* is asking if they can slowly start their landing process. It must be tight quarters up there, and they're probably bored."

"I don't have a problem with that. The Rover is running perfectly." Mike rapped the console and moved the steering wheel as if he had been steering the whole time.

"Good, then I'll authorize their landing. Sweet dreams, Mike," Sarah said with a chuckle.

Mike rubbed his temples and examined the map. He still had four hours to go. It was time to make a call.

"Rover to MfE module, please come in."

It took a while for them to answer.

"Ewa here. Any news?"

The boss. Lance was right. There was something about her. *She seems a little distracted*, he thought. No, that wasn't the right word. She was aloof. You couldn't accuse her of not being prepared to fight for her people. She was doing an excellent job as commander, despite the fact she hadn't been trained for that position. However, there seemed to be a distance between herself and the world. Or was he just imagining that since he had only encountered her indirectly via a screen? He was quite interested to see what his impressions would be when they met for the first time.

"I just wanted to ask for a status update. I should arrive in four hours," he replied.

"Everything's fine here. We're looking forward to you getting here with the Rover, and we're extremely grateful for this."

Ewa smiled as she said this, but there it was again—the distance. Maybe she was just an introvert? He had witnessed his fair share of introverted people holding others off at arm's length even though they would have been happy to be included in the group. He was like that, too, sometimes. He got along well with Sarah, Sharon, and Lance because they had known each other for so long. They had become a kind of family.

"If I can do anything," he offered.

"We still don't have any idea about how to get our animals into the Rover. But we have some time to brainstorm before the second trip."

"I understand. I'll give this some thought, too. Maybe there's an old wives' trick we could use."

Ewa laughed. "I doubt there are any old wives out there who've ever had to solve such a problem."

"Oh, the stories I could tell you! My Mama grew up in Italy. Sicily, to be specific. She claims that she invented the pressure cooker after observing Mount Stromboli for some time."

"Does that mean your actual name is Michele, not Michael?"

"Mama was the only one who ever called me Michele."

"And what about the pressure cooker?"

"It was already around before my mother was born. But she refused to ever admit that. At some point, she showed me an ancient, obviously homemade pressure cooker in her mother's shed. In their village, they had distilled schnapps in pots like that."

"Fascinating."

"Yeah, well, that doesn't help us any."

"That's true. We would rather keep the animals alive and not have to cook them."

"I could send a message to my mother."

"Sure, why not? We'll see you in four hours."

He glanced at the clock. "Three hours and fifty-six minutes."

EWA'S FACE DISAPPEARED, AND THE SCREEN AUTOMATICALLY turned itself off. Mike started thinking about options. He had plenty of time. Maybe he really should send his mother a note. It would reach Earth in twenty minutes. How late was it right now in Baltimore? Since a day on Mars was forty minutes longer than a day on Earth, it had been a long time since Mike had possessed any sense of what time it was at home. The crew had already started adjusting to Martian time on their outbound flight.

He activated the voice input program. Everything had been easier in the past. On previous vacations, he had simply bought a postcard, written 'I got here and am doing well' on it as large as possible, and trusted the delivery to the good old U.S. Postal Service. What should he tell his Mama? Everything felt so complicated. He didn't even know if he was doing well. It looked like he was at present, but maybe the material in the base's airlock was already developing a hairline tear that would cause an explosive ventilation of the base in the next three days.

Mike shook his head. Mama wouldn't want to hear about that. So he decided to describe for her what his day was like. He talked about his colleagues and explained how boring the Mars desert looked. That took up about fifteen minutes. He hadn't been that talkative in a long time. In the end, he told her about the problem they had with the animals. How could they move a creature without a spacesuit through a deadly environment? She would like feeling part of what was going on in his life. Mama had always felt her best when she was giving advice.

Mike saved the message and forwarded it through the base to the Deep Space Network. He imagined the high-gain antenna on the base searching for the position of one of the three orbiters. Then his message would shoot, virtually, into space to be picked up by the satellite, which would reformat and strengthen it before streaming it to Earth. His message and question would fly at the speed of light through frigid space until it was caught by one of the large dishes, maybe in Spain or Australia. It depended on which one was pointing in Mars's direction at the time. The message would eventually reach Mission Control in Florida, where someone would listen to it, label it as private, and then send it on as an email attachment.

He guessed that all of this would take less than an hour. And then it would just depend on when his mother checked her messages. In all honesty, nobody could say that the two of them were all that far apart. The first explorers of Antarctica had had it much worse when it came to sending news home. Some of them never even returned. It was only later when someone found their bodies that the relatives knew for sure what had happened. In contrast, the entire world would know by the next day if something happened on Mars—unless somebody didn't want them to.

"WE CAN SEE YOU!" EWA EXCLAIMED OVER THE RADIO channel.

Mike was surprised since it was already dark outside. His navigation lights must be more visible at night than the unlit vehicle was in the haze of day. He switched on his camera. She was right. Far in front of him was a blinking light that could only be on the module.

"Will it be a problem for you to board in the dark?" he asked.

"Not at all," Ewa said.

"And do you need my help?"

Mike hoped that Ewa would say no. But then he remembered that the boarding process would have to occur without the pressurized tube attachment. He would have to exhaust the oxygen and open the airlock. That would mean he would have to pull on his spacesuit, so he may as well help with the transition process.

"It would definitely go faster with your assistance," Ewa replied, "but I don't want to take advantage of your good will."

"No, I'm already changing, so that's not a problem."

Mike reached for his suit, which he was able to pull on quickly thanks to its flexible material. He tugged on his backpack and connected all the cables and hoses. By the time he finished with this, the Rover had reached its destination. It automatically parked three meters away from the module. Mike put on his helmet and started the pump. It was a shame about the breathable air. He then opened the emergency exit located at the rear of the Rover. It consisted of a heavily-insulated double door. The inner panel swung inside, while the external one swung out. Mike stepped into the passage. "Shit." The word escaped his lips before he could stop himself. The ground was over a meter below him. That wasn't how he remembered it.

"Ewa? You're going to need to climb some. I'll wait for you at the hatch to help you up."

At least he didn't have to go out into the chilly night. He glanced at the multi-display on his arm. The temperature had already fallen to minus 80. It would get a lot colder than that before sunrise. They could expect minus 130.

A glimmer of light bobbed back and forth in front of him. That had to be the helmet lamp of one of the approaching astronauts. It didn't take long for him to see the contours of the suit. It looked old-fashioned. *MfE must have bought those at a flea market!* he thought. Nobody had used spacesuits like that in the past twenty-five years. The fluid movements of the person inside the approaching suit reflected real athleticism. Mike could now see that the person was carrying a box that was hugged against the torso of the suit. The astronaut wasn't just hauling him- or herself along, but also a load. Mike's opinion of the newcomer rose even more.

"Hi, I'm Ellen."

Mike caught sight of a very youthful face. Its owner looked like she couldn't even be eighteen. Surely MfE hadn't sent children on this one-way trip?

"I'm Mike," he replied. "Physicist and commander of the NASA mission."

"At your age, already? Congrats," Ellen said. "Could you give me your hand?"

Mike reached out to shake her hand. She grabbed it and gave it a tug. Mike almost lost his balance.

"I meant so you could pull me up," Ellen said.

Mike stabilized himself and pulled harder. In her suit, the woman didn't weigh more than thirty Earth kilos, but she felt twice as heavy. He really needed to work out more, especially his arms. *Not just the bike*, he thought. The suit was so bulky that he had to press himself against the cabin wall to give Ellen enough space. She dropped the box.

Mike felt the vibration under his shoes. "Please be a little careful," he said. "This is our only Rover."

"Sorry about that!" Ellen said. "I'll go get a few more crates. So you'll stay here to give everyone a hand?"

"Otherwise, none of you will be able to get up here," Mike replied, gesturing apologetically at the distance below them.

Ellen jumped back down to the Mars surface, her knees gracefully flexed for the landing. She then turned around and reached for something located right below the hatch. It was a ladder. Mike flushed. Fortunately, nobody could see *that* in the dark. He hadn't even thought about the ladder. Ellen pulled it out to its full length and jammed the end into the ground.

"That'll feel a little better than your hand," she said.

FORTY-FIVE MINUTES LATER, THE ROVER WAS STUFFED SO FULL that Mike and his six passengers could barely fit in their seats. Would it have been better if they had all taken off their spacesuits? In the bustle, Mike had a hard time locating Ewa. He finally caught sight of her blonde hair. "Kowalska" was written on her name tag.

"How does it look in the module?" he asked.

"We won't be able to avoid a second trip, but we already knew that. It definitely won't be so tight the next time, though."

"And the animals?"

"They're behaving themselves. We have locked them in a wire cage."

"So all that's missing is a plan," Mike said.

A head appeared at the hatch. It was Rebecca. "I just wanted to say goodbye," she said.

Ewa walked over to the opening and knelt down. "Want to tell me something?"

"I... no," Rebecca answered. "Just a funny feeling in my gut. It's probably just that for the first time in eight months I'll be all alone. You all can sometimes be a real pain in the ass, but it feels like I'll actually miss you once you're gone."

"We'll be back soon," Ewa said.

THERE WAS NO QUESTION ABOUT IT. SIX INDIVIDUALS WHO hadn't really showered in a long time weren't any less odorous than a few goats and sheep. Mike's sense of smell wasn't especially sensitive, but the range of new aromas in the Rover didn't escape his notice. However, this situation confirmed the fact that the sense of smell is one of the most adaptable of the senses. What had made him feel nauseous right after the removal of the spacesuits was hardly noticeable after an hour of their drive.

His passengers had scattered themselves across the boxes and the floor. There wasn't enough space for all of them to lie down. Some of them were dozing. Gabriella, the doctor, was snoring loudly. Mike knew he wouldn't be able to sleep under these circumstances anyway. He would just have to tough it out.

He then noticed that Andy had wrapped his arms protectively around a large monitor. Mike nudged him. "Want to watch a film or two? Mission Control regularly sends us a small library to use in our free time. We're supposed to delete them after watching them, but I just override the copy protection and save them on my personal server."

"Cool!" Andy replied. "I also have a little collection, but I downloaded them before we left and have already seen them a hundred times each."

"All that's missing here in the Rover is a large screen, but the one you have...," Mike pointed at the one Andy was holding.

"Probably has the largest dimensions for a million kilometers around," Andy declared.

"That should work." Mike stood up, opened a small door in the wall, and pulled out a cable. "Would this work?"

Andy studied the plug at the end of the cable. He looked skeptical. "Doesn't look good, but we could make it work with an adaptor," he replied. "May I?"

"Sure, but make sure you don't cause an electrical short. We would be dead in the... um, desert without power."

"Got it. I know what I'm doing."

Mike watched Andy for a moment, but the guy really did seem to know what he was doing. They should be able to watch films together soon, which would help them get through the final hours. He suddenly noticed that an incoming message was blinking on the console. He climbed over several boxes and hit the answer button.

Rebecca was gazing into the camera, and Mike could tell right away that she wasn't feeling well.

"Sorry to bother you, but I'm afraid my stomachache had

nothing to do with my mental state. I've caught something," Rebecca informed him.

"Come over here, Ewa," Mike said.

Rebecca's boss joined him, but after casting a quick glance at the image on the screen, she went and fetched Gabriella.

"Can you describe your symptoms to me?" the doctor asked.

"Stomachache, nausea, vomiting, weakness, tremors," Rebecca counted off, though she had to cover her mouth for the last half of the list.

"How long has it been like this?"

"It started right after you left. I thought maybe I'd eaten something that didn't agree with me and that a little time in the bathroom would take care of it."

"Considering what I'm seeing, I don't think that's the case."

"It comes in waves. Napping helps a little, but I feel so weak."

"It could be food poisoning, but it's also possible that we brought something with us from Earth. I'll need to take a closer look at you."

"The most important thing is that it's not a Martian illness. Otherwise, my stomach might explode so an alien could creep out. Or I might turn into a zombie."

Mike was glad her sense of humor seemed to be intact.

"You've watched too many movies. Some viruses are tough and can lie dormant for months. But it might also be something we've caught from the animals. We were in pretty close contact with them," Gabriella said.

"Shouldn't I have been the first one to get sick then?" Ewa asked. "I'm the one who spent the most time with the animals."

"Your immune system might be stronger. Or maybe the virus remained asymptomatic in your case, despite the fact you were taking care of them. I can only speculate about that."

"And what is your medical advice?" Ewa asked.

"To the patient, rest and lots of liquids. To you and Mike, we can't leave her in the module. If Rebecca loses consciousness, she'll need someone to take care of her and get her circulation back up."

"Lose consciousness? I feel weak," Rebecca said, "but it doesn't seem that serious. Can't I just take something?"

"I can't suggest treatment by just guessing. To determine what you have, I need to examine you, and run stool and blood analyses."

"In other words, we need to go back for her?" Mike asked.

He glanced at the map. It was fifty-three kilometers back to the module. "It'll take three and a half hours," he said.

"Yes, that's what I would recommend," Gabriella said. "It's up to you to decide what to do with this advice."

"One more question," Mike replied. "Isn't there a chance that we'll bring the illness onto the Rover?"

"I can't rule that out as a possibility, but we can try to prevent contagion through hygiene. And anyone who's really worried can wear a spacesuit."

Everyone will love that, Mike thought. *Who wouldn't want to wear their suit for the whole way back?*

"So, it looks like we'll have to replace Rebecca in the module. I need a new volunteer," Ewa said, turning to the others.

Nobody spoke up. When the silence started to turn uncomfortable, Andy's finger rose into the air.

"Fine, I'll do it," he said, "but only under one condition."

"What's that?"

"Mike makes a copy of his film library for me."

Ewa looked over at Mike. She seemed relieved by Andy's volunteerism.

Mike's mind whirled. *If Andy leaves, his screen goes with him.* And he would be left here with nothing on which to watch his films. Of course, he could offer to keep Andy company. But no, no way. He would have to forego the comforts of the base for even longer if he did that. That was out of the question.

"Sure," he said, "but you have to swear you won't spoil any of them for me."

THEO AND GABRIELLA ASSISTED REBECCA FROM THE MODULE to the Rover as Mike watched. The patient had wrapped her arms around her assistants, but she was walking on her own two legs. The rest of the crew waited for them inside the Rover. Like before, all were wearing their spacesuits. After the external door slid shut, Mike realized that he hadn't told Andy goodbye—and that the air now smelled considerably better after being completely swapped out. There were pros and cons to everything.

Space was cleared for Rebecca at the back of the Rover. Theo helped with that, but to be safe, he kept his suit on. Gabriella, on the other hand, exhibited the typical doctor behavior, the kind that caused non-medical people to believe doctors were magically immune to infections.

"It's all a matter of hygiene," Gabriella declared. "These wipes here could kill anything that might infect me. I just have to be a little extra careful."

Mike smiled apologetically. She must have noticed his gaze. There was nothing for him to do back here, so he moved up to the front seats where it was even tighter than it had been before. He checked the fuel gauge and was glad he hadn't chosen to drive faster on his way out to the module. If he had, they would now be close to running out of methanol. Thanks to thinking ahead, he still had a hundred kilometers' worth of fuel in reserve. They were set. What could go wrong?

It was just unfortunate that now he couldn't even watch films on the mini-screen built into the front console. What was the best way to kill the next few hours? At least Gabriella, the loudest snorer, was no longer an issue to contend with since she was occupied with the patient. With nothing better to do, he decided to check on them, carefully moving across the floor and climbing over the sleepers.

"Have you figured anything out?" he asked Gabriella.

"Rebecca is stable. I think she'll be in the clear in about three days, but it's a good thing we went back. I just gave her IV fluids, so she'll hopefully get a little of her strength back."

"And the cause?"

"I haven't completed all the tests yet. I brought a test set along," she said, pointing at a shiny silver, cube-like case. "I bought that for the trip with my own money. It contains twenty reusable tests that react to various kinds of proteins."

"What can you learn from knowing which proteins Rebecca has in her bloodstream?"

"I'm not just testing her blood, but also her stool. See, here are two samples. Would you like to stick them in the test containers?"

Gabrielle held out two small tubes which were closed on the ends with metal fasteners. "The outsides are sterile," she said.

"Thanks, but I don't want to intrude on your work."

"Your call. The final results will be drawn from the cumulative results of all the tests. If I know that her blood contains proteins A and B but not C and D, while her stool has E and F but not G in it, then hopefully I can make a conclusive diagnosis. After that, the only other question will be the cause."

"'Hopefully?'"

"Our options are limited. I will only be able to distinguish the more common germs. However, the odds are relatively slim that Rebecca picked up some kind of rare virus."

"But what about the viruses and bacteria on Mars? Extraterrestrial life forms?"

"Don't you start, too. You know, the general consensus is that, if these exist, they only do so in fossilized form. They used probes to search for so long..."

"But they still sent us after them. Doesn't that make you wonder?"

"It would be exciting to excavate Martian fossils, wouldn't

it? That would enlighten us a lot about the evolution of life on Earth."

"And if there's still life on Mars?"

"Then it wouldn't be in any position to infect Rebecca. Her organism would be as alien to Martian germs as yours would be. What do you think would be the most alien aspect of life down here, Mike?"

"The women," he replied. "The women."

"GOOD MORNING, FOLKS!" ANDY SEEMED ESPECIALLY cheerful on the screen.

"Where is your good mood coming from?" Mike asked. "I hope it's not catching. One sick person on board is enough for me."

"I slept better last night than I have in ages. Just me and a few friendly animals. Look, Petey would like to wish you all a good morning."

Andy lifted a goat up for the camera and waved his front hoof.

"That isn't even Petey. That's Eliza," Ewa said, suddenly appearing beside the screen. "Can't you tell the difference?"

"What do you think I am? A biologist? It doesn't matter. I just wanted to tell you that I'm about to take a short morning constitutional. My old bones need to adjust to the gravity here."

"Old bones? You were born in 2006! According to your personnel file, that makes you thirty-six."

"Almost thirty-seven," he said. "What else do you know about me?"

"I know everything," Ewa replied. "For example, I know that your real name is Andrej and that you were born in Georgia."

"That doesn't count as a major secret. You could dig that up online."

"I don't want to compromise you with the other things I know."

"That's awfully nice of you, Ewa. But you should know that if there was anything in my electronic MfE file that I didn't like, I would've deleted it a long time ago."

"Good to know. So the only things I know about you are what you wanted the organization to know?"

"You know a lot more about me than that," Andy replied. "We've spent the past six months in a flying shoebox. You even know what my farts smell like, and that isn't in any file anywhere."

"I've suppressed that," Ewa shot back.

"In that case, I'm going to head on out. The weather looks nicer today than it did yesterday."

"Be careful," Ewa said. "All outside recons are supposed to be done in pairs. But unfortunately Petey doesn't have a spacesuit. Please don't move beyond sight range of the module."

"Aye-aye, captain." Andy cut the link.

Mike stared out the Rover's porthole. The veil of dust really did seem thinner today. You could almost describe it as a sunny day. That would make the solar-powered batteries happy. He turned around in search of Gabriella. His eyes fell on Ellen, who was in the corner busy with the urine bottle. He quickly turned away. And, there stood the doctor.

"How's our patient doing?" Mike asked.

"She slept a lot and is drinking well. However, she can't keep any food down. She instantly vomits even the dry crackers I've been giving her. I suspect this won't improve before tomorrow."

"Have you figured out what caused this?"

"Everything *looks* like a norovirus infection, but the tests aren't indicating that virus. Three of the typical markers are missing."

"And if it's a mutated variety? The viruses on board the ships have been subjected to the ionizing radiation of space, just like all of us."

"Theoretically possible, yes. But the mutation would have to distinguish itself in three different markers and still cause the same illness. That seems unlikely to me."

"Do you have any other suspicions?"

"Yes, I'm wondering about a poison. There are several that manifest similar symptoms. Nausea and vomiting are quite typical. But my test set wasn't made to test for toxins, just germs."

"You think that someone poisoned Rebecca?" The MfE commander had joined them.

"I think that Rebecca consumed a poison. I can't say if it was administered to her or if she took it herself."

"Why would she poison herself?" Ewa asked.

"I'm sure she didn't mean to. Maybe it was an accident. Some foods can be toxic under certain circumstances, like cucumbers and zucchini, for instance. If one of those or something similar spoiled in our supplies and she ate one of them, then that could explain what happened."

"You don't sound all that convinced, Gabriella," Mike said.

"I'm not. I'm surprised at Rebecca's serious reaction. The concentration of those kinds of toxins is usually so low that people rarely ingest enough to be life-threatening."

"The cooking or the freeze-drying process might have increased the concentration," Ewa suggested.

"That's possible. If she dumped a bag of zucchini powder into her tea, perhaps mistakenly... We'll have to ask her once she wakes up."

"We will," Ewa said.

Forty-four kilometers to go. Sarah had just radioed in from the base to inform him that the *Endeavour* had landed. There were congratulations all around. However, they wanted to wait to disembark until the Rover could be used for the transfer—that would be the more comfortable option.

"Before I forget... your mother responded," Sarah said at the end of their conversation.

"Oh, that's... good," Mike replied.

"Come on, a little more enthusiasm! This is the woman who breastfed you and changed your diapers. I wouldn't have done it."

"You're right. Please forward the message to me."

"It's on its way."

Three minutes later, the data package was in his inbox. It contained a video and a text file, so he started with the video. In it, his mother described what she was up to these days and how she had been so glad to receive his message. *Yes, Mama, I know that already*, he thought, before feeling a pang of guilt for his impatience.

"As for the problem you described to me, the animals for which there aren't any spacesuits... I didn't know you'd even taken animals along. They never mention that in all the reports they're constantly featuring about you."

That's because they belong to the MfE folks, Mike thought.

"Anyway, I've been thinking about this, and I think I have a solution. On Sundays, there's a crime series I always watch on TV. Two weeks ago, I watched an episode in which a woman was murdered when the killer wrapped plastic wrap around her face. This struck me because we use various foils and wraps so often. Did you know that bananas won't ripen so fast if you wrap their stems in plastic wrap? You can even roast a goose breast in aluminum foil or poach an egg in plastic wrap. Anyway, when you work with plastic wrap, you quickly notice what all it can withstand, even though it is so thin and transparent. This was why I was thinking that maybe you could wrap the animals in lots and lots of plastic wrap! You would need to leave a balloon or some kind of sack filled with oxygen around their heads so they wouldn't suffocate. I'm sure this won't be comfortable for them, but dying is even less comfortable. What do you think? Please write again soon. Love you!"

With that, the video ended. The accompanying text file

included instructions on what all you could do with plastic wrap. Mike considered this idea. The tip about the wrap wasn't all that wacky. If they transported the animals to the Rover as the last thing, the poor things would only need to stick it out in the wrap for ten minutes max.

He called Ewa over and explained the potential solution to her. "Do you think the animals would let us do it?"

"I'm sure they'll fight us, but before we kill them, I'd like to try to transport them safely. Tell your mother 'thank you' for us! She might've just ensured the survival of the first human colony on Mars."

"She'll appreciate knowing that," Mike said, feeling slightly proud of his Mama.

"The only question is if we have enough plastic wrap in the module. If not, we'll need to bring some over from the base."

"I'll ask Andy to check." Mike opened a connection to the module via the console. The call went through, and the Rover's sender and the module's receiver established a stable connection.

However, there was no answer.

"Andy, please come in," Mike spoke into the microphone. Maybe he was relieving himself, or he was standing in the airlock and couldn't hear anything. "Andy, please come in... Andy, please come in."

Ewa noticed that something was off. It was pointless, but she tried it anyway: "Andy, come in."

No response.

"Andy, this isn't a joke." Ewa's stern voice reflected her increasing anxiety. "If you can hear us, please respond immediately."

Mike increased the volume, but the only thing they heard was the crackle of static electricity.

Sol 8, MfE landing module

Petey looked around. He couldn't see the daylight, of course, but his stomach told him that the night was over. Usually one of the Two Legs came along about now. It was almost always the same one who refilled the food dispenser. Petey touched the lever with his nose, hoping some food would fall out, but nothing happened. He nudged Eliza, who was acting like she was sleeping. She made a little noise. Hadn't she noticed that something wasn't right here? Petey tried the dispenser again. The Two Legs never filled it up more than halfway. Why not all the way? If he had filled it up, Petey would have something to eat right now. Or maybe not, since he probably would have stuffed himself full yesterday. The Two Legs knew what they were doing.

His stomach rumbled again. He pressed up against the wire that the Two Legs had set on top of them. It was very efficient. For a long time, Petey had thought that the cage was just meant to pen them in, but a while back something heavy had fallen from the sky. It had landed directly on the cage, right where Eliza had been standing. Without this barrier, she would now be dead.

It wasn't like they couldn't leave the area they'd been assigned. Is that what the Two Legs thought? Petey had tested that some time ago. He had put his front hooves on a small box sitting on the floor and had pushed his head against the top of the cage. He then stood up on his back legs. The wire wasn't as light has it had been, but it wasn't too much for him to handle. He lifted the frame and moved it until the side panel rested on the box. He could now get in and out of the enclosure whenever he liked.

Petey glanced at Eliza again. He bleated softly, but she didn't respond. Well, he would go off on his own then. The space he found himself in, beyond the wire, didn't look any different than it had from inside the cage. The solution to the mystery of the missing Two Legs wasn't in here. But he had seen where the Two Legs came from. There was a round opening in the ceiling. That must be where the Two Legs lived. Petey stood under the hole and tried to push himself upward, but nothing happened. A few days ago, that would've been enough to make him float straight up. But he could also try it the old way. Petey took a running start and jumped. The effect was amazing. He never would have thought he could jump that high! Was he really that strong?

He reached the upper floor. After all that effort, he needed to relieve himself. He left a puddle behind in a corner. It didn't really look all that different up here than it did below —boxes sitting all around and a few strange tables with colorful, blinking lights. Petey had hoped that there might be some fellow animals living up here, but there wasn't a single creature in sight. He couldn't see any food either, and that was the actual problem. Maybe he should try the feeder again.

The Two Legs might have just come in through the other door, and perhaps Petey had missed him. Suddenly worried, Petey hurried to the round hole and jumped back down to the lower floor. His landing was somewhat louder than he'd expected. Eliza leaped up and whipped her head around in fear. He glanced over at the door, to the one that had been closed for so long, but which the Two Legs had used the day before yesterday. It was shut, unfortunately. However, he hadn't noticed until now that there was a red light burning right beside it.

Sol 8, NASA base

"NASA AND THEIR COALITION PARTNERS DENY ANY responsibility for the events connected with the Mars expedition funded by the private initiative Mars for Everyone," Sarah read aloud from the official statement just issued by Mission Control in Florida.

"Contrary to expressed expert advice," she continued to read, "the organization launched its ship, the *Santa Maria*. This flight never should have been allowed to take place, since none of NASA's high standards were met, at any stage, by this mission. The MfE bears sole responsibility for the five people who have already died due to insufficient planning, and the recent disappearance of another astronaut from the MfE landing module indicates that the chain of unfortunate events is not over yet."

The six people who had just transferred from the ship to the base stood before her, their heads bowed. Sarah wouldn't have wanted to be in their shoes. They had taken considerable risk, and they had failed—or were, at least, about to. But she knew that the message from Mission Control wasn't over yet. The attorneys must have insisted on the formulation of the first sentences. But pragmatism always triumphed in the end. And this time wouldn't be any different.

Sarah jumped over a few sentences full of blah-blah, and then read the critical sentences aloud. "Nevertheless, NASA and all the coalition space organizations have decided to make available the surveillance capacity of the satellites in Mars orbit to aid in the search for the missing *Santa Maria* crew member. At this very moment, the module's landing site is being measured at a five-millimeter resolution. If the astronaut is located within a five-kilometer perimeter, the cameras will locate him. That also goes for any clues he might have left behind, or equipment parts. The four-person crew at the NASA Mars base has been authorized to operate at their own discretion in utilizing their capacities for the search and rescue operation."

"That's good news," Ewa said.

Sarah didn't quite know what to make of the blonde woman. Mike seemed to be keen on her, even though he wouldn't admit it. He could hardly take his eyes from her.

"They'll find him!" Sarah declared.

"When can we head back?"

"The Rover will be ready to go in thirty minutes."

THEY HAD SPENT A LONG TIME DISCUSSING WHETHER THEY should just turn the Rover over to the MfE people for the second transfer excursion. Mike was firmly for that idea, since it would mean that he could finally sleep in his own bed again. However, he had subsequently turned down Sarah's offer to take over the navigation. Now there were three of them returning to the module. Ewa was on board, and Theo. The Rover was tanked up again. Their mission was straightforward—to rescue Andrej Pugashwili, known as Andy, from whom nothing had been heard in at least four hours. But they also had rolls of plastic wrap on board. Ewa had insisted on that. They had to keep going. Unlike NASA, she refused to view the MfE project as a failure. Their mission wasn't beyond salvage yet.

The autopilot had been instructed to maintain an average speed of 20 kilometers per hour on the outbound drive. The risk of a lower distance capacity seemed to be less dire than the possibility that Andy urgently needed their help. Mike's feelings were mixed. He was afraid that the missing man was long dead. Otherwise, wouldn't he have reported in by now? The radio in the module was still intact. At least, the receiver was in a state to establish a connection with their sender. *What else would keep an astronaut from answering their calls?*

"I have no idea," Ewa said, cutting into his thoughts.

Mike flinched. Had he spoken aloud?

"Oh, did I say that out loud?" Ewa asked as she noticed his surprise. "I was wrapped up in my thoughts."

"I was just wondering what reasons there might be for your colleague's silence," Mike said.

"I was wondering the same thing. Funny," Ewa replied. "The only thing I could think of was he's either unconscious or dead."

"I'm sorry," Mike said, "but I don't have any better ideas. Wasn't the last thing he said that he was going to take a walk?"

"Yes. Maybe he fell down a cliff?"

"There's nothing to fall down around here. Take a look at this desert, Ewa. NASA spent a long time searching for a spot as safe as this for our landing. We should be close to the equator, too, and the soil supposedly contains aqueous minerals. That's why the land's so boring. I wouldn't even want to be buried here."

Mike snapped his mouth shut. That was an insensitive thing to say, but Ewa didn't react. She looked distracted.

"Safety first," he continued. "The geologists don't care if they get bored. But they should've sent a remote-controlled probe down here first. What are we doing here besides proving to the world that the Americans were the first ones able to put four people on Mars?"

Ewa didn't respond. What was she thinking about?

"Maybe Andy was abducted by Martians," he suggested.

Ewa's face remained impassive. He might as well be talking to the wall. Theo wasn't offering any companionship, either. The German had been sleeping practically the whole time. Exasperated, Mike turned around and stared at the navigation console. If only he could sleep, too! But he wouldn't be able to rest under these circumstances. To do that, he needed peace and quiet, and room to stretch out. And since he had a mission to fulfill, there was no way he would find the 'peace' part of that recipe right now.

A CHIMING SOUND STARTLED HIM. HAD HE REALLY FALLEN asleep? His body had desperately needed rest. Mike activated the screen, and an impatient Sarah popped into view. He hadn't responded quickly enough.

"Can you hear me, Michele?"

Now she was calling him Michele as well. No one except his mother ever called him that. "I'm here," he answered.

"We've analyzed the satellite photos."

Mike woke up his passengers. "Ewa, Theo, you need to hear this."

"There isn't a single trace of your colleague within the search area," Sarah said.

"Not even footprints?" Ewa asked.

"When you landed, the engine blew away most of the dust, so there's nothing to be seen. Even if there were some slight traces, the contrast was too small for the satellites to pick up from three hundred kilometers up," Sarah replied.

"Maybe we'll see something once we're there," Mike said.

"Yes, you'll have to take a look on site. That's our only option right now. One more thing," Sarah said. "We heard some noises coming from the module earlier. The microphone seems to be on. Something was moving around, but nobody answered us."

"Could it be the animals?" Mike asked.

"The microphone is located up on the command level, and the animals are locked inside a cage," Ewa remarked.

"Then you must have visitors—or it's Andy who for some reason doesn't want to talk to us."

"That would be good," Ewa said. "We'd know he was alive, at least."

Mike gazed at the navigation screen. They still had 60 kilometers to go. That meant he'd been asleep for almost four hours.

"Thanks, Sarah," he said. "We should know more in about three hours."

THE ROVER SLOWED DOWN AS IT APPROACHED THE LANDED module. Mike had by now taken control of the steering. He wanted to get the hatch as close to the airlock as possible so they wouldn't have too far to go during the loading process. Ewa and Theo were waiting at the hatch in their spacesuits.

Mike was also wearing his suit. He'd had to help the other two get dressed. Thank goodness NASA had switched over to the more modern suit version years ago. He closed his helmet. "Let's go," he said. "Are you ready?"

"Yes," Ewa assured him.

Theo mumbled something that Mike took as a yes. He opened the external hatch. The breathable air gusted out, condensing into a whitish, shimmering cloud. It looked rather cinematic as Ewa and Theo climbed down the ladder through the mist. They reached the module in three strides.

"There's a problem," Ewa said.

"Oh?" Mike asked.

"The airlock's blocked."

Damn it. He had no experience at all with this ancient technology. Where could they quickly find a specialist for airlocks from the Stone Age?

"I can break into it," Theo declared.

"Will we be able to make it airtight again?" Ewa asked. "If not, the only way we can get in is if we let the breathable air out of the module. The animals—"

"It wouldn't be good for Andy either, if he's lying inside without his suit on and we let the air out," Mike interrupted.

"Then I shouldn't," Theo replied. "A crowbar isn't exactly a precision instrument."

"Could we get the module's navigational software to release the airlock?"

"That seems to be the only possibility, Mike," Ewa said.

"I have to say up front that I really don't know my way around with these old programs," Mike said. "Do you, Theo?"

"I prefer hardware," the German said. "If we could ask Andy, we'd be set."

"I can try," Ewa cut in.

"You? I thought you were a chemist and an agricultural technologist," Theo replied. He sounded sincerely surprised.

"I had a life before MfE," Ewa shot back. "I'm already thirty-five."

"And you were a programmer? That puts a whole new spin on things."

"Something like that, Theo. Programming was part of what I did."

Mike heard someone climb up the ladder at the back of the Rover. It was Ewa.

"Can you get me a data link to the module?" she asked.

"Sure, but I don't have any login information," he replied.

"I have Chuck's login, so it shouldn't be a problem," Ewa said.

She leaned over the keyboard. She couldn't type very fast with her thick, rigid gloves on, so she looked like a retiree trying to work on a computer.

"Would you like me to type for you?" Mike asked. "My gloves are more flexible." Ewa shook her head. From where he was standing, Ewa's body was blocking the monitor.

"I've found the problem," she said. "The system diagnosis

has determined that there's something located in the airlock. Since the system can't ascertain the condition of the object, it won't let the door be opened from the outside."

"Good call," Mike said. "Whatever is stuck in the airlock might require air, and if we come in from the outside..."

"Could it be Andy?" asked Theo.

"No, don't think so," Ewa replied. "I took a look at the oxygen level in the airlock. It's been constant for hours. Nothing in there is breathing. If it's Andy, he must be dead."

"In that case, there shouldn't be any risk to the object in the airlock if we open the external door. Can you override the system and get it to open the hatch for us?"

"I think so, Mike. Just a second."

Ewa typed an entire row of commands. Then she warned, "Theo, please stand right in front of the airlock. If it opens, enter as quickly as you can, and I'll shut it behind you."

"Got it."

"Why such a complicated procedure?" Mike asked. "Didn't we just agree that there's nothing living in the airlock?"

"I just want to be prepared for anything. We've already made enough mistakes. By 'we,' I mean those of us with MfE," Ewa replied.

"I'm ready," Theo announced from outside.

"On the count of three. One two three."

Mike heard a huffing sound over the headphones. It had to be Theo.

"I'm in," Theo said. "Andy's here."

Shit. They'd been wrong. Again. *No, I hope we've been wrong,* Mike thought, hoping Theo had found Andy still alive in the airlock.

"Shutting door," Ewa said.

"The closing mechanism can't overcome the air pressure," Theo said. "The airlock is trying everything it can to keep the pressure in here constant. Wait. I'll try to leverage it shut."

For a few seconds, all they heard was the clatter of metal against metal.

"Oof," Theo finally said. "The door is shut. Andy is lying on the floor. He's alive, but unconscious. I can't make sense of his biodata."

"We'll bring him over here," Ewa said. "And then we'll take him with us."

ANDY'S CONDITION APPEARED TO BE STABLE. HIS HEART RATE was even and regular. Theo transferred the biodata to the Rover, and Mike forwarded it to the base.

"I can't make any kind of diagnosis," Sarah said over the radio. "The oxygen saturation is okay. Can you elevate him carefully, Theo?"

"Sure," Theo said. "Now."

The image on the monitor didn't change.

"He doesn't seem to be in pain," Sarah said. "I suggest that you take him to the Rover where we can check a few of his responses."

"We have a practical problem here," Mike interrupted. "The Rover is depressurized right now. Should we go ahead and fetch the rest of the stuff from the module?"

"Rats. I wish he could get to me as quickly as possible, but I suspect that twenty minutes more or less won't change anything. Andy's probably been unconscious for quite a while."

Ewa helped Theo carry Andy to the Rover. They laid him out near the front of the cabin across three tall crates. Then they quickly carried the rest of the cargo over to the Rover. Mike broke out in a sweat, but he didn't complain—at least he could still walk. The animals were the last things. They rebelled against the idea of being wrapped in the plastic wrap, but they weren't given any alternatives. The packages all thrashed around a little, looking eerily ghostlike, which was why Mike was happy when he could finally shut the Rover's hatch and pressurize the cabin. That had been a lot of work. Hopefully, Gabriella and Sarah would find a way to help the unconscious Andy.

What could have happened? Ewa thought. *Did he somehow inadvertently cause this condition, or was this another case of sabotage?*

Sol 9, NASA base

"TURN DOWN THE VOLUME. IT'S DRIVING ME CRAZY!" MIKE said, rubbing his temples. He had a headache, and hadn't yet caught up on his sleep after the long drive.

Sarah glanced at him, then pushed the button on the machine that was tracking the unconscious man's vital signs. The beeping stopped.

"Thanks," Mike said.

Andy was stretched out in the lounge on a mattress they had rolled out across three boxes, putting him at a height of 1.2 meters. He had an IV in one arm. As the supervising doctor, Sarah had decided that he needed to be hydrated and nourished. Mike and Sarah stood at Andy's 'bedside' with Ewa, the MfE commander. Theo, who had practically become Ewa's shadow, and Gabriella, the other doctor, were there, too.

"Could you tell us what you've found out so far?" Ewa asked.

Sarah swapped looks with Gabriella. "You go first," Sarah said. To Mike, this sounded like the two doctors didn't agree. The doctors had sent the three others out during their examination.

"There really isn't much to say," Gabriella explained. "Andy is doing fairly well. He doesn't seem to have sustained any organ damage. His heartbeat is regular, and the heart is operating at full capacity. There's no reason why he couldn't get up on his feet any minute."

"Then why is he still lying here?" Mike asked.

"We can't see inside his head. We assume oxygen deprivation caused damage to certain areas of his brain. However, we don't have a tomography unit here with which we could verify that. His brain might be in the process of coping with the damage. In other words, the functions of the injured areas are being taken over by undamaged zones. We know that can occur, but we can't say how long it will last."

"And you're not sure about that?"

"No, Ewa, we don't know what's going on in there," Gabriella said while pointing at Andy's forehead.

Mike pressed on. "Can he hear or see us?"

"Our measurements are showing activity in multiple areas, which is good. This means he isn't brain dead—and that the activity isn't limited only to the brainstem. However, he isn't showing any reaction to external stimuli. It's possible that these aren't being relayed to the brain," Gabriella explained.

"He might be stuck there inside his head, completely alive, but the outer world has disappeared?" Ewa asked with an odd smile.

Mike wondered why she was smiling. She had to be forcing herself to do that.

"We can't preclude the possibility, but it might also be that he's living inside his own world, like in a dream. We just don't know."

"Yes," Sarah said. "We have to give him time. There's a chance he'll come back to us."

"And how high is that?" Ewa asked.

"In this case, the statistics can't help us much. This is an individual fate, and I have to be clear about this... we don't know."

"Can't Earth help us?"

"They have their own problems, Ewa. It seems there were

widespread power outages across the US yesterday. They passed along the data to the experts, but the experts seem to be as perplexed as we are. If Andy were down on Earth, we could examine him more closely and figure out in which areas of his brain there is still some activity, but even that wouldn't get us any closer to answering the question about his future."

"And what about the past? How did this happen?" Ewa asked.

Their conversation was being transmitted to the *Endeavour* where most of the MfE expedition crew members were temporarily staying. The NASA team wouldn't need the ship any time soon—before their next flight, they would have to produce enough methane to use as fuel.

Mike turned toward the camera. "Theo and I examined Andy's equipment closely," he explained. "Although the suit is as old-fashioned as they come, it's in excellent condition. This means that Andy's collapse had nothing to do with a physical defect in the connectors."

Mike hesitated, waiting on the prompt that was bound to come.

"But?" Ewa delivered the nudge he was waiting for.

"But, through a software error. The problem was linked to the gauge on the oxygen tank. We tested it and discovered that the tank shows that it's full, even though it's only at one-quarter capacity. You know what it would mean if someone set off for a short walk thinking he had an hour's worth of air in his tank. Andy was very fortunate he didn't get any farther away from the airlock. He must've pulled himself back inside with his last bit of strength."

"If he made it, why is he in this condition?" Ewa asked.

"We wondered that, too," replied Mike. "If the suit ran out of oxygen he should've suffocated, whether he was in the airlock or not. It would be like pulling a plastic bag over your head. However, in the last second, Andy managed to yank out the plug connecting the oxygen tank to his suit. That could've happened when he entered the airlock. I imagine he hauled himself for the final meters on all fours. The disconnected hose is what saved his life. Enough breathable air from the airlock flowed through the hose and into his helmet to keep him from suffocating."

Mike wasn't sure if Andy would count himself lucky. A happy ending seemed quite unlikely at this point.

"He was fortunate in his misfortune," Gabriella chimed in.

"Then you weren't really listening," Theo shot back, his voice furious. "Excuse me, but Mike hasn't gone into full detail. This software error was only linked to Andy's suit. Before our departure, all our suits were updated with the same software. That doesn't mean that this software was flawless, but any error we've found should be present in all the other suits. Or..."

"Or?" Ewa asked.

"Or we're talking about a targeted attack. I'll find out who's responsible for this, and I swear I'll make whoever it is pay," Theo said.

With that, he spun around and left the room.

"Sharon has the floor," Mike said in his capacity as commander of the NASA base.

"Thank you. We need to discuss the future," Sharon said. She was speaking to a small group right around her and to the eleven on the *Endeavour*, who were watching via the camera. "I'm mainly concerned about how our cohabitation will function, and about your—and our—plans for the coming weeks."

Of course, this wasn't the first time they were having a conversation like this. Mike had spent the entire day thinking about nothing else, despite the fact he really wished he could take a nap. But now they needed to agree on an official solution.

"First of all, I would like to thank NASA and its partners in all of our names for your hospitality and assistance," Ewa began. "Without you, we would have been finished. The goal of the Mars for Everyone Initiative has always been to establish an independent settlement here on this planet. I'm deliberately not calling it a colony, since it isn't meant to ever function like that. We don't have a comprehensive plan and strategy, but as far as I can see, there is no reason for us to abandon this goal. However, we will need sporadic assistance, especially since our machinery is now lost to us. This is why it seems reasonable for us to change our minds about the original intended site for our settlement. Instead of utilizing the one on the other side of the planet, how would it be if we selected one relatively close to your base, perhaps a little farther to the north, closer to the giant ice reservoir?"

"We will support you with our equipment. Mission Control has already granted us permission to do that," Sarah said.

Mike knew this wasn't true, but the four of them had agreed to ignore this part of their instructions. "This means we won't be able to continue expanding our base as we had planned," he said. "However, we would like to at least complete our greenhouse. That will require an additional eight days of machinery usage,"

Their own fresh vegetables! Mike couldn't wait. With the specially cultivated, fast-growing varieties, they should be able to enjoy their first meal in about five weeks.

"In the meantime, we will continue to enjoy the *Endeavour*'s hospitality," Ewa replied. "Besides that, it would be helpful if we could borrow the open two-person Rover to make some recon trips up north."

"That would be fine," Sharon answered.

Mike was amazed at how easily everything was going. That was the advantage of not needing to take political expediencies into consideration.

"What are your plans for the patient?" Sharon asked.

"I think he'll receive the best care at the base," Ewa said. "But I would understand if you might consider him a burden, which is why I would be fine with leaving him here under

Gabriella's supervision. We will be located very nearby, so we wouldn't have to do without her medical abilities for too long."

"That sounds reasonable," Sharon replied. "Is there anything else we need to clarify?"

"I can't think of anything," Ewa said.

"It's all sweetness and light?" Mike asked. "Is there really nothing that we might potentially argue about? Low-key conversations like this make me concerned that perhaps something hasn't been expressed fully."

"I'm sorry, Mike, but I really can't think of any problems," Ewa said. "At the same time, I'm sure some will pop up, and we'll discuss them when they do."

Mike shrugged. He couldn't help feeling like everything felt much too harmonious. There was no way that nineteen people could live together without any conflicts arising. Well, he needed to take Andy out of the equation. Make that eighteen, who would have to struggle against jealousy, grudges, depression, and homesickness. None of this had been mentioned, but perhaps that was due to the nature of official meetings like this. He vowed to keep a close eye on the *Endeavour* to make sure that everything was alright. The fact that he would run into Ewa there simply amounted to an additional motivation. Mike wondered if perhaps the lack of conflict was because the two crews possessed very different perspectives. One crew wanted to stay here forever, while the other one planned to stay as guests for another few months and then return home.

Sol 9, MfE expedition

THEO WAS SITTING BEHIND THE LARGE ROUND STEERING WHEEL of the open Rover the NASA crew had lent them. With its large, solid rubber balloon tires attached to its four axles—two of which were on the drive module—the vehicle looked like someone had hitched three ATVs together. This construction made the vehicle a good candidate for off-road travel while maximizing its load-bearing capacity. And thanks to its modular design, the three sections had been easy to transport through space in the *Endeavour*'s hold.

"Recon team to Commander, ready to depart," Theo announced into his helmet microphone.

"Copy. Have a good trip," Ewa said.

The *Endeavour* was roomier than the old Dragon landing module, but there were now fourteen people on board a ship that had been built for four residents. Fourteen people had to share two restrooms and one shower. They were rotating the use of the four tiny cabins. Each person was supposed to be able to enjoy the luxury of a little privacy, even if only for one night at a time.

Ewa had turned down the crew's offer of reserving one of the cabins for her personal use as Commander. This had wrought a positive effect on the crew's morale, and Ewa was now working on activity schedules for the entire team so that nobody would get too bored. They wouldn't be able to construct their own accommodations until the NASA crew lent them the equipment they would need. This was why the most critical task at the moment was the selection of an optimal building site. It needed to provide the greatest number of resources, including mineral-rich soil, as well as water and sunlight, and moderate-enough temperatures.

Initially Ellen was supposed to accompany Theo on the Rover expedition, but then Rebecca had asked to go along. She had recovered surprisingly fast after her suspected food poisoning. Theo was glad to have a chance to get to know the South African better. She hadn't been there for the mission briefing, so he needed to fill her in on a few matters.

"Let's drive a few kilometers first," he said, "at least until the base is out of sight."

"Works for me," Rebecca said from her seat behind him, similar to a motorcycle, rather than side by side.

The eight-wheeled vehicle set off slowly. Theo deliberately took it easy at the outset. This was his first time to drive a Rover, so he needed to start by getting a feel for how it operated. Since each axle was propelled separately, the vehicle had to be more steerable than it seemed at first glance.

They were heading north. Like on Earth, Mars's sun rose in the east and set in the west. The reddish surface seemed to stretch in front of them forever.

"IT LOOKS LIKE WE'LL BE DRIVING FOR THE NEXT THREE weeks," Theo declared.

"Oh, it's just an illusion," Rebecca said. "Mars's small radius means the horizon is much closer than you'd think. I'd guess it's only about three kilometers away. We won't even be able to see the *Endeavour* in another fifteen minutes."

"Are you a geologist?" he asked.

"I'm actually an architect. For the MfE expedition, I

studied up on geology. But I also spent six months working on a survey team."

Theo was surprised at how little he knew about his colleague. After all, they had spent six months together in very close quarters. Obviously, it had taken the catastrophe to shift the team's dynamics. Before that, they had mostly been in their own cocoons.

He glanced back. The *Endeavour* really was gone from view.

Like its enclosed equivalent, a methane fuel cell powered the open Rover. The vehicle came to a stop, and Theo climbed out. His thigh muscles were aching. He saw that Rebecca was also stretching her legs.

"Yours hurt, too?" he asked with a laugh.

"The spacesuit isn't exactly good for driving or being the passenger," she replied. "I hope we'll get used to it."

Theo caught sight of an almost cube-like, one-meter-high boulder. "That would make a good table," he said.

"If you can whip up some coffee and cake, we could have a picnic," Rebecca quipped.

"Unfortunately, we can't take off our helmets. We'd have to suck everything up through a drinking tube."

"Maybe next century," Rebecca said, "if our terra-forming efforts are a success."

Bracing his arms against the stone, Theo boosted himself up and sat on top of the rock. Rebecca followed suit. They stared toward the Southeast as the sun approached its zenith.

"Do you believe in it?" he asked.

"In what? Oh, the terra-forming? I don't know. It is the ultimate goal, right? A second Earth. That's why I joined MfE."

"But as a geologist, it must be obvious—"

"—that Mars doesn't have enough mass to maintain an atmosphere like Earth's? Yes, that's true. I also think we aren't in any position to envision our future. Maybe we won't transform the entire planet, but we'll end up adapting ourselves to better exist here."

"You mean like the Inuit who dress warmly to survive in the Arctic?"

"More than that. I mean our actual biology. Perhaps our skin will eventually function like a pressurized suit."

"We'd still have to carry breathable air around," Theo said.

"I'd prefer that to having to live permanently in underground caves, as some have suggested."

"I couldn't live without the sky," Theo conceded. He looked up and saw several delicate feathery clouds drift northward. They were made up of frozen steam. "See that? There's the water we're looking for," he said.

"Then we should just follow the clouds," Rebecca replied, jumping nimbly down from the boulder.

IT WAS TIME TO SPEED UP THE DRIVE A LITTLE.

"Hang tight!" warned Theo as he pushed the throttle forward.

This Rover weighed much less than its enclosed variation, which meant it could be driven faster without negatively impacting the fuel usage. And, the area in front of them looked level. They quickly realized that there were all sorts of little humps and dips in the surface. It took all of Theo's skill to avoid the more massive boulders which a giant had obviously scattered across the surface like grains of salt.

It was a wild and crazy drive. The Rover sprang up into the air in Mars's low gravity, like a bouncy rubber ball, landing over and over again on its eight wheels with a thud. They were kicking up a stream of dust behind them. Theo imagined that if someone could see them from afar, they would look like one of those giant sandworms that had plowed through the desert in the science fiction novel *Dune*. But here it was the reality.

"I'm... afraid I... won't make... it much longer!" Rebecca

squeezed out the sentence in rhythmic blocks as they jolted up and down. "But... it's fun!"

"Tell me... when that happens... You can just... stand up... and jump lightly... up and down," Theo said. He glanced over his shoulder and saw Rebecca changing her position.

"That's... better," she said.

Of course, she was right. After about thirty minutes, Theo could feel the toll being taken on his thigh muscles. It wasn't easy to keep them loose. By sundown, in about nine hours, they would have covered around two hundred kilometers. However, he wouldn't make it that long at this tempo. He eased the throttle back slightly. At only twenty kilometers per hour, the Rover's leaps were no longer quite so high that bruising could only be avoided by standing up. He sat back down. His rear end would definitely be hurting by evening, but that was the future. This was now.

"I wish I could take off my helmet and let my hair wave in the air," Rebecca said, after resuming her seat as well.

"I'm afraid nothing much would happen in this thin atmosphere," Theo declared.

"Oh yeah," Rebecca replied, slapping her hand against her helmet. "You're right again. We'd have to be going one hundred to see anything happen."

"Just barely," Theo said. "But it's nice to imagine racing across the Mars landscape wearing sunglasses against the dust."

"Would it be enough to just wear a breathing mask?"

"Definitely—during the day, when it's warm enough," Theo said. "The story that our eyes would pop out is utter nonsense either way."

"It may be hard to believe, but my mother actually told me old wives' tales like that. She didn't know much about the world, but she worked hard and made it possible for me to go to college and, later, grad school."

"Passed on?" asked Theo.

"Yes, my mother and my brother were killed in a car accident," Rebecca explained softly. "That's why I'm here. We were a happy family before that happened."

"And your father?"

Rebecca didn't answer immediately. Theo regretted having asked. Rebecca had flown to Mars without any prospect of returning. It should have occurred to him that things might not be all that great with her father.

"My father...," she finally said after Theo had stopped expecting a reply. "My father was the one at the wheel. Someone cut him off. My father wasn't responsible for the crash, but he blames himself for having switched off the autopilot so that he could practice his driving skills. After the accident, the system diagnosis determined that the autopilot had noticed the approaching vehicle one second before he did. It might've been enough to avoid the collision."

"That is hard," Theo said. "And obviously no one can ever be the same after something like that."

"Sadly true. It destroyed my father, who turned to alcohol to forget."

"And you couldn't watch anymore."

"I tried over and over again to get him to break the cycle, but I eventually realized that he was pulling me down with him. That was when I applied for the initiative."

"You didn't put this on the application, did you?" During the tedious selection process, the psychologists had diligently weeded out anyone who wasn't completely mentally stable, anyone who carried any major baggage.

"Of course not," Rebecca said. "I made up a beautiful story for them. You're the only person here—or there—who knows the truth."

Theo was touched. He couldn't recall anyone ever telling him such a personal life story. What had he done to cultivate Rebecca's trust? He was just doing his job.

"You could tell me about our destination," Rebecca said, clearly ready for a new topic. "I wasn't at the briefing."

"Right. The most crucial resource for our settlement is water."

"Sure."

"There's a lot of frozen water up at the North Pole, but it's too cold for us there. According to some theories, there's stable ice located less than one meter beneath the surface as far down as the 40th parallel. On Earth, this is located on about the same latitude as Ankara, Peking, or Philadelphia. We want to find this ice. We won't need to dig, since we've brought along a GPR."

"And you have me," Rebecca replied. "There are certain terrain features that are more likely to be situated by water reserves."

"I honestly didn't know that."

"For example, the base of craters, or northward-facing hillsides. Actually, pretty much anywhere that there might've been water in the past or where glaciers could have slid, but now the area is covered with soil."

"Good. Then we know where we should look. Is that why you asked to come along?"

"No, I just longed to spend a few nights under the open sky," Rebecca said.

"You'll get more than just a few. The 40th parallel is unfortunately about 1,450 kilometers from the NASA base."

"Oh."

"Didn't they tell you that?"

"Uh... not exactly. Only that we'd be traveling for a few days, and I should bring a few changes of clothes."

"That wasn't misguided. The drive will take about two weeks all told, plus however long it takes us to find water."

"A two-week camping trip. Sounds great!"

"Maybe we'll be lucky and find something sooner. It would be alright if the ice was located at a lower depth. Our radar can reach down about five meters."

"WE'VE DONE 220 KILOMETERS," THEO SAID. "THAT'S enough for the first day."

"I agree," Rebecca replied.

"Do you want to take a look around outside? Once we're inside the tent, we'll have to stay there through til morning."

"And if nature calls?"

"Believe me, you won't want to go out at eighty below, even if it's urgent."

"That explains the single-use bags."

"Sorry about that. Camping out here isn't nearly as comfortable as our five-star spaceship," Theo said.

"How does the tent work?"

"Just a second," Theo remarked as he walked to the rear of the Rover. An almost two-meter by one-meter board was secured between the two axles. He unfastened it. "This is our bed," he said.

Rebecca felt the material. It was cushioned on one side, while the flip side felt like hard plastic. "Looks quite comfortable. Very cozy, too," she commented.

Theo chuckled. "Yes, it isn't very wide, but there isn't more space underneath the Rover. How tall are you?"

"One-meter seventy-eight."

"Then you're lucky. The mattress is one meter eighty. I'm two centimeters short of two meters tall."

"How will you fit on it?"

"In a fetal position, I suppose. There's a reason why NASA will only accept candidates who are one meter ninety or less."

"I can't wait to see what comes next!" Rebecca said. She scanned the Rover's interior, obviously searching for the tent.

Theo smiled. She had the wrong idea about what their lodging would look like. He opened a crate on the Rover's loading area and tugged out something that looked like a sack.

"We're sleeping in a sack?" Rebecca asked.

"Almost. But it doesn't quite work that way. First we need to find a spot that is relatively flat."

Rebecca looked around and pointed at a spot in front of the Rover. "There?"

Theo glanced in that direction. "Why not?" He set the plastic board down there. "Everything we need yet today has to fit on the mattress."

Rebecca removed a small bag from the Rover and set it on top.

Theo fetched a bag of provisions and another clothing bag. He also picked up an oxygen bottle and a device that looked like a blower. "Do you have any electrical devices in your bag? We should leave them outside. Since we'll be sleeping in pure oxygen, there'll be a higher risk of fire."

Rebecca shook her head. "I assume the suit doesn't count."

"It would be a bad idea outside," he said.

"What about watching the romantic sunset, just you and me?" Rebecca winked at him.

"I suspect we won't sleep particularly well anyway," he said.

Theo started to unfold the sack, which was surprisingly large. He then slid it under the board until the board was centered on the fabric. "Last chance to do anything well tonight. We could watch the sunrise instead."

"Either way," Rebecca replied, and Theo thought he detected a note of disappointment in her voice.

"Come on, then. Kneel up there at the front." He pointed at the head of the bed, before pulling the sack up over their heads.

"Now somebody needs to seal the top up there," Rebecca said.

"Pretty much. Do you see the drawstring at the edge? When I tighten it, the sack will be closed off."

"And it'll hold?"

"A small engine will help me with the last little bit. I'll fill the final tiny gap with a special foam that will instantly freeze when it comes into contact with the outside air."

Theo fastened the drawstring, finally letting it go so it fell lightly onto Rebecca's shoulders. "Wait... I'm not done."

"Good to know."

It was almost dark inside the sack. Theo could only make out Rebecca's silhouette. He looked over his shoulder and reached for the oxygen bottle before opening it.

"What's that hissing sound?" Rebecca asked.

"I'm letting the air out for us."

One more step and he'd be finished. Mike had explained everything to him in great detail, but in reality, it all felt very different, especially under the watchful eye of an attractive woman. He thought about what she had said earlier about the sunset—but she'd probably only been joking. Where had he put the exchanger? He ran his hands along the mattress.

"That's my leg," Rebecca said.

He finally located the device and pressed the large, round button on its front edge. "The exchanger will monitor, purify, and dehumidify the air inside here," he explained. "It will also serve as a light source. If it glows red, then something's not right. Wake me up immediately if that happens."

"In other words, it's going to burn all night long?"

"The regulations stipulate that, for safety reasons."

The air pressure inside the tent was slowly increasing. The sack was gradually taking its true, spherical form.

"Like an ugly duckling turning into a swan," Rebecca said.

"Yeah, not bad. This is the first time I've seen it, too."

Ten minutes later, they were lying inside a two-meter tall balloon. It wasn't a perfect sphere because of their weight, but it was still a majestic sight. The more the fabric stretched, the more outside light it let in. The sun hadn't completely set yet. From inside the ball, they could still see it as a blurry spot.

"And if I accidentally prick the balloon with something sharp?" asked Rebecca.

"The material is quite strong. You'd have to intentionally cut away at it with something. It's made from some kind of nylon, kind of like pantyhose."

"That doesn't make me feel any better. Have you ever worn hose?"

Theo shook his head. "My taste runs in other directions. But we could get undressed now."

"Well, I think you should go first," Rebecca quipped with a laugh.

Theo was glad he still had his helmet on. Otherwise she might have seen him blush.

For a few minutes, the only sound was rustling. Theo imagined what it would look like if someone could see them from the outside darkness—two silhouettes gradually growing thinner.

"If you need it...," he said, pointing at a waste container. It then occurred to him that he was still wearing his diaper. A grown man in diapers. This profession really did have its downsides. Theo sighed.

"Are you alright?" Rebecca asked, obviously having heard the lament.

"Just fine," he replied. He realized this wasn't exactly true. Considering how forthright Rebecca had been with him earlier, she deserved better than this. "I felt lonely for a second."

"Because we're so far from the others? Have you gotten used to the group?"

Theo snorted. "Not at all. I'm glad to be away from them. I always feel like we're a crew, but nothing more than that. When you were telling me your story earlier, it was the first time in many months that I actually felt close to someone."

"Thank you," Rebecca replied.

For whatever reason, he never felt comfortable complaining about things. He saw himself as hands-on and practical. What was the practical value in regretting that things weren't different than they were? And yet, it felt good to voice these thoughts. "What bothers me especially—or more like *who,* instead of *what*—is our commander."

He looked over at Rebecca and found a smile spread across her face. Maybe he shouldn't talk to her about other women. Wouldn't he destroy everything by doing that? He had to stop while he was still ahead.

"I always thought you worked well together," Rebecca declared.

"That's definitely true. But... it feels like I don't know anything about her. Sometimes she seems to be totally lost. Do you know what I mean? Like someone who is going down a certain path but has forgotten why. At the same time, that person knows that at the end of the path, some catastrophe is waiting for them. And yet it never occurs to them to turn around. Why is that? Because the person has already gone so far down the path that the end seems closer than the beginning, I suppose."

"That's a horrible feeling," Rebecca commented.

In the glow of the lamp, Theo noticed that there was a glittering tear at the corner of her eye.

"I think my father spent a long time on that path. He's already reached the end, though."

Sol 10, NASA base

A TRENCH MEASURING FOUR METERS DEEP, THREE METERS wide, and five meters long stretched in front of him. It had smooth walls and a solid bottom as far as he could tell. The robot had done an excellent job. Lance could still recall what this site had looked like on Sol 4. The drill on its two chains had just begun to work, and now it was almost time to put the roof in place.

Sol 4 had been six Martian days ago, but it felt to him like ancient history. He must have aged at least three years since then. Once again, they had seen how quickly their best-laid plans could go awry. Once the lab was finished, the robot would help them build the greenhouse. In the new construction, the robot would only need to dig down to a depth of half a meter, and instead of a roof composed of melted rock, the covering of the greenhouse would be made of transparent plastic. They would still need to shine artificial light on the plants, but they would be able to use the sunlight, in part, to convert the carbon dioxide from the atmosphere into biomass.

Lance tried to imagine what the future would be like. Would humans be able to run around the surface someday without suits on? "Couldn't we use the plants in our terraforming efforts since the atmosphere is so full of carbon dioxide?"

Sarah touched his shoulder. Their combined biologist-and-doctor was standing behind him. “You overestimate the density of the atmosphere,” she said. “You’re right that it’s almost completely composed of CO_2, but because the atmosphere is one hundred times thinner than what surrounds Earth, it still wouldn’t be enough for the plants. We will enrich the air inside the greenhouse with additional carbon dioxide from the air we’ll be exhaling.”

“You mean that we’ll be separating the CO_2 from the rest of the air?”

“We won’t need to take that step. We’ll just conduct the used air back into the greenhouse. Some of the microorganisms that live in the ground need oxygen. A pure CO_2 atmosphere would kill them off.”

“All the things you have to think about...”

“You’re telling me! I’m interested in seeing how long it’ll take us to get the greenhouse stable and functional. If the pressure is too low, the water will evaporate faster and the relative humidity will rise... Did you know that the dry Mars air can sometimes reach one hundred percent humidity? Considering how thin the atmosphere is, a little water is all it takes.”

Lance studied his colleague’s profile. Sarah wasn’t all that talkative, but when she got started on a biology-related topic, her enthusiasm was evident. He scratched his knee. He was finding the women on Mars distracting. Was that normal? His girlfriend was waiting on him—but he was always wondering if he felt more attracted to Ewa, Sarah, or Sharon. He should focus on his work instead of mulling over such questions.

Before they could connect the new room to the base, he needed to build a roof that would protect the lab against the radiation and cold. The robot operated autonomously most of the time, but he now needed a new tool.

“Could you help me?” he asked Sarah.

“Of course.”

They walked over to the depot situated on the other side of the base. It was comprised of various small containers that weren't airtight. This was where the special nozzle for spraying off the roof had to be located. Besides that, the metal sheets for the base layer of the roof were stored here.

"Would you carry one of those sheets, Sarah?"

His colleague leaned down to pick up a sheet. Lance once again appreciated the fact that their suits were so form-fitting, but his pleasure quickly turned into feelings of guilt. He bit his tongue. He had almost said something he shouldn't.

He picked up the robot tool. It was made of steel, and he wouldn't have been able to carry it on Earth. However, here it weighed less than two buckets of water. He trudged over to the machine with it and set it on the ground.

"Simply slide the sheet onto the edge of the trench," he said.

Sarah carried it over to the construction trench. Lance followed to make sure the installation went smoothly. Along the two long edges of the hole, the robot had dug out a thirty-centimeter indentation. This was where the sheet would be installed. Sarah handled this easily and marched right back over to the depot to fetch the next sheet.

Lance turned to the robot. He unfastened the drilling tool that the machine had used to remove the rocks and collect them into a cauldron. It was now heating the stone until it was viscous. Once it was done it would use the new tool Lance had attached to apply force to spread the molten rock onto the metal substrate. This was how a roof was created, crafted by human hand into a giant block of artificial stone.

He tried to jiggle the newly mounted tool, but it was solid. He pulled up the new program on the control panel and started the machine. The robot knew automatically what to do, so he could now help Sarah carry the sheets. They were done in five minutes.

Their interview was supposed to start any minute. That was the only reason Sarah was outside with him right now. The camera was set up on its tripod beside the base's external hatch. They would be filmed together. The station had claimed that the majority of the audience would be men.

This was why Sarah would be the one asking the questions that the station would send her in real time, and he, the rescuer of the Mars for Everyone crew, would answer them.

"Mike, have they been in touch?"

"No, the station hasn't checked in yet."

"Can you contact them?"

"Why—are you in a hurry, Lance?"

"I want to get this behind me. I hate giving interviews."

"Alright, I'll ask, even if I don't see the point. It'll take forty minutes for us to get the answer. By that time, we'll already have the questions."

"Just do it."

"Yeeaah. In process. Have fun outside, you two."

"MIKE THINKS WE SHOULD BE HAVING FUN OUT HERE."

Sarah put her hands on her hips. "Does he honestly not think I have anything better to do than this?"

"He thinks the questions will get here any minute. It doesn't make sense to go back inside."

"That's true. And how should we kill time?"

"You could tell me a story from your younger days." *Oh, that was stupid*, Lance realized. It sounded like he was referring to Sarah's age. "I mean, from your past."

"I have a better idea. Have you ever danced on another planet?"

"Ever what?"

"Danced! Based on the verb form 'to dance,' meaning 'to move to the music.'" Sarah laughed.

"What in the world made you think about that?"

"I tried it on our way out, in zero gravity. Didn't work well. But here? It should be lots of fun in this low gravitational field."

Great, she wants to dance. That wasn't one of the core competencies of most mechanics. He had taken two months of weekly dance lessons before graduating from college. Those were horrible memories.

"Trust me," he said, "someone else would make a better partner."

Rhythmic music started to pulse through his helmet headphones. Sarah must be transmitting it.

"You're in good shape," Sarah said. "I'm sure you're a great dancer. Let's give it a try."

"Fine, but you lead," Lance said.

"Gladly!" Sarah crowed, reaching for his right hand as she placed her right hand on his left shoulder.

"Close your eyes, listen to the music, and follow my movements," she said.

Lance shut his eyes. He let the music seep into his consciousness. Other thoughts vanished in its wake. He then noticed her pattern. To the back, the side, he only needed to stay alert. If he didn't try to intentionally set his feet anywhere, everything happened automatically.

"Hey, you're good at this," Sarah said.

Lance felt flattered. She led very well. He didn't need to listen to the beat. He just had to follow wherever she moved. His legs followed his body all on their own. "You're amazing at this," he said.

"Thanks."

The music was inside his head, and Lance felt himself relaxing, his muscles loosening. They didn't have a choice, but he didn't collapse either. *Thank you for this experience, Sarah,* he thought. He didn't trust himself to say this thought out loud. She might have misinterpreted it.

THE MUSIC FELL SILENT, AND SARAH CAME TO A STOP. LANCE had no idea how much time had passed.

"That was lovely," she said.

"I thought so, too." *Thanks a lot,* he thought, but the words stuck to his tongue. It truly had been lovely. They had danced, no more, no less.

"How much longer, Mike?" he asked over the communications channel.

"The answer should be here in ten minutes."

"And who was right this time?"

"You."

"Was it a good idea to check in?"

"It was, Lance."

Maybe he should check on the camera again. Lance moved toward the airlock. The camera was an older model, but it was particularly durable and suitable for something like this. The newest chips had such small electronic structures that under the cosmic radiation they produced digital artifacts. The good news was this old model functioned everywhere. He wondered from which museum NASA had taken this camera.

Lance unscrewed it from the tripod and pointed it at the sun, which was considerably smaller-looking here than it was on Earth, but if he looked right at it, it could still blind him. He observed it on the small screen on the back side of the camera. He then zoomed in as far as he could. The image grew blurry, probably because of the movement in the atmosphere.

He focused the camera on Sarah. In the encroaching dusk, her silhouette looked like a paper cutout. She was just standing there. Had she ever pursued any competitive sports? She looked relaxed and tense at the same time. He might be physically fit, but he would never get this combination. People could always tell when he was getting close to his limit.

"Lance? Sarah?"

It was Mike's voice. It sounded breathless. He had probably just climbed off the stationary bike after his workout. Lance fastened the camera back onto the tripod. Sarah started to run toward him. It should be starting any minute.

"Did you finally get the questions?" Lance asked.

"Uh... I can't exactly answer that."

"What do you mean?"

"I mean that I don't have them. Why don't the two of you come in first?"

Mike sounded extremely tense. Lance had never heard him like this.

"They'll be calling in in five minutes. I know these press idiots. First, they make sure everyone is on pins and needles, and then they make you wait. We should just wait out here for the interview."

"You're not listening, Lance."

"What am I supposed to make of your cryptic comments?"

"I want to tell you something inside, face to face."

"What's going on, Mike? All this secrecy isn't helping anything. What's wrong? Did someone die or start a revolution?"

Lance was slowly getting upset. Why was Mike making such a huge fuss?

Sarah placed a hand on his shoulder.

"There won't be a fucking interview. So just get back inside."

"Mike, your tone is out of line. Can't you hear yourself?" Suddenly, Lance was calm again. Was that because of Sarah's hand?

"Fuck my tone, Lance. This is about Earth. They aren't transmitting, not even a peep. If it were a living creature, I'd say that it was dead."

"What does that mean? Is the line dead? Is one of the satellites defective?" Lance couldn't grasp what Mike was saying.

"No, it's Earth. It isn't responding anymore. Nobody's there. Something terrible must have happened, but I don't know what," Mike said quietly.

Lance suddenly sensed how cold it actually was on Mars. The thermometer hadn't dropped down to zero yet. The cold spread through him, and he lifted his foot because the chill seemed to creep along his leg like a disgusting, damp worm. It reached his hip, chose a path along his spine, and reached his head. And then he stopped feeling anything.

MIKE WAS SHIVERING ALL OVER. LANCE WISHED HE COULD give him a hug. Wished? That was nonsense. He stood in front of Mike and wrapped his strong arms around his commander. The trembling slowed down. Lance could feel Mike's muscles go limp.

"I'm going to let you go now," Lance said as he nudged Mike lightly in the abdomen.

"Thanks," Mike said.

And just like that, everything had been said. Lance felt hollow. Shouldn't he miss his girlfriend, their mutual plans, the children they planned to have? Had his entire future just dissolved into thin air? It was still too early to sense that, and he wasn't upset yet. If there was anything he needed right now, it was to keep a cool head. It might be that all of this was nothing more than *idée fixe*. Ideas change, mutate, disappear into nothingness. No conservation laws applied to them.

"I still can't believe it," Sharon said, her back against the wall. She was sitting on the floor and scraping her feet against it.

"You've really checked everything?" Sarah prodded.

"Yes, everything. Every little cable. There's nothing from Earth. Nothing from the four orbiting satellites, either."

"Why didn't we pick up on this earlier? Maybe we could've done something?"

"No, Lance. The twenty-minute transmit time. We didn't expect anything. Why would we've been upset if nothing came in?" Sharon said.

"And the satellites?" Lance asked.

"We wondered about them. MRO 2 and ExoMars 3 came into view first, and then the others, once they emerged from the dead zone behind Mars. But this incident fell beyond all expectations. The satellites weren't programmed to report to us in the case of a total communication collapse. On the other hand, if we were to stop reporting in, they would raise an alarm."

"And there weren't any warning signs?"

"No, Lance. Yesterday evening, I received the next day's briefing from Earth," Sharon said.

Mike scuffed back and forth through the room, and finally decided to take a seat next to Sharon on the floor. Sarah stood very quietly beside Lance, who didn't know what to do next.

"We have to find out what happened on Earth," he said.

"But how?" Sharon asked. "We don't even have a telescope. Earth is damned far away. The observation satellites in orbit are watching Mars, not Earth."

"Couldn't we send one of the satellites back to Earth to try to see what's going on?"

"Yes, but we don't have enough fuel for that. And the next start window won't open for six months. That's our flight window to get one of them into Earth-bound trajectory."

"We can't just give up on Earth. Maybe they need help."

"And we're supposed to be the ones to help?"

"Who else?"

"We won't need to discuss that before the next start window opens," Sarah cut in. "Until then, we have other things to do. We have to help ourselves."

Nobody replied. Lance wanted to just shut his eyes, but he did all he could to keep them open. He wasn't willing to give up yet. Or was Sarah correct? Did they need to take care of themselves first? They had enough resources to last them for just under three years, but they wouldn't stretch forever. If Earth didn't reply before the next start window, they would have to stay up here longer than expected. Sarah had made an important point. They had no time to waste. They had what they needed to survive, but they would have to use their tools and wits, too.

"That's true, Sarah," Lance replied. "It looks like we might be here longer than we'd thought. It's time to start planning for that."

Sol 10, MfE base

"Are you coming? Mike's waiting."

Ewa heard Ellen's call, but she couldn't instantly stop what she was doing. It had taken her a long time to calm Germaine down. Now she was sitting behind her against the wall, holding her tightly. The woman from Cameroon was still weeping quietly, but it was no longer the hopeless sobbing from before. And she wasn't the only one who had broken down when the NASA base had informed them that Earth had fallen silent.

"Ewa? Should I put him off for ten minutes?"

Put him off... *No. At this point, that would go down about as well as a slap to the face*, she told herself.

"No, that's okay. I'll be right there."

Somehow they would have to keep going. Frankly, nothing much had changed for her own crew. They had each punched a one-way ticket. They had known, every one of them, that they would never again see their parents, their siblings and other relatives, or any of their friends—they had told them goodbye forever. Why was it that for some of them this news still made such a great difference? Their farewells on Earth had already been for eternity. They really shouldn't kick up such a fuss! It was quite possible that all of this would prove to be a big misunderstanding. However, the situation was too puzzling to make that likely.

She gently pushed Germaine away and got up from her spot. *Your work isn't done*, a voice deep inside her warned. It sometimes took her by surprise, but at this moment its timing was perfect. Despite the loss of half their cargo in the bowels of the *Santa Maria*, they still had everything they needed to set up their settlement. However, they required the NASA crew to do that, and that was why she was now at the video console.

Ewa brushed a few strands of hair out of her face. It never hurt to look your best for whomever you were talking to. She had a sense that Mike found her interesting.

"Hi, Mike," she said. "Nice to see you. Please excuse the delay. The situation has been a terrible shock for some of us."

"Understandable," Mike said. "I'm pretty upset myself. My mother..."

"I'm sorry. Should we postpone our conversation?"

"I'm keeping it together. Have to keep going." Mike sniffed slightly. "Do you have..."

"I don't have any living relatives on Earth. I *didn't* have any, I should have said. It will take some getting used to. And I purposely avoided making any close friends once I'd applied for MfE."

"Now I'm the one feeling sorry."

Ewa was annoyed. Why should he feel sorry? It had worked out well for her. That was probably why she felt so calm. Everything was still running as planned, despite a few small bumps in the road. The silence from Earth wasn't any kind of loss for their mission. In reality, she hadn't expected any support or contact from there anyway.

"Thanks," Ewa said. "I'd like to chat about our collaborative work. It looks like we'll have to put up with each other longer than we'd expected."

"I'm not sure that we're quite willing to accept that yet. I honestly think there's some kind of temporary problem going on. However, I'm also aware that we need to be prepared for anything."

"Good. Will it still be alright for us to borrow the robotic drill from you?"

"Yes. But we would like to agree to terms in a signed contract. Our food production will be fairly low over the coming months."

"Understood. You'd like guaranteed deliveries. I can offer you four-nineteenths of everything we cultivate on Mars. That corresponds with the relative sizes of our crews. Along with your own produce, your provisions will be larger than ours."

"Agreed," Mike said. "And you'll return the robot to us as soon as you're able to meet your own nutritional needs, right?"

"Mm-hmm. There is one other problem, though. We would like to build as close as possible to an ice deposit. However, the direct sunlight in the northern zone is lower than down here. We'll need an energy source that will function independently of the sun."

"Are you thinking about a KRUSTY?"

Yes, she was thinking about a KRUSTY, the NASA acronym for a Kilopower Reactor Using Stirling Technology. "I know that you have more than one KRUSTY," Ewa said.

Actually, she wasn't sure of that fact, but she had to try at least. The current model produced one hundred kilowatts of power, and it was maintenance-free for the first ten years. That would be a fantastic treasure for the settlement. However, when ten years had passed, all the fuel would be gone. If Mike was thinking strategically, he would keep all the KRUSTYs he possessed for as long as possible. Even if there were no children, the adults could expect to spend at least fifty or sixty years here.

Ewa could hear Mike whispering. He was probably discussing her request with the others.

"Fine, we'll agree to that," Mike said finally.

She was surprised. Mike had struck her as having a cool,

calculating head on his shoulders. She had been wrong about him, which was why she now allowed herself a smile.

"Oh, you've taken a load off my shoulders," she said. "You have no idea how much better I feel now. We will return the favor as soon as we can."

"I'll look forward to seeing how you do that," Mike said.

"Well, we have something you definitely don't."

"The animals? A little fresh goat milk would be welcome."

He was assuming that she meant the animals. He was mistaken! Ewa felt her spirits rise. "I didn't mean them," Ewa said. "We have guns—three pistols and ammunition."

"You have what?"

"You heard me correctly."

"But I always thought that MfE was a nonprofit organization that wanted to build a just, new world."

"We might be a little disorganized, but we're not stupid. We always wanted to survive on this planet. And at some point, other people will come. That's always been obvious. So we have to be able to defend ourselves. If that ever happens, you can count on us."

Mike didn't look all that pleased at her promise. He was probably one of those people who rejected violence in general. He might have also interpreted her offer as a threat. She wouldn't mind if he did.

Sol 11, NASA base

"Is it possible that the blonde Ms. Ewa and her charming smile have pulled the wool over your eyes?" Lance asked.

Mike shook his head. "We have to find a way to get along together," he said, defending himself.

Lance was pissed off. Mike might be the official mission commander, but all fundamental decisions were supposed to be made as a group. It bothered him that Mike had practically given away a robotic drill and a KRUSTY without adequate compensation and without previously seeking the other NASA crewmembers' agreement. That was why he had spent the previous night inventorying their supplies.

"I'm afraid that the mere presence of MfE is going to jeopardize our own survival," Lance declared. "Take a look at this list."

He displayed the results of his survey on the monitor.

"Per person, we need a daily supply of 0.2 kilograms of oxygen, assuming that you can rely on a rate of eighty percent reprocessing. Besides this, you can plan on a half kilogram of dehydrated food, one kilogram of canned food, and four liters of drinkable water, of which we can recycle about 3.2 liters."

"Those are the known NASA figures. What are you trying to say?" Mike said.

"Just a second. You seem to be ignoring the fact that the situation has drastically changed. There were only four of us, and we'd planned for two years, including unexpected emergencies. But now we have to project ahead to the end of our lives."

"But we have plenty of time to do that."

"You think so? It's no longer just the four of us. We're now providing for nineteen people."

"We can cultivate most of our resources here."

"To a certain extent, yes. We can get oxygen by splitting the carbon dioxide in the atmosphere, but we need energy to do that. And you've now given away one of our KRUSTYs. We also need power to produce methane as fuel and to grow the plants. The hundred kilowatts that one KRUSTY can produce isn't really all that much."

"You're exaggerating, Lance. Since when have you been so skittish?"

"Since learning that we're never going to receive new supplies again. Follow these figures. We have about 650 kilograms of oxygen in bottles. That will last about 800 days for four people. But for nineteen people, this will barely cover 168 days. Less than six fucking months! And this doesn't even take into consideration the spiked usage, such as when we have to vent the Rover cabin."

"We can extract the oxygen from the *Endeavour*'s drive system," Mike assured him.

"Which will make it incapable of future flight. But I'm not done yet. Let's get back to the food situation. We have just under five tons of food that were also supposed to last for two years. At least for four people. If we share this with the MfE people, we'll run out completely before we hit the six-month mark."

"They brought their own provisions along."

"Really? We transported all their worldly goods in our Rover. That was less than a ton of stuff."

"Some of their supplies came on the *Endeavour*."

"Have you forgotten everything you learned in math? There are almost four times as many of them as there are of us. Just for themselves, they wouldn't need five, but rather twenty tons of food for a two-year period."

"We'll figure it out," Mike said glumly.

Lance looked at him. Mike looked like a little kid whose balloon had been stolen. Sarah and Sharon were simply watching.

"It's time for the two of you to say something," Lance declared.

"What should I say?" Sarah replied. "You're right, Lance. But Mike is, too, somehow."

"We can't both be." Lance was slowly getting angry. "Should I bother you about the water, too? Just the four of us each need 3.2 liters of fresh water a day. Not to speak of the plants. At this point, we're only getting two liters a day from the minerals."

"The MfE folks plan to build their settlement close to ice deposits. They could provide us with water."

"Deposits they haven't even found yet. And if they do, we'll have to transport that water over a thousand kilometers."

"Your figures are right, Lance, but you're looking at all of this pessimistically. These are solvable problems," Mike said.

"Ones we wouldn't have if you hadn't—"

"Lance, I have to cut in," Sarah said quietly. "Whether we give them away or not, our provisions will eventually run out. That's a given. We have to find ways to replenish them, faster now than before. We can do it."

Lance scanned the group. Sharon was nodding in agreement with what Sarah had said. Maybe she was right after all. However, the time pressure that Mike's decision had put them under really rankled.

"Okay," Lance finally said, his anger spent. "Then we should get started working as soon as possible. As I see it, our main problem is energy. If we have enough of that, we can produce enough oxygen and water.

"Food cultivation is a close second," Sarah replied. "As the biologist, I'll take this piece. Lance, you should take charge of the power production. Do you have any ideas?"

"Absolutely. I'd like to build some turbines."

Sol 12, MfE expedition

"THEO, IT'S GOOD TO SEE YOU."

It was so dark in their bubble that the screen was blinding them. Theo dimmed the brightness to keep from waking up Rebecca, who was still asleep.

"Hello, Ewa," Theo said softly.

"Are you making good time?"

"Very good. If we can maintain our speed, we'll reach our destination a day early."

"Don't forget that you should start searching for ice before then. It'll just be at a greater depth."

"Of course. But I suspect you haven't called before dawn in order to remind us of that?" Theo felt hope flicker up briefly. *Have they perhaps made contact with Earth again?* he thought.

But he was wrong.

"You're right, Theo. I wanted to warn you that the satellite has detected a dust storm heading your way."

"When?"

"The highest wind speed should reach you in about four hours."

"Thanks for the warning. We'll set off anyway."

Ewa laughed. "I thought you would. That's the Theo I know. Good luck!"

She ended the transmission.

THEO DECIDED TO AWAKEN REBECCA. THERE WAS A CHANCE they would lose some time today, so it would be best for them to set off earlier.

His colleague was sleeping on her stomach, her head propped on her arm. This only left him one-third of the mattress, but since he had to sleep on his side, it didn't bother him.

"You blow on my neck during the night," Rebecca had declared on the second night.

"I can turn and sleep on my other side," he had replied.

"Don't worry about it. It doesn't bother me. I actually find it somewhat comforting, as if someone is taking care of me. When I was a kid, I had a dog that always slept next to me in my small bed. I fell asleep to the sound of its panting."

A dog. Theo had laughed aloud at the thought. However, if it helped her to fall asleep, he would be a dog. He had probably been smelling like one for a long time already, anyways. The opportunities for them to wash up during their camping trip were quite limited. The methanol fuel cell produced water they could use to wash, but the amount was limited, and they refused to squander the drinkable water they had brought along.

"Time to wake up," he said, tapping her leg.

Rebecca moved slightly, but she seemed to still be dreaming. She turned over on her back but didn't open her eyes. A crease line ran across her right cheek, which had been resting on her arm.

"I'm sorry, Rebecca, but we have to get going," he said louder.

She opened her eyes. "Oh, is it morning already?" she asked, her voice sounding soft and a little husky.

"Almost. A storm is heading our way, which is why we have to set off earlier."

"Okay, give me ten minutes."

Theo turned around. He spooned instant coffee powder into the water kettle, added water to it, and set it on the warming plate. The drink was heated to precisely 37 degrees. The brew's taste was far from real coffee, but the caffeine never failed to have its effect. He cranked the clasps to the right on the aluminum cans containing the bread dough. The contents were heated chemically. After forty-five seconds, he could open the cans all the way. The clumps of bread that he dumped out of them looked like rolls. They were warm, but not crusty.

"Jelly or chocolate spread?" he asked.

"Jelly. Strawberry," Rebecca replied.

He cut her roll in two against the edge of the can and drizzled a tube of red cream on it, before pressing the two halves of the bread back together. He spread a brown cream onto his own roll.

"Ready," he said."

"Me, too," Rebecca answered.

Theo turned back around and held out her roll and coffee. Only then did he begin on his own breakfast.

THE SKY WAS BEHAVING STRANGELY TODAY. THEO WOULD HAVE been worried if he hadn't known what was coming. He hadn't seen the sun come up. It was already a washed-out spot in the sky when they emerged from their tent balloon. Although it was now eight o'clock, it was difficult to judge direction by the brightness of the sky. It hadn't grown brighter over the past half hour, it had actually become darker.

"Shouldn't we stop somewhere and take shelter?" Rebecca asked from behind him.

"That won't be necessary unless our visibility gets too bad," he replied.

Ewa radioed in. "Are the two of you all right? The satellite has reported that the storm has almost reached you."

"It's only gotten a little darker," replied Rebecca.

"That's the dust floating in the air," added Theo.

"Why hasn't it hit you?"

"It's coming up from the South, and we're directly north of you," said Theo.

"You're forgetting the rotation of the planet. It disrupts the airstreams," Rebecca noted.

"That's right," Theo said. "I should've thought of that myself."

"But be careful anyway!" Ewa advised.

"Of course," they both responded at the same time.

He terminated the connection. Theo's thoughts drifted to his childhood. Whenever they had driven home from his grandmother's house at night, white walls of fog had often blocked the streets. His father had driven straight through them with no hesitation. That had always impressed him greatly as a child. *Another world is hidden inside the fog,* his child's mind had thought. *Will we be able to find our way back out again?*

He had imagined dust storms on Mars to be like that, but of course, they weren't similar at all. The visibility was definitely limited, but he could still see for at least 150 meters. This was why he hadn't dropped his speed even a little. The dust seemed to be swirling above their heads primarily. However, that was an optical illusion. When he glanced upward, he could see a brownish wall, actually a thick layer of dust, many kilometers in depth. The illusion didn't function on the ground level because the scattered boulders provided a sense of perspective.

"It's rather unnerving, that wall above us," Rebecca said.

"The air isn't any thicker than it is down here."

"I know," she replied.

But she was right. It was as if they were driving underneath a gigantic boulder that was gradually descending on top of them. In the direction they were driving, their perspective caused the boulder to look like it was sinking closer and closer to the surface, and yet the farther they actually drove, the higher the boundary between sky and surface seemed.

Theo glanced at the clock. Nine-thirty. "It's nine-thirty," he said. "This is the worst of it."

The Rover's gauge indicated that the wind speed was about 80 kilometers per hour. Since they were driving in the direction the wind was blowing, the storm seemed to be blasting them at 60 kilometers per hour, but at most, it felt like a gentle wind on Earth. He really hadn't needed to worry. Next time, he'd let Rebecca sleep in. A thin atmosphere had its advantages.

Theo was glad that the storm hadn't stalled out somewhere else. The atmosphere was hypnotic. He was no longer on Mars, but rather, caught in a painting by an Expressionist painter. He would now steer for eternity toward a destination that sat just beyond the edge of the picture, while a giant tried to squash him under his foot.

Sol 19, NASA base

Due to the dust floating in the air, it hadn't really grown any brighter since they'd awakened. That was normal for this time of year. Sharon, the trained meteorologist, called it the northern Autumn. As the southern region, where significant deposits of frozen carbon dioxide gathered during the chilly winter, gradually grew warmer, here, north of the equator, it was slowly becoming colder. The temperature extremes were equalized by the airstreams that carried the dust with them.

Lance gazed up. If the sun remained missing for yet another day, his depression would deepen. But his project was even more critical. The solar panels they had brought with them had only produced half of their typical output for days now.

Today there wasn't even a little breeze. It was a strange atmosphere, like before the onset of a storm. If only it would rain! Lance imagined how the raindrops would scrub the dust out of the air. The sky—how he missed the blue on Earth!—would be clearer than it ever had been, and once the storm had passed, a rainbow would stretch across the horizon.

Lance sighed. He would never experience rain again. Even if they managed to change Mars's climate, there wouldn't be rain on this planet for another thousand years.

He was making decent progress with his turbine. Because of the low dynamic pressure that the wind here generated, he couldn't build a machine with massive propellers, like on Earth. He had based his design on memories of a childhood toy. His pinwheel had consisted of paper blades folded into a common center, their points secured—with a sturdy pin—to a stick. They maintained their form as a result of the material's internal tension. And since they were so lightweight, even the mildest breeze had set the pinwheel in joyous motion. To young Lance, that had seemed so magical. If you stared at the spinning blades, the colors would suddenly start to blur. He had always hoped that the enchanted process would lead to something new and wondrous, but the pinwheel had eventually come to a stop, every time.

He wasn't working with paper in this case. For the dimensions he needed, it wouldn't have been stable enough. Along with Sharon, he had worked in the new lab and synthesized a soft plastic that met the requirements for his endeavor. They had used methanol as their base material, since they could produce an ongoing supply of this from carbon dioxide. How many times had they had to start over again? Many!

The material had to be stable, and had to bear up even when shaped into a surface area of ten square meters with the lowest wall-thickness possible. It wasn't enough to make it as pliable as a sheet of paper, whose lower edge you could curve and attach at the top. It was on this point that they almost failed, until Lance started to experiment with actual paper. The paper proved to be less pliable if you bent or rolled it up beforehand. That was the moment he altered the form of his turbine. It would now consist of two curved, U-shaped plastic elements. They would each be five meters long, and along two sides they would be mounted to a pivoted mast. A generator would be located at the foot of the structure. He had already repurposed an electric engine, the spare for the open Rover, into the generator.

Now he was in the process of attaching the blades to the metal pole. They had constructed it from various replacement parts and fused them together. Once that was done, he had cut slits into both sides of the pole into which he was now slotting the plastic blades. Lance had thought up a trick to keep them from working their way loose. Thin wires were running through the pole, and he would send an electrical current through them. When they grew hot, the plastic touching the metal pole would melt a little and weld onto the metal to keep the blades from slipping out.

For this final step, he needed help, which was why Sarah was on her way. In exchange, he had promised to water their first garden beds.

"Tell me what to do."

Oh! She's already here. Lance wiped the dust from his helmet window.

"You need to pick up the end of the pole and pull the wire inside it taut. Just a sec. Not until I say when."

He leaned down and lifted his end of the pole. "Now."

They lifted it simultaneously.

Lance felt Sarah start to pull on the wire. "That's just right," he said. "I'll now send 330 volts through the wire."

The wire twitched in his fingers. His announcement must have startled Sarah.

"The charge won't do anything. The resistance in your gloves is too high for you to feel anything. At most, the wire gets a little hot, but I'll turn off the electricity after a few seconds."

"Got it," he heard Sarah say over the helmet radio.

"Alright, now."

This time, the wire remained still. Lance pushed the power switch on the mobile methanol generator with his toe. He couldn't see anything, which meant he'd have to guess. How long would the wire need to heat up and melt the plastic?

Exactly this long, he decided as he cut the power back off. If that hadn't been long enough, he could always heat it for longer.

"You can put the pole back down."

Sarah carefully set the pole back down on the ground.

"Still need me for anything, Lance?"

"Let me just check quickly to see if it worked."

He walked along the pole and tried to tug the plastic blades out, but they didn't budge. His plan had worked. He stopped right in front of Sarah, who was gazing toward the East. He followed her gaze, which was when he noticed it—a flickering reddish light up in the sky.

"Do you see that?" he asked, pointing toward the light.

"See what?"

"There was a light over that way."

"A light?"

He didn't reply, but then the light reappeared.

"Oh," she said. "I thought maybe you were joking."

"Is that a polar light?" Lance asked.

"The magnetic field on Mars is much too weak to produce a polar light."

Lance radioed Sharon back at the base. "Do you know what's glowing out there on the horizon?"

"The red lights?" she asked.

"Exactly."

"It's a storm. Or the Martian version of one."

Lance cranked his external microphone up all the way. He heard his feet crunching through the dust, which he had never noticed before. However, no sound followed the next flash of lightning.

"It's a shame there's no thunder," he said.

"There's a little, but the atmosphere is so thin that it seriously dampens the sound," Sharon explained.

"Pity," Lance replied.

"That doesn't matter. We're probably the first people to observe such red discharges in the sky from the Mars surface. I think it's quite romantic," said Sarah.

Lance wanted to say, 'You're right,' but the words, which felt both stubborn and unwieldy, did not cross his lips. He would have liked to slide his arm around Sarah's shoulders, but what if she didn't want to be touched? *Wouldn't that make working together awkward?* he thought with a sigh.

"Go ahead and do it," Sarah said.

Uh, what? He was stunned. Had she just read his thoughts? He cautiously placed his right arm around her shoulders.

Sarah started to laugh.

"I was actually talking to Mike," she said. "He wants to come out and watch the weather. But this is very nice. Don't stop." She carefully leaned back until he was supporting her.

Sol 20, NASA base

The night shifts were stressful. Lance was supposed to spend eight hours watching something that had never failed because it had been designed for long-term functioning without supervision. The base had been here long before they had arrived, and after their departure, it would... No, they wouldn't be departing, at least not as they had planned. How could he have forgotten that for even a moment? Was it normal that he had adjusted so quickly to this situation, or was he still in some state of denial?

Lance turned onto his side in the seat. He had reclined the back as far as it would go. It wasn't a completely flat surface, but he slept even worse sitting upright. He had tested that theory on his last night shift. He pulled the thin blanket over his body and closed his eyes. His girlfriend materialized on his mental movie screen. He still remembered how sweet her face had been. Sweet—that was what came to his mind. But he couldn't recall the color of her eyes. *Don't worry*, he thought, *you just need to take a look at one of her photos, and then everything will come back.*

But he didn't listen to his own advice, and his memory dissolved. This hadn't happened even once during their six-month flight to Mars, but now it was starting. *What does this mean? Don't I still love her? Yes, I do.* Just the thought of Freda made him feel warm.

Something began to vibrate suddenly. Lance jerked, and his right foot brushed against the control panel. He leaped up. 'Transmission declined' stood in red letters on the screen. His foot must have touched the transmission button. Lance quickly pulled up the details. Mars Express 2b, which had been orbiting the planet for the past ten years, was notifying the base that it had received a signal. It wasn't from NASA, but from a distance that corresponded with Earth's location. The signal strength indicated that. *Is it back again? Has everything just been a mistake, an experiment, a disruption? Freda has brown eyes,* he suddenly remembered. *Or does she?* Lance tapped at the screen wildly. He had to countermand the dismissal! But it was too late. The satellite was just sinking below the horizon. They would have to wait until it reappeared over this hemisphere.

Should he wake the others up? Absolutely. Regardless of what Mars Express 2b had picked up, it was something relevant to all of them. Lance left the control center. He needed to deliver this news in person. He woke the others up gently, starting with Mike as the commander.

"The satellite won't show back up for several more hours. Why did you wake me up?" Mike was all cool.

Sharon dashed right to the control center. She had to see the message with her own eyes.

Sarah impulsively hugged him. Startled, Lance turned red. He hadn't deserved that. On the contrary, if he hadn't reacted so clumsily, they would already know what Earth wanted from them.

Of course, there was a chance it hadn't come from Earth. *But if not, from where?*

SEVERAL HOURS LATER, MIKE WAS SITTING IN THE commander seat as Mars Express 2b climbed over the horizon. Lance, Sharon, and Sarah were standing around him, following every movement he made.

Mike requested that the satellite resend the transmission. Everything ran smoothly. The parabolic antenna transmitted what it had received, and the computer decrypted it.

"This is Rick Summers, the administrator of the space ship *Spaceliner 1.* Our task is to develop Mars as a colony for Earth. Just like us, you must now know that our home planet is no longer responding. We few survivors are on our own. In the name of our president, I would like to offer you the opportunity to join us once we reach Mars in about five months. We possess all the resources necessary to make the planet permanently habitable, and we are prepared to share these with you, if you are willing to place yourselves under our command. Please send us your decision as soon as possible."

The message hadn't come from Earth, after all, Lance thought grimly. He watched as Sharon and Mike's faces fell by the end of the first sentence. Sarah pushed the replay button. Rick Summers's voice repeated his speech.

"I don't know about you, but I don't like that man," she said finally.

"It doesn't matter. It's the most logical thing for us to do. The *Spaceliner* project was privately funded, and they have very different resources than we do," Mike said.

"We can't just agree to submit to them! We don't even know who they are," Lance interjected as he started to pace up and down the control center.

"Lance is right," Sarah agreed. "My gut tells me that this Summers isn't everything he seems to be."

"What do you think, Sharon?" Mike asked.

"I... don't know. I have to admit that, for a moment, I felt real hope again."

"Our chances of survival would be greater if we had access to what *Spaceliner I* is bringing with it," Mike remarked.

"That might be true, but we can't give up our independence so quickly," Lance protested. *What was wrong with Mike?*

Had that brief flicker of hope swept him along to the point of preferring to abdicate his responsibility? he thought.

"We don't have to make a decision today," Sarah suggested. "You can formulate a polite refusal. If they land and behave themselves, we can still decide to join them."

"I can live with that," Sharon said.

"Fine," Mike shrugged. "That's what we'll do."

He leaned over the monitor.

"In theory, we are open to whatever your idea of collaboration might be," he spoke into the camera as he rubbed his chin. "There are bound to be areas in which we could profit from one another's experiences, or in which an exchange of knowledge or technology would be helpful. As a crew, we agree that the formal structures you have in mind are not necessary for us. We see ourselves as an independent operation, as our contracting authority intended for us to be, which means we are not part of the private enterprise that you represent."

"Perfect," Lance was about to say, though he was able to bite his tongue just in time. Mike needed to be the one to express the concluding greeting.

"I wish you a safe journey," Mike continued. "Please contact us again shortly before you land. Perhaps, with our equipment, we can help you find a good landing spot."

Mike pressed a button. Lance followed the progress bars on the send icon. It only took a few seconds for the message to start its long trip.

"You did a good job, Mike," he said.

"Thanks." His colleague and friend's voice sounded weary, observed Lance.

Sol 21, MfE expedition

"OUCH! I TOLD YOU TO BE CAREFUL AROUND THAT SPOT!"

"I'm sorry, Rebecca."

"Man, Theo, it hurts terribly as it is."

"I know."

The insides of Rebecca's thighs were covered in bruises. However, the raw spots were even worse. They had first appeared on her body four days ago. Theo's had shown up two days later. He already hated what was coming next. As soon as he was done spreading medicine on Rebecca, they would have to climb back into their instruments of torture, their spacesuits. The wounds had first developed on their joints, where the fabric ridges inside the suits rubbed against their skin. As they drove for hours in the Rover, these spots were scraped raw. They were also unable to sit any longer, since blisters had now formed on their thighs and backsides—a recent development.

He squeezed a dollop of cream out of the tube and spread it lightly across Rebecca's skin. To reach one of the abrasions, he had to push her underwear a little to the side. However, his thoughts were occupied with their medical supplies.

"I'm sorry that I yelled at you in the tent earlier," apologized Rebecca. "I know you didn't mean to hurt me."

"No problem," Theo replied as he maneuvered the Rover between two boulders.

For the first time yesterday, he had shouted as well, because she had taken longer than usual to climb into the Rover. *This is all normal*, he said to himself. It had been days since they had been able to get away from each other. They spent their days and nights together. By this point, Theo was convinced he knew Rebecca better than he had known the three or four serious girlfriends he'd had back on Earth. At least he and Rebecca weren't at each other's throats—yet.

Their routine might help with that. Theo valued sticking to their plan. They set off at the same time every day, reset the ground-penetrating radar every ten minutes on the dot, and never stayed more than ten hours in one spot. They should've already located ice four days ago. They had driven over 2,000 kilometers northward, even though they had only figured on 1,500. They would eventually have to call it quits.

"Rebecca, I think we need to give some serious thought to whether or not we should turn back," he said.

"If we do that, Mars for Everyone is finished," she replied. "Is that what you want?"

"Ewa thinks we can find another way to procure water."

Ewa had already started advocating for their return three days ago, but he had been against it. He was now wondering if he had made the right call. *Maybe Mars doesn't want to make it so easy for us?* They had trusted one specific theory, perhaps too much—underground ice could exist around the 40th parallel. However, that didn't mean that it had to.

"You can do the math yourself, Theo. Extracting water from minerals requires way too much energy input. We'll be suffering from a chronic energy shortage as it is, a decade from now at the latest, once the KRUSTY the NASA people plan to give us runs out of fuel."

"Ten years is a long time. We'll find alternatives by then."

"By then we might have moved our settlement, which won't be cheap. Let's stay around here for another few days.

"The farther north we go, the colder the winters will be, and that will cost more energy and decrease even more the efficiency of our solar panels."

"Only a few percentage points. We'd be able to recover the loss if we found an ice deposit."

Rebecca was right. If they failed to locate any ice deposits, the previous plans for their settlement would be obsolete. They might have to find some way to remain with the NASA people in that case. Wouldn't that be the wiser course anyway? Did they really have to build their own Mars for Everyone settlement? Who was the *Everyone* if Earth remained silent?

"Our medical supplies won't last for the entire return trip. The last days will be hell," Theo declared.

"We'd get through it, if we have a good report to bring back."

"And if not?"

"Oh, Theo, I've never heard you so pessimistic."

"I start every morning by staring at the open sores on your backside."

"I can promise you that, although I can't see them, I feel them with every bump in the ground."

"And you really want to keep going?"

"Give us three more days, alright? Then we'll head back."

"Two days, as a compromise?" Theo offered.

"Agreed," said Rebecca with a sigh.

Sol 22, MfE base

"HAVE YOU SEEN WHAT THE NASA PEOPLE SENT OVER?"

Gabriella was sitting in front of a monitor in the *Endeavour*'s command center, her eyes on Ewa, who had just climbed up the ladder.

"I just woke up," Ewa replied. She hadn't slept so poorly in a long time. *Why aren't Theo and Rebecca finding the ice?* As a group, they had discussed this for a long time. It could just be dumb luck, or the lack thereof. There might be giant ice deposits on either side of their route, but not directly on their way. Or the models generated by the planetary scientists had simply been wrong.

"They've received two messages from *Spaceliner I*," Gabriella said.

"That American multimillionaire's privately funded ego project? What was his name?"

"Yep, that's the one—I don't recall the guy's name. *Spaceliner I* will be here in five months."

"Well, hopefully, not right here. They must have launched before Earth went silent."

"Looks that way," Gabriella said. "It sounds like you have something against them."

"What they're doing is the complete opposite of what we imagined for our settlement of Mars. They want to build a colony that will function according to economic considerations."

"Considering there might not be any more assistance from Earth, isn't that perhaps the model which will ensure the highest likelihood of survival, even if it isn't the better concept?"

"You can't be serious, Gabriella. But what did they have to say?"

"In the first message, they offered to formally incorporate us into their endeavor. You'll especially like the second one, though. Just a sec."

Gabriella pushed a few buttons, and a thin face appeared on the screen. The man had to be in his late thirties. Ewa based this estimate on the few wrinkles she thought she could make out on his forehead. His clean-shaven face made him seem younger, though. His ears stuck out a little. The speaker introduced himself as Rick Summers, administrator of *Spaceliner I*.

Gabriella turned up the sound. "I meant this part," she said.

"You might be interested in this offer I'd like to make," Summers began. At this volume, his voice sounded unpleasant.

"If any one of you agrees to support our mission, I will name you my non-terminable representative. If you would prefer, you don't need to tell anyone about your decision. It can remain between the two of us. All I require is your loyalty, and you won't regret this decision. Take all the time you need to consider your response. However, you should understand that I can only keep this offer open until I receive the first positive response."

Ewa laughed. *The man is obviously seeking a spy among my crew,* she thought. His gall impressed her. It wasn't coincidental that Summers was in charge of a private spaceship. Whatever his specific function, it seemed to come with a certain amount of power, as otherwise he wouldn't be in a position to make such enticing offers. Ewa's first impulse was to have Gabriella delete the message, but that would indicate that she didn't trust her crew.

Would any of them actually fall for this primitive manipulation? she wondered. They were all caught in a state of relative emergency, but Ewa had never once thought that the crew's loyalty to the mission had suffered as a result of it. And yet, she felt uncertain. Most of them would reject the offer flat out. But hard times were coming, without a doubt. Over time, Summers's offer might sink into the crew's thoughts like a slow-acting poison. Ewa shook her head. Her questioning of the other crew members simply made Summer's work easier.

"Go ahead and play it for the others," she told Gabriella.

"Shouldn't we vote on our response? The NASA people already sent Summers their refusal."

"I don't think that will be necessary. But if anyone on the crew thinks differently, we can certainly take a vote. I think the outcome would be quite clear."

Sol 22, NASA base

"YOU PROMISED TO HELP ME WITH THE GARDENING."

Lance glanced up at Sarah from his monitor. He had just been planning his first wind farm. The turbine he had set up was producing less than 30 watts on average, which was only enough to power a single LED panel. But with one hundred turbines they could generate three kilowatts, which would be enough to actually do something significant. However, Lance was facing two problems.

He had to raise enough for the initial investment. The methanol that they were processing into the plastic for the turbines required a significant energy input for its production. He also needed a large number of pipes, as lightweight as possible, to set up the mini-power plants, as well as several generators that could take the angular momentum and convert it to electricity. He was using his computer to experiment with how to lay out a hundred turbines so that they wouldn't negatively impact each other. This was where Sarah's request cut in.

Biting back a groan, Lance stood up. He had indeed promised to help with the gardening. Sarah smiled, and Lance suddenly realized that maybe he didn't mind working in the garden.

"It won't be all that much fun," she cautioned.

"I bet that's not true," he answered. "After all, you'll be there." He instantly turned as beet red as a schoolboy, but Sarah seemed to be flattered by this awkward compliment.

"Then, come on."

Sarah led the way to the greenhouse. It was located beyond one of the airlocks. Before stepping inside, Sarah pressed a breathing mask into his hands. "Because of the special atmosphere," she said.

Though the explanation was unnecessary, Lance nodded anyway. The plants they had brought with them thrived especially well in carbon dioxide-enriched air.

Sarah also pulled on a mask before climbing down the three steps to the airlock and continuing on her knees. He followed her. The airlock's ceiling was low, which was why they couldn't walk upright. The greenhouse was also less than adult height. Lance could only work there by ducking his head. A cloud of foul-smelling gas was waiting for them beyond the airlock door.

Sarah pointed at the mask, and he nodded.

"Yeah, unfortunately, it doesn't hold the scent molecules at bay. At least, they're not toxic," she said.

It smelled like feces, and Lance could guess why.

"In case you're wondering," Sarah said, "we didn't have enough dirt for the spores we brought along."

Lance caught sight of a giant four-shelf unit. Each level held a thirty-centimeter thick layer of reddish-brown material.

"That is Martian dirt," Sarah explained. "I've injected it with the spores to help enrich it. However, our greenhouse is larger than planned, which is why I have to avail myself of the life support system."

"You spread our shit across the beds?" Lance said, laughing.

"No, not directly. First I dried it and ground it up. That way I could distribute it more systematically than if what I had was thick chunks of it."

Sarah held a bag out to him. "What does it look like?" she

asked.

"Coffee grounds?" was Lance's best guess.

"Then, *bon appetite*. This is the result of your time on the toilet yesterday."

"Great. What would you like me to do?"

"I've prepared something for you over there to the side."

"Almost sounds like a cooking show."

"Haha! I injected this dirt two days ago. I need you to take a series of samples and analyze them."

"I have no idea how to do that."

"You insert the samples into that tube there and the machine will do the rest."

"And how many samples do I need to take?"

"Do you see the little sprouts? They're all cataloged on the computer. You should take a sample from each plant, and this will help us determine the optimal growth conditions."

"Not just warm and damp?" Lance asked.

"No, we want to produce as much food as possible with as little energy input as is necessary. Back home, the best results were 420 grams per kilowatt-hour. The better my values are, the less electricity your turbines have to produce."

"Interesting. I didn't know that you worked with values like that. In other words, for each four-kilowatt hour, I could cover a day's rations for one crew member?"

"Only if we want to eat Rambo radishes and nothing else. Watercress, carrots, and lettuce aren't nearly as efficient, the grains even less so."

"That has to be linked to the least-consumable components of the plants."

"At least in terms of the grains. But we can also eat cooked radish leaves, and they're high in nutrients. Plants benefit the most from strongly carbon dioxide-enriched atmospheres."

"Good. Well, should I go ahead and start?"

"Yes, thanks. I'll be on the other side of the shelves. I have to prepare ten square meters of dirt today so that I can plant some carrots tomorrow."

Sol 23, MfE expedition

"YOU KNOW WHAT WE'LL BE DOING AFTER TODAY'S excursion, right?" Theo asked.

"We'll be turning around," Rebecca replied. She gazed into his eyes as if she had something on her mind.

"But?" he asked.

"I would like to take a little drive westward."

"According to the theory, our chances of finding ice should be greater if we keep heading north."

"That's true. But I caught sight of a crater on the map with a southern edge that looks shadowy."

"You mean the sun never reaches the bottom of the crater on that side? The edge of the crater has to be fairly steep, then. Craters like that are rare."

"Yes, it must be fairly young. That makes it a potential location for ice. The impact of the meteor removed the top layer of dirt, and the reduced exposure to sunshine might have caused the ice to last longer in there."

Theo gave this some thought. There was no reason not to give this a shot. Odds were odds. "Okay," he said. "We'll head that way."

With a groan, he resumed his seat in the Rover. He gritted his teeth, since the new sore on his left buttock was pressed right against the edge of the Rover's seat.

"Ready?" he asked.

Rebecca moaned quietly.

He turned back to look at her. She was still trying to find a bearable position.

"Ready," she finally said.

Theo turned the ignition and pressed the pedal. If he stood up, his suit would chafe other spots. They were rubbed raw, too, but not as severely as the skin on his inner thighs.

THEY WERE APPROACHING THEIR DESTINATION FROM THE EAST. The map had been excellent. The crater was located precisely where it was indicated. They arrived at noon, when the sun was at its zenith.

Theo parked the Rover. They climbed out and began to carefully scale the eastern crater wall. It was about eighty meters high and littered with loose gravel. "Watch out," Theo said. "With the low erosion-rate here, there could be larger boulders just waiting for the right vibration to roll down on top of us."

"I can just imagine," Rebecca replied.

Theo quickly grew short of breath. Rebecca passed him, climbing with considerable skill. It looked as if she hardly broke a sweat as she did so. Theo trudged laboriously, step after step up the incline. Considering the low gravity, he had assumed climbing uphill would be easier than it felt.

Rebecca made it to the top. She stood on the ridge and waved at him. "Looking good," she called.

He finally made it to the crest of the hill. He felt dizzy, but Rebecca noticed and caught hold of him. The ground fell away again, right at his feet.

"It's only eighty meters," she said soothingly.

"Eighty?" He could hardly believe it. Thanks to the unaccustomed exertion, Theo felt as if he had climbed a kilometer.

"Do you see that?" she said, pointing at the shadow.

His eyes followed Rebecca's arm. The southern crater wall threw a 150-meter-wide shadow into the crater, and this was at noon when the sun was at its highest. Fortunately it was fall, not high summer, but even in the summer the shadow had to be at least 100 meters wide, creating a perpetually dark area in which the temperatures presumably never rose much above minus 50.

"We need to take a closer look," Rebecca said as she started to descend the other side.

"Wait. We need the radar, but it's too heavy to carry."

"Maybe the ice is sitting right below the surface, and we'll be able to see it."

"But it might not be."

Theo pointed at the north wall of the crater. At that spot, the wall gradually sloped off until it met the surface. "We can drive the Rover in through there," he said.

"But that's so far out of our way."

"Forty kilometers. We can manage that."

"If I keep climbing, I'll be there in ten minutes," Rebecca assured Theo.

"No solo expeditions, Rule Number 1," he reminded her.

She nodded, then said, "I'm coming."

IT TOOK THEM TWENTY MINUTES TO REACH THE ROVER AND another two hours to get to the northern access point to the crater.

"If we end up building our settlement here, it would be easy to defend," Rebecca said.

"Against whom?"

"Who knows?"

"You've seen too many action films."

The Rover reached the shadow. It was now two-thirty, which meant the shadow must have lengthened some. They drove an additional hundred meters. Theo checked the thermometer on his suit.

"Minus 65," he said before bringing the Rover to a stop.

Rebecca climbed down from her seat and moved forward a few steps. It wasn't completely dark because the hazy sky was illuminating the landscape. She pulled out her flashlight anyway.

Has she found something? Theo wondered. Rebecca walked a little farther, knelt down, and moved her hands across the surface. *What is she doing?*

Theo watched her. The ground where he was felt harder than usual. His thoughts wandered to what it must have been like here when the crater was formed.

At some point, one of the countless asteroids must have entered Mars's gravitational field. The thin atmosphere had heated it, but not to the point of causing it to burn up. And then the chunk of stone had crashed into the surface at a sharp angle. The crater had a circumference of about ten kilometers, reflecting a relatively minor impact.

Rebecca was thinking too. *What happened to the water that would eventually have collected in the bottom of the crater? Either the heat evaporated it—or the meteorite had gouged away enough of the surface area so it could...* "Theo, come here! Quick!"

"What?" He began to run despite the fact his pain increased as he did.

Reaching Rebecca, he knelt beside her. She was rubbing her glove back and forth across the surface, which was covered by a thin layer of dust. Rebecca picked up some of the powder and illuminated the sample with her flashlight. "Look," she said.

Theo studied her palm. In the beam of light, little crystals glittered in between the small mineral grains.

"Are they ice crystals?" she asked.

"They do look like it, but they could also be just some other glittering material."

"Come on, let's test them."

Rebecca closed her fingers around the small pile of dust and led the way back. He could guess where she was going. The Rover's engine still had to be warm. Theo jogged behind her, panting. She waited for him somewhat impatiently. There was a small, level surface on the side of the Rover, a projection of the engine cover.

Somewhere along the way, although Theo could no longer recall which day, they had melted carbon-dioxide snow on it. They had found that sort of snow one morning in the shade by the side of their track. The snow had instantly sublimated into gas. Rebecca held her fist up over the same place and slowly opened it. Theo held the flashlight steady. The mixture of dust and crystals slowly drifted down. Theo had yet to get used to how long it took things to fall here. He wished he could hurry it along.

"Hold the light on it," Rebecca said.

He pushed the power button, and the beam lit up the engine surface. Before their eyes, the small crystals turned into tiny droplets.

"We found ice!" Theo shouted. He dropped the flashlight and hugged his companion.

Of course, a few ice crystals weren't proof of anything. They could have been created by the water vapor-saturated air, similar to the condensation of dew on Earth. If the water vapor settled on shaded ground that the sun never reached, it would remain as ice crystals. In the crater's shadow, the crystals would eventually form a thick layer of snow as the centuries passed. *Or not quite,* Theo thought. Since the wind would constantly blow the dust around, it would produce a dust-snow mixture. They wouldn't be able to adequately provision their settlement in the long term with just that.

"We need to check it with the GPR," Theo declared.

"Sure—this might be no more than a layer of dust-ice," Rebecca replied.

"Can you read minds?"

"No, but I can think."

Score one for her. He had to stop underestimating her just because she was the younger of them. Theo walked over to the center section of the Rover where the GPR unit was stored in a crate. It had its own four-wheeled base that was propelled by a battery-powered electric engine and operated by a separate handheld controller. This feature allowed them to take measurements without needing to put themselves at risk, an important consideration if they eventually ended up on the North Pole glaciers.

Theo liked to run the radar as he walked along. He had a remote control which enabled him to operate the detector like the remote-controlled car he'd had as a kid. In theory, they could send the device out on its own to search for water without accompanying it. The radar could cover about six kilometers on a full battery.

"Do you mind?" he asked, waving the remote that was already in his hand.

"I know how much you enjoy driving that thing, even if I don't really get why," Rebecca said. "I'll watch on the monitor."

The screen sat on a small console next to the transport crate, ready to display what the GPR transmitted.

Theo drove the small buggy he had dubbed 'Husky' to the area where Rebecca had discovered the crystals. "Can you start the readings?" he asked.

"Right away."

The box-shaped device sent radio waves into the ground that then bounced back to varying degrees when they encountered some kind of boundary, such as the transition between two unique substances whose distinctive characteristics had different influences on the radio waves. For example, this might be the spot where granite transitioned into basalt, a boundary between layers of varying depths, or a foreign element of some kind, or even a transition from ordinary Martian ground to a concealed layer of ice, a remnant from the time when giant oceans had covered Mars.

Theo had never waited so patiently. It took a while for the

receiver to pick up enough reflected waves. So much hinged on the results of this measurement. Would they finally be able to return to the base? Would this moment mark the starting point for the Mars for Everyone Initiative as originally planned?

"Do you see anything yet?" he asked. "Should I take Husky somewhere else?"

"Just wait. Don't rush me," Rebecca replied with a laugh.

Is that a good sign? The image would be building slowly in front of her. *She wouldn't laugh if there was nothing to see, right?* he thought.

"It looks alright," she finally said.

She sounded extremely cautious. *Why isn't she shouting for joy?* "What's wrong?" he asked.

"Nothing."

"Spit it out."

"Drive Husky fifty meters farther."

"I'll do that. But first, talk to me—why are you *torturing* me?"

"To be honest," Rebecca said, "the results are better than okay. They're almost too good to be true. I don't want us to celebrate winning the jackpot until we know for sure the lottery ticket is in our wallet."

"'The jackpot?' What do you mean?"

"The layer I see on the radar images is very, very thick. The radar isn't picking up its edges, even at the highest sensitivity setting. That means it's at least a hundred meters thick. If that's really ice, we're sitting on a 'gold mine.' We'd be able to provide water for our children's children."

A shiver ran down his spine. Could they really be that lucky? But wasn't it about time for the tide to turn after the loss of their five crewmates and practically all their equipment, as well as Andy's accident?

"It's good to be careful," he said. "Let's check out the entire area before we draw any conclusions."

"I would prefer to take a look myself. That's the only way we can make sure the radar isn't malfunctioning."

"Good idea. How deep do we need to dig?"

"The upper edge of the ice layer should be a meter below the surface," Rebecca said assuredly.

IT TOOK THEM AN HOUR TO FINISH MAPPING THE AREA UNDER the surface. In the permanent-shade area, the ice layer started a meter below the surface. In those places touched by the warming sunbeams, the ice appeared to be at a greater depth. Perhaps the models by Mars researchers were incorrect. However, the ice layer appeared to resume a short distance from there, underneath the crater's edge. If they could access the directly reachable deposits, they could extract even more water through mining.

If it was actually water that was down there. Everything seemed to indicate this, but only direct evidence would dispel the last doubts.

Theo packed the GPR back into its crate while Rebecca busied herself with the drill. It had a 150x15-centimeter drill rod, the function of which wasn't immediately obvious.

Rebecca set it down on a randomly selected spot close to the place where she had found the crystals. "Start the drill," she said.

The term 'drill' had taken root among the crew, although technically speaking it wasn't a drill, but rather a kind of hammer. The chisel-shaped head didn't bore into the substrate with a circular motion, it was instead repeatedly rammed into the surface by force, similar to a jackhammer. Theo could feel the vibrations of the rapid hammering under his feet.

Rebecca did not need to hold onto the rod once it had reached a depth of 30 centimeters. It took 20 minutes for the drill rod to achieve the desired depth. Now only a small piece of the rod was visible. At that point, the drill head was given a little rest to let it cool down. Then tiny, electric-powered shavers began to gather material from the area immediately around the head. This process lasted an additional ten minutes.

"We have a sample," Rebecca said.

"Let's pull it out."

"As you wish, sir."

Rebecca pulled the bar out of the substrate. She unscrewed the sample container, which was sealed and airtight, before carrying the rod and sample to the Rover. Hopefully, the mobile lab would provide them with the desired answer. Rebecca screwed the sample container into the lab's filler neck until the material fell into the analysis chamber.

If only the lab could know how vital its actions are, Theo thought. He balled his hands into fists. Four eyes stared at the weakly-glowing line that still bore only the word 'PROCESSING.'

But then the display changed. The first information the machine provided was the fact that it had not found any sign of life. This was because the device had been primarily developed to help search for life forms. It then supplied the percentage of organic and inorganic combinations, classified by physical states and pH values.

Only at the end did the machine produce a complete list of all discovered chemical combinations. It reported '97.2 percent H_2O.'

Rebecca processed the information faster than Theo did. She was already wrapping her arms around his neck while he was still registering what this meant. "Water!" Rebecca cried. "We've found water!"

It was a strange feeling. Theo had forgotten what such pure, unadulterated joy felt like. They had found water. Hurrah! He murmured incoherent sounds and danced with Rebecca across the crater that would soon become their new home.

Sol 24, MfE base

It was unbelievable. Theo and Rebecca had finally succeeded. The entire crew was ecstatic. They had all needed this good news. The expectations were obviously high now.

Ewa rubbed her temples. She had to present the crew with their relocation plans, which had to remain realistic while also bringing the establishment of their settlement within arm's reach. Without the NASA building robot, for example, those plans wouldn't come to anything, so for the time being they would need to wait until the NASA people were done with it. Then they would have to transport their equipment about 2,000 kilometers to the north. How would that function when the enclosed Rover could only drive a distance of 500 kilometers at a time?

Ewa wished that Theo was already back. He would have had a suggestion ready to go. Ellen helped Ewa with the day-to-day details, but she seemed to lack the talent to think outside the box. Unconventionality was the only way for them to make any headway in this tricky situation.

Could the Rover's range somehow be increased? If they carried along additional methanol, the available load quantity would be the limiting factor. Unlike the distance to the landing module, which they had needed to cover twice, they would have to travel back and forth across those 2,000 kilometers at least five times. If they could reach 25 kilometers per hour... no, that was utterly unrealistic.

What would Theo suggest? Ewa wondered. He would be spending at least ten more days in the open Rover, so he wasn't available as a discussion partner. *But wait a moment.* The open Rover had already driven the distance to the crater once. Although the vehicle had the necessary range, it wasn't suitable for transporting fragile cargo, among which Ewa included the still-unconscious Andy. Or should they leave him here? Couldn't the NASA crew take care of him? It would be a practical solution since, objectively speaking, he would be a hindrance when it came to building the settlement. However, the MfE crew would probably see it differently.

Maybe they could use both the open and the closed Rovers! The open one could simply tow the closed one behind it, conserving most of the fuel that would have been consumed by operating the closed one independently. Their speed would presumably be reduced, but this solution would make the move realistic, though tedious. If only they could snap their fingers and transport everything straight to the crater, Star Trek-style!

They must be jinxed. Ewa tried to sort out her thoughts. Then it occurred to her. They really could snap their fingers —so to speak—and the *Endeavour*, their current abode, would rise into the air. They wouldn't have to reach orbit. A suborbital route to the crater wouldn't consume much fuel. The entire move could be accomplished within a day! The perfect solution... except for one small glitch. The *Endeavour* didn't belong to them, and it was doubtful that the NASA crew would give them permission for this. *Ewa, Ewa,* she thought. *Your creative solutions are going to land us in a huge mess—or else enable us to cover the 2,000 kilometers to the distant crater with its giant ice deposits in the matter of a few minutes.*

Sol 45, NASA base

"ENJOY!" SARAH CROWED AS SHE GAZED PROUDLY AROUND THE group.

Lance carefully trickled two drops of dressing onto his lettuce leaf. He then picked it up by its firm, bright green stem and slowly pushed it into his mouth. He closed his eyes, then his mouth, until he could hear the crisp, fresh snap. He hesitated. The dressing spread across his tongue, the light acidity here, the smooth fat of the oil there, and a hint of sweetness at the tip. He began to chew. A lettuce leaf consists primarily of water and cellulose, its nutritional value hardly much more significant than a piece of paper. However, it felt marvelous in his mouth, especially since for months all he'd had to eat was prepackaged foods.

He swallowed, opened his eyes, and picked up a radish. It was smaller than he had expected. "What are these called again?" he asked.

"Rambo radishes," Sarah replied.

Lance chuckled and took a bite. His teeth cut through the tender skin. He stuck the entire bulb in his mouth and crunched down on it. He could feel the sharpness of the radish all the way up into his nose. "Rambos have a kick to them!" he observed.

"That was my hope," Sarah declared.

Neither Sharon nor Mike said anything. They seemed to be lost in the pleasure of this first fresh meal.

Lance thought about what all they could cultivate once they had enough space and energy. Nobody had expected for Earth to fall silent, which was why they had only been given a few seeds. Once they ran out of oil and vinegar there wouldn't be any more. They would need to talk with the MfE crowd. They might have brought along a greater variety of plants. He thought there might be good chances of growing rapeseed to make canola oil, but it would be harder to produce vinegar.

"Sharon, once we've used up the vinegar, could we possibly produce a chemical replica of it? In principle, it's just citric acid, right?" Lance asked.

"It's mainly acetic acid, which should be easier to synthesize, in theory. But I'm afraid I don't know the process. On Earth, it's produced from natural materials. This problem shouldn't be hard to solve, though."

"We absolutely need to expand our cultivated area," Lance declared. "If we're going to spend the rest of our days here, we need at least one highlight a day."

"We will," Mike replied. "But the MfE folks get the robotic drill first. We promised them that."

"I was thinking about that, and won't argue against it. They really haven't had it easy," Lance said.

"In the meantime, we could expand our electrical production."

"I'm already on it, Mike, or do you have a new idea about that?"

"Solar cells."

"But, we lack the resources to produce those ourselves."

"We wouldn't have to. Think about all the abandoned Rovers sitting around here on Mars," Mike said with a raise of his eyebrows.

Lance put down his fork. How many automated exploratory Rovers had landed here over the past 40 years? There had to be 20 or more of them, just sitting around and waiting for someone to repurpose them. "That's a splendid idea," he said. "We just need to gather them up. Most of them belong to NASA anyway."

"We should harvest all the equipment from them. For spare parts," Sharon suggested.

"Could we please discuss this later? I would like to concentrate on this simply amazing meal for now," Sarah implored.

"Of course. Sorry for the disruption," Lance said. "We'll talk about it later." He shut his eyes again and shoved the next lettuce leaf into his mouth.

"WAS THERE ANY DATA KEPT, BACK THEN, ABOUT WHEN AND where the probes landed?" Mike asked.

They were all rubbing their full stomachs.

What I'd give for a postprandial brandy, Lance thought. If they could produce methanol, why not ethanol? He and Sharon, the chemist, should take a look at the system together. Ethanol also worked great as a fuel source. "Unfortunately, we don't have any. On Earth..." Lance said, then stopped in thought.

Nobody said anything. Again. As soon as a conversation touched on the silent Earth, moods instantly darkened. Would that get better as the years passed? The problem was that they hadn't been able to say goodbye properly. Lance's thoughts turned to his girlfriend, who was waiting for him. No, who had been waiting for him. *She's dead, Lance*, he told himself. On the other hand, Sarah was still alive. He needed to cut himself more slack.

"We could just set off and look for them," Sharon suggested eventually. "It is always better than just sitting around here."

"The surface of Mars is larger than the entire land surface of Earth," Mike said. "We won't just happen across the Rovers."

"There are some high-resolution photos of Mars that the probes took while in orbit," Sarah replied. "They are so sharp that the old Rovers are recognizable on them. At the same time, it might take us a really long time to locate them on the images."

"I could try to write an algorithm that could search the photos for traces of the landed probes," Mike said.

"Then let's get started! How long do you think this will take?" Lance asked.

"Just give me two Sols."

Sol 46, MfE base

LANCE MANEUVERED THE ROBOTIC DRILL INTO POSITION RIGHT outside the entrance to the *Endeavour*. Enclosed in his spacesuit, he was sitting in the open Rover and steering the robot by remote control. Someone climbed out of the spaceship's airlock. He recognized the ancient suit model being used by the MfE people. It was probably Ewa. The height was about right. At the same time, the suit was so bulky that the figure of the wearer was concealed.

"Ewa, is that you?" he asked over the frequency used by the MfE people.

"Yep," she replied. "I wanted to thank you in person."

"That wasn't necessary," Lance said. "We promised you could use it."

"Still..." Ewa raised an arm, and he could see that she was holding a small box. She walked over to the Rover. "As a small token of our gratitude, we wanted to give you this." Ewa held out the box to him

Lance took the surprisingly lightweight box.

"No worries," she said. "The family jewels aren't packed inside."

"So what is it?"

"Something much better. Seeds."

"Oh," Lance said. "That's really a wonderful gift. What kinds?"

"Have fun checking them out. The sacks are all labeled."

"Thank you, Ewa, that really is very kind of you. Our own seeds are in pretty short supply. We had never planned to be here for very long."

"We *had* planned on that, but our plans didn't work out all that well in the end."

"Maybe we'll still find a happy ending somehow."

"I have my doubts about that," Ewa admitted, "but it's nice that you can stay optimistic about it. Here's hoping you won't be too disappointed."

"Thanks. How long will your drive take?"

"It's only about five hundred kilometers. We'll manage that in about three days."

"Then we'll see you again soon. We're already making plans to expand our base. We'll be able to plant your seeds after that."

"I wish you the best of luck."

Lance thought he saw something flash in Ewa's eyes, but the woman spun around quickly and hurried back to the *Endeavour.*

THE NASA CREW UNWRAPPED THE BOX FROM THE MFE people after supper. Around twenty small bags were sitting inside of it, each of them inscribed in blue ink.

"Pansies," Lance read aloud.

"We can't eat them," Mike said. "We can put those seeds away for later."

"Oh, flowers!" Sarah exclaimed. "And, Mike, pansies are edible. And they taste pretty good."

"Barley."

"Woohoo! We can make beer!" Mike cried.

"We shouldn't celebrate until we find the hops seeds," Lance countered.

'Hops' was written on the next packet.

"See!" Mike chortled as Lance grinned.

"Carrots."

"We have those already," Sarah said.

"Tomatoes."

"Perfect," Mike replied. "I can make us a pizza that will make you lick your fingers clean."

"What about yeast?" Lance asked.

"It won't be hard to make that from dried fruit," Mike said.

"Caraway... mugwort... wild garlic..."

"It's just getting better and better," Sarah said. "We'll soon be able to plant an entire botanical garden."

"...cannabis."

"That's just like the MfE folks," Sharon said.

"Us, too. At some point, our painkillers will run out, and then we'll be glad to have something to smoke," Sarah said.

Sol 47, NASA base

Mike was pointing at a blurry spot against a reddish-brown background. "What does that remind you of?"

"Is this a Rorschach test?" Lance asked.

"I'm being serious."

"A three-leaf clover missing its third leaf?" Sharon suggested.

"'Clover' on Mars? Not even close."

"A fly someone squashed with a fly swatter?" Lance said.

"Haha!" Mike laughed. "Guess for real."

"Well," Sharon said, "I'd say you've tracked down the *Phoenix* probe. It must've been sitting there for more than 30 years by now."

"Not quite the answer, but close."

"Then it's the *Insight*, which was based on the same design as the *Phoenix*. When was that? 2018?"

"No idea. I was still a baby," Mike said.

"So how did you recognize the *Insight*?"

"From the photos of the probe. I found a book in our electronic library that describes the most important Mars probes up to 2030. The *Phoenix* looked very similar, but the *Insight* was the only one that landed so close to the equator, so it has to be that one."

"How far is it to that location?"

"About 2,400 kilometers."

"Just a stone's throw from here," Lance quipped. "When do we leave?"

"You'll have to cross through a fairly major trench system to get there," Mike warned.

"A few ditches aren't going to stop us."

"I'm talking about something many times larger than the Grand Canyon, Lance."

"Then we need to be adequately prepared. Can't you write an algorithm that will take us along the least treacherous route?" Lance asked.

"Can do."

"And there's nothing closer than that?"

"No, Sarah. This is the best I can do for now."

Sol 48, MfE

Theo had waited a long time to catch Ewa out of earshot of the other crew members. "Why weren't you honest with the NASA people about the location of our settlement two days ago?"

"What do you mean?"

"When you met Lance to get the drill, you told him it was only five hundred kilometers away. Right?"

"Oh that. I don't know. At the moment, it seemed like the right thing to do. I didn't want them to have second thoughts about their agreement. They won't be getting their enclosed Rover and robotic drill back for at least three months."

"I don't think that was a good idea. They'll start to wonder when we keep them longer than they're expecting."

"We'll be long gone by then."

Ewa's words sounded cold. He hadn't known her to be so calculating. He knew that she would fight like a lioness for the MfE project, but was she capable of going too far?

"Nonetheless, this won't enhance their trust in us," he said.

"Theo, in case you haven't noticed, trust isn't exactly our most urgent problem. Right now, our main priority is survival. The NASA base is excellently equipped. We don't need to worry about them."

Thirty minutes later, Ewa called the entire crew to the command center. It was very tight. For the very first time, Theo missed the weightlessness that had enabled him to just float above the others. What was Ewa up to, and why hadn't she told him about this beforehand when they'd been chatting? He had always thought she trusted him. Was this because he hadn't given his blessing to her deception of the NASA people?

"I won't keep you long, I promise," Ewa began, "but I need your input on an idea. You all know how far away the crater is that Theo and Rebecca so amazingly found for us. Applause for the two of them, please!"

Everyone clapped.

"If we travel there by land, the trip will take us an eternity, and once we get there, we—fifteen people and more than a few animals—will have to live inside the cabin of the enclosed Rover until our first accommodations are ready. I think that's inhumane."

Theo suspected he knew what Ewa was about to suggest. He couldn't help hoping though that she had a completely different idea up her sleeve.

"It is particularly inhumane because there is one possible alternative. We could launch the *Endeavour*, and in a few hours we could land at the site of our future settlement. We would have instantaneously functional lodging, and perhaps within four weeks or so, we could even return the spaceship if we wanted to."

Theo cut in loudly. "You want to steal the *Endeavour*?"

"I want to *borrow* it for a period of time. The NASA people don't need it either way."

"Then why don't we just ask them?"

"Because they might say no and prevent us from being able to implement this plan."

He couldn't think of a counterargument to this logic, except for the moral one. "Those people saved us! Without them, we'd be stranded up there in space and presumably long dead. They've lent us two Rovers and their robotic drill. And you want to repay that by stealing their ship?"

"This has nothing to do with gratitude or ingratitude. Our lives are at stake here. The NASA base is excellently provisioned. In the short term, they will be able to do without what they're letting us borrow, including the *Endeavour*. It won't hurt them, but it will help us enormously. What's the harm in that?"

"I'm sorry, but this is just too underhanded for me." Theo realized he no longer understood Ewa. How could someone argue so cold-bloodedly for betrayal? This wasn't the Ewa he knew.

"That's your prerogative," Ewa shot back. "This was why I didn't make this decision on my own. I would like to put this to a vote. There are 14 of us, 14 votes. If the majority vote for my plan, we'll carry that out. If there's a tie, I'll abstain."

Ewa really was clever. She was giving the no votes a tiny advantage. In reality, a tie wasn't a 'yes' for her, but she had painted the situation as if she would graciously sacrifice her right to vote.

"Does anyone here want a secret ballot?" she asked.

No one spoke up.

"I would like to suggest that you call off this insane plan without putting it up to vote," Theo declared. "It is deeply immoral, as well as incompatible with the goals of our initiative. We want to establish a settlement in which we don't repeat the mistakes of the old world. Theft isn't the right way to begin everything. Where will it land us?"

"If we don't do this," Ewa replied, "there might not be anyone left to build the settlement you've been dreaming of. We can't just think about the future. The future will take root in our brave decisions today. Let's vote now."

Theo shook his head. They were about to make a huge mistake, but the others seemed to agree with the vote.

"How do things stand? Who is for my plan?" Ewa asked, lifting her own arm.

Theo looked around the group. Two, then three arms raised. Gabriella, the doctor, also voted yes. He hadn't seen that coming.

Soon there were ten yes votes. Ewa had won. She asked for the no vote anyway. Theo raised his hand, as did Rebecca. He was glad for that. Iris and Ellen hesitated, but they then added their hands to his side. He gazed at them gratefully, even though the result was clear.

Maybe he was naive. He had always assumed they shared a mutual vision of how to shape a better world that was no longer possible to achieve on Earth, but was attainable on Mars. This dream had just shattered in front of him. Rebecca placed her arm around his shoulders.

Sol 48, NASA base

"That's our goal," Mike said, pointing at a small, black 'x' on the blue background.

"As you can see from the color, that spot is on a similar elevation to our base, located in an elongated valley. But unfortunately...," he gestured at a crosshatched, yellow-and-red area, "between here and there, there's a small obstacle—a spur of the Valles Marineris, a huge trench system."

"A spur?" Lance asked.

"The area is called Hebes Chasma. It isn't connected to the Valles, which are located south of it, so it isn't a spur in a real sense. It's also only six to eight kilometers deep."

"Only six kilometers? Child's play!"

"The Valles are up to nine kilometers deep, Lance."

"And there's no way around them?"

"I have mapped it all carefully. Of course, you can get around any obstacle, but in this case, this would significantly prolong your travel time. If you cover two hundred kilometers a day, including the detour, it would take you about a month to get there and back."

"So what? We've got the time. There's nothing to do right now as it is," Lance replied.

"That's true," Sarah agreed. "We should find a way to

productively use the time we're waiting until we can get the drill back."

"Sounds like an offer," Mike declared. "Do the two of you want to make the trip?"

"If you'll take care of the garden while I'm gone," Sarah said.

She glanced at Lance, and he nodded. This would make a nice change from the base's daily routine.

"Since the enclosed Rover's on loan to MfE, you'll have to take the open one," Mike warned. "You won't be able to get out of your suits until nighttime."

"That's fine. The open Rover is easier to maneuver, and it has an almost unlimited range," Sarah said.

"And we'll see something of the landscape," Lance added.

"I just wanted to mention that so you knew what you were getting into," Mike explained. "The route I've calculated should be relatively safe. The only place you'll encounter significant changes in elevation is in Hebes Chasma. The erosion should be advanced enough that you should be able to get up and down the hillsides just fine."

"That makes me feel a lot better," Lance said. "When do we start?" He would have preferred to set off right away. He held nothing against the other crew members, but the thought of crossing through the solitude of Mars electrified him. This would probably change to irritation once a few days in his suit had rubbed his backside raw, but at the moment this seemed like a splendid idea.

"If we all get to work, the Rover should be ready to go by tomorrow," Mike said.

Sol 50, MfE base

"We have a problem, Ewa," Theo said.

"Just spit it out," she snapped back, her eyes closed.

Ewa's nerves seemed frayed today. Was she perhaps trying to squelch her guilty conscience? That was just wishful thinking. This unscrupulous woman who was willing to steal a spaceship didn't coincide with his prior image of her.

"The two Rovers won't fit onto the ship," he said.

"Not even if we take them apart?"

"Not a chance."

"Hmm. We definitely need the enclosed Rover. Otherwise we can't move the animals over to our new base."

"So we'll leave the open one here?" Theo suggested.

"It's perfect for the exploration we need to do. It would be a real loss."

"But we still have the ship. Let's at least leave the NASA crew the second Rover."

"Ah, so that's where this is coming from. We already discussed that in the group. What we're doing is in the interest of our mission. The NASA base will be just fine."

"You know my feelings on this, Ewa."

"Yeah. But on a different topic, Ellen had an idea. An old NASA probe is sitting west of us, and it contains solar panels and other materials. I was thinking we could salvage it from the new base, but the distance would be shorter from here. If we can't take the Rover anyway, we should go ahead and start on the salvage operation."

"I hope you're not counting on me, Ewa. I'm still recovering from those thousands of kilometers I just spent in the Rover."

Ewa gazed at him in evident astonishment. No, he wouldn't be volunteering for this mission despite how good the trip with Rebecca had been.

"Fine. Shashwat and Guillermo will do the run. Shashwat's a good mechanic. He'll be able to take the probe apart in no time flat. It would be best if they set off today."

"I'm sure they'll be thrilled." Theo couldn't keep the sarcastic edge out of his voice. "You'll do the briefing, right? I need to take care of getting the enclosed Rover on board."

"ALL SET?" EWA ASKED.

Ellen had taken over the job of pilot. Her talents really were multifaceted. Ewa had first asked Theo if he wanted to pilot the *Endeavour*, but he had declined. As it turned out, back on Earth, Ellen had gone through simulator training on a capsule similar to the *Endeavour*. That would have to suffice, Ewa decided.

"Looks good," Ellen said. "Prop, LG, FC, everything at one hundred percent."

Deep furrows ran across the young woman's forehead. Theo was glad he wasn't in her shoes, because this wasn't a standard launch but a suborbital flight. This meant that the spaceship wouldn't reach orbit around Mars. Shortly after they took off, Ellen would have to hit the brakes.

An automated voice came out of the console and started to slowly count to zero. Theo tightened his fingers around his armrests. He inhaled and exhaled deeply. This was his first launch without a trained pilot at the controls. He wouldn't have been so scared if Chuck was still here. Chuck wouldn't have permitted such insanity to take place. After they landed, he needed to warn Ellen about Ewa. Was she being hounded by ambition or by fear of death?

A deep vibration reverberated through the ship. The ship's steel panels groaned as the engines strained against Mars's gravitational pull. Theo watched Ellen as she focused intently on what she was doing. Her face was completely emotionless. The trajectory was pre-programmed, but she had to be ready to intervene at any moment if any deviations from the plan arose. The programming was based on conjectures drawn from the literature—they had been forced to prep for their launch without asking the NASA crew for the latest data or instructions.

Theo was pressed back into his seat by his own inertia. He now folded his hands over his stomach. With each passing second he felt more and more nervous. Very soon, it would be time for the trick for which the *Endeavour* had never actually been designed. The primary engine would be turned off. He started to mentally count down the seconds.

This was it. The pressure on his back vanished. They were weightless. Ellen was leaning far over the control screen. She steadied herself with one hand as she activated the vernier thrusters. The *Endeavour* had to pivot 180 degrees until the primary engine was pointing along their trajectory. An empty sack floated through Theo's field of vision, slowly drifting up to the ceiling. That had to be the effect of deceleration in the thin atmosphere.

"The engine will be reactivated in ten nine eight...," Ellen said into the microphone.

Restarting an engine within such a short time wasn't all that easy. It typically would need a more extended rest period, but they couldn't give it that if they didn't want to overshoot their destination.

"...three two one ignition."

At that very second the vibration returned, and the inertia of his own mass once again pushed him back into his seat cushions. Somebody behind him applauded, although it was still too early for that. The *Endeavour* had performed an impressive solo, but the concert—the flight—was far from over.

"Congratulations! We're right on course," Ewa said.

Did she really have to say that? Theo wasn't the superstitious sort, but such predictions could only bring bad luck. He pulled up the flight data on his seat monitor. Within thirty minutes, they would land at the spot where it would have taken them many days to travel to on the surface. If they had enough fuel, they could comfortably travel from start to destination. But after they landed, the *Endeavour* would have to wait for a long time to be refueled.

The first priority would be to construct the base.

The NASA people would be furious, and he could hardly blame them.

THEO WAS RELIEVED. ELLEN HAD BROUGHT THEM BACK DOWN cleanly. They were now at the place that would be their new home. He brought up the images from the external cameras on his screen. There was still a lot of dust in the air, but he instantly recognized the crater he and Rebecca had visited three weeks ago. The great treasure—water in the form of ancient ice—was sitting there in the black shadow. It might have come from a sea that had frozen more than three billion years ago. Considering the environment, it was more likely that the deposit had formed at a later point, whenever the comet fragment had struck and formed this crater. They were lucky that, first, the permanent shadow and, second, the layer of protective sand had spread over it. Otherwise none of the ice would be left today.

Ellen stood up and walked past him to Ewa, pride in her accomplishment written large across her face. She hugged the older woman. Ewa smiled as if she wouldn't harm even a fly. The only thing that stood out was her nose, which looked as if it had been broken multiple times.

He heard loud laughter behind him. A woman started to sing a song he didn't recognize. Ewa's smile remained strangely stiff. It looked frozen, unresponsive to the jubilation around her.

It was at that moment that Theo realized with certainty that Ewa had a secret, a dark one at that.

Sol 49, NASA expedition

AMAZING, LANCE THOUGHT. THEY HAD MADE THE DECISION yesterday, and by today, they were ready to leave. That was the advantage of being on a small team. Every other hour or so, Sarah and he would swap out as drivers. Sarah was going to drive the Rover for the first forty kilometers. Their vehicle consisted of three segments with a total of four axles. They were sitting up front, while the provisions and fuel were stored in the middle section, and the tent was strapped to the last one. There was also room at the back for whatever they could salvage from the old probe.

Sarah hit the gas hard. You could tell that she was enjoying this unaccustomed pleasure.

Lance tightened his fingers around the armrest between them. This grew uncomfortable after the first half-hour. "May I?" he asked without further explanation.

Sarah seemed to know exactly what he meant. "Sure," she replied.

Lance leaned forward against her back and locked his hands around Sarah's waist. It had been a long time since he had ridden a motorcycle, but he could still recall the feeling clearly. It was surprisingly similar. Instead of feeling Sarah's body through motorcycle gear, he could feel her through the flexible NASA suits. They weren't wearing safety helmets, but rather breathing helmets. However, the most significant difference was in the driving experience itself. Instead of an asphalt strip, a track of loose dust and stone stretched out before them, jostling and rattling every part of them.

They took a short break after three hours. Lance had dozed against Sarah's back for almost an hour. His mouth was dry, his voice raspy. They hadn't spoken a word since leaving the base, but he felt neither awkward nor weird.

Lance looked around. The landscape had already changed. It was now fairly hilly. He could make out several oddly shaped boulders on the horizon. "Do you see them?" he asked.

"It looks like a giant tossed his dice on the ground," Sarah said.

"They must be as large as an apartment complex," Lance added. He sat down on a smaller stone, but stood right back up again. He would be sitting soon enough as it was. "Where do we go from here?" he asked.

"Straight ahead for the next while. We won't reach the Chasma for another five days," Sarah replied.

Lance stared up into the sky and discovered a bright dot. "Is that Venus?" he asked, pointing at it.

"That would be very romantic, but I don't think we can see it during the day. That must be Deimos."

"Mars's moon? It's that tiny?"

"Yeah, even in its lower orbit. It's supposed to look about three hundred times as bright as Venus does from Earth."

"And here I thought you were a doctor and biologist."

Sarah chuckled. "Didn't you do the survival training course in Death Valley? They told us something about that there."

"All I remember is the roasted snake they served us."

"Ready to keep going, Lance?"

"Yeah, let's go."

This time Sarah rested against his back. It was a pleasant feeling, pleasant and familiar. About 20 kilometers later, the radio beeped. The call was coming from the base. Lance put the Rover in park. Neither Mike nor Sharon would contact them without good cause. Sarah climbed down and stood next to the steering rod, while Lance remained seated.

"Something terrible has happened!" Sharon shouted. "Mike is as mad as hell, and I had to send him outside to calm down. Otherwise he would've taken the base apart into little pieces."

"What happened? Did the *Spaceliner I* guy call back in and make more arrogant demands?" Lance asked.

"Worse. The MfE criminals stole the *Endeavour*, and all we could do was watch."

"Whaaat? That's... but they all made such a decent impression."

"And we rescued them," Sharon said. "That's what upsets Mike the most. We put our lives at risk, and they turn around and steal our ship. He wants to drive out and take it back by force."

"That might be a little challenging. There are fifteen of them and only four of us," Lance said.

Sarah turned around and strode a few meters away from the Rover, her shoulders hunched.

"What's wrong, Sarah? Do you need help?"

"It's just... the shock. I suddenly feel nauseous. I have to make sure I don't throw up inside my helmet."

Lance felt himself growing angry. It didn't bother him so much that the ship was gone, but those bastards were responsible for making Sarah feel sick. His hands clenched involuntarily into fists. He was probably wrong to think of them all as bastards. The only one who would have dared to do this was Ewa. But no, he wouldn't have expected such unequaled treachery from her, either. That's not how you repaid someone who saved your life! This was unbelievable.

"Now what? Can you keep Mike there, Sharon?"

"We're lucky you're out with the Rover. We don't have any others here. Mike also isn't crazy enough to actually chase after them. But it's possible that he will contact you soon and ask you to break off your trip. Please tell him 'no,' or he'll just put himself in harm's way."

"Should we just leave everything as it is, then?" Lance asked.

"What would you want to do? We're at a disadvantage. We could ask them to return the *Endeavour*, but even if they agreed, they wouldn't have enough fuel for the return flight."

"You're right, Sharon. But when I think about this deception, it makes me want to break something."

"Be careful out there. Don't break anything you might still need. Without the *Endeavour*, we'll have to be even more careful with our resources."

"Understood."

"And whenever Mike calls in, you'll know the reason why."

"Sure, we'll know," Lance said.

THE ROVER COVERED THE NEXT FIFTY KILOMETERS IN HALF the time. Lance drove as fast as the motor would let him. This way he didn't have time to stay upset about the theft. The route was challenging, and the vehicle bounced up and down like crazy on its solid rubber tires. If the Rover had resembled a plump caterpillar before, creeping comfortably toward its destination, the vehicle now reminded him of an eight-legged lesser Egyptian jerboa out hunting.

Sarah spent the whole time holding on to Lance for dear life. He wasn't sure if it was her arms or the fact he had to concentrate so hard on their wild ride, but either way he gradually felt calmer. They would be able to get over the material loss. There wasn't a destination they could have used the *Endeavour* to reach anyway. The enclosed Rover was more comfortable for its crew, since during the drive you could take off your spacesuit, but it was considerably slower and less maneuverable, and its range was more limited.

The main problem was that he would have to adjust to a new future again. Only a few weeks ago, he had seen himself as a future father and husband. And then suddenly the human race had shrunk down to a mere 20 people. He could have imagined working cooperatively to build a new life with the MfE crew, but now they were on their own... their number was down to four. After this breach of trust, any potential collaboration with Mars for Everyone was an impossibility. He would spend the next 40 or 50 years living with Sharon and Mike, and with Sarah. One of them would eventually bury all the others and would face death alone. Lance hoped he wasn't that person.

Mike didn't call in as Sharon had expected him to do. She must have managed to convince him to give up his plan for revenge. After they set up their tent and had removed their suits, Sarah and Lance made love for the first time. It felt right and almost effortless.

Sol 55, MfE base

Ewa was standing beside a rectangular ditch that the robotic drill had dug into the Mars surface. It was twelve by eight by five meters deep. A big pile of sand and gravel was sitting only a few meters away. "May I introduce you to our new base?" she said.

"It's not very beautiful," Rebecca remarked, pointing at the pile.

"Most of that will be used to cover our base. It's the perfect shield against cosmic radiation," Ellen explained. She was standing right beside Ewa.

Theo had already noticed that the two of them were spending a lot of time together. Ellen was an extraordinary planner, and Ewa persuaded the crew to accept their mutually conceived plans. The construction of the base was proceeding more quickly than they had thought it would. They had already started to mine the ice as well. Since their *Endeavour* landing, something inside their community had changed. Theo wasn't sure exactly what it was. You could perhaps describe it as a fissure, although there hadn't been any arguments or discussions. However, groups were forming that spent more time with one another than with the people in the other groups.

Was this perhaps the evolution that always occurred when an extreme situation slowly transformed into a new normalcy? thought Theo. He and Rebecca spent so much time together that the others probably assumed they were a couple, though they really weren't. Why not, though? Theo didn't know why, but he also didn't feel any urgent need to alter the situation. Could a true, unromantic friendship exist between a man and a woman?

Ellen walked around the trench, studying the edges as if she needed to check on something.

"When can we move in?" Rebecca asked.

"In seven sols, at the latest," Ellen replied. "I suspect we might be able to speed that up by a day, but I have to discuss that with Ewa first."

The blonde commander joined Ellen. The two of them stood close together, and Theo could see their lips moving. That meant they must have switched over to a private radio channel.

THEO TURNED TOWARD THE *ENDEAVOUR*, WHICH STOOD glittering in the sun about 500 meters away. Today was an especially low-dust day. He waved at Rebecca and walked over to the enclosed Rover that was parked beside the ship. He couldn't climb into it from the outside, but had to first re-enter the ship and then access the Rover through the pressurized tube.

The cabin was their medical station. If you ever needed to find Gabriella, she was almost always in there. She had set up her bed beside her most critical patient, Andy, who was still unconscious. Gabriella was tending to him with great devotion. She was a good doctor.

"How's Andy doing today?" Theo asked.

"Speak to him yourself, please. It's important that I'm not the only one he has to listen to," Gabriella urged.

"Do you think it helps?"

"I can't prove it, but imagine being trapped inside yourself. You can perceive everything, but don't have the power to actually react. You would be happy if someone talked to you."

"That's what it's like for him?"

"Oh, Theo, I don't know for sure. He might never regain consciousness, but I'll take care of him as long as I can."

"And how are things for you?"

"Is that really important? I'm a doctor, so it's my profession. And it's nice to do more than just distribute bandages and headache medicine. But I appreciate your question. Now talk to him."

"I'll do that."

THEO LOOKED OVER AT THE ENTRANCE TO THE ROVER'S cabin. It would be nice if Rebecca would materialize there. Conversations like this were more comfortable for her, but she didn't appear on mental command. He walked over to the head of the cot, pulled a stool over, and sat down.

"Hi, Andy. It's me, Theo."

Of course, Andy didn't answer. Theo watched his face, but nothing moved. He might as well be talking to a wall.

"I don't know if anyone told you yet, but we've just arrived at the site of our new settlement. You'd like the crater."

Theo decided to include the less savory bits of news as well.

"To speed things along, Ewa arranged for us to hijack the NASA spaceship. Steal it, to be more precise. I didn't agree with that, but the majority voted for it. What would you have said to that?"

Andy didn't respond.

"Yes, it's a difficult question, I admit. But we always wanted to establish a new, free society based on morality and justice. And now our settlement has a birth defect. It wasn't right for us to steal the ship from our rescuers, even if they didn't necessarily need it right then."

He brushed a strand of hair from Andy's face and then caught sight of a damp rag in a shallow bowl. Theo dabbed the patient's dry lips with it.

"I'm sorry you have to listen to my whining, but I really am worried about the evolution of our crew."

On which side would Andy have stood? They were two very different people. Andy's behavior had always been cool, logical, and cautious. Theo, who saw himself as a survival artist, didn't always give a lot of thought to his actions, but he was bold. Nonetheless, he felt like he and Andy shared one particular characteristic, that they were both obstinate and preferred to not have other people's opinions foisted upon them.

Andy presumably would have voted against the theft. But that might be nothing but wishful thinking on his part. It was impossible to know.

"What I would really like to hear is who did this to you," Theo said.

This was the one thought he kept trying to suppress. The surface of Mars was a lethal place, that was a given. In that light, you could say that Andy had been very fortunate. However, the presumed way in which the accident had occurred seemed more and more unlikely the longer he thought about it.

"Man, Andy, did you really go outside without checking your oxygen supply? You're always so careful about everything. Solo excursions outdoors aren't even permitted. You really ignored all the rules about that?"

And yet, that had to be what happened. The facts seemed incontrovertible. If that wasn't true, then they must have missed something. Theo propped his arms on his knees. Andy was breathing very evenly, as if he were just sleeping. If Theo pinched his arm he would wake up, and the nightmare would be over, right? They wouldn't have stolen the *Endeavour*. They could begin their new lives without any stain.

What if he assumed that Andy's condition wasn't due to dumb coincidence? Theo tried to stay on this line of thought. In that case, there must have been some deed that had at least paved the way for the accident to happen. But the trail of evidence had long since been swept away. Theo wouldn't have an opportunity to examine the landing module. However, there had to be a second precondition for his theory to work —a motive. Andy must have been an obstacle for someone. Maybe it had to do with something in the past. If that were true, Theo might as well give up. He didn't know Andy well enough, and he didn't have access to the archives on Earth anymore.

But what about a reasonable motive? Everyone knew that Andy was an excellent programmer. Had he discovered something that had condemned him to this? There was only one way to figure that out. He would have to go through Andy's notes, but in such a way that the potential culprit wouldn't realize what he was doing. Could he enlist Rebecca's help in this? Theo would have liked to share his suspicions with her. This might help him get his ideas off the ground, since he trusted Rebecca's opinions. But there was also a risk tied to this course. Although he couldn't imagine her guilty, she was also a potential suspect, objectively speaking. So he was on his own in this. He was used to flying solo, but he had also now learned how much he enjoyed sharing things with Rebecca.

"Take care of yourself, Andy," he said. "It's time for me to see if there's anything I can do to help you."

He thought, for a microsecond, he saw Andy's right eyelid twitch, but he might have been wrong.

"I'll see you later, Gabriella," he said in farewell to the doctor.

HIS NEXT DESTINATION WAS THE *ENDEAVOUR*'S COMMAND center. Theo glanced at his watch. His visit with Andy had lasted twenty minutes. Ewa and Ellen had to still be out inspecting the building site. This might be an excellent opportunity to get started.

He climbed up the ladder and found the center empty. Perfect! He sat down in the pilot's seat, pulled the keyboard in front of him, and activated the screen. He selected Andy's user name before hesitating in surprise. He was sitting in the *Endeavour*, but Andy had never flown this ship. Why would his data be located here? Maybe someone had transferred the data from the *Santa Maria*'s system into the new system onboard here. That would be convenient for everyone.

Beeeeep! The computer was now asking him for the password. Theo felt relieved. That really wasn't a problem. He had watched Andy type in his password once and had been amazed that he'd used a series of adjacent keys.

"We're the only ones here," Andy had said with a laugh. "The system is protected from an outside attack, and I have such a lousy memory for passwords."

Theo entered *12345678,* knowing the system required that passwords be at least eight characters in length.

"Access denied."

23456789.

"Access denied."

34567890.

"Access denied."

Now he had to wait thirty seconds until he could try another password. He studied the keyboard. There were about twenty possible combinations of adjacent keys. He would try them all. As the countdown ran, Theo leaned back.

He suddenly heard footsteps behind him. "Is someone up there?"

It was Gabriella's voice. Theo hit the keys required to close the input screen and then straightened up in the seat.

"Oh, it's you, Theo. I didn't think you'd be up here."

"I'm waiting on Ewa," he said. "Have you seen her?"

"No. I thought she'd be here. I wanted to ask her something, too."

Theo was surprised. If that were the case, why had

Gabriella just asked if someone was up here? If he were looking for someone, wouldn't he ask if that particular person were somewhere? The doctor was acting oddly, but she probably thought he was, too. After all, they had both heard Ewa praising the building site over the ship's radio system. Just like him, Gabriella might have assumed that the center would be empty. Should he confide in her? Could she possibly be looking for the same information he was? But the risk would be too high for him. If she was responsible for the accident... Theo didn't want to go there. A patient in the hands of his murderer—hadn't that been the plot for far too many thrillers?

Theo stood up at the same moment that Ewa stuck her head through the hole in the floor that led to the lower level.

"A secret conversation, or are you waiting for me?" she asked.

"Gabriella wanted to ask you something," Theo said. "I'll give you two a little privacy." He walked over to the floor hatch, planning to leave the spaceship. Hopefully, the doctor wouldn't delay him. He didn't feel up to concocting a plausible excuse for Ewa about why he presumably wanted to talk to her.

"It's about Andy," Gabriella said. "I'd like to run a few more tests on him."

"Really?" Ewa replied, clearly interested in what this might mean.

Theo was glad he was no longer needed. He climbed through the hole and down the ladder before exiting the ship via the airlock. He would have to try to access Andy's data some other time.

Sol 56, Hebes Chasma

SARAH CAREFULLY LET THE ROVER ROLL TO A STOP. LANCE gazed over her shoulder. The map on the control console indicated that the escarpment must be somewhere close in front of them. It was a good idea for Sarah to stop here until they could figure out the condition of the slope.

Lance got out first. He stamped his legs and stretched. His thighs throbbed, but they felt better than they had yesterday. His body seemed to be getting used to the new strain. And the custom-tailored NASA suits were worth their weight in gold. Back on Earth, they had trained in the old, bulky EVA suits. He had never known before then how many places one could develop bruises or abrasions.

Sarah followed him. She turned back, leaned over the control panel, and pushed a few buttons. She then extracted the ignition key and stuck it in her pocket.

"You don't need to take it with you. Nobody will steal it."

"Sure about that?"

Bullseye. If only she hadn't reminded him. And yet, the existence of an ignition key still struck him as weird. The modern electric cars on Earth only needed their drivers' fingerprints to operate the doors. But Lance remembered the arguments of the NASA engineers, 'the more modern the technology, the more quickly it could fail.' In an emergency, a real key could be recreated from a piece of iron.

"No," Lance said aloud as they reached the escarpment.

"No?"

"We can't cross this in the hours left today."

Sarah nodded. Hebes Chasma stretched before them, a gigantic canyon. It ran for several thousand meters downhill. The bottom was about 20 kilometers wide, and in the middle of the canyon rose a mesa that was almost as tall as the opposite side of the Chasma.

"That's insane," Lance said. "The Grand Canyon would fit inside it."

Sarah pointed downward. "Our route will take us west, past the mesa. About 90 kilometers beyond that point, we should find a drivable passage that will take us back up to the plateau."

"I don't see anything here I'd call drivable," Lance declared.

"Mike sent us the latest satellite pictures. We came in a little farther south than planned. We'll need to head that way to find the spot to descend with the Rover."

Lance knelt down on the ground and brushed the surface with his gloved hand. This area was covered with a very thin coating of dust. As he rubbed at it, a hard, dark material appeared. "Could be volcanic," he said.

"The scientists think that, too. At some point during the greatest period of tectonic activity, a fissure was created."

"But one so wide?"

"That could've been caused by the water that might have flowed along here at one time. That's at least the theory," Sarah explained.

"Back then, Mars must've looked damned different."

"Maybe. We don't know. If life never developed here, then it probably looked like it does today, just with water."

"That's what you believe, Sarah?"

"I believe you're a nice guy, but that's all I believe for the time being. At some point in the near future, I hope we can find the time to seriously look for traces of lifeforms."

Lance started frantically stirring up the sand. Sarah moved closer, curious. He waited until her foot was within arm's reach, and then he struck. "Hey, I've found life on Mars!" he exclaimed as he stood up and hugged her.

"Should we perhaps continue our research inside the tent?" Sarah asked after a minute of silence. "I've heard that life thrives better in oxygen atmospheres."

"Who am I to contradict anything a degreed biologist says?"

Sol 57, Hebes Chasma

Lance tugged on the strap that held the tent to the Rover's bed, making certain it was tight. He took a step back while Sarah checked to make sure everything was secured. They had agreed to do things this way. If they lost the tent—or any part of their provisions—on their descent, it would be a real disaster. Regardless of how comfortable their suits were, spending two weeks in them would be absolute torture, if even possible.

"Looks good," Sarah said.

She then climbed into the driver's seat. They had drawn straws to see who got to drive the Rover first—and he had lost.

Compared to the desert tour of the past few days, the trip down to the base of the canyon promised to be a real adventure. Lance took his seat behind Sarah and then clipped his safety line to her. If the Rover tipped over, they would need to be able to jump out quickly to keep from being buried underneath it. The line would provide at least a little security from plunging all the way down to the bottom. But both of them were fully aware that they simply couldn't make any mistakes.

THEY STARTED OUT DRIVING NORTHWARD ALONG THE EDGE OF the canyon. Lance appreciated the view of the Hebes Chasma. The mesa in the middle of the valley really looked out of place. Its sides were as steep as those of the canyon itself. It looked as if a giant had thrown a chunk of dough into the Chasma. It was a shame they weren't on a research mission. He would have enjoyed examining the surface of the mesa. It had supposedly been formed by the sediment deposits from a body of water. That had to be the ideal site to search for fossils from Mars's fertile period!

"I think this is it," Sarah said, breaking into his thoughts.

His eyes followed her outstretched arm. The edge of the canyon seemed to be missing a kilometer-wide chunk, as if a plummeting meteorite had grazed the slope. But this wasn't just a simple collapse of the canyon wall. It was more likely that a side valley had developed over a more extended period of time.

Sarah steered the Rover a little toward the east to enter the gap at a more optimal angle. From this perspective, it was apparent what had created the valley. A massive gush of liquid water must have flowed into the canyon. Lance tried to imagine what the landscape must have looked like 3.5 billion years ago. Early on, perhaps there had been a spectacular waterfall here. The spray must have been full of rainbows on clear days. As the years passed, the water had eroded more and more of the hard substrate. The climate on Mars had eventually changed so much, growing increasingly colder, that the once-denser atmosphere had frozen, making the process irreversible.

"Can't you just imagine the giant waterfall that must've existed here once?" Sarah asked, seeming to read his mind once again.

"It's a shame we got here three billion years too late," Lance replied with a smile.

"Or a few centuries too early."

"Do you think that water will flow here again someday?"

"Maybe not up here, but perhaps down there?" Sarah said, pointing at the canyon floor.

"We'll never manage that. There are way too few of us."

"Don't say that. Homo sapiens started its trailblazing on Earth with relatively few individuals."

"So we're something like Adam and Eve?"

"If you want to put it that way. In any case, there are realistic projections about how we can reestablish the carbon dioxide atmosphere. The greenhouse effect would elevate the temperatures so much that water could exist in liquid form on the surface."

"I've read about that," Lance said. "We'd have to build giant mirrors and launch them into orbit over the South Pole to concentrate the sun's rays and thaw the frozen carbon dioxide. But with just the four of us?"

"Yes, that would be a problem. We couldn't do that without the MfE people."

"Or with them, either."

"You're right about that, I'm afraid."

"I SUGGEST THAT YOU HOLD ON TIGHT NOW," SARAH SAID.

Lance followed orders and then felt the Rover tilt forward. Sarah was driving at a walking pace as the surface grew steeper with each meter. Lance sat up straight. He felt a strong need to lean back. The substrate was comprised of a thin layer of loose rubble. The Rover weighed enough that the tires spun the sand, dust, and gravel to the side, finding traction on the volcanic stone. All four axles had brakes, which meant that the back section with its load didn't shift much. After approximately 300 meters, the incline was so steep that Sarah began to drive in a serpentine pattern. Lance had to commend the Rover's builders. The vehicle's axles gave the tires enough play that the machine moved down the slope like a mountain goat. The view was still magnificent. Lance couldn't see enough of it.

But then it was suddenly dark. They had driven into the shadow cast by the hillside of the side valley, which sliced deeper and deeper into the canyon. The temperature dropped drastically, and Lance turned up his suit heater. The mesa at the center glowed all the brighter, but their line of visibility along their track shrank to less than ten meters. Sarah switched on the headlights. The substrate looked much different in the artificial light. The thickness of the dust layer also diminished, with some areas being completely free of dust. They rose out of the ground like giant roots or muscles.

"Those are ancient lava flows that the wind keeps clear," Sarah explained.

The temperature continued to fall. Were they already in the area of the permanent shadow?

Sarah brought the Rover to a stop. "Do you see that?" She was pointing ahead of them. In the light of the right headlight, thousands of tiny diamonds were glittering. "Those have to be ice crystals. They must be crystallizing directly out of the air."

"Could we collect them?" asked Lance hopefully.

"It wouldn't be worth it. It can't be more than a paper-thin layer of ice crystals. They must've been gathering here for millennia. I'm just a little surprised at this considering how close we are to the equator."

Sarah restarted the motor. The Rover's tires buried the crystals beneath them. What had taken such a long time to form was destroyed in a matter of seconds. *We humans really have that down*, Lance thought.

It was gradually growing brighter, as the canyon walls receded. They were no longer driving on stone but on a large spit of debris that stretched into the canyon. The river that had gouged out the side valley must have deposited all the stones and sand along there. Lance tried to see if the gravel had been polished and formed by the water, but that didn't seem to be the case. Maybe the river hadn't had enough time for that.

His helmet's external microphone picked up a muffled,

scraping sound. It was coming from the rear. Lance quickly looked back. Sarah must have also heard it because she slowed the Rover to a stop. *Shit*, he thought. The rear section of the Rover was slowly skidding downward.

The thin atmosphere altered the scraping noise. Sarah had also realized what was happening and had hit the gas. They couldn't let themselves be pushed down the hillside by the Rover's mass. Lance felt his fear mount as the tires on the front axle spun, but Sarah seemed to remain calm as the Rover tilted sharply toward the valley floor. She shifted down to first gear and let the tires roll slowly. Her response was perfect.

Lance estimated that it was still two kilometers down to the base of the slope. If the Rover eventually went into a slide, there would be no stopping it until it hit the canyon floor. In an emergency, they would have to leap free. However, if they jumped too soon, they would reduce the mass over the front axle, and the tires really would just spin in vain. *Frying pan or fire*, Lance thought, *frying pan or fire*.

But Sarah's strategy was working. The back part of the rover was pointing straight downhill, but the two front axles had now regained their traction. Sarah was driving back uphill on the diagonal. She had to find a way to free the two back axles, or at least one of them, from the loose debris. The Rover's slant lessened.

Lance considered what he could do to help. Would it help if he pushed from the valley side? But then his body mass would no longer be on the Rover, and that might make the tires spin again. All he could do was let Sarah handle it.

After ten minutes of what felt like slow motion, they reached solid rock. Sarah cut off the engine and slumped over the wheel.

"Thank you, Sarah," Lance said, hugging her from behind. She turned toward him, and he saw that she was crying. "Hey, you did it."

"I'm so relieved," she admitted.

"You need a break. Should I drive for a while?"

"Gladly," Sarah replied. "But before we set off, let's load the Rover down with all the rocks we can find. We'll consume more methanol, but it will help the tires grip better. At least until we get past the strip of debris."

"Good idea," Lance said. He climbed down and began to collect some smaller stones.

"If we have room," he said, "we should take them back with us to the base. Maybe we'll find some signs of life in them."

LANCE HAD TO STAY FOCUSED. HE ADMIRED SARAH'S accomplishment all the more now that he was the one in the driver's seat. He could sense what he hadn't noticed as a passenger, the feedback from each individual wheel. Was it gripping the substrate—or starting to slip? If he paid close attention, he could keep the Rover stable as they drove. The two-kilometer altitude difference sloped off at ten-percent grade, and that had to be driven at a walking pace. They reached the floor of the canyon approximately one hour before sundown.

"Should we go a little farther?" Lance asked.

He wanted to make up at least part of the time they had lost. The best route to take would be through the middle of the canyon. Along the right side ran a depression that looked like a former river bed. The ground was quite sandy to the left. The mesa wasn't composed of volcanic stone, but of unevenly compressed sand. The individual layers were easily distinguishable. The stone was eroding much faster than the volcanic material in the side walls of the ravine. Lance was now glad that they hadn't planned to investigate the top surface of the mesa. It would have been almost impossible to drive the Rover up the slope. The lowest third or so of the incline reminded him of a steep sand dune—the only difference here was that the slope ran uphill for two kilometers.

"How much longer do you think it'll take us to reach our destination?" Sarah asked.

"If I believe Mike's itinerary, we're about three days out."

"Okay."

The ground grew bumpier. The river bed now reached to the middle of the canyon floor. Lance studied the hillside. It looked like a river of lava had come down at this point, causing the river water to recede away from the basalt. He steered the Rover over to the left. The layer of sand on the surface was thicker and the tires sank deeper. It would be best for them to keep going so he wouldn't have to drive back onto this surface later.

As a child, Lance had hated riding his bike through damp sand, but now he had four axles beneath him. It was unlikely that all of the tires would get stuck in the sand at the same time. He looked up. They were now driving along the bottom of a gigantic wall. Unfortunately, it was too dark now for any geological observations of the strata. The material along here had to be harder, though—otherwise it would be more substantially eroded.

Something suddenly crashed behind him. There wasn't much sound, but it had been very close at hand. Lance looked back, but he couldn't see anything. *Let's get past this wall*, he thought, *and then we'll set up the tent.* He was already looking forward to continuing his search for life on the desolate Mars surface along with Sarah.

They reached a niche in the canyon wall. An almost circular, sandy area was located at the center of it. The mesa had receded into the distance.

"All that's missing are the palm trees," Sarah declared. "Let's stop here."

Lance nodded and brought the Rover to a stop. Sarah was the first one to climb out. She walked around to the back, planning to fetch the tent. Lance followed and saw her suddenly snatch her hand back mid-reach.

"Shit," she said. "Take a look at this."

"What is it?"

He joined her and immediately saw what had happened. That must have been the crash from earlier. Their radio was strapped down near the back end of the Rover. It was stored in a sturdy metal container, but it hadn't stood a chance against the force of the object that had fallen onto it.

"We've been lucky again," Sarah said.

"Lucky?"

"If it had been a half-meter closer to the front, it would have ripped the tent. And another meter and a half ahead, it would've hit me."

Lance felt cold. He had only been thinking about what the loss of the radio would mean to them. "You're right," he said. "We were very fortunate. Tomorrow we need to keep away from these steep walls."

"I hope Mike and Sharon won't get worried when they don't hear from us," Sarah added.

"That's wishful thinking. Of course they'll worry. But once we get back, all will be forgiven. But there's one other problem."

"Yes?"

"The four active satellites in orbit were tracking our position via the radio. We'll have to come up with some other way to navigate now. Unfortunately, Mars doesn't have a magnetic field, which means that trying to navigate solely by the sun is very imprecise."

"Don't worry about that," Sarah said. "I have another idea. I'll explain it to you in the morning."

Sol 58, Hebes Chasma

"SO HOW ARE WE GOING TO FIND OUR WAY NOW?"

It was still dark. In the headlight beams, Sarah put a finger up to where her lips were. It was a symbolic gesture, though, since she was already wearing her helmet. This was how she had reacted to every one of his questions, at least at those times when she didn't respond by asking him why he hadn't paid attention during survival training. Despite his best efforts, Lance couldn't recall that manual navigation had ever been taught during that course. Had Sarah gone through the same training as he had?

After securing the tent, she walked to the center section of the Rover, which was where a well-stocked toolbox was stored in case they needed to do emergency repairs on the vehicle. Sarah flipped the toolbox's latch and opened it. After rummaging around in it, she eventually turned around triumphantly and showed Lance a tool. "A sextant," she said.

He recognized it.

"I could've built you one if it had been necessary," she said. "All I would've needed was a little sheet metal, a compass, and two mirrors. But this is easier."

"Show-off!" he said with a laugh. "Let's see what you can do with it."

"We first have to figure out our line of latitude. Mars doesn't have a polar star, unfortunately."

"So we're lost for good?"

"Of course not. We need Deneb, the first-magnitude star in the constellation Cygnus, and Alpha Cephei, also known as Alderamin, the brightest star in the constellation Cepheus. The north celestial pole is located halfway between them."

Lance looked up into the sky. It was crystal clear. "Good thing we don't have a dust storm right now," he said.

"We'd really be up a creek then."

"I don't see Cepheus," Lance said.

"It looks a little like a house with a steep roof."

He stared up hard into the stars, but couldn't find anything that looked like a house. Maybe he wasn't imaginative enough.

"You shouldn't be looking right up at the zenith. We're fairly close to the equator, so the north celestial pole should be low over the horizon. But don't strain anything. I know where it is," Sarah said. She held the sextant up to her right eye, tweaked the device, and read the value from it. "Good, now for the longitude. That will be easier."

"I'm really not smart enough to figure that out," Lance declared.

"That's nonsense. You can do it. For the longitude, we need either the sun or one of the two moons."

Lance looked up at the sky again and saw a bright object he recognized. "I found Phobos. No, Deimos." He remembered that Deimos was the dimmer of the two moons.

"Good." Sarah handed him the sextant. "Now measure how high it is over the horizon."

He took the device, held it in front of his helmet, and gazed through the eyepiece. He adjusted its angle so the horizon was visible through it. Now he had to turn the screw on the measuring armature until Deimos appeared in view and came to rest on the horizon line. "What's this armature called again? I can't remember the right word," he said.

"The alidade."

"Thanks." And there it was, Deimos, Mars's moon. Lance was astonished at how bright the chunks of rock in Mars's sky looked. He turned the screw until the two halves of the image were aligned. He must have actually practiced this earlier since the procedure seemed familiar to him.

He handed the sextant back to Sarah. She read off the angle and double-checked the measurement.

"You don't trust me, huh?" he asked.

"You were the one who thought he'd never held a sextant before. I'm just making sure."

"Smart."

"You did a good job," she commended him. "I got the same result." She then moved up to the Rover's control console.

It took Lance a moment to remember why she needed to do that. She had to check the angle of the moon against a data table. She tapped the screen and then nodded.

He stood next to her. Sarah had obviously saved their coordinates in the map software program.

"We've actually made very good time," remarked Sarah. "We should reach the probe the day after tomorrow. We still have a stretch to do through the Chasma and then up through the notch. After that, it's straight onward to the probe."

By early afternoon, they were standing at the spot that Mike had pointed out on the satellite photos as ideal for ascending from the canyon. Lance was sitting at the wheel, looking up. He thought that what they were planning to do sounded insane. There was nothing like this back on Earth. It was as if they had to climb directly from a beach up an 8000-foot escarpment.

Just like on the other side, a side valley sliced down into the Chasma at this point. However, it looked even less like a long-vanished river had gouged it out. Parts of the European Alps looked like this, in those spots where glaciers had receded. But Mars wasn't supposed to have ever had glaciers like that. There had never been a time in which Mars had been completely covered in snow and ice, at least according to the planetologists' climate models. And when would there have ever been a glacier here at the equator?

"We really want to go up there?" he asked Sarah.

"We should've considered that yesterday before we drove down here."

"Well, hold on tight."

The first part of the ascent was still relatively level. Lance tried to forge ahead hard. Lance knew the tires must not be given an opportunity to get buried in the debris. The grade was still less than forty-five degrees, which meant the Rover wasn't at risk of tipping over. They were able to cover the first 2000 meters surprisingly fast.

After that point, the slope grew much steeper. Lance was amazed that Mike had considered this passage drivable. He must have thought they were experts at the wheel. The greatest danger now was that the Rover would begin leaning toward the valley. If it started in that direction, they would be hard-pressed to keep it upright. Lance couldn't give the vehicle as much gas anymore, and he was having to avoid the more substantial obstacles in their path. This also meant that they kept getting stuck. When that happened, they had to get out, shovel the tires free, and then wedge something flat underneath them so that Lance could make even a little bit of forward progress.

After the fourth stop like this they decided that Sarah would go ahead on foot, so they could at least save a little time from climbing in and out of the vehicle. Sarah was also able to figure out which spots were especially sandy and could warn him to steer clear of them. They swapped these roles out every 30 minutes. Lance wasn't sure which was the more stressful job, the tense, unrelenting concentration needed to drive or the sweaty climb as the scout. At least the strain wasn't all one-sided this way.

They had now reached an altitude that was close to the

level of the mesa plateau. According to the satellite images, the substrate here should be harder. They had reached the original granite, which was older than the volcanic rock they had driven over to enter the canyon, and the sediment that had formed the mesa. *Too bad Mike's not with us*, Lance thought. *With his background in geology, he would have enjoyed seeing all these different formations.* Thanks to the extremely slow erosion process, it wouldn't have been all that difficult for a stonecutter to reach the most interesting spots.

They finally neared the top of the slope. Both stopped.

"Look at that," Lance said.

"Unbelievable," Sarah sighed.

Above their heads stretched a 50-meter, perpendicular wall face. It was as if they were supposed to drive the Rover up the facade of a 15-story high-rise. Lance measured the height with the laser rangefinder and then studied the satellite pictures. The wall didn't show up on them. According to their images, all they supposedly needed to do to reach the top of the canyon was drive a few more meters to the west.

"The satellite's angle was poor," he said.

"Yeah, that's not Mike's fault," Sarah agreed.

"Look, we could take a detour," Lance said. He traced an alternate route with his finger.

"That would cost us half a day at least, and we might end up facing another wall like this one," Sarah said.

Where did she want to try to get out? "We'd just need to drive back a thousand meters and then head north for two hours. There's another narrow way to get up there."

"The sun is going to set in two hours. Would you prefer to make our ascent in darkness, or to spend the night in the wall again?"

Sarah was right, he thought. Neither alternative seemed all that appealing. "So what do you want to do?" he asked, interested to hear what she would suggest.

"Well... we have a windlass, including a pulley and a high-tensile rope. The Rover only weighs a third of its Earth weight. One of us can climb up and secure the winch, and then we can haul the Rover up. We've strapped everything down, so what could go wrong?" Sarah asked.

Sure, what could go wrong, Lance thought. They would be trying to haul a bus on the end of a rope up to the top of a high-rise. Standard procedure with no risks at all. He was at least aware of his skepticism.

"I'll do it," she said. "You wait down here and release the Rover's brakes when I give you the signal. You can then climb up after me. The wall doesn't look like it should be too hard. No overhangs."

"Yeah, sure. Not hard at all," he mumbled. Sarah had to be crazy. And he was, too, since he had just agreed to her idea. In the face of her enthusiasm, he didn't have it in him to argue with her.

"If we start now, we should be at the top in forty-five minutes," she said optimistically.

"Let's get cracking," Lance said.

Sarah started rummaging for the winch in the toolbox. She clipped it onto her back and then attached herself to the safety line. And just like that, Sarah started up the slope.

Lance watched closely as she struggled up the wall. It would be good for him to memorize the route she took. She moved assuredly, like an experienced climber. And here he had thought she was a typical scientist who never left the laboratory.

"You're doing great," he said.

"Eh," she exhaled loudly, "I'm a little out of shape. Fifteen years ago, I pursued speed climbing as a hobby."

"Take your time. This isn't a competition."

"I know that."

And with that, she reached the top. The most critical phase started now. Sarah had to find a way to secure the winch so that the weight of the Rover wouldn't be able to pull it loose. Lance couldn't help her. He couldn't even see what she was doing, but she was taking her time, which was a good thing. If she made even the smallest misjudgment here, the Rover would plunge to the bottom of the canyon.

"That's it," she said. "Heads up, here comes the rope.

Lance caught the rope and tied it to the front of the Rover. "The rope's secure."

Now or never, Sarah thought. "Starting the winch."

Lance released the Rover's brakes, and Sarah began to turn the winch. Thanks to the winch's gear ratio, she was strong enough to slowly raise the vehicle. The front axle dangled in the air, and the rest of the vehicle crept closer to the wall. The Rover swung side to side a little, but that stopped when the front two wheels met the wall.

"It's working," he shouted.

Centimeter by centimeter, the rope was pulled upward. The Rover's joints creaked as the vehicle assumed a sway-backed shape. The Rover hadn't been constructed to be bent like that, but as long as unusual noises were the only things breaking the silence, Lance was satisfied.

The Rover's eight tires were now pressed against the wall. It was a strange scene, one in which it looked as if someone had switched off the gravitational pull. Lance's tasks below were over, so he also started to climb. For a two-legged creature, the steep wall didn't really present a problem. There were enough footholds, and the stone hadn't eroded much and was stable. He finally propped his arms on the upper edge and pulled the rest of his body over the top. *Did it!*

Sarah was still cranking the winch. She had placed it far enough back that when the Rover crested the wall, it would roll to a stop in front of her.

"Need any help?" he asked.

"Not right now. Could you check on the Rover, though?"

Lance stood on the edge of the cliff. A thick, plump caterpillar twinkled its headlights at him. "Looks great," he said, giving Sarah a thumbs up.

The next moment, she began to sway unsteadily. He was about to run to her, but she caught herself in time.

"Ooof. I lost my balance because the Rover suddenly grew lighter. Did you see anything fall off?"

"I'm sorry. I was looking at you."

“That’s alright,” she said.

Ten minutes later, the Rover was standing beside them. They had saved at least three hours—and another night spent camping in the wall—by following Sarah’s advice.

Together they checked their cargo. Nothing obvious was missing, but then Lance recalled, “We had packed those rocks on the Rover for better traction. They must’ve come loose,” he said in relief.

“Of course,” Sarah answered. “Why didn’t I think of that before?”

Sol 59, NASA base

"HAVE YOU HEARD ANYTHING FROM SARAH AND LANCE?"

Sharon gave a start as Mike poked his head into the command center. It was only 5 AM. "No, nothing new," she replied. "But I told you I would wake you up immediately if they called in."

Mike dropped into the seat beside hers. He reeked of sweat.

"Maybe you should take a long shower. Why are you up already?" Sharon asked.

"I couldn't sleep anymore. How could anyone sleep with all this bad news? I bet the MfE backstabbers have done something to Sarah and Lance. We'd have heard from them otherwise!"

"We can't know that. Their settlement is located in the other direction, and they don't even know that Sarah and Lance are out and about."

"Maybe they've been listening in on our radio communications. I'd believe anything of them. We need to encrypt our communications from now on."

"Mike, anything could've happened. Maybe a sun flare hit Mars and scrambled the ionosphere. Or their radio had a short circuit. There are plenty of innocent reasons why we might not be hearing from them. The two of them can look out for themselves."

"There are also enough reasons that make my blood run cold. I'm the one who suggested they take the route through the Hebes Chasma. That was a huge mistake."

"They got down into the canyon just fine. The contact broke off after that point."

"See! Something must've happened when they tried to drive out of the Chasma. If the MfE scum hadn't robbed us blind, we could've checked on them. But now we can't help them at all."

"We could ask the MfE people for help if it's necessary."

"Ask them? Just what we need. So they can betray us one more time? Lance and Sarah are better off without them."

"I'll bet they're feeling bad about what they did, Mike. At least a few of them probably are. They have two Rovers and plenty of people."

"Only over my dead body," Mike snapped back.

"You know what, I'm going to go lay down for a little while. The night shift was tense, and your griping isn't helping. What's happened to your optimism?"

"How could anyone remain an optimist under these circumstances?"

"Goodnight, Mike."

"Goodnight, Sharon."

ALTHOUGH SHE WAS DEAD TIRED, IT TOOK SHARON A LONG time to fall asleep. At this rate, Mike was going to drive her totally crazy. The boy was so hardheaded! And he now expected only the worst from the MfE group. But it was impossible for 15 people to all mutate into assholes overnight. *What's that old saying? Ah, yes, 'A fish rots from the head down,'* she recalled. The theft might not have been Ewa's idea, but she was the one who had approved and then implemented it. Sharon had a hard time believing that the entire crew had been in agreement. They needed to make contact with the ones who hadn't agreed with Ewa. But how? The reality was that it didn't help anything to condemn the entire crew, as Mike was willing to do.

The first thing she had to do was tend to Mike. Sometimes she felt like he was a big baby, and she was his mother. At those times, she felt a little jealous of Lance and Sarah, who had found common ground as peers. Were they also sleeping together? They would be spending a lot of time together as a foursome. It made sense if they could fulfill each other's needs like that. However, Mike—who felt more like a son—wasn't the right one for her.

How could she distract him, moving forward? Mike needed an outlet for his energy. Now that they weren't working with the MfE people any longer, they had to rely on each other for survival. One valuable resource was missing for their long-term plans—easily obtainable water. MfE was deliberately building their settlement at a location that possessed this resource. They couldn't transplant their base so easily. That meant that they would have to find another way to access the vital water.

WHEN SHARON WOKE UP, THE CLOCK INDICATED THAT IT WAS noon. She slipped into the shower and put on fresh clothing before joining Mike in the command center. She noticed instantly that he still hadn't showered. He was wearing earphones and seemed to be searching through all the frequencies for signals.

She sneaked up behind on his left side and tapped him on his right shoulder.

Mike flinched and spun around toward the wrong way. "You got me!" he said with a laugh. He always fell for that.

Sharon gazed at him sternly, then said, "If you don't get into the shower this instant, I will stick you in your spacesuit."

Mike sighed. "Okay," he said as he stood up to shuffle into the bathroom.

HE WAS BACK 15 MINUTES LATER. IT WAS LIKE NIGHT AND DAY. He was wearing clean clothes and smelled like a freshly-bathed baby.

"That's better," she said. *Children liked to be praised.* "Before I fell asleep I had a major idea that I'd like to discuss with you."

"Lance and Sarah didn't radio in while I was gone?"

"No, Mike. What I wanted to say was, now that MfE has left us high and dry, we have a big problem to solve."

"I know. We need water. I've been thinking about that."

"Oh?" Sharon was surprised. Mike was obviously still in a condition to think about other things besides their betrayal.

"Yes, and I have an idea of where we can find some."

"Sounds good."

"The MfE scum took our Rover with the GPR, so we can forget about that. But we could construct our own radar. We have everything we'd need to do that right here." Mike pointed at the radio. "I have to admit I already got started while you were sleeping," he added.

"A radio?"

"Yes, we don't need more than that. Depending on the frequency, we can use it to explore up to a thousand meters below the surface level. When the radio waves encounter the separation levels, they will bounce off of them at varying intensities."

"That seems like a brilliant solution."

"The main problem is that we will have to somehow calibrate the radar. The GPR on the Rover is already calibrated. In other words, the device knows which material the signal is encountering based on its reflection factor. We don't have that information."

"What will we need to do that?"

"Ideally, we could deposit water and ice samples at various depths, but to do that we need the drill the MfE scum stole from us."

"What's the second-best option?"

"We might just get lucky."

"That's exactly what I was thinking," Sharon said. "But what does that look like in a concrete sense?"

"At some depth between five hundred and a thousand meters, there must be a water table. The water there is warm, due to its depth, and it will contain numerous admixtures, which will make it very conductive. If our radio waves hit it, we should hear a clear echo."

"Geothermics. That would be marvelous, since we could also obtain energy from it. But what could possibly go wrong with this approach?"

"If there's something else down there that functions as an equally strong electrical conduit, then we'll end up drilling a five-hundred or thousand-meter deep hole for nothing."

"What else could be down there?"

"No idea. Maybe an iron deposit?"

"Metallic iron? Not very likely."

"You asked, Sharon."

"It doesn't matter. We have to take that risk. When do we start?"

"Give me an hour. I'll convert the radio into a portable GPR. Sarah and Lance seem to be incommunicado for the time being anyway."

"Hopefully you didn't ruin your suit," Sharon said skeptically, eying Mike's homemade connector between the converted radio and his spacesuit.

"You don't think I can show up at the Captain's dinner in this, after all?" he shot back.

"Smartass."

They were waiting for the airlock to open the external hatch.

"But seriously," Mike explained, "I had to find a way to connect the radio to my helmet's earphones. Now I can hear if we hit a conduit layer below the surface."

"You'll hear it?"

"The receiver will filter out the reflected part of the signal, amplify it, and make its rhythm audible to the human ear."

"Ah. So if nothing's being reflected, you won't hear anything, but if there's water right underneath us, it will beep loudly."

"Something like that. Though I don't really expect us to find groundwater anywhere nearby."

The light in the airlock switched from red to green. Sometimes Sharon suspected the base's computer listened in on their conversations and waited to start the next activity until they were done talking. *Very courteous*, she thought. But that was nonsense, of course. This expedition had deliberately not been equipped with an AI system. NASA had discussed this for a long time, but in the end, they decided against it—it was either deemed too expensive, or too risky. Nobody had ever told them the exact reason for the decision.

"After you," Sharon said.

"Ladies first," Mike countered.

"You weren't paying attention during training, were you? Upon exiting a vehicle, the gentleman goes first, holds the door, and opens the umbrella for the lady."

"Is it supposed to rain today?"

"The entire week."

"I hate this constant rain."

In moments like this, Sharon actually liked her colleague. You could kid around with him very easily.

"Go on now. Get out," she said, hands on hips.

Mike climbed up the ladder.

THE SKY ABOVE THEM WAS REMARKABLY CLEAR TODAY. IT STILL wasn't blue—nor would it ever be that color in the future—but the grayish-brown looked fresher than usual, tinged as it was with a generous dash of pink. One might even wonder if rain had just passed through.

"Watch out for the puddles," Sharon advised.

"I was just about to jump in one. They always splash so nicely."

"There'll be hell to pay if you get your newly-washed suit dirty."

"Sure."

Sharon walked around the base. Since the *Endeavour* had been stolen and the Rover was gone, the human presence on Mars was barely noticeable. The structure was a rectangular hole in the ground. The roof was covered with slag to shield its occupants from cosmic radiation. Observers would undoubtedly realize that the hill was a relatively recent addition to the Mars surface, but it probably wouldn't occur to them that this was where NASA had built its first and only base.

The sole structure that looked manmade was the greenhouse, thanks to its vaulted plexiglass dome. Lance had constructed his turbine behind it. It was turning very slowly. She suddenly remembered that Lance had asked her to knock the dust off it from time to time. She walked over to it and did just that. From the turbine, a thick cable ran westward to where their KRUSTY, their small nuclear reactor, sat at a safe distance.

This was now their new home. Sharon was still having a hard time accepting that. *Small but mine*—didn't people say that? She would never again see a green meadow or smell the resiny air of a forest. Worse still, she would eventually forget what that was even like. Memories couldn't last forever. *It was actually a practical mechanism*, she thought. It would help make life easier for her on this dusty, red rock, but there was still something achingly sad about this.

Maybe they should meet to share memories for an hour

or so a week. Sharon imagined all four of them sitting at the table, talking about their loveliest memories. While their own memories faded, they would be inspired by their visions of the others' stories. In 30 years, their recollections might become a collective trove as they lost the ability to distinguish who had contributed which memory. Isn't that how humanity's great myths had been created, by people gathered around a fire? It was a strange feeling, but if they found a way to survive on Mars, their memories might form the foundational mythology for a future Mars Nation.

"Should we get started?"

Sharon glanced around. Mike's voice sounded clear in her headphones. He was moving away from her in the opposite direction. He already seemed far away, but she knew that the perspective was deceptive. She unconsciously still defaulted to Earth's scale with its much greater distance to the horizon. "I'm coming," she said.

"I've already started."

Sharon sprinted to catch up with him. Her heart was racing. Mike pointed at his helmet, about where his ear was located. It looked as if he was listening to the planet's heartbeat. Mike walked along slowly, and Sharon followed. But then he stopped.

"Do you want to listen in?" he asked.

"Yeah."

"I'll crank the volume up as high as I can and switch on my helmet mic."

"Alright."

There was the sound. Sharon heard a high ping that repeated every ten seconds. She recognized it from an old film she had seen that had been set on board a World War II sub.

"But that's not the echo, is it?"

"No. It's nothing more than a fake, or really more like a symbol. I'm not sending sound waves into the ground like the U-boats did when they used sonar to search for obstacles. These are radio waves that the receiver is transforming into audible sounds."

"And the echo?"

"To a certain extent, the material is absorbing the radio waves, but some of them are also being scattered or reflected. They are being picked up by the receiver, though with a certain amount of delay and distortion which is dependent upon the materials they're crossing through and being reflected by."

"So you're hearing a lot of echoes?"

"The receiver is filtering out all the weak returns. I'm not hearing any of them. But if the waves hit a conductive layer, a larger percentage of them will be reflected. That's also the reason why mirrors function as they do. They reflect the largest percentage of light waves. Interesting bit of trivia—the water on Mars is supposed to have a high saline content."

"So the receiver should only indicate the especially-strong reflections because of that?"

"That's the idea. To be honest, though, I have no idea what their expected values are, or how strong the reflection should be if we encounter a layer of groundwater. I simply don't know enough about what lies beneath Mars's surface."

"But you're still going to keep trying?"

"As I walk all over the place, I think I'll eventually get a feeling for what counts as a normal reflection, and where we should actually try to bore a hole."

"That sounds like a reasonable plan," Sharon said.

"At least I'll get some exercise out in the fresh air."

"Just make sure you don't catch a cold, and come back inside before the sun goes down, alright?"

"Sure, Mama."

BECAUSE YOU COULD NEVER STRAIGHTEN UP COMPLETELY, THE work in the greenhouse was strenuous. If she had been in charge, Sharon would have had the robotic drill dig down an extra 30 centimeters. But it was true that if that had happened, they would have had more space to warm and fill with air for the plants, both of which would have consumed more energy. Maybe Mike would get lucky and find hot water. They could make good use of a continually-bubbling energy source.

Lettuce plants. Check. Sharon worked down the list that Sarah had left for her. The entire greenhouse was still functioning as a lab, as they tried to figure out the optimal conditions for each plant variety—nutrients, irrigation, illumination... Sarah had set up small, transparent foil tents over some of her samples. These were being supplied with significantly more carbon dioxide via thin tubes. Not all of the crop plants were benefiting from this. The main problem was that they only had enough supplies to last a maximum of 18 months, but now that time had suddenly turned into years. At some point, they would run out of the fertilizer they had brought with them, and when that happened, they would have to start producing it from the resources available to them.

Sharon didn't want to imagine the consequences of that time-factor on the other things they needed, such as medicines. How would they produce basic painkillers on Mars? And what about antibiotics? They'd all been hale and healthy when they arrived, but potential pathogens were slumbering inside every person. The bacterial population just inside herself was huge. If her immune system ever wavered, one of those bacteria could quickly gain the upper hand.

Radishes. Check. The last plant on the list. Sharon was sweating. She could finally leave this sauna. Two hours of gardening seemed more tiring than a day spent on the stationary bike. She climbed through the lock and made a beeline to the shower. There was one distinct advantage to Lance and Sarah being gone—her daily water ration had doubled. Showering twice a day would have been an unnecessary luxury otherwise. A few new hairs were sprouting under her arms. She considered shaving them, but decided there would be enough time for that tomorrow.

A little bulb was flashing in the command center. Mike

had tried to reach her. The greenhouse still wasn't connected to the base's communication system. Sharon called him over the base's radio. "I just got done in the greenhouse," she said.

"I thought so," Mike replied.

"What's going on?"

"I want to show you something."

"You want me to get back into that sweaty suit? I just took a shower."

"Sorry about that. You should've checked with me before getting in the shower. We could've showered together afterward."

"Keep dreaming. You know how small the stall is."

"Are you coming?"

He gave up on the shower topic of his own accord—she'd expected another snappy comeback. Whatever this was seemed to be quite important to him.

With a sigh, Sharon agreed.

SHARON WAS STANDING IN THE RED DUST OF MARS, BUT MIKE was nowhere to be seen. The sun was already sinking close to the horizon. "Where are you?"

"Just head due east."

"And how do I do that without a compass?"

"Obviously you have to keep the sun directly behind you."

Sharon sighed and set off. Mike's decision to move beyond sight range of the station on his own was against the rules. They hadn't brought along any navigational aids. She kept looking back to see if the sun was still behind her. The base disappeared soon, and she couldn't see even the turbine. The sun would set shortly.

"How far do you think you are, Mike?"

"Uh, I'm not sure. I just kept walking. You should see me soon."

Sharon thought back. Mike had departed over two hours ago. He could have covered ten kilometers or more. Hopefully, he hadn't done something that stupid. If he had, they would have to find their way back to the base in the dark.

But then she caught sight of him, a thin, gray line standing in the barren landscape. Mike looked lost. Now she felt like hugging him. He waved at her.

"How did you get here?" she asked.

"I walked."

"Nice."

He pointed to the tablet he was holding. "Look, I just followed the gradient," he said.

Sharon saw the rising line. "What does that mean?"

"I walked along the course in which the reflection grew steadily stronger. For example, if I veered to the right and the strength decreased, I went back to where the signal was stronger."

"I understand. And now?"

"Regardless of which direction I take from here, the reflection decreases. We're standing above the local maximum reading."

"That's great."

"It is! Look around. We're standing in a depression. It seems to have been a drainage area." Mike pointed northward, and Sharon saw a low spot. "So, maybe this was once a lake with inlets and outlets, 3.5 billion years ago or thereabouts. Back then, the most optimal conditions were supposed to be around the equator, right where we are."

"And what does that have to do with the gradient?"

"The deep water might reflect the conditions from back then. If this had been the location of a lake, then the water table was situated closer to the surface and it still would be."

"You can determine that from your measurements?" Sharon asked.

"Yes, and from the topography. If there's anywhere around here we should investigate, this is the spot," Mike replied.

"Does this mean you think you've found groundwater?"

"I think the odds are fairly high, so I suppose you could put it that way."

"Just spit it out! That's wonderful!" Sharon hugged Mike. He might have just found a solution to their biggest problem!

"It's premature to do that. We won't know for sure until we actually strike water," Mike said.

"You can also celebrate a preliminary finding. We don't exactly have lots of good news these days."

"Don't remind me about that."

The moment was over. They were back in the world of hard realities.

"At what depth do you think the reflection is being created?" asked Sharon.

"At least three hundred meters," Mike replied.

"That will be a pretty deep hole."

"We'd need years to dig that by hand, Sharon. We have to get our robotic drill back."

"That might take some delicate negotiations."

"If they don't give it back willingly, we'll take it back by force."

THEY MARCHED BACK TO THE BASE IN SILENCE. IT TOOK longer than Sharon had expected. Had they gotten lost?

"Don't worry," Mike said. "If I have to, I'll convert the receiver again so we can use the satellites to navigate."

But then Sharon caught sight of the lonely, yellow positional light they had attached to the highest point on the base. They had made it back.

Sol 59, Hebes Chasma

Their destination was within reach. Lance drove the Rover across the arid landscape as fast as he could. It almost felt as if a tailwind was propelling them. They had even set off before sunrise. And now they were finally able to choose their own course. The satellite images didn't show any real obstacles between them and the NASA probe, so they were racing along the straightest path possible.

He changed spots with Sarah hourly. It was too strenuous to drive at this breakneck speed for longer than that. They had to keep swerving around rocks, both large and small. The Rover kicked up a long trail of dust behind it. Lance wondered if this whole trip had been worth the trouble. How much capacity did the solar cells have, anyway? At the same time, the probe probably contained parts that they wouldn't be able to build themselves for the next ten or twenty years.

They wouldn't be able to repair failing technology unless they had access to replacement parts. Lance could see himself as a modern-day junk collector, driving his Rover all over Mars in search of stuff. It would be a worthwhile task, and they made a good team. Considering what all the nations of the Earth had fired up to Mars over the past 60 years, there had to be several tons of junk down here. Even the probes that had crashed into the planet harder than expected could be a source of usable replacement parts.

It was time for a little break. Lance let the Rover roll to a stop. The sun was at its zenith, and they were now sitting in a shallow depression. "Let's stretch our legs a little, okay?" he said.

Sarah looked at the screen on the console. "Only three hours to go! We could take a longer break."

"I don't want to. I'd like to finally get there."

"That works, too. We could go on a nice evening walk then. You and I, alone in the light of the setting sun..."

"Oh, to finally be alone!" Lance laughed.

"Someday we'll be able to walk around without our suits."

"I'm not so sure about that. The atmosphere will never be as thick as it is on Earth."

"If not us, then our children." Sarah smiled at him.

Lance gulped. "Our children..."

"No, I'm not pregnant, at least as far as I know. But I know you know what can happen when you have unprotected sex."

"I... no. I assumed that you..."

"Did you see me take any pills?"

"Not directly."

"NASA assumed that we could all control ourselves. It was only supposed to be for a certain length of time, though. And we all had other plans than to establish families here."

"True," Lance remembered with a twinge.

"Just so you know and can't say later that you had no idea. We shouldn't do that to each other." Sarah smiled at him.

Lance had a feeling that it was too late for this warning. The thought of creeping into the tent with her and not being able to touch her seemed like torture. "Sure. I know now," he mumbled through gritted teeth.

About 30 minutes from their destination, they checked their position one more time. Everything looked perfect. The old probe was sitting right in front of them. What condition would it be in? If they were unlucky, it would be buried under the dust. The probe wasn't very tall.

But all their fears proved to be unfounded. They recognized the probe long before they reached it because its solar panels reflected the sun in the southwest.

Sarah parked the Rover about ten meters away from the probe. "Some of its parts might've come loose, might be scattered around here," she explained.

"Good call," Lance said.

They climbed out of the Rover. The probe looked as if it might reactivate at any moment. If he remembered correctly, NASA had broken off contact with it after three years because it had achieved all its scientific goals. Now 20 years later, it showed hardly any wear and tear. They should definitely be able to make good reuse of the solar panels. The one still hung perpendicular above the surface, while the second one was a little bent.

"The site didn't treat it all that kindly," Lance said, pointing at the crooked panel.

"Did you already find the HP3?"

Mike had been especially enthusiastic about this instrument. It consisted of a hammer that could drive a measuring probe into the ground. Since they no longer owned a drill, this was one alternative that would enable them to check on deeper strata. The HP3 could only drive something down to a depth of five meters, but they might be able to alter that. Or they could use it as a model on which to base a larger hammer drill.

"There it is," Sarah said, and he now recognized it as well.

The instrument looked like a miniature version of a drilling rig. A small housing was attached to its side. A flat cable led from the HP3 to the inside of the probe. They located the SEIS, the seismometer, a few meters farther on, close to the other solar panel. Lance took the cover off. This instrument could detect the smallest imaginable vibrations. There was no telling what they might be able to use this for. He cautiously picked it up and set it carefully on the driver's seat of the Rover.

"It would be best for us to start the disassembly process according to Mike's suggested procedure," Sarah said. "I'll unscrew the separate parts, and you can store them safely on the Rover. The probe weighs at least 350 kilograms."

"I thought it was heavier."

"The tanks are empty, which is too bad, but the chemical engine will still be beneficial for us," Sarah said.

They started to work. The first items on the list were the solar panels. Lance pulled the tent off the Rover and fastened the bulky panels to its spot. Sarah was already busying herself with the inside of the probe. They wouldn't leave anything behind, but the guts—all of the electronics—were the most valuable elements. With its high-gain antenna, the probe could even link into the NASA Deep Space Network. The probe's computer was utterly outdated in terms of technology, but it could still do its job.

They wouldn't have any problem replacing the *Endeavour*'s computer and flying back to Earth. *The only problem is that nobody is waiting for us anymore*, Lance thought.

"DONE." SARAH HANDED LANCE THE PROBE'S LANDING LEG, which she had carefully taken apart into three sections. Even the nuts and bolts might be quite valuable at some point. There was no telling when they would be capable of pouring iron.

"Very good," Lance said. "With twenty minutes to spare until sunset. It's been a pleasure to work with you."

"Glad to return the compliment. What about our walk now?"

"It would be my honor, Miss Jaeggli, to invite you to take

a turn before the sun sets." Lance bowed and held out his hand."

"Enchanté, Monsieur," Sarah replied.

Hand in hand they slowly strolled westward. The sun favored them by tinting the sky violet. In its own unique way, the landscape was spectacular, Lance had to admit, but the woman who had taken his hand and was now nimbly walking across the flat sand with him was even more so.

"About our conversation from earlier...," he said.

"Yes?"

"In case you got the impression that I would be displeased if you were pregnant..."

"Yes?"

"That isn't true. I've never been in that situation, and this might not be the most ideal environment for a child, but it's not going to get better than this any time soon. I think I would be glad if that happened... Very."

Now it was out. Sarah stopped walking. She was bound to be on the verge of laughing at him. *It was just a stupid joke*, she would say. I can't even get pregnant. It's been fun sleeping with you, but under these circumstances, I'd choose to have an abortion. *Yes, that would be what she would say*, he thought.

Sarah took his helmeted head in her hands, pulling him to her and blowing him a kiss. "Someday," she said, "we'll kiss each other at twilight. For real. Not our children, us. I believe that with all my heart."

"That would be wonderful," Lance said.

There was nothing else to say. No other words came to him. He was speechless, but that wasn't really a problem.

THE SUN SANK BEHIND THE HORIZON. THEY TURNED BACK. It was time to set up the tent. They strolled slowly back to the Rover. The probe was gone, but Lance noticed two gray lines that seemed to be messing with their vehicle. They weren't alone.

Lance grabbed Sarah's arm. "Wait here," he said. "I'm going to find out who they are and what they want."

"No way. We're going together." Sarah yanked her arm free and made a beeline for the two figures who were standing with their backs to them and hadn't seemed to notice them yet. They were wearing cumbersome, old-fashioned space-suits, like the ones the MfE group had.

"They have to be MfE people. How did they find us?" Lance said in a lowered voice, although there was no way the newcomers could hear them. If they were using the same frequency, they would have realized they were coming before now.

"The Rover back there looks familiar," Sarah said.

A second Rover was sitting about ten meters away from theirs. It was the same vehicle model as their own. A NASA production. The two visitors were members of the group that had stolen their ship, and at the moment they were obviously trying to make off with the probe parts from their Rover. *That figures*, Lance thought, but he had no intention of making this easy for them.

He switched on his external loudspeaker, cranking the volume up high. If he didn't do that, anything he said would travel through the thin Mars air and reach the two thieves as a whisper. "Hey! Take your hands off our Rover!" he shouted.

The figure on the left spun around immediately, but the other one didn't seem to hear anything, since he kept trying to untie the rope in his hands. The left-hand figure tapped him on the shoulder.

Lance strode toward the two of them. He couldn't tell from the bulky suits if they were men or women, but it really didn't matter. They didn't have any business taking things off their Rover. Sarah tried to hold him back, but he couldn't just stand there! If they refused to leave voluntarily, he would have to force them to go. In their old-fashioned spacesuits, they didn't have a chance against him. If you were stuck in one of those, it took you three times as long to hit back.

At about three meters away, he could make out the names

stitched onto their suits. It was two men, Shashwat on the left and Guillermo on the right.

"Guillermo," Lance yelled furiously over the loudspeaker, "take your hands off our vehicle!"

Guillermo suddenly reached into his suit pocket and pulled out a black object. In his oversized gloves, it was hard to tell what it was.

"He has a pistol!" Sarah cried, just as he recognized it. Lance stopped in his tracks, as the man pointed the gun at him.

"Shit, they're armed," he said over the helmet radio.

"Don't provoke them, Lance. Please, it's not worth it," Sarah said. He turned toward her. She had raised her arms and was slowly walking toward them. "Tell them that you want to talk to them on Channel 22," she said quietly over the radio.

"Why? We're using Channel 15."

"Don't ask."

Lance activated his external mic. "Channel 22. Can we talk?" he asked loudly.

The two men seemed to understand him. They pressed a button on their helmets.

Lance heard a voice. "This is a surprise." He didn't recognize the accent, so it was probably Shashwat.

"Yeah. What lousy luck," the second man said with a Spanish accent. *Definitely Guillermo.* He was the one pointing the pistol at him.

"Couldn't you lower that thing, pal?" Lance tried.

"So that you could put me out of action? You must think we're really dumb. Typical NASA arrogance. No, the gun stays where it is."

"And what do you want?" Sarah asked.

"The same as you. The probe," Shashwat replied.

"And while we're at it, anything else you can do without," Guillermo said. "The third segment of your Rover would fit perfectly onto ours. All NASA manufactured. How practical. Hahaha! I'm also sure you have more supplies packed than you'll need for your return trip. Isn't it NASA routine to pack twice as much as you might need, in case of emergency?"

Shashwat gestured at his colleague. They had presumably not discussed this. Scavenging the probe was one thing, but to rob the competition... Shashwat might have a problem with that. Or Lance might just be imagining things, and Shashwat actually wanted them to hand over the entire Rover. That would be a death sentence for them.

"Just slow down. You can't really think that you can cause any damage with your puny pistol, Guillermo. Where would the oxygen come from that you need to ignite the gunpowder in your bullet?" Lance spoke with deliberate calm, hoping the MfE guys wouldn't know that he was lying to them. He didn't raise his arms like Sarah, but he didn't move any closer to Guillermo either.

"What does he think he's doing?" Guillermo asked his partner.

"Don't get too cocky," Shashwat said to Lance as he pulled his pistol out of his pocket. "This pretty little thing shoots great. The propelling charge holds its own oxygen. The lower gravity and the thin atmosphere give the bullet even more oomph."

The bluff hadn't worked, unfortunately, but they couldn't just let the MfE guys walk all over them! First the *Endeavour*, then the probe and their supplies. Would they follow this up by showing up on their doorstep and demanding that they surrender their base?

"Whoa, everyone just take a deep breath. Nobody has to get hurt here," Sarah interjected. "You have guns and we don't. What choice do we have? We'll give you what you want, and we don't need to argue about it."

What was this? Had Sarah already given up? She was right though, there was no point in arguing with two guys with revolvers. Why had NASA stopped arming their astronauts? Lance was furious, but maybe there'd still be a chance to turn the tables on them. Guillermo might not feel up to shooting someone, but then again, he could be an ex-Mafia hitman for all Lance knew. Hadn't the MfE application process been open to anyone?

"Your colleague seems very sensible," Shashwat said.

"We really just want the best for you," his cohort said with a laugh.

The guys really weren't making it easy for him to accept his humiliation. He saw Sarah amble over to the Rover out of the corner of his eye.

Shashwat must have also noticed her movements. "What are you doing?"

"I'm unfastening the back section for you," Sarah replied. "I didn't think you wanted to draw this out any longer than necessary."

"Very true."

Sarah unfastened the coupling on the one side, then walked around the Rover to take care of the other side. Was she up to something? Shashwat's view was blocked by the cargo in the middle section, and Guillermo wasn't looking her way since he was still pointing his gun at Lance.

It was growing darker minute by minute. Suddenly a shadow came flying out from behind the MfE guys. Lance had only seen something that crazy done by stuntmen in ninja films, but this time it was real. Sarah had used the low Mars gravity and nailed Guillermo in the lower back. The man collapsed on the ground. He tried to turn over and point his gun at Sarah, but she snatched it out of his hand as quick as a cat and pulled his body up as cover against the other MfE man.

"Sorry, Shashwat," Guillermo groaned. Sarah was holding him tightly from behind.

"I think we have a stalemate," Shashwat said as he aimed his pistol at Lance.

At the sound of the shot, Lance instinctively dropped to the ground. He then heard a shout of alarm.

"A stalemate? I wouldn't be so sure about that," Sarah replied as Lance got back on his feet.

"Help! Help!" Shashwat cried. "My suit has a hole in it. I'll suffocate!"

Lance realized what Sarah had done. The man's spacesuit now had a hole in the upper sleeve where Sarah's bullet had penetrated the suit. Shashwat dropped his gun and was now trying to hold the hole closed with his other hand. Guillermo, who was still lying on the ground, didn't react.

"Do I really have to do everything myself?" Sarah asked.

She strode over to Shashwat and kicked the pistol that was lying at his feet over to Lance who picked it up. She opened her tool bag and pulled out her emergency spray.

"You don't have something like this with you? I guess it's one of those fucking NASA luxuries," Sarah said, "but sometimes it comes in handy. Shall I?"

"Yes!" the man shouted. "Quickly!"

"Say 'please.'"

"Please."

"And you won't ever steal anything again."

"I won't."

"What won't you do?"

"Steal anything."

"Won't those parts fit in a complete sentence?"

"Please, I won't ever steal anything again."

"Good," Sarah said as she pressed the spray nozzle. A white repair foam welled out of the nozzle. "Turn around, please."

The man turned. Sarah lifted his arm a little, and he cried out in pain.

"I have to do that. The hole is located in a wrinkle," she said. "The spray can only seal it if the fabric is pulled straight. But I'd be lying if I said I felt particularly sorry about this."

"Thank you," the MfE man said.

"And now for you," Sarah said as she walked over to Guillermo. "What should we do with you?"

"Please don't do anything to me. It wasn't my idea. The theft, I mean."

"Yes, it was," his colleague blurted out.

"In that case, I'll have to blow your brains out," Sarah said, though she didn't raise the gun.

"Please don't," Guillermo said. "I'll do anything you ask me to."

"Good idea, though that wasn't what I was thinking. That was just revenge for the fear that had to be pumping through my colleague Lance's veins. I suggest that you two pretties drive back to your settlement and convince your boss that it would be a good idea to give the ship back to the NASA people."

Lance was impressed with Sarah's performance. He had never seen her like this. All that was missing was a whip dangling from her hand.

"That... won't be so easy," Shashwat declared.

"At least try. I'm sure you aren't the only ones who'd like to do that. If I come and visit our ship and hear that you didn't even try, I'll remember that you owe me. Got that?"

"Yeah," Guillermo replied.

"Oh, by the way, I'll need a small token of collateral from both of you."

Lance wouldn't have been surprised if she demanded they hand over their little fingers or the souls of their firstborn children.

"Yes?" Shashwat asked.

"Our radio bit the dust on our drive out here. We haven't been able to communicate with our base for the last part of our journey, and you won't be able to do that during your return trip. That seems fair, right? Coincidentally, it should fit perfectly in our Rover. After all, it's all NASA technology."

"Of course," Guillermo said. "We can manage without it."

THEY DROVE THROUGH THE DARKNESS FOR HALF AN HOUR before they set up camp. Despite how the altercation had panned out, it didn't seem like a good idea to spend the night close to the MfE people. After all, they didn't know if the two men had other guns hidden in their vehicle.

"Rover to base, please come in." Sarah was speaking into the microphone. They could finally relieve their friends' anxieties.

"Base to Rover. Sharon here. It's great to hear from you! What happened? Are you two alright?"

"Everything's just fine. We've had a few interesting days, but we'll fill you in when we get back."

"Understood. Mike was convinced that MfE had something to do with your disappearance."

"That's not quite what happened. A rock destroyed our radio."

"But you were able to repair it?"

"Kind of."

"Alright. Well, I'm just glad you're safe and sound. We were really worried."

"I'm sorry about that."

"It wasn't your fault, but it's good to be back in touch. We have some interesting news for you as well."

Sol 61, MfE base

"We haven't heard from Shashwat and Guillermo for two days now. We have to do something," Rebecca said.

The group had gathered in their new command center for the first time. Even Gabriella was there, having decided to leave Andy alone on his sickbed for a short while. They were still only twelve in number. *If this keeps going*, Theo thought, *our Mars for Everyone project will literally be dead by the end of the year.*

They had to do something. Today. He had filled Rebecca in on his suspicions and asked her to prolong the discussion about the disappearance of the open Rover as much as possible. He was planning to do something that he didn't want anyone to witness. Theo looked around the group. Ewa was sitting on a stool with her arms folded, while Ellen sat cross-legged beside her on the floor. She had become Ewa's personal aide-de-camp.

Theo belched loudly and deeply, something he had practiced for a long time. He then grabbed his stomach, and without another word, ran out of the center.

"Do you need help?" Gabriella called after him.

"This morning he..."

He couldn't catch Rebecca's last words. The subterranean passage that connected the command center in the finished base with the *Endeavour* had a bend to it. Theo ran as fast as he could. He would have the ship to himself for the next few minutes. Rebecca would send him a signal when the meeting ended.

He climbed up into the ship and then into the *Endeavour* command center. Breathless, he sat down in the pilot's seat and pulled the keyboard in front of him. He clicked on Andy's user name and waited for the password request. The last time he had been here, he had tried three more of the twenty possible combinations of eight adjacent characters. The computer would still only allow him three attempts before it would temporarily lock him out. Theo was on pins and needles. He was already up to the 17th variation! But what if Andy had used a combination that involved a line change, like *890-QWER?* No, he was too lazy for that. Hopefully!

Theo had reached the nineteenth combination, *ZXCVB-NM<*, and it finally worked! He now had access to Andy's projects and files. What had he been up to? Most of all, what had been so sensitive that he had decided against saving it among the publicly accessible files?

Theo went through the lists. There was a directory with personal photos. He glanced through them. Andy might have concealed other files there, but these really were just pictures. An older, gray-haired woman flashed by. Was that Andy's mother? Right underneath the photo folder was one for music, which Theo also checked. The Eagles? He chuckled. He wouldn't have taken the gifted programmer for one of their fans. He, at least, had stopped listening to such old music by the time he turned twenty-five. It wasn't surprising that Andy had an extensive video folder. What also didn't surprise Theo was the fact that Andy was a fan of the old *Star Trek* movies. He briefly considered copying the videos, but that wasn't why he was here.

The fourth primary folder was simply titled 'Projects.' It contained a wide array of document types—software source texts, sketches, tables, texts, and a few data types that Theo didn't recognize. Where should he begin? There had to be around 900 files here. It would take way too long to work through them, so he plugged in a memory chip he had brought along and copied the documents. He would go through them this evening at his own pace.

His communicator vibrated. It was Rebecca's signal. He didn't have more than 20 seconds left. The memory chip was full, and Theo logged out of Andy's account. What about the clues he was leaving behind? The system log would indicate that someone had accessed the unconscious Andy's files on this computer today. If Ewa noticed that, she would immediately remember his absence from the meeting, but he was out of time.

Theo pushed the keyboard back in place, jumped up, and climbed down the ladder. It still smelled like the animals that had lived down here for some time. The toilet was attached to the wall of the lower level. He quickly locked himself in the tiny cabin, and when he heard the sound of footsteps outside, he loudly gagged several times. He decided not to rinse himself off. His rushed actions had made him sweaty, but that would just substantiate his story about having indigestion.

He slowly made his way back down the corridor to the base. Ellen passed him and wished him a speedy recovery. He then ran into Rebecca, who noisily expressed her concern for him before dragging him into his new cabin.

"Did you do it?" she asked after she had shut the door.

"Hopefully I got all the pertinent data out," he replied.

They had to be careful. For all Theo knew, Ewa might have installed listening devices in the walls during the construction phase.

"I hope you feel better soon," Rebecca said. "Should I check on you this evening?"

Theo reached into his pants pocket. It was empty, and he felt the room grow hot. In his hurry, he had forgotten to extract the memory chip. "Shit," he gasped.

"Oh, that too?" Rebecca asked.

He drew the outline of the chip in the air, but she didn't get what he meant. He searched frantically for his tablet. He typed, 'Memory chip still in the computer,' showed it to Rebecca, and deleted the text.

Rebecca grew pale and sat down on his bed.

"Have you caught what I have?" he asked.

She shook her head and then stood up quickly. "I'll get you something from the doctor," she said.

Theo was about to protest. She shouldn't put herself in danger because of him! But Rebecca had already left the room.

Now he'd done it. He walked up and down the room. Three steps to the left, three to the right. That was all the space he had. He sat back down on his bed. His knees began to tremble of their own accord. He pulled off his boots and stretched out on his mattress. It was torture to have to just sit here and do nothing. If only he could see what was going on! He massaged his wrists and leaped to his feet just to sit back down again.

An eternity later, someone knocked at his door. "Please come in," he said.

It was Rebecca. She closed the door behind her and held her fist out to him. "Your pills," she said as she triumphantly opened her fingers.

Theo saw the two white tablets—and his memory chip. "Thank you," he said. "Thank you so much. I should hug you for that."

"I'll take a rain check on that," Rebecca replied.

For another eternity, nobody said anything, but then they sat down next to each other on the bed.

"I ran into Ewa with the doctor when I went to ask for the pills. Their conversation was pretty interesting. Gabriella was explaining that she had run an EEG on Andy a few days ago and that she had detected some conspicuous activity in his frontal lobe."

"Is that good news?"

"Gabriella thinks so at least. Sometimes patients wake up after such indications. Ewa was skeptical. She thinks it might just be one last gasp."

"That is really interesting," Theo replied. "I think I'll take the pills now and sleep a little while. I'm sure I'll feel better by this afternoon. Want to meet outside around sunset?"

"Sure, Theo," Rebecca said, smiling.

THEO ACTIVATED HIS TABLET AND SWITCHED IT OFFLINE before plugging in the memory chip. Almost 1,000 documents made for a ton of stuff. He wouldn't be able to make sense of the software source texts anyway. Those probably had something to do with Andy's hobby programming projects.

Two of the file names looked interesting, 'MainEngine.diff,' and 'Module.diff. That had to be related to the *Santa Maria*, their spaceship. He opened the smaller Module.diff file first. It was empty. Andy had saved it that way, which was strange.

On the other hand, MainEngine.diff contained at least 300 lines. Most of them held terms that Theo didn't understand, but Andy had added notes to some of them, such as 'Unnecessary loop' and 'Missing break statement.' The software that had steered the main engine had made several mistakes that had led to the *Santa Maria*'s first catastrophe. And that was what Andy had speculated the following day when the failed uncoupling process had caused the landing module to almost squash him. That was the day they almost missed the final opportunity to enter Mars's orbit.

Theo tried to remember. He had pushed as hard as he could against the crowbar to separate the module from the ship. He recalled that, but everything after that was blurry.

A software error—isn't that also what they had discovered from Andy's suit? Three program errors in a relatively short time that resulted in varying degrees of disasters. They had lost five people the first time, and he had almost been killed the second time. And then Andy's number came up after he had tracked down the errors, as these documents were showing. Could it all just a be a coincidence?

And how had Andy used his information? He had obviously not discussed it openly. But had he taken someone into his confidence or even blackmailed them? Only one thing was certain—Andy hadn't caused the error himself. There wouldn't have been any reason to track down and document all this if he had.

Who else was a possible suspect? Theo scrolled on through the files. There had to be other clues! In one text document, Andy had described how the first catastrophe had played out, second by second. Ewa had almost been killed, too, but she had left the module shortly before the accident and had shut the hatch as prescribed by the regulations. That had saved all the rest of them since an open hatch would have meant that the air would have suddenly been released from the entire ship. And yet, Theo recalled clearly that most of the time, the hatch had been left open. The crew had moved so often between the main space and the command module that most of them had been too lazy to continuously open and shut the hatch.

No one could fault Ewa for setting an example for the others. Unless she had known what was going to happen!

THEO NEEDED TO DISCUSS ALL THIS WITH REBECCA, BUT NOT here. He checked the clock. It was already time for their agreed-upon walk. He left his cabin and went to the tiny training room. Twenty minutes of pre-breathing would have to be enough. They had become a little lazy by this point, but that wouldn't change until somebody got the bends. Rebecca was nowhere in sight. He thought he could smell her scent, but that was probably just his imagination. Theo pedaled the allotted time and then squeezed himself into his spacesuit. If only they had some of the modern NASA suits!

But these old ones were still better than not going outside at all.

The base planners deserved praise for the airlock. Unlike the NASA base, this one was sized to accommodate two individuals in voluminous suits. Since he was the only one here, it felt like he was walking through a palace.

And then he was outside. The sky was almost clear, grayish-brown as always, but clearer than usual. The sun was still high enough that you couldn't look at the disc directly. Theo stepped off the roof of the base. He caught sight of a figure about 50 meters away. It had to be Rebecca. He walked slowly toward her. She was holding a piece of paper that she now raised up.

27, he read.

Very smart. That wasn't the general base frequency. The likelihood that someone would be listening in on this band would be fairly low. He switched his helmet radio to Channel 27.

"Good to see you," Rebecca said.

"Exciting times," he replied.

"In every way," she said.

What did she mean? He decided to ignore the hint. "I have learned some things," he declared, switching gears, "and I need your advice."

"Gladly."

He pointed in front of them, and they started to stroll through the desolate landscape. Rebecca tucked her arm through his.

"Andy obviously figured out what caused the first two so-called accidents, and then he was the target of the third one," he said after a few minutes.

"That's certainly strange, Theo. It could just be dumb luck on his part. But if not?"

"Do you know who he might've shared his information with? Who did he trust the most?"

Rebecca came to a stop and stared at the ground as if she could find additional clues there. She started to scratch the dust with her boot. "I'm trying to think back," she explained quietly.

Theo waited. He tried to recall the situation on the *Santa Maria* as well. Andy had always seemed to keep to himself, which was why Theo had considered him a kindred spirit of sorts.

"I only remember two or three situations in which I saw him talking privately with Ewa," Rebecca finally said. "The two of them seemed to be on the same wavelength."

"I didn't pick up any of that," Theo admitted.

"I'm not surprised."

Theo nodded. *Had Andy confided his suspicions to Ewa and inadvertently fallen into the saboteur's clutches?* "It would be horrifying," he said, "if our commander, of all people, was the one sabotaging our mission."

"It's possible even if I never would've thought Ewa capable of that," Rebecca replied. "But..."

"But?"

"If that's the case, then we really need to watch out for Andy. Gabriella told her that he might wake up soon. If that happens, Ewa will have a real problem on her hands. She'll need to try to prevent that from happening."

"You think—"

"—she will try everything within her power to keep Andy from waking up again," Rebecca said before Theo could say it.

"GOOD THING WE'VE ALREADY LAID THE GROUNDWORK WITH your illness," Rebecca declared.

She kissed Theo on the cheek, then pressed the emergency call button. The doctor responded right away.

"He's feeling worse than he was this morning," Rebecca said.

"Did he eat something?" asked Gabriella.

"Not since this morning. We went outside for a little while. Maybe a case of the bends?"

"I need him in the sickbay immediately. Can you bring him here?"

"Yes, I can."

Rebecca stepped out of the cabin, leaving the door open. "Help me, please!"

Theo heard her speaking with someone before she returned with Ketut in tow. The two of them picked him up, Rebecca grabbing him underneath his arms and Ketut holding his feet. They then hauled him through the base and down the subterranean passageway into the ship, and from there into the closed Rover that was functioning as the sickbay.

Theo was glad once they arrived since his back was hurting from the transport. He kept his eyes closed and hyperventilated to seem more convincing. He was tucked into a soft bed.

"Do you still need me?" Ketut asked.

"No, but thanks," the doctor replied.

Gabriella started her examination. Her cold instruments tickled him, but Theo stopped himself from laughing.

"I haven't found anything acute going on," Gabriella said after a while. "His blood pressure is high, but everything else seems normal. It might be gallstones, but nothing's showing up on the ultrasound. The stones might still be too small. Are you still in pain, Theo?"

She touched his lower abdomen, and Theo winced.

"Okay. I'm going to give you a shot of painkiller. We still have enough of that on hand. I'd like to know how things will look three years from now."

Theo didn't say anything. He clenched his jaw as the needle pierced his upper arm.

"I'd like for you to spend the night here," Gabriella declared. "Everything might be different by tomorrow morning. I'll check up on you from time to time, but if anything comes up, press the emergency bell."

Theo acted as if he were trying to nod.

"Just rest. Rebecca and I will leave the sickbay now, right, Rebecca? The medicine should act quickly, and it will make you a little sleepy."

Shit. He couldn't fall asleep. That might cost both of them their lives.

THEO WOKE UP BECAUSE EWA WAS PRESSING A PILLOW AGAINST his face. He couldn't see her, but he was absolutely certain that she was the only one it could be. He turned his head back and forth to escape the pillow, but it was much too large. Ewa was smothering him with tremendous strength. She must be sitting on his arms because he couldn't move them. He sensed that he only had a few seconds before she reached her goal.

Theo wrenched his head back and forth like crazy, and suddenly, he woke up. He was drenched in sweat and was breathing rapidly. He tried to stand up, but he felt instantly dizzy. *Slow down, Theo.* He knelt on the floor and felt a soft mat beneath him, one that Gabriella had spread out there. Was this a side effect of the painkiller? What had she shot into him? Theo took a deep breath in and out. The stabbing feeling in his chest slowly faded.

He steadied himself on Andy's cot and pulled himself up until he was on his feet. Theo glanced around. Several medical devices were spreading dim light with their colorful little bulbs. He checked Andy's vitals, but he was breathing as evenly as ever. *It must've been an actual nightmare*, he thought. He had never experienced one that felt so extreme and real.

Theo sank back onto the mat. Everything seemed to be alright. He wouldn't go back to sleep, but would keep watch over Andy as they had planned for him to do. As soon as he sat down, he began to struggle to breathe. He jumped back up and his breathing settled back down. Something was wrong, after all. He hadn't just imagined it!

There was something close to the floor, a gas that was heavier than the rest of the air. If it was carbon monoxide, he and Andy would already be dead. It must be carbon dioxide. What was more readily accessible on Mars than the gas that was the primary element in its atmosphere? Carbon dioxide was heavier than the air they could breathe. If his nightmare hadn't woken him up...

Theo frantically checked on Andy. The gas had presumably been slowly seeping into the Rover cabin for a while already. Its surface would gradually rise, like during a flood. The only difference was that this danger remained invisible. If the gas rose above Andy's cot, he wouldn't be able to breathe anymore either.

The cabin wasn't large. Theo checked the exit. It was locked. What had Gabriella said about the emergency bell? The button was located at the end of Andy's cot. Theo pressed it but nothing happened. Whoever had planned this attack had obviously cut off all means of contact with the rest of the base. It wasn't difficult to disconnect the Rover, since all that took was removing one cable.

But if the cabin was completely cut off, how was the carbon dioxide getting inside? Theo flipped on the light. It still worked. The Rover had its own life support system that should be filtering out the CO_2. Why wasn't it doing its job? And where was it located? He didn't know this NASA model.

Theo scanned the area close to the ceiling. If he could find the air ventilation openings and follow the channels that connected them, he should be able to figure out where the life support system was situated. He finally located a fan. A pair of scissors sat on a shelf next to it. He jabbed the blades into the seam in the wall cladding and levered one of the panels free. There was a tube. He followed its course, tearing more and more of the wall panels off as he went along.

The NASA crew would be furious if they ever got the Rover back, but he found what he was looking for. The filtration device looked like the radiator in a refrigerator, a very large refrigerator. It had to contain one component that extracted the CO_2 from the air and another that injected oxygen into the air. 'Attention! Corrosive material!' was printed on a rectangular container. Maybe that was where the soda lime that absorbed the CO_2 was located.

Theo yanked the cover off. But somebody had been thorough! The grainy mass was no longer white but purple. That meant that it was completely used up! Theo could see little water spots inside the holder. The assailant had simply filled it with water. Any contact with moisture made the material unusable.

Theo heard a wheezing sound behind him. He glanced over at Andy, who was clearly breathing more rapidly than he had earlier. The carbon dioxide must have reached him, but that couldn't be the result of their breathing alone. There had to be a CO_2 source inside the Rover. Theo picked the scissors back up and continued dismantling the wall panels. And there it was—a metal bottle. It was attached by a hose to the outlet of the life support system. The bottle's neck was pointing downward, and it was gray. Theo didn't need to read the label. Gray indicated that the bottle contained carbon dioxide. The bottles containing oxygen had white necks. He reached for the valve on it. It was open, and Theo quickly cranked it shut.

It wouldn't be so easy to get the gas out of the cabin. Even if no new gas was being pumped into the space, he still needed to bring Andy to safety. He grabbed his shoulders, but he couldn't lift the other man despite the low gravitational pull. He finally managed to raise Andy's head! Theo shoved the cot toward the external door. Andy was breathing heavily. His eyes seemed to be bulging out of his skull. He was probably having a similar nightmare to what Theo had experienced. He had to rescue him from this nightmare.

Theo elevated the head of the cot so that it angled upward. The external door had a narrow ledge that ran along its lower edge. He just had to jam the cot's wheels underneath it, and then the Rover would help him keep the cot at an angle. Andy's head was now close to the height of his own.

He slid down the mattress a little until his feet hit the door. Now just one more jolt forward and the cot would be stuck. He just needed to maintain his own pressure against the cot to keep it from sliding back down to the floor.

He checked on Andy, whose breathing had returned to normal. Had he just rolled his eyes? Theo thought he must be seeing things. He was exhausted, but he gradually felt himself relax. The acute danger was over for now. Somebody would eventually check on them. He would make it until then.

He just hoped the person who came wasn't Ewa.

Sol 62, MfE base

THEO HAD JUST CHECKED THE TIME. IT WAS SHORTLY AFTER three AM when the external door opened. He didn't react fast enough, and the cot, with Andy still aboard, crashed to the floor. Fortunately, Andy was only jarred, not thrown off. The heavy carbon dioxide rushed out of the Rover. Like water, it flowed downward and dissipated throughout the *Endeavour* and the base, where the life support system would quickly neutralize it.

"Who's there?" he asked.

"It's me. I had a bad feeling and wanted to check on you."

"Glad you did, Rebecca. I've never been happier to see you."

"Is everything alright in there? What's going on?"

"Everything's just peachy, Madame Doctor. Only a minor attempt at murder."

Someone pushed the cot inside and stepped into the sick-bay. It was Gabriella with Rebecca at her heels.

"It looks like a war zone in here!" the doctor exclaimed.

"Yes, me against the gas."

"Which gas?"

"Carbon dioxide." He pointed at the depleted mass in the absorber and the carbon dioxide bottle.

"How bizarre," Gabriella said.

"It looks like an attack to me," Theo said.

"Where was there an attack?"

He went cold at the sound of Ewa's voice. The woman really was brazen. Or innocent. She now pushed past Rebecca and the doctor.

"Ah, the absorber. I think Guillermo fixed it before he left." She ran her fingers along the wall. "See that? A water line runs along here. He must've damaged it making the repairs."

How convenient that Guillermo and Shashwat were incommunicado at the moment. The man couldn't defend himself.

"We probably hadn't noticed anything because of the constant exchange of air between the Rover and the station. And when the door was shut tonight—"

"The door was locked from the outside, and all the communication channels were blocked," Theo cut in.

"Yeah, I did that," Ewa admitted. "I looked in on you right before midnight. Both of you were sleeping so soundly that I didn't want anyone to bother you. So I shut the door. I had no idea that the absorber was defective."

"And the emergency bell?"

"Oh, does its signal use the cable, too? I didn't know that. The wakeup alarm was supposed to go off two hours after I stopped by, and I wanted to spare you that. My intentions were good."

Ewa shot him an ingenuous smile. Theo shook his head. She really was cunning, but she wouldn't get off that easily.

"A bottle of carbon dioxide was attached to the life support system. That couldn't have anything to do with Guillermo, since otherwise it would've been empty a long time ago," Theo protested.

"I need to see that myself," Ewa exclaimed. "Maybe you're right, and it really was an attack! We shouldn't dismiss that possibility so quickly."

She removed more of the paneling and checked the tube connectors.

"I think we've been lucky in these circumstances. We can forget about the possibility of an attack. Look at this. The gray bottle is hanging from a fire suppression system. The sensors probably detected a CO_2 surge and an unusually-high temperature reading, and concluded that there was a smoldering fire in here. It tried to smother the fire with the carbon dioxide."

"Without an alarm going off?" Theo asked quietly because he already knew the answer.

"That was my fault because I had unplugged the cable. I'm really very sorry. I'm prepared to accept the consequences and resign as Commander."

"No, Ewa, that won't be necessary," Gabriella interjected. "It really looks like a chain of unfortunate events."

"Yes, but don't you see...," Theo trailed off.

No, Gabriella hadn't noticed what was going on here. And he wouldn't be able to convince the others either. Ewa had already proven that she would fight heroically for this mission. She couldn't be the bad guy here—that was what they'd say. He was probably lucky that she hadn't twisted things in such a way that he looked like the sole culprit. But the story Ewa had spun was actually much more plausible with her openly admitting the errors she had made and claiming ignorance about the communication system cable.

"May I interrupt your little chat?" Rebecca asked. "There's something interesting going on over here."

Everyone turned toward Rebecca, who was pointing at Andy. Andy, who had slept through the past few weeks, had suddenly begun to move his mouth. It really looked like he wanted to say something.

"Andy, don't!" Ewa cried, launching herself at him.

Her hands covered his mouth in an attempt to keep him from talking. However, Theo succeeded in pulling the thrashing Ewa off the other man.

Andy opened his mouth again. His tongue was bleeding. He had probably bitten it while Ewa tried to hold his mouth shut. Gabriella started to staunch the blood, but Rebecca intervened. “Let him be,” she said. “He wants to tell us something.”

Gabriella stopped in her tracks. Ewa took a deep breath and seemed to accept the situation. All four of them stood there as Andy finally formed the three words he wanted to say.

“Ewa is lying.”

THE HEARING TOOK PLACE IN THE BASE’S LARGE CONFERENCE room. They didn’t have a formal court system in place yet. They hadn’t thought they would need to discuss legal structures for another year or two. The initiative had assumed that capital crimes wouldn’t be a factor so early on. After all, everyone had volunteered and sworn allegiance to the mission.

Andy was still having a hard time speaking. He could only construct the most basic of sentences and had to take extended breaks between them. This was why Theo was the one recapping the conclusions from Andy’s analyses. If he spoke slowly, Andy could understand what was being said, so he was able to confirm Theo’s explanation. Nonetheless, the evidence wasn’t clear cut, as even Theo and Andy had to admit. Ellen corroborated that Guillermo really had been asked to repair the absorber on the Rover. On the other hand, Andy declared quite clearly that Ewa was the only one he had confided in. She was the only person who’d had a motive for wanting to see him harmed.

But there was one incident that had been witnessed by four crew members. Everyone who had been in the Rover had observed Ewa’s attempt to prevent Andy from speaking. Gabriella’s statement finished tipping the scales among the other crew members. Most of them had been aware that Theo and Rebecca were at odds with Ewa, but the doctor had been considered one of her allies.

By the vote at the end of the hearing, eleven of the fifteen crew members were convinced that Ewa was guilty of sabotage. Only the accused and Ellen voted not guilty. Even if Guillermo and Shashwat had, contrary to expectation, voted for Ewa, she still wouldn't have stood a chance.

Ketut spoke up. "Two months ago, I accompanied Shankar and Asha on their final journey. I saw you weep for our dead comrades back then, Ewa. It touched me deeply. Now I've learned that you were responsible for their deaths. That means you were crying for yourself. Either that or you are an actress without any scruples. Either way, there's no longer a place for you on this crew. I think we should vote on what should happen to you next."

"Do you have a suggestion?" Rebecca asked.

"I don't believe in the death penalty," Ketut replied. "Ewa targeted the community with her lethal acts of sabotage. For that, she should experience what it actually means to be alone."

"And exactly what does that mean?"

"We will provide her with a generous amount of supplies and breathable air, and banish her."

"But isn't that a death penalty of sorts, Ketut?"

"No, Rebecca. She isn't worth us putting a hand on her. She is no longer one of us, plain and simple. We will just be carrying her own plans out to their logical conclusion."

"I don't know. That seems inhumane to me," Rebecca said.

"I would like us to vote," Ketut continued.

"Yes, let's vote," Nance agreed. The others nodded.

"Then go ahead and vote," Ewa interrupted, getting to her feet. Her eyes were gazing into the distance. Theo was sure that at this moment she really wasn't herself. She turned around completely where she stood, then swayed. He was about to jump up to steady her, but she regained her balance.

"I... I didn't do it," she said quietly. "Or maybe I did, I'm not sure. I don't know anything. You're right. The evidence is clear. I'm a murderer."

The conference room fell silent. Was that a confession? Theo was confused. The others seemed to share his feelings.

"Ewa, are you sorry?" Ketut asked.

"Does that matter? I should say 'yes,'" she continued, "but I can't. I don't feel guilty. I watched myself as I tampered with the absorber, but it felt like I was observing someone else. I wanted to stop. I could tell that I was on the verge of making a huge mistake, but I couldn't do anything. I couldn't make that other person stop."

"That sounds to me like some kind of dissociative disorder, like schizophrenia," Gabriella chimed in.

"Or an excuse that we could never verify," Ketut countered. "Or is there some ironclad way to diagnose this disorder?"

"Of course not," Gabriella admitted. "It would take months to establish a precise diagnosis."

"And in the meantime, she'll keep killing more of our friends?" Ketut asked. "That's unacceptable. We have to protect ourselves from her."

"We could lock her up somewhere," Theo suggested.

"Do you really think that would work? We don't have any secure holding cells. We have to give the *Endeavour* and the Rover back. All we'll be left with are a few rooms underground. We can't afford to keep Ewa here with us. If she hadn't sabotaged our mission, it would look different, but as it is..."

"Ketut, you can't just banish her."

"We don't know if she's sick or not. She admitted that the evidence is impressive, and she confessed to everything and tried to act like she was mentally ill. That is very cunning, just like Ewa. She said she knew fully well what she was doing was wrong. But why didn't she let any of us know?"

"That usually isn't possible for patients during such episodes," Gabriella explained.

"I'm not changing my mind," Ketut declared. "At this point, we aren't in a position to care for someone who poses a threat to our community. She has access to resources we don't. And I personally don't believe her in the slightest. There's more behind this than schizophrenia."

"But what?" Theo asked. "I would like to understand what she did."

"We should vote now," Nancy said.

Nobody objected. Theo and Rebecca raised their hands against banishment. All the others, included Ewa, voted for it.

As Ewa left the base the following day, Theo pressed a radio into her hands. She stuck it into the outer pocket of her heavy backpack.

"In case you need help," he said.

She didn't look at him. "I won't need help, but the rest of you might," she replied as she walked out.

Those words hadn't come from Ewa, Theo was sure of that. He wanted to hold her back, but what good would that do? Was he supposed to die with her out in the Martian desert? He had to let her go, even if the thought of that was painful.

Sol 62, NASA base

"Mike, you won't believe this, but the MfE people just radioed in."

"Let me guess. We're supposed to rescue the Rover they used three sols ago to attack Lance and Sarah?"

"No, the opposite. They want to apologize."

"Whaaat? What kind of trick is that? I don't believe anything they say anymore."

"At least come over here and listen in."

Sharon was whipping her foot up and down. She hoped this wasn't another empty promise. All her previous attempts to get Mike to talk to the initiative had failed.

A young woman, almost a girl, was smiling from the screen. She had introduced herself as Ellen Blake.

Mike finally appeared. "I'm Mike Benedetti, Commander of the NASA mission."

"I'm Ellen Blake from MfE."

"Are you a spokesperson? Where's Ewa?"

"Ewa.... isn't with us anymore. That's why I'm the one reaching out."

"Is she dead?"

"She just left the base, permanently. As it turned out, she was responsible for numerous acts of sabotage."

Sharon was shocked. Ewa of all people? She had never found her particularly warm, but a multiple murderer?

"Oh, that's interesting news," Mike remarked.

"That's not why I radioed in. I would like to apologize in the name of the entire MfE initiative."

"Ah, to apologize."

"We made a really terrible mistake. You rescued us, and we betrayed you in return. I wish I could claim that this was Ewa's fault alone, but that wouldn't be true. Most of us stood behind her. We are very sorry."

"You're sorry?"

"We would like to return what we stole. Unfortunately, the *Endeavour* doesn't have enough fuel for the return trip, but we will send the enclosed Rover and the robotic drill back as soon as possible."

"As soon as possible?"

"We need to wait until our open Rover gets back. The range for the enclosed one isn't far enough, so we'll need to send the other one along to carry additional fuel."

"Understood."

"The crew of our open Rover—"

"—attacked two of our astronauts three sols ago."

"What? We haven't heard about that!"

"Don't worry, nothing happened to them. We guaranteed safe passage in exchange for their radio. Your people tried to rob us."

"That won't happen again. We should be perfectly clear about that. Anyone who threatens other people will be punished."

"Those are nice words."

"We will back them up with actions. If it's alright with you, I would like to accompany the Rover back to your base. We would also like to sign a formal contract with you. On this planet, nineteen people out of almost nine billion humans continue to survive. We should make our lives easier for each other, not harder."

"That is true. I look forward to your visit."

Sol 70, NASA base

"THEY'RE COMING!"

For the past hour, Mike had been standing on the roof of the base, keeping watch for the Rover. He had obviously caught sight of something.

"How far away?" Sharon asked.

"Ten minutes?"

"I'll hurry." She slipped into her spacesuit. She had already finished her pre-breathing training. After climbing through the airlock, she joined Mike. A dot on the horizon was speeding toward them with a tail of dust behind it.

"Are you the one at the wheel, Lance?" Sharon asked.

The helmet radio should be in range of the two travelers. They were within sight, and the air was amazingly clear today.

"Lance is sitting behind me, dozing as usual," Sarah replied.

"I wish I was, but that's impossible when you're the one driving," Lance quipped. He sounded like he was standing right next to Sharon—and as if he had never been gone.

"If we had driven the whole way at your speed, Sharon and Mike would still be waiting for us at this time tomorrow," Sarah shot back.

"I saved us at least seven blowouts," Lance replied.

"Why seven?"

"Because it sounds good."

"The two of you sound like an old married couple," Sarah said.

"If you only knew!"

"If I knew what, Sarah?"

"Later. We first need to shower."

MIKE WAS RIGHT. THE ROVER TOOK ABOUT TEN MINUTES TO reach the base. They waited on the ground for the adventurers. Lance jumped down first and Sarah followed. They walked with a rolling gait like cowboys, their suits covered with a thick layer of dust.

"Nice to have you back," Mike said. He had planned to shake Lance's hand, but the latter hugged him instead. "Oof," Mike gasped.

"I'm so happy you made it back in one piece," Sharon said as she hugged Sarah.

Sarah turned to Mike, who didn't even try to shake hands this time around. Sharon moved toward Lance. He looked weary, but also somehow... content. They wrapped their arms around each other, and then the four of them walked to the base, arms linked.

"I can't tell you how much we missed being here," Lance sighed. "The two of you most of all, of course."

"This place is pretty dreary for two. We were about to place an ad for new roommates, but the rental market here seems fairly dead."

"Come on, Mike. You know what they say. 'Location, location, location,'" Lance said.

"What do you think are our best-selling points? Great view, neighbors a thousand kilometers away..."

"Speaking of which, how are things going with the neighbors?" Sarah asked.

"I'm not taking their apology seriously until the things they stole from us are sitting outside our door."

"Mike is always a bubbly mass of pessimism," Sharon replied. "We never heard anything more from Ewa, but the others seem to have their heads screwed on right. They got their Rover back yesterday. They sent their thanks for your fair treatment of their crew members, and they supposedly set off the same day with both Rovers, as well as the robotic drill."

"How long until they get here?" Sarah asked.

"They guessed it would take two weeks," Sharon declared.

"Good," Lance said. "That will give us enough time to rest up. You have no idea how many blisters are covering my entire body."

"THAT SMELLS AMAZING," SARAH SAID. SHE, SHARON, AND Lance were sitting at the table as Mike carried the casserole in.

"Anything would smell great to me as long as it didn't come from a tube," Lance said. "Having only prepared food to eat eventually kills any appetite you might have."

Mike set the dish on the table and used a large spacesuit glove to remove the lid. "Be careful, it's hot," he said. "I present to you a potato-leek casserole à la Benedetti. Everything in it is fresh, except for the artificial milk I used for the sauce. That came from a bag Unfortunately, we don't have any cows, but maybe we'll be able to produce soy proteins soon."

"This is great!" Sarah exclaimed. She really looked excited, her eyes sparkling. "You did an excellent job taking care of my garden!"

"That reminds me of something," Sharon said. She had forgotten the present! She'd hidden it in the walk-in refrigerator so that Lance and Sarah wouldn't see it beforehand. It was wrapped in thin paper, and she carried it into the large room. "May I introduce you to our first flower?" Sharon said as she removed the wrapping.

"A pansy! How marvelous!" Sarah crowed.

"I spent a day considering if we could afford this luxury," Sharon explained. "It cost us a lot of energy, but what is life without flowers? So this is supposed to be a gift for all of us. By the way, they grow amazingly well here."

"Thank you, Sharon. What would we do without you?" Lance asked. "I'll need flowers if I ever decide to propose to Sarah!"

"What are you talking about?" Mike asked. "Propose?"

"He's just joking, Mike," Sharon said.

"I said *if*."

"Are you a couple now?" Sharon asked. "If you don't mind my asking," she added with a laugh.

"We... we are," Lance replied, reaching for Sarah's hand.

"Yes, we are," Sarah agreed.

Sol 84, NASA base

"Ah, that feels good."

Lance was lying face down on his bed. Sarah was sitting on his calves as she rubbed lotion onto his backside and thighs. The wounds from their long drive still hadn't completely gone away. Sarah spanked him lightly and stood up.

"Thanks a lot, Sarah."

"Do you hear that? There must be something going on outside," she said.

Lance turned his head and listened. He heard a hissing sound. "Somebody must be in the airlock," he said.

"I'm going to take a look," Sarah said as she left his cabin.

Lance stood up to search for his pants, which had fallen under his bed. He pulled them on. He had slept a lot over the past few days, though he had also helped Mike sort through the souvenirs from their trip. They had decided to keep the solar panels for whenever their fortunes changed—in case the KRUSTY eventually broke down. The panels would enable them to keep their life support system going during the daylight hours. At night, they could plug in a methanol generator.

His door opened again.

"Hurry! It's the MfE people," Sarah announced. "I'm going out right now."

"I'll just wait in here," Lance said, although he knew she couldn't hear him. He put on his shoes and strolled over to the conference room. He heard sounds in the airlock and stood right next to the hatch.

The light beside the door changed to green and the airlock opened from the inside. A figure in one of the bulky MfE suits climbed into the room, followed by Mike. Lance read the name on the MfE suit. 'Ellen.' This had to be the new commander, Ellen Blake. He remembered her as a delicate person who hung on every word Ewa said, but maybe he had been wrong about her. He closed the door again to make room for the next newcomers.

As Ellen and Mike climbed out of their suits, the next pair appeared. Lance took a step back. This time it was Guillermo, the bastard who had threatened him with the pistol.

"Everything's good," Sharon said as she stepped out of the airlock behind Guillermo and noticed Lance's expression.

"Lance?" Ellen asked. "Please excuse this surprise. I brought Guillermo along on purpose because he would like to apologize face to face for what he did to you."

Lance relaxed. Either Guillermo had really lost control at their last encounter, or Ellen had her people solidly under her command.

The man removed his helmet and stepped toward him. "I *would* like to apologize," he said. "I was a real asshole out there. I didn't even realize it, which was the worst part. I always thought I had some kind of moral compass, but over the past few weeks, it seems to have become quite skewed. I was only thinking about ourselves and our mission, something that Ewa had sold us on hard recently. But that's not really an excuse. I'm glad that Sarah was able to put me out of commission. Where is she?"

"Thank you," Lance said, taking Guillermo's proffered hand. He still wasn't completely won over, but the apology seemed sincere. "Sarah should be coming through the airlock right behind you."

Guillermo turned toward Sarah. He waited until she had taken off her helmet. "I'd like to thank you for your literal kick in the pants out there," he said. "I really deserved it. In a way, you saved my life. I don't know how I could've kept living if I had actually harmed you."

"Gladly done!" Sarah replied. "If you ever need a kick like that again, you know where to find me. How's Shashwat doing?"

"It was a clean in-and-out shot. The wound is healing nicely, but the drive down here would've been too much for him."

"Could you all make a little more room? Ketut will have to stay in the airlock if you don't," Mike pointed out. He moved closer to Ellen to help unfasten the sections of her suit. "That'll help us maximize the space."

Lance noticed that Mike could hardly take his eyes off the young woman. Poor Sharon's chances were shot to hell now. Ellen was about Mike's age, and Lance had heard that she had even more Ph.D.'s than Mike did.

"Please move aside!"

Lance didn't recognize this voice, which meant it had to be Ketut who was still stuck in the airlock. Lance now realized why. The MfE member was carrying a stack of five-sided somethings. The material couldn't be all that heavy, though, since it was taller than Ketut's head.

"This is our hospitality gift to you," Ellen said. "These are the remnants from the large dome we'd planned to build over our settlement. Please set the pile on the floor, Ketut."

Ketut knelt down, which wasn't all that easy in his suit, and placed the honeycomb-shaped stack on the floor. It swayed slightly. Ellen reached for one of the thin, transparent panels at the top.

"This is Kevlar fabric, under one millimeter thick. We intended to build our dome out of these, but unfortunately, this was the only stack we could save from the *Santa Maria*.

The rest of the panels are flying around the sun in our shipwreck. However, this material should be enough to construct a smaller dome. Or you can cover a garden with it."

"Thank you very much," Mike said as their official spokesperson. "I have a great idea for what we can do with these. But now it's time for you all to freshen up, and then we can eat."

Sol 88, NASA base

THE PROJECT WAS SLOWLY TAKING SHAPE. FIRST, THE ROBOTIC drill had dug a circular hole into the ground, as Lance stood nearby and supervised. The walls were already hardened. The hole measured 1.2 meters in diameter and was four meters deep. A ladder would provide access for a person to climb up into the new section.

They were now in the process of digging a passageway from the base to the lower edge of the hole. Lance had spent the entire previous day shoveling, but the others were taking their turns today. He could hear the sound of their axes and spades underneath him. Unfortunately, the robot was unable to drill around corners, nor could it fit through the base's airlock. This was why they were having to dig the corridor by hand. At least they were being energetically assisted by the three MfE guests.

Lance's task today was to tend to the robot. It was busy digging a round trench around the hole. The channel was about a meter deep. The lower end of the dome would be anchored, sealed, and stabilized in this trench. They were making good progress. Occasionally, the robot sucked up an especially hard stone and needed Lance to dislodge it with a crowbar, a mechanical version of the Heimlich maneuver.

These occurrences were far enough apart to leave him with ample time to study the landscape.

After they'd landed, Lance had thought the scenery was monotonous. He had been mistaken, he now acknowledged. The landscape had simply needed some time to reveal its intricacies. Or was it perhaps the humans who took longer to value Mars's simplicity, because of their acquired tastes and customs? For example, the hill to the north—Lance enjoyed watching it through a telescope as it changed with each passing day. In the mornings, it sometimes glittered because water or carbon dioxide ice crystals had settled on its surface the night before. A week ago, he had even spotted a trail leading down from the ridge of the hill to the bottom. Sharon guessed that a piece of carbon dioxide ice had slid all the way down before literally evaporating—technically, sublimating—into thin air once the sun rose.

Lance had to chuckle as his mind wandered. Sarah had recently started acting a little strangely. She lost her temper more easily, or burst out crying at the slightest thing, but thirty minutes later, there was nothing left of the odd mood.

The robotic drill beeped, having finished its task. Lance checked the trench. He used his spade to shovel out rocks from two different spots where they must have fallen once the wall had been dug. Tomorrow the robot would start digging a new garden plot. Sarah wanted to try out a few new techniques. They had come to the conclusion that their current methods were still consuming too much energy. If they hoped to someday be able to meet all their food needs through their own cultivation, they wouldn't be able to continue using their present techniques.

After this, they wanted to start in on the deep drilling project. But they would have to convert the robotic drill in order to do that, so they needed to first wrap up their current projects.

"Heads up, Lance," Mike radioed in.

"What's going on?"

"According to my data, we're about to break through."

"Alright. I'll set the cover in place and watch."

Lance walked over to the deep hole at the center of the round trench. He pulled out his flashlight and shone it inside. Everything looked the same as it had before. He took a couple of steps to the side to where a transparent panel that was larger than the hole was sitting. He picked it up and covered the opening in the ground with it. He sprayed its edges with repair foam. That should suffice as a temporary isolation method. As a security measure, he set two heavy stones on top of the panel to make sure that the air pressure wouldn't lift it even a little.

"Alright, you're on!" he called.

His friends down below were probably now hammering like crazy on the stone in front of them. He then saw a rock from the wall tumble onto the floor of the hole. The beam of his flashlight fell onto shining metal behind the rock's former location. The connection to the base was almost complete!

Sol 92, NASA base

THE SEVEN OF THEM WERE STANDING AROUND A SMALL TABLE and toasting each other with champagne, except for Sarah, who had opted for water. The panorama was marvelous. The Mars surface was underneath them, but when they lifted their heads, they could gaze into the grayish-brown sky. The sun had almost reached its zenith. They were wearing neither spacesuits nor breathing masks since the tent of transparent Kevlar panels guaranteed them a breathable atmosphere.

Lance took a sip. Ellen was talking, but he wasn't listening. Too much had happened! The sheer fact that they were standing here, protected by less than a millimeter of Kevlar, was a miracle. What would it look like in a year? In a century? Would green someday be part of the Red Planet's palette?

It was a given that they would continue to make mistakes in the future. That was the nature of humans. The small table counted as one. None of them had thought about the fact that they could only easily transport into the dome those items that fit through the narrow corridor from the base. They should have built some furnishings beforehand. Lance, however, had sworn that he would somehow manage to bring a comfortable chair up here. No, make that two of them, even if he had to completely dismantle them and rebuild them inside the dome.

"I propose that we sign the document now," Ellen said.

Sarah clinked her glass against Lance's.

Right, thought Lance, *the official part still has to take place.*

Over the past few nights, Mike and Ellen had prepared a Declaration of Independence that would also function as a kind of constitution. They had discussed every aspect of it for a long time. Ellen had let the entire MfE vote on it, and they had all agreed to sign it.

Lance thought it had turned out as a nicely blended document that could be summarized as *Freedom, Equality, Fraternity.* They had deliberately left out concrete structures, such as governmental frameworks. The NASA expedition and the MfE initiative would continue to make their own decisions, but would take the other group into consideration. They had also discussed how cooperation with the crew of the private *Spaceliner I* might look. However, since the ship wouldn't land for a few months yet, they had decided to put off any resolution on this until later.

"You're up," Sarah said, handing him the pen and the document.

Lance signed his name. The two words, 'Lance Leber,' looked odd on the paper. He couldn't recall when he had last signed his full name anywhere.

Guillermo and Ketut were the next in line. Lance had spent two days toiling in the base passageway with Guillermo. The Mexican really did seem to be a reasonable person.

"Mike, Sharon, Sarah, Lance... I would like to thank you once again in the name of the Mars for Everyone Initiative," Ellen finally said. "We wouldn't be here if it weren't for you."

"And we'd already be bored out of our minds without you here," Mike replied. "There's really nothing worse than boredom on a lonely planet you won't ever be leaving."

They clinked their glasses again.

"To the Mars Nation," Mike said.

"To all of us," Ellen replied.

"There is one more bit of exciting news," Sarah said. They all looked at her.

"Lance and I," she took his hand, "are going to be parents. The first native-born Martian is on its way."

As the others clapped, Lance felt a strange feeling churn inside him—a combination of anticipation, pride, and fear.

Sol 99, NASA base

TOMORROW WAS GOING TO BE A RED-LETTER DAY. SOL 100! They had spent 100 Martian days here already. MfE and NASA had decided to celebrate the day together. They were spatially separated, of course, but they would set up cameras and screens, and play the same music—a virtual party of sorts. Lance was in the process of clearing some space in the conference room to create a small dance floor. *We definitely need more storage space*, he thought, *especially if we want to scavenge the other old NASA probes over the coming weeks*. This time there wouldn't be any fights. The MfE people were now concentrating on the materials that all the other nations had shot up to the planet. That was a fair division since NASA had ultimately been more successful with their probes than the other space agencies.

"Lance, could you come here?"

Sharon was calling him from the command center. What could be going on now? He moved one more chair before doing as she asked.

"I've received a strange signal," she said as he stepped into the room.

"Don't tell me—it's coming from Earth?"

"It is."

Lance sighed. Over the past three days, there had been

numerous false alarms because one of the Mars probes was going berserk for some reason. Mike was still trying to figure out what was causing the problem.

"Has Mike finished his analysis yet?" Lance asked.

"I don't think so, but he's still asleep. Should we wake him up?"

"No, it's not worth it. I'm sure it's another of those error messages."

He replayed the signal. It wasn't coded in NASA standard language. All he could hear was a whooshing sound. He changed the code filter, and suddenly the noise vanished.

"Wǒmen yāoqiú liánxì."

What language was that? He thought it sounded like Mandarin. Luckily, the speaker switched to English.

"This is the spaceship *Long Trip 2*, seeking contact."

"Whoa! I'll go wake up Mike. Could you notify Sarah?" Lance called as he hurried off to fetch their commander.

IT TURNED OUT IT WAS MANDARIN. THE CHINESE SHIP WAS still too far away for an actual conversation. They would have to wait 40 minutes for each reply to reach them. The crew had also indicated that they needed to conserve energy as much as possible. Apparently their launch hadn't gone as planned, and there were six people on board instead of the intended four.

"Can you tell us anything about what has happened on Earth?" Mike asked before sending off his reply.

Over the coming days, they waited in vain for a response.

Author's Note

Finally! I have been waiting very eagerly to be able to get Mars Nation in your hand as a book or an e-book. You must know I wrote the trilogy back in the summer of 2018 after Audible, the audiobook company, had asked me for it. They wanted it exclusively in audio format for six months. As they took three months between each part, this meant they had to wait until the autumn of 2019.

But there is an upside: I had enough time to get both versions, English and German, ready at the same time. This is my first simultaneous global release. I think even large publishers rarely manage such a feat. Also, I will not let you wait for three months for the next installment. You can order it here:

hard-sf.com/links/790047

Compared to my other books, Mars Nation is set in our nearest future. In the late 2020s, we will have ships cruising to the Red Planet. This is about ten years from now. There are good chances we all will be able to witness the first TV coverage of one man or woman stepping into the red sand. I think it will be at least as memorable as the first moon landing 50 years ago. Did you watch it? You can bet I did. And if I can, I'll try to be aboard one of those tourist ships that Elon Musk from Space-X is trying to build. Would you come with me?

What will happen to the involuntary colonists over the next few years? Although Lance, Sarah, and the others believe that figuring out Earth's fate is their greatest problem, real danger draws closer from two completely different directions.

Before I let you go to your dreams, I have to ask you one favor – if you liked Mars Nation 1, please leave a review at this link:

hard-sf.com/links/762773

Thanks a lot!

Best regards from my nightly desk

Yours, *Brandon Q. Morris*

Register at hard-sf.com/subscribe/ and you will be notified of any new Hard Science Fiction books that I will be publishing. Also, you will get a beautifully illustrated version of the Guided Tour to Mars.

facebook.com/BrandonQMorris

amazon.com/author/brandonqmorris

bookbub.com/authors/brandon-q-morris

goodreads.com/brandonqmorris

Also by Brandon Q. Morris

The Enceladus Mission (Ice Moon 1)

In the year 2031, a robot probe detects traces of biological activity on Enceladus, one of Saturn's moons. This sensational discovery shows that there is indeed evidence of extraterrestrial life. Fifteen years later, a hurriedly built spacecraft sets out on the long journey to the ringed planet and its moon.

The international crew is not just facing a difficult twenty-seven months: if the spacecraft manages to make it to Enceladus without incident it must use a drillship to penetrate the kilometer-thick sheet of ice that entombs the moon. If life does indeed exist on Enceladus, it could only be at the bottom of the salty, ice covered ocean, which formed billions of years ago.

However, shortly after takeoff disaster strikes the mission, and the chances of the crew making it to Enceladus, let alone back home, look grim.

2.99 $ – hard-sf.com/links/526999

The Titan Probe (Ice Moon 2)

In 2005, the robotic probe "Huygens" lands on Saturn's moon Titan. 40 years later, a radio telescope receives signals from the far away moon that can only come from the long forgotten lander.

At the same time, an expedition returns from neighbouring moon

Enceladus. The crew lands on Titan and finds a dangerous secret that risks their return to Earth. Meanwhile, on Enceladus a deathly race has started that nobody thought was possible. And its outcome can only be decided by the

astronauts that are stuck on Titan.

3.99 $ – hard-sf.com/links/527000

The Io Encounter (Ice Moon 3)

Jupiter's moon Io has an extremely hostile environment. There are hot lava streams, seas of boiling sulfur, and frequent volcanic eruptions straight from Dante's Inferno, in addition to constant radiation bombardment and a surface temperature hovering at minus 180 degrees Celsius.

Is it really home to a great danger that threatens all of humanity? That's what a surprise message from the life form discovered on Enceladus seems to indicate.

The crew of ILSE, the International Life Search Expedition, finally on their longed-for return to Earth, reluctantly chooses to accept a diversion to Io, only to discover that an enemy from within is about to destroy all their hopes of ever going home.

3.99 $ – hard-sf.com/links/527008

Return to Enceladus (Ice Moon 4)

Russian billionaire Nikolai Shostakovitch makes an offer to the former crew of the spaceship ILSE. He will finance a return voyage to the icy moon Enceladus. The offer is too good to refuse—the expedition would give them the unique opportunity to recover the body of their doctor, Dimitri Marchenko.

Everyone on board knows that their benefactor acts out of purely personal motivations… but the true interests of the tycoon and the dangers that he conjures up are beyond anyone's imagination.

3.99 € – hard-sf.com/links/527011

Ice Moon - The Boxset

All four bestselling books of the Ice Moon series are now offered as a set, available only in e-book format.

The Enceladus Mission: Is there really life on Saturn's moon Enceladus? *ILSE*, the International Life Search Expedition, makes its way to the icy world where an underground ocean is suspected to be home to primitive life forms.

The Titan Probe: An old robotic NASA probe mysteriously awakens on the methane moon of Titan. The *ILSE* crew tries to solve the riddle—and discovers a dangerous secret.

The Io Encounter: Finally bound for Earth, *ILSE* makes it as far as Jupiter when the crew receives a startling message. The volcanic moon Io may harbor a looming threat that could wipe out Earth as we know it.

Return to Enceladus: The crew gets an offer to go back to Enceladus. Their mission—to recover the body of Dr. Marchenko, left for dead on the original expedition. Not everyone is working toward the same goal. Could it be their unwanted crew member?

9.99 $ – hard-sf.com/links/780838

Proxima Rising

Late in the 21st century, Earth receives what looks like an urgent plea for help from planet Proxima Centauri b in the closest star system to the Sun. Astrophysicists suspect a massive solar flare is about to destroy this heretofore-unknown civilization. Earth's space programs are unequipped to help, but an unscrupulous Russian billionaire launches a secret and highly-specialized spaceship to Proxima b, over four light-years away. The unusual crew faces a Herculean task—should they survive the journey. No one knows what to expect from this alien planet.

3.99 $ – hard-sf.com/links/610690

Proxima Dying

An intelligent robot and two young people explore Proxima Centauri b, the planet orbiting our nearest star, Proxima Centauri. Their ideas about the mission quickly prove grossly naive as they venture about on this planet of extremes.

Where are the senders of the call for help that lured them here? They find no one and no traces on the daylight side, so they place their hopes upon an expedition into the eternal ice on Proxima b's dark side. They not only face everlasting night, the team encounters grave dangers. A fateful decision will change the planet forever.

3.99 $ – hard-sf.com/links/652197

Proxima Dreaming

Alone and desperate, Eve sits in the control center of an alien structure. She has lost the other members of the team sent to explore exoplanet Proxima Centauri b. By mistake she has triggered a disastrous process that threatens to obliterate the planet. Just as Eve fears her best option may be a quick death, a nearby alien life form awakens from a very long sleep. It has only one task: to find and neutralize the destructive intruder from a faraway place.

3.99 $ – hard-sf.com/links/705470

The Hole

A mysterious object threatens to destroy our solar system. The survival of humankind is at risk, but nobody takes the warning of young astrophysicist Maribel Pedreira seriously. At the same time, an exiled crew of outcasts mines for rare minerals on a lone asteroid.

When other scientists finally acknowledge Pedreira's alarming discovery, it becomes clear that these outcasts are the only ones who may be able to save our world, knowing that *The Hole* hurtles inexorably toward the sun.

3.99 $ – hard-sf.com/links/527017

Silent Sun

Is our sun behaving differently from other stars? When an amateur astronomer discovers something strange on telescopic solar pictures, an explanation must be found. Is it merely artefact? Or has he found something totally unexpected?

An expert international crew is hastily assembled, a spaceship is speedily repurposed, and the foursome is sent on the ride of their lives. What challenges will they face on this spur-of-the-moment mission to our central star?

What awaits all of them is critical, not only for understanding the past, but even more so for the future of life on Earth.

3.99 $ – hard-sf.com/links/527020

The Rift

There is a huge, bold black streak in the sky. Branches appear out of nowhere over North America, Southern Europe, and Central

Africa. People who live beneath The Rift can see it. But scientists worldwide are distressed—their equipment cannot pick up any type of signal from it.

The rift appears to consist of nothing. Literally. Nothing. Nada. Niente. Most people are curious but not overly concerned. The phenomenon seems to pose no danger. It is just there.

Then something jolts the most hardened naysayers, and surpasses the worst nightmares of the world's greatest scientists—and rocks their understanding of the universe.

3.99 $ – hard-sf.com/links/534368

Mars Nation 1

NASA finally made it. The very first human has just set foot on the surface of our neighbor planet. This is the start of a long research expedition that sent four scientists into space.

But the four astronauts of the NASA crew are not the only ones with this destination. The privately financed 'Mars for Everyone' initiative has also targeted the Red Planet. Twenty men and women have been selected to live there and establish the first extraterrestrial settlement.

Challenges arise even before they reach Mars orbit. The MfE spaceship Santa Maria is damaged along the way. Only the four NASA astronauts can intervene and try to save their lives.

No one anticipates the impending catastrophe that threatens their very existence—not to speak of the daily hurdles that an extended stay on an alien planet sets before them. On Mars, a struggle begins for limited resources, human cooperation, and just plain survival.

3.99 $ – hard-sf.com/links/762824

Mars Nation 2

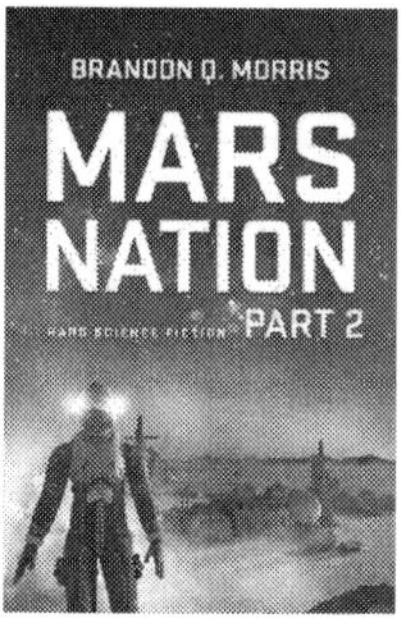

A woman presumed dead fights her way through the hostile deserts of Mars. With her help, the NASA astronauts orphaned on the Red Planet hope to be able to solve their very worst problem. But their hopes are shattered when an unexpected menace arises and threatens to destroy everything the remnant of humanity has built on the planet. They need a miracle—or a ghost from the past whose true intentions are unknown.

Mars Nation 2 continues the story of the last representatives of Earth, who have found asylum on our neighboring planet, hoping to build a future in this alien world.

3.99 $ – hard-sf.com/links/790047

Mars Nation 3

Does the secret of Mars lurk beneath the surface of its south pole? A lone astronaut searches for clues about the earlier inhabitants of the Red Planet. Meanwhile, Rick Summers, having assumed the office of Mars City's Administrator by deceit and manipulation, tries to unify the people on Mars with the weapons under his control. Then Summers stumbles upon so powerful an evil that even he has no means to overcome it.

3.99 $ – hard-sf.com/links/818245

The Death of the Universe

For many billions of years, humans—having conquered the curse of aging—spread throughout the entire Milky Way. They are able to live all their dreams, but to their great disappointment, no other intelligent species has ever been encountered. Now, humanity itself is on the brink of extinction because the universe is dying a protracted yet inevitable death.

They have only one hope: The 'Rescue Project' was designed to feed the black hole in the center of the galaxy until it becomes a quasar, delivering much-needed energy to humankind during its last breaths. But then something happens that no one ever expected—and humanity is forced to look at itself and its existence in an entirely new way.

Mars - A Guided Tour

If we ever have to abandon Earth, Mars would probably be the only possible place to seek refuge. The planet offers manageable temperatures and vast water reserves. All it's missing is oxygen in its atmosphere.

For almost 100 years, the existence of a non-human civilization on our neighboring planet was considered a safe bet. After the astronomer Giovanni Schiaparelli used his telescope in 1877 to discover mysterious channels—mistranslated into English as 'canals'—which appeared to cover the entire planet, Mars was imagined at that time to be a drought-prone world, whose inhabitants were trying to ensure their survival with gigantic, planet-wide civil engineering projects.

It was, coincidentally, also a period in which humans had undertaken huge canal projects. Mankind's picture of Mars has changed with the times. When tensions between nations were increasing before World War I, but also between the two world wars, public opinion about Mars suddenly shifted toward the idea that it might be dangerous. Wouldn't the Martians want to take over our fertile and bountiful land? When, on October 30, 1938, the radio network CBS aired the drama *The War of the Worlds* by Orson Welles, its storyline based on 'live reporting,' for a Halloween special, the broadcast led to a nationwide panic, despite a disclaimer aired at the beginning that the show was an adaptation of the famous book.

No civilization, maybe life

Improvements to telescopes, and eventually the first landings of probes on Mars, finally proved that there were neither canals nor civilization on Mars. Researchers, however, have not given up on their search for life on our neighboring planet. This is because the conditions might not be optimal, but they are not entirely hostile to life.

Like Earth, Mars is a rocky ball. Its diameter is approximately half that of the Earth, and the planet has a bit more than ten percent of the Earth's mass. On the Martian surface, an astronaut would weigh in at 62% lighter than on Earth. Its nickname 'red planet' was rightfully earned—Mars appears reddish not only in the sky, but also close up.

This is due to the relatively high iron oxide content, colloquially called 'rust,' in the surface rocks and in the dust resulting from erosion. Mars orbits the sun at a distance 1.52 times farther than the Earth. Every two years it comes especially close to our home planet, although it's still 56 million kilometers away. At its farthest distance from the Earth, it is 401 million kilometers away from us.

Choose your launch time wisely

Therefore, if you want to launch a spaceship to Mars, you need to be smart about selecting when you go. Choosing a good launch time can reduce the amount of time you spend in interplanetary space, where you would be exposed to cosmic radiation.

Cosmic radiation, however, will still be your main problem even after you arrive on the red planet. This is because Mars lost most of its magnetic field 4 billion years ago, so it has no protection from solar wind. This contributes to the fact that the Mars atmosphere is even thinner than would be expected based on the low mass of the planet.

If you land in the temperate zones of Mars, your visible landscape would include wide, crater-scarred plains. The sky would appear yellowish-brown because the air carries a high content of dust particles in it. If you're really unlucky, you might even land in the middle of one of Mars's dust storms, which sometimes circle the planet for months at a time. The average atmospheric pressure corresponds to that found at an altitude of 35 kilometers above Earth.

It would be necessary for you to keep your helmet on, because the atmosphere contains almost no oxygen, only 0.13 percent. It consists of 95.3 percent carbon dioxide. Researchers at the German Aerospace Center showed in 2012 that lichen and bacteria could survive for 30 days under Mars conditions, and thus should be able to thrive and prosper. So, if you've brought along a potted plant, you could safely put it outside. At least during the day, when it can warm up to 35 degrees Celsius.

You'd want to bring your plant in at night, however, because it can get cold. One Mars day is 24.623 Earth hours long, with temperatures dropping to minus 85 degrees at night. This is due to the thin atmosphere, which cannot store heat very well. A heated greenhouse would be a good idea if you wanted to stay for a long time.

Spring, Summer, Fall, Winter

A greenhouse would also help save you from the effects of the seasons, which on Mars are significantly more pronounced and longer than here on Earth. Mars follows a more eccentric orbit around the sun, lasting approximately 1.9 Earth years, with 'more eccentric' meaning that it is much farther away from the sun at some points in its orbit and much closer to the sun at other points. Especially during the parts of its orbit that bring it closer to the sun, when Mars receives up to 40 percent more energy, this can produce intense dust storms with wind speeds up to 400 kilometers per hour at the surface and 650 km/h in the upper atmosphere. Under some circumstances, these storms can envelop the entire planet and cause higher temperatures at the surface.

Noticeable vortices, or twisters, which considerably exceed similar storms on Earth, have also been observed. During the times farther away from the sun, clouds of water ice can form in the atmosphere, beneath which it can be up to 10 degrees colder. Sometimes, in the early morning hours, it can even snow, as laser measurements have shown, both summer and winter, just like on Earth.

The make-up of Mars

Like the Earth, the red planet was created from a cloud of matter around the sun. It contains a somewhat higher proportion of lighter elements that were driven by the solar wind into areas farther from the sun. Approximately four billion years ago, Mars must have been impacted in its northern hemisphere by a celestial body about the size of Pluto—an event that left behind a humungous impact crater with a diameter of almost 10,000 kilometers.

Today it is still recognizable through a strange difference between the northern and southern hemispheres. While the north consists of relatively flat lowlands, the south is dominated by mountain ranges.

Mars's core consists of iron and nickel, with relatively high sulfur content. At a temperature of 1500 degrees, it might even still be largely molten. Above the core is a thick mantle made of rock that is barely active today. The heyday of volcanoes on Mars was about three billion years ago. Most of the lava-flow regions that are still recognizable today were created at that time. However, definite, but weak, signs of volcanism still seem to occur today. Mars's crust is about as thick as Earth's crust, so it is considerably thicker in terms of the relative size of the two planets.

A paradise for mountain climbers

A large part of the Martian surface is covered by dust, so any traveler to Mars had better get used to it. The red planet, however, does offer a vast array of sightseeing attractions that are worth the strenuous effort to get around. If you are impressed by the Grand Canyon in the Arizona desert, you should definitely have a look at Valles Marineris. This giant system of canyons is 4,000 kilometers long, up to 700 kilometers wide, and up to 7 kilometers deep. In the west, it merges into the fractured Noctis Labyrinthus, where the valley walls are closer together, but the canyons are still up to 5 kilometers deep.

Farther in the west is the Tharsis Rise, which rises to about 10 kilometers above the lowland and is crowned by the three extinct shield volcanoes: Ascraeus Mons—480 kilometers in diameter, 18 kilometers of elevation; Pavonis Mons—375 kilometers in diameter, 14 kilometers of elevation; and Arsia Mons—435 kilometers diameter, 16 kilometers of elevation. On the flanks of Arsia Mons, probes have discovered cavities that are probably former lava tubes. There also appear to be extensive glaciers on the slopes of this mountain.

Mars's largest volcano in terms of surface area is named Alba Patera. It is only 6 kilometers high, but its surface area has a diameter of 1200 kilometers. That is also a Solar System record, just like the elevation of Olympus Mons, which rises 26 kilometers above its surroundings. However, Olympus Mons rises only 21 kilometers above 'middle ground,'—the equivalent of sea level, which is the zero point we use on Earth—so it might need to give up its gold medal to the 22 kilometers tall Rheasilvia Mons on the asteroid Vesta. The summit of Olympus Mons extends above the atmosphere of Mars and into space and thus would be the perfect location for a telescope. It's not completely clear, however, whether the volcano is still active or not. It appears to have last erupted two million years ago.

But let's return to Valles Marineris. At its ends are broad

valleys that were shaped in the past, researchers believe, by rivers. Where these valleys open into craters, deposits that are reminiscent of typical river deltas can be detected in some areas. Maybe, at some time in Mars's past, underground ice supplies were melted by global volcanism, and huge amounts of water had to be drained away. That these deposits are actually sediment, however, has not yet been verified. The youngest of these valleys were formed just a few million years ago. The most significant example, Ma'adim Vallis, is up to 700 kilometers long, 20 kilometers wide, and 2 kilometers deep.

Dark streaks can be seen on many of the crater walls, and they change with the seasons. Their chemical makeup is presently undetermined. Perhaps landslides in these areas are exposing the dark rocky layers underneath. The erosion gullies that are also frequently found on steep slopes in the southern hemisphere appear to have a connection to liquid or melting water, especially because they seem to form only at certain latitudes. However, they could also originate from carbon dioxide ice or movements of dust.

Visually, the sand dunes that you can see near the north pole are particularly impressive. They also change with the seasons. In the winter they are covered with a centimeter-thick layer of carbon dioxide ice. When spring starts, the ice breaks down little by little, so that the dark sand underneath becomes visible. With increasing warming, lower-lying CO_2 also evaporates and carries the sand with it, depositing it on the tops of the dunes. From there, the sand moves downward when the winds blow.

Water on Mars

Most of the Martian surface today looks like a dry desert. But if you take a closer look, closer than using only your own eyes, you'll find that water might be closer than you would think. NASA's Curiosity rover, for example, found some minerals with a water content of up to four percent. At the middle latitudes, there might be water ice below the surface that was transported there by glaciers during Mars's ice ages.

Other vast water reserves have been detected under the ice caps at the north and south poles. These caps, which are up to 5 kilometers thick at the North Pole and 1.5 kilometers thick at the South Pole, are mostly made up of carbon dioxide (what we call dry ice), but they also have a water ice component. Radar measurements by the Mars Express probe show that there must be large areas of ice that are under the surface around the south pole and reach down to a depth of 3.7 kilometers and correspond to approximately two-thirds the volume of the Greenland ice sheet. Melted, they could cover all of Mars with an ocean 11 meters deep.

However, currently it would be counterproductive to set up a giant melting furnace at the South Pole. Due to the low atmospheric pressure, liquid water cannot exist on the Martian surface for any length of time—it simply evaporates too quickly. As mountain climbers know, the boiling point of water decreases with lessening air pressure—unfortunately, when it comes to Mars.

Life on Mars

The conditions overall do not sound favorable. Mars is at the edge of our Solar System's habitable zone, which is defined by the tolerance limits of known lifeforms. In principle, certain extremophile species could survive under the conditions on Mars. Greening the planet with lichen, for example, doesn't have a very utopian appeal.

Another question is whether any native Martian lifeforms survived the billions of years of dry conditions. There are scarcely the necessary prerequisites for survival on the surface: big temperature swings, intense ultraviolet radiation, and the thin atmosphere without liquid water are all points against it. And if Mars is geologically dead, that is, has no more volcanic activity, the possibilities of survival decrease even more—without a source of heat from the interior of Mars, life under the surface is unlikely. Researchers, however, believed they had detected active sources of the hydrocarbon methane, which could have been of either volcanic or bacterial origin. Either one would be good news, because in either case it would mean that there are locations in which primitive life is possible.

Recent measurements by NASA's Curiosity rover, however, are making this hope sound more and more unlikely. In the scientific journal, *Science*, researchers have reported that the rover's laser spectrometer could find absolutely no traces of methane. The earlier measurements from Earth and from Mars orbit appear to have been faulty, because Curiosity's instrumentation is significantly more accurate, and tuned specifically for methane. The overall values are so low that it would make the existence of life as we know it unlikely, both right now and also in Mars's past. In their paper, the researchers also discuss what makes the earlier methane detections so unbelievable. It appears that the previous scientists let their desire to discover life somewhere out beyond Earth influence their interpretations of the results.

The Mars moons

Mars has only two sad, little moons, Phobos and Deimos, which have irregular shapes and were probably originally from the Asteroid Belt. Phobos, which has dimensions of roughly 26.8 x 22.4 x 18.4 kilometers, is the larger of the two, and its orbit takes it to a distance of only 6000 kilometers above the Martian surface. Due to tidal forces, it is moving closer to the planet on a spiral path—in 50 million years it might finally collide with Mars, or the tidal forces might tear it into smaller chunks that will then form a ring around Mars.

The smaller Deimos, at 15.0 x 12.2 x 10.4 kilometers, in contrast, is well on its way to escaping Mars—sometime in the distant future it will rejoin the Asteroid Belt.

Off to Mars?

The large-scale Mars program that President George W. Bush announced in 2004, and that was to be capped by a human-crewed mission to Mars, has for a long time fallen victim to more and more budget cuts. NASA is now targeting flights in the 2030s, just like the European Aurora program. Such a journey might happen first with a one-way ticket and no return flight.

There seem to be plenty of volunteers. A Dutch non-profit organization, Mars One, published a call for volunteers in the spring of 2013 and received responses from more than 10,000 interested persons. Mars One would like to use private funds to finance the expedition planned for 2022, and estimates that six billion dollars would be needed. For comparison, NASA's Spirit Mission cost around 2.5 billion dollars.

Travelers to Mars, however, would have to be okay with increasing their risk of cancer because of their exposure to cosmic radiation during their flight. During the Curiosity mission, NASA measured a daily dose of 1.8 millisieverts from cosmic radiation. On a trip to Mars, which would take more than 500 days, a traveler would be exposed to approximately 1 sievert and thus an increased risk of 5 percent of developing some form of cancer.

There's also at least one moral problem that humankind would need to solve before setting foot on Mars—it would be almost impossible for the first astronauts to *not* contaminate the planet. And as a result, bacteria from Earth would almost certainly eradicate any remaining survivors of Martian life... who would have had to survive 3.5 billion years of very harsh conditions, just to be wiped out by us.

Register at hard-sf.com/subscribe/ and you will be notified of any new Hard Science Fiction books that I will be publishing. Also, you will get a beautifully illustrated version of the Guided Tour to Mars.

Glossary of Acronyms

AI – Artificial Intelligence

ERV – Earth Return Vehicle

EVA – ExtraVehicular Activity

FC – Flight Control

GN&C – Guidance, Navigation, and Control system

GPR – Ground-Penetrating Radar

HP3 – Heat flow and Physical Properties Package

HUT – Hard Upper Torso

IV - IntraVenous

KRUSTY – Kilopower Reactor Using Stirling TechnologY

LG – Landing Gear

MfE – Mars for Everyone

MRO – Mars Reconnaissance Orbiter

NASA – National Aeronautics and Space Administration

Prop - Propulsion

SEIS – SEISmometer

Metric to English Conversions

It is assumed that by the time the events of this novel take place, the United States will have joined the rest of the world and will be using the International System of Units, the modern form of the metric system.

Length:
centimeter = 0.39 inches
meter = 1.09 yards, or 3.28 feet
kilometer = 1093.61 yards, or 0.62 miles

Area:
square centimeter = 0.16 square inches
square meter = 1.20 square yards
square kilometer = 0.39 square miles

Weight:
gram = 0.04 ounces
kilogram = 35.27 ounces, or 2.20 pounds

Volume:
liter = 1.06 quarts, or 0.26 gallons
cubic meter = 35.31 cubic feet, or 1.31 cubic yards

Temperature:
To convert Celsius to Fahrenheit, multiply by 1.8 and then add 32
To convert Kelvin to Celsius, subtract 273.15

Brandon Q. Morris
--
www.hard-sf.com
brandon@hard-sf.com
Translator: Rachel Hildebrandt
Editing: Marcia Kwiecinski, A.A.S., and Stephen Kwiecinski, B.S.
Cover design: Audible Germany

Printed in Poland
by Amazon Fulfillment
Poland Sp. z o.o., Wrocław

23443326R00206